MIRROR ME

A NOVEL

LISA WILLIAMSON ROSENBERG

Published by Little A, New York

www.apub.com

Amazon, the Amazon logo, and Little A are trademarks of Amazon.com, Inc., or its affiliates.

ISBN-13: 9781662521263 (hardcover)
ISBN-13: 9781662521256 (paperback)
ISBN-13: 9781662521270 (digital)

Cover design by Mumtaz Mustafa
Cover image: © Malte Mueller / Plainpicture

Printed in the United States of America

First edition

PRAISE FOR *MIRROR ME*

"*Mirror Me* is an exquisitely rendered meditation on race, family, and memory. With stylish prose and tender storytelling, Williamson Rosenberg explores what it means to have your identity divided at the root and ultimately answers the question we all have about where we truly belong."

—Nancy Johnson, author of *The Kindest Lie*

"Boundaries of consciousness blur and twist in Lisa Williamson Rosenberg's compulsively readable second novel, *Mirror Me*, a heart-pounding exploration of identity, family, and the interconnected webs of the human psyche. Eddie Asher's desperate journey through the echoes of memories not entirely his own will keep readers mesmerized until the final reveal. Perfect for fans of *Behind Her Eyes*, Williamson Rosenberg's unputdownable novel delves into the many ways a person can be Other—even to themselves. Get ready to question everything you thought you knew about the nature of the self in this thrilling and thought-provoking read."

—Anne Burt, author of *The Dig*

"*Mirror Me* is a mesmerizing mind bender. Love, betrayal, secrets, and one man's quest to decode his fragmented memories had me on the edge of my seat as I made my way through this gripping exploration of the human psyche."

—Deborah Copaken, *New York Times* bestselling author of *The Red Book* and *Ladyparts*

"With boldness and grace, Williamson Rosenberg offers a powerful and gripping story of identity, power, and belonging. Her subversive storytelling lets readers embody the characters of *Mirror Me* with insight into their challenges, desires, and struggles."

—Diane Marie Brown, author of *Black Candle Women*, a Read with Jenna Book Club Pick

"A haunting story about a man trying to find his true identity, *Mirror Me* weaves together his fragmented memories with the tortured relationships in his life to bring together a truly beautiful and twisty tale."
—Lyn Liao Butler, bestselling author of *Someone Else's Life*

"*Mirror Me* is both a riveting page-turner and a thoughtful exploration of psychological adaptation, the complexity of families, the weight (and richness) of biracial identity, and the enduring mysteries of friendship, connection, and love. You'll stay up late to finish, but you won't soon forget this gripping and classic tale."
—Laura Sims, author of *Looker* and *How Can I Help You*

"*Mirror Me* by Lisa Williamson Rosenberg is an intricately plotted and sensitive exploration of identity, race, family, and fate. Combining all the elements of a psychological thriller with deeply emotional, literary prose, Williamson Rosenberg delivers a fascinating story that keeps us reading until the very last page. Full of visceral grief and hope, *Mirror Me* is a thoughtful reminder that while there is no such thing as a perfect family, some connections can never be broken."
—Lynda Cohen Loigman, bestselling author of *The Matchmaker's Gift*

"Lyrical, captivating, and full of the unexpected, Lisa Williamson Rosenberg's *Mirror Me* will keep you on the edge of your seat. A tale of self-perception versus reality through the lens of memory and loss, this page-turner is the kind of story that lingers in your mind long after you've finished. Gorgeous and haunting."
—Xio Axelrod, *USA Today* bestselling author of *Girls with Bad Reputations*

"*Mirror Me*, the sophomore novel by Lisa Williamson Rosenberg (*Embers on the Wind*), opens with a bang. Eddie, a troubled young man of mixed-race heritage, sprints on a subway platform, grappling with the twin fears that his brother's fiancée may have been murdered—and that Eddie's alter ego may have done it.

"Williamson Rosenberg, a licensed psychotherapist and former ballerina, draws from experience to paint a richly detailed portrait of a deeply disturbed protagonist, the dynamic New York City art scene into which he is thrown, and a diverse cast of characters who bring him both love and torment.

"Like a trained dancer, *Mirror Me* is taut, nimble, and so compelling that I couldn't tear my eyes away. Just when I thought the story was about to wrap up, Williamson Rosenberg throws in one last twist. I didn't see it coming."

—A. H. Kim, author of *A Good Family* and *Relative Strangers*

MIRROR ME

ALSO BY LISA WILLIAMSON ROSENBERG

Embers on the Wind

For Jon, Zoe, and Theo.

The patient [primary] and his alters switch out and replace one another, depending on "who," or which aspect of the self, can best address a stressful circumstance. This rotation can occur multiple times in an hour.

The splitting off is adaptive in childhood, serving to shield the youngster from experiencing trauma. The alter steps in to "front," meaning to become the spokesperson for the body (like the front man of a rock and roll band), when it deems the primary is unable to manage the stimuli.

—Dr. Richard Quentin Montgomery, *The Splintered Self: Challenging the Origins of Multiple Personality Disorder*

Do I contradict myself?
Very well then I contradict myself,
(I am large, I contain multitudes.)

—Walt Whitman, "Song of Myself"

PART I

1.

PÄR

1993

Eddie's wild heart and shaking legs propel him down the subway platform, up the stairs, and into the bitter cold. One with the wind, he races toward the park, long the site of his and Lucy's rendezvous. Is he hoping to find her there? As if the past few hours, weeks, months were a dream?

Eddie tries to conjure September, when they walked here together, hands entwined, immersed in one another, only mildly distracted by their betrayal of Robert—Eddie's brother, Lucy's fiancé. There was guilt, yes, but no sense of danger, no universe in which Eddie could have conceived of harming Lucy. When the memory fades, Eddie flees the park, plunges himself into the bowels of the subway once again, lands on a C train as the doors are closing. He cannot sit. He paces the car until a woman with children hustles them off the train at West Fourth Street and ushers them into a neighboring car that doesn't have Eddie in it.

Along the journey home, something clicks for Eddie. Though I have only recently revealed myself to him, Eddie identifies me as the culprit, which kicks off a harangue: *How could you do it? Why? Why? Why?* and the like, all vocalized aloud. As I lack both substance and voice, this performance only enhances Eddie's perceived derangement, frightening more fellow travelers. Like a chemist stepping back to view an unfolding reaction, I observe what I've sown: *madness*. See what power I have? Not just over Eddie's body but his mind too! How shall I use it?

Eddie's hysteria coupled with my own navigation carries us back to his apartment, where he calls Joanne, his mother. After ranting gibberish into her answering machine, Eddie paces some more, shaking loose the recollection that Joanne is away visiting friends in Tel Aviv. It is 9:15 p.m. in Brooklyn, which—if Eddie were inclined to calculate—brings Israel to 4:15 a.m.

He discards his next impulse, which is, absurdly, to call Robert. Robert! To whom Eddie believes he owes what little sanity he has but whom he's wronged beyond forgiveness. Eddie wails aloud, then hops up to storm about the place again, pulling at his hair.

"*You* pushed her!" He does not know my name. To Eddie, I am still *You* or *The Other*. "*You* killed her! How could you? Why? *Why?*"

Rabid, he hurls our body about, crashing into furniture, flinging papers, mail, magazines, books, anything that isn't nailed down. He throws open cabinets, searching for alcohol, of which there is none. (Only a single beer in the fridge, where it does not occur to him to look.) I'm riding this out at first, letting it go on, observing his utter lack of competency, considering how I might take advantage. But then Eddie ransacks the medicine cabinet for pills, pouring any and every kind he can into his hand. I shake these away before they get to our mouth. What's next? Razor blades, which I knock to the floor.

I didn't think Eddie was capable of suicide, but now I reassess, ready to fight for our life. To think that I'm the one who wants to save it. But I do. His eyes land on the only sharp kitchen knife he owns. He raises the blade, aiming it toward our throat. *No!* We struggle. He falters; my will is stronger. I make him hurl it far across the room.

"Enough of that!" I tell him. "No more!"

Whether he hears me or not, Eddie gives up—at least for now—on offing himself, myself. Ourself. We stand amid the chaos he's made of the apartment. A book is splayed, face down at our feet, the title catching Eddie's eye. He kneels and picks it up. Ha! *The Splintered Self.* I swear I didn't orchestrate this; how could I have? Call it happenstance, a higher power, fate, or what you will; occurrences like this make me believe. I seize the moment, will Eddie to open the book and investigate, let him think, *So this is what's wrong with me!* attributing me to yet another mental disorder. Good. Let him call me an "alter ego," a different "personality," a "dissociative identity." Give him the hope that he might be fixed, that there might be a life without me. Drop his guard. How easy it will be for me then!

But my fantasy of a coup comes under threat before I can formulate a plan. As Eddie lists against the wall, reading—first the blurb, eyes welling, then the introduction through flowing tears—his atoms readjust, like a Rubik's Cube or a rotary safe, turning, churning, until: click! A physical staunchness I've never known in Eddie cuts off my power, rendering him—at least for the moment—complete and singular. In charge. The room dims, fades to darkness.

When the fog lifts from my eyes, I am running; Eddie is running. I am breathless, with no idea where we are, as the body hurtles up a dirt road that turns paved only once an unfamiliar building looms into view. It's huge, like a medieval castle left to the elements.

At least, I reassure myself, I am still here, still capable, if deeply shaken. Whatever happened to Eddie under the influence of that book was a warning to me, a preview of my own obliteration. Never have I conceived of such a thing. All along, at least since our adulthood, I've been able to determine when to take over, *whether* I am present with Eddie or not. I have never faced the threat of oblivion. That damn psychiatry book! I should have disposed of it when I had the chance.

Now Eddie pulls himself up a stone path through weedy, overgrown terrain, mounts the front steps of the building, and rings a bell at the side of a heavy wood and wrought iron door. When there's no answer, he knocks, then heaves himself against it, crying out in desperation for someone to let him in.

At last, the door on our right swings open, presenting the form of a large Black man, a few shades darker than Eddie, our age, maybe younger, dressed in white scrubs. He holds out his arms, palms up.

"Easy. Easy, man. I got you."

It's Eddie who lets us fall into him, trusting easily, either because the man is also Black, because he's young, or calm and even-throated, or because Eddie is forever in search of a savior. I, on the other hand, resist, fight against being "gotten," screaming till Eddie's voice grows hoarse, dry, and finally extinguishes itself.

"Hey!" The man is stronger, skilled at restraining people, gets us into a hold we cannot defy. Darkness drinks us in once more.

2.

EDDIE

I see Lucy flying. I see Lucy's face, her eyes cold and hard. My Lucy—she *was* mine, more than she was ever Robert's. I see the train, my fist full of feathers. Did I do this thing?

"Edward?"

I open my eyes to see Dr. Richard Montgomery in the flesh. I know it's him by his square white face and piercing blue eyes. This guy is my best chance of solving what happened last night, of solving *me*.

He looks way older than he did in the author photograph: blond hair going gray, shadows under his eyes, creases by the mouth and between the eyebrows. Dr. Montgomery looks like the token old guy from some outdoorsy sportswear catalog: sturdy blue-and-red polo shirt, beige corduroys, and an expensive-looking watch. No white lab coat. I bet his pay grade puts him above those.

A quick gander down at my own presentation reveals what I had on when I got here. Shouldn't I be in a hospital gown or something more institutional than faded jeans and a They Might Be Giants *Dial-a-Song* T-shirt?

He's here too—The Other—who takes over whenever he wants, who hurts people I love—*loved*—most. I need Dr. Montgomery to figure out who or what he is and blast him out of me. Does it even work like that? I can feel The Other constantly now, whereas before I could only see and hear him some of the time. I swear to God, he's inside my lungs, breathing my breath. And any emotions I feel—rage, fear, whatever—seem to come from him but make *my* heart pound. And then—Lucy. What he did or I did. I cannot take it.

"Edward." The doctor repeats my name, inching closer. He doesn't want to freak me out or make me shut down. "Can you hear me? Can you respond?" A soft voice, I learned years ago from my stepmother, is a psychiatrist's favorite tool. But I need to trust him.

When I open my mouth, no sound comes out. Not even a rasp. What the fuck? Instinctively I go to grab my throat, but of course, my arms are strapped down. What did The Other do to make them restrain us? Or was I the crazy one? I've been in and out of consciousness since I got here—thanks both to the sedatives and The Other switching in with no notice.

"You were calling out to Lucy, Edward."

Her name rises in my chest, smashes against my brain fog. There is the train again, the lights. It must have been Lucy: Lucy on the Tracks with Feathers. I saw her fly.

"Who is she?" the doctor says, and it's like picking a scab. I can still feel the warmth of her; smell her smell; see her face, her dark hair, the slight hollows and hills of her body. Lucy, Lucy, fucking hell, what happened to you?

"Tears, Edward? Is it difficult to talk about Lucy?"

My body jolts. I'm out; he's in.

3.

PÄR

"—and Robert." Montgomery is midsentence, which gives me a start. "You mentioned him as well. Who are Robert and Lucy?"

"Robert is Eddie's brother," I share. "Older by four years. And oh, how Eddie *loves* his big brother." I pause, giving Montgomery a moment to point out that I've skipped over Lucy. In my experience with shrinks, during initial sessions, most will follow where the patient leads. Challenges and tough love come later. So I treat Montgomery to our smile, dazzling in my execution, merely pretty in Eddie's, but even he has learned to use it to his benefit. The teeth, flawless, thanks to the Ashers' orthodontic budget. The cheeks and jawbone a celebration of our genetic potpourri.

"Why do you speak of Eddie in the third person?" Montgomery, as predicted, leaves Lucy aside for now.

"How should I speak of Eddie?"

Montgomery graces me with his own smile: broad, stretching through the gray-blond stubble on his upper lip, cracking skin robbed of its bloom by time. "To whom am I now speaking if not Eddie?"

You'll pardon me for savoring this moment. No one has asked me this before. I have never introduced myself aloud. Not even to Eddie.

"My name . . ."—I indulge myself, drawing it out—"is Pär. Pronounced like the fruit: pear. It's Swedish, the name our birth mother chose for us."

"You did indicate in your intake forms that you were adopted." A reaching for files, a shuffling of papers. "Biracial. Swedish and African?"

"Eddie filled those out."

"And *Pär* is the name you chose for yourself."

"It's the name our mother chose for Eddie. The Ashers renamed him."

Montgomery pulls his chair—leather, swivel—closer to the recliner I'm strapped to. He adjusts his glasses—wire rimmed, but only on top. I catch a whiff of his cologne, the same one Eddie's stepfather, Michael, uses. I bookmark this. Familiarity with the doctor's taste in scent might be useful one day. Intellectually, we circle one another. Montgomery takes my measure, eyes squinting, head tilting, a staunch believer in his own competence, convinced that he's the smarter man. I won't disabuse him of this until it's necessary. "In response to the presenting problem question, Eddie has written 'memory lapses.' Do you have any insight into those?"

"I do."

Montgomery lifts an eyebrow as if to say *Gotcha*. Well, he hasn't got me. I count to five and raise an eyebrow of my own. Establishing my authority. I'd feel more effective if he would remove these restraints from our arms.

The doctor queries, "Would you say you're responsible for Eddie's so-called lapses?"

"Perhaps."

Montgomery slides the chair back to his desk to make notes. "Is it spelled P-e-r?"

"P-ä-r. Umlaut over the *a*, thank you."

He makes a show of marking the two dots, then calculates his next question. "You say that Eddie loves his big brother."

"Eddie believes the sun rises and sets with the presence of Robert. It has always been thus."

"And how do you feel about your brother, Pär?"

"My brother? Robert is not my brother. The Asher family adopted Eddie, not me. And no, I do not adore Robert. Eddie does only because he sees what I let him see."

"You protect Eddie. Is that your job?"

"I have a number of jobs."

"Can you tell me when you first emerged?"

"In good time."

I won't give myself away. I'll let Montgomery associate me with some crisis from Eddie's adolescence, or else implicate Robert—clever, generous, personable, popular, tall, and rotund Robert—from whose dark side I shielded Eddie for so many years, cooling my figurative heels until the moment was ripe for vengeance.

"Meanwhile, you might release my arms and legs. It's easier to converse unbound."

Montgomery reaches for an intercom and speaks into it, summoning Sylvana, a white nurse with an imposing form, hair in a silvery French twist. She releases my limbs and exits without making eye contact.

"And whose idea was it to come here?" Montgomery says. "Yours or Eddie's?"

This is my Achilles' heel, my shame, the leak in my levee. If I respond with the truth, I'll expose myself. I lost control. Eddie brought us here. I don't know how. He forced me out for the first time in our life. Yet, due to Eddie's decision, his facility, here we are. To be *solved*.

I flounder for a moment, then right myself, hypothesizing that Montgomery will be susceptible to flattery.

"Actually, it was your book that brought us here."

"My book?" He glows. Ah! Jackpot!

"None other," I say. "*The Splintered Self: Challenging the Origins of Multiple Personality Disorder.* Guilford Press, 1988. Eddie received it as a gift several months ago."

"An interesting gift," Montgomery says. "It hardly sold more than a few thousand copies. I didn't know anyone outside the field knew it existed." I detect a bruised ego.

"Well, clearly someone did. As I said, it was a gift. A lady friend thought Eddie might benefit from your research."

"So this lady friend was aware of Eddie's lapses?"

"Indeed."

"And was this lady friend Lucy?"

"No." I say it without thinking. Damn. I should have gone with his error, rewritten our story, relegating Lucy to a mere one-night stand, a single evening of drinking, weed, sex, and a book recommendation. And now he's scribbling in his pad. Montgomery will want to know about Lucy. He'll push, especially if Eddie keeps talking in his sleep—or worse, finds his voice in these sessions.

"Who is Lucy, then?" he asks.

"Who, indeed?" I search my wits for a good riddle to keep him off track, coming up empty. I'm weakening. There is no doubt about it. This place, this pompous white expert, is not good for me. My only hope is keeping him and Eddie in the dark.

4.

EDDIE

"—is it you?"

Dr. Montgomery just called me some other name that I missed, then says, "Eddie?"

I nod. Still can't speak. Wait—so I'm Eddie now? Which means The Other must have gone to the trouble of telling him that no one calls me Edward.

"Shut your eyes if that helps," Montgomery urges. "Bring up anything you can of the night before you arrived here."

I shake my head, pointing to my throat to show I still have no voice. I bet The Other does.

Dr. Montgomery tells me, "Write." He hands me a pen and a lined pad of paper. The pages are stark white like everything else in this room, Montgomery included. Lucy was the opposite. She came in bold, bright colors: reds, purples, greens, like that vintage flapper hat she was wearing the last time I saw her. The one with the feathers. My fingers still remember the texture of it, the felt, the place where the satin ribbon made a dent.

My hands are sweating now; I have to grip the pen tightly to keep it from slipping. As I fill the page, the doctor rises from his seat and hovers, which does not help my nerves. Still I write, describing how I waited for Lucy, lurking outside their building. I followed her down the subway stairs. We fought. And then. And then what? Lights, faces, feathers . . .

"Eddie, stay with me," Dr. Montgomery commands, raising a hand as if to hypnotize me. "I need this part of you to stay."

I write *"Okay,"* because I am a compliant guy. At least part of me is. I come in parts, according to Dr. Montgomery's book, which was originally slipped to me by a woman I had sex with, or more accurately, who had sex with me. This woman had shockingly thin thighs, bobbed hair, and gravitas, much older than me. Montgomery was an acquaintance of hers maybe? Someone associated with her husband? Some things are clear while others are—not just murky, but *absent.* There is no *coming into clarity,* no *just out of reach,* nothing vague about my memories. They are accessible or they are not. There is a big, dark hole in my memory after the train and the feathers. I didn't look down at the tracks. Instead I fled, ran outside into the park, then back to the subway. Next, I remember tearing up my apartment, pouncing on the book. I found my way to this place, Hudson Valley Psychiatric Hospital, where I knew Dr. Montgomery was the director and chief psychiatrist. I pounded at the heavy doors.

There was a guy named Dwight, either a doctor or a guard, I couldn't tell which. He wore white. Then, an oldish woman with red chipped nails, lips twisted in judgment, who handed me a clipboard full of forms.

Montgomery takes his seat again and snaps his own pen into action. His is fancy and monogrammed. I bet it was a gift from his wife. He wears a thick gold wedding band.

"You followed this Lucy down the subway stairs," he says. "You confronted her. Why?"

How do I explain it? The rage, the fear of losing her. Her evasive bullshit, the pain of becoming an afterthought—less than an afterthought—when we were finishing each other's sentences just a few months ago. I write it like this:

"You can't imagine how close we were, me and Lucy." It's the best I can do to say "you can't imagine." Because if I tried to describe what we were like, I'm scared it'll cheapen what we were. "We were one" is how it felt, but that sounds like the worst of clichés. There was so much more to us than that.

What I come up with next is:

"Fuck you, Lucy." As I write those words, I see myself reaching for her. My arms ache with the muscle memory. What I wanted was to reclaim her. To bring us back to the times in Central Park, when sheets of rain sent everyone else running, leaving us drenched but free and happy. So happy. Lucy, my Lucy.

There's just no way I—as myself, as Eddie Asher—could ever hurt her. It was The Other if anyone. I believe that with my entire soul. But what if I am dead wrong?

❧

Time passes, hours, I think, though it may be a day. I am in and out. Hands free now, Dr. Montgomery at my side, still or again.

With shaky hands I write to Dr. Montgomery, *"How long have I been here?"*

"Two days, almost three."

Almost three days. My rusty brain plays back more snatches. Nurses in white serving pills in paper cups. Men in white scrubs, strapping and unstrapping my wrists.

When Dr. Montgomery smiles, the corners of his eyes crease. The Other studies him over my shoulder. "His face," The Other says in my ear, "will be hanging off itself soon, whereas the Black in us will stave that off for years." His words set me to wondering about things that rarely cross my mind. For example, what is "Montgomery"—English? Scottish? "Montgomery" comes with crystal-blue eyes and a straight nose—not too long, not too broad or narrow—which I bet the doctor takes for granted. A "goyish" nose, my mother would say with a twinge of mistrust.

But why does The Other need me to notice this? Why does he need me to wonder what it feels like to gaze out at the world from the safety of those eyes, over a nose like that nose? He's not good-looking in any sense, but his eyes and nose can take him anywhere. Dr. Montgomery, whose whole being is the color of the beach—white sand, yellow sun, blue sky, and water. "He would fit in with her," says The Other. By "her," I know he means our birth mother, Britta. "He would fit in with her whole family. He could pass for a Swede. He could *be* a Swede."

"Eddie?" Dr. Montgomery's voice breaks through. "Do you know why you were so agitated when you arrived?"

"I don't remember being agitated." Though the images I remember are more than enough to explain agitation.

"You were quite explosive, posing a risk to staff as well as to yourself. You arrived at four o'clock Sunday morning. Dwight, one of the orderlies, brought you in. You were disheveled, demanding to see me."

"I looked you up." I remember sitting in my apartment, taking in the blurb of the book and bits of the introduction, which dangled the promise of wholeness, or "integration." Reading, I thought: if The Other and I become "integrated," we'll no longer have to share this body. The lapses will end. I'll stop missing out on the life that was mine first. Maybe that was the change: I uncovered something, and now I'm a threat to The Other. Is that why he's stolen my voice?

"My theories resonated for you?" Dr. Montgomery smiles slightly. "How many alters do you have, Eddie?"

"Only one I think."

Montgomery's pale eyebrows arch higher. "So just Pär?"

I start. *"Why did you say that name?"*

"'Pär' is how he introduced himself to me. Did you give him that name?"

"No!" I underline it several times. *"No, I did not!"* I am agitated, breathing hard. I see Dr. Montgomery straighten up, glancing at the

restraints. My head aches; chills creep up my back. *Pär?* How the fuck can The Other call himself Pär? How dare he steal all I have of my biological mother? But of course he would. He is not my strength, like I thought at first, not my friend at all. Fucking Pär. I hold myself steady and write, *"I didn't know he had a name."*

"He said it was the name your Swedish birth mother chose for you." Dr. Montgomery studies my face. "Fascinating. He took the name your adoptive parents cast aside. And you had no idea?"

I can only stare, feeling violated, robbed of the one thing that was mine alone.

5.

EDDIE

I spent the night strapped into the recliner again. I can't remember why, but this morning, Dwight released my arms and legs and took me for a shower. Once I was dressed in the beige uniform, he brought me a tray of eggs, toast, and mediocre coffee. Now I sit in an ordinary chair in Dr. Montgomery's actual office, facing him across his wide leather-topped desk. His degrees and awards preside from the walls in gleaming gilt frames.

"Your distress level spikes each time we try to get at what exactly happened on the night you arrived," Dr. Montgomery tells me. "Why don't we put that aside for now, until we've got a more complete background, including anything you might know about your parents' psychiatric history."

I assume he means my adoptive parents, seeing as I know nothing about my birth parents' mental health. Montgomery produces another pad and pen, but when I reach for them, my arm snaps back against my will. Pär, of course. And it's he who speaks:

"Eddie is unqualified to give a history of any kind. I told you that."

I can actually hear him as though he's sitting beside me. How? It's one thing to whisper in my ear, but for Pär to speak—using my own defunct voice—while I'm conscious is new territory. Either he's evolving or I am.

"Ah! *Pär.*" Dr. Montgomery smiles with recognition. "How are we this morning?"

Is he shitting me? Just as I write the word *"We?"* underlining it three times, Pär replies, "Never better. Ask me anything."

"You claim Eddie is unqualified," says Dr. Montgomery slyly. "But you also told me that you are prone to fabrication and embellishment. If I am to help you—and Eddie—it's important that I start out with the truth. What would it be like for you to be candid with me?"

"Candid? Oh, Monty!" Pär laughs, slipping back inside. But my awareness of him remains sharp. He's here beside me, behind me, around me. Fucking everywhere I am.

"It's me, Doctor," I write on the pad, awkward as it is to address him like that on paper, *"but Pär is here too. It's never been this way before."* I try to explain that I've never witnessed what Pär does while he's doing it.

"It's fascinating, frankly," says Dr. Montgomery. "In all my years of practice, I have never had the occasion or good fortune to meet with two of a patient's identities simultaneously." He makes a note. "Ah, and I must have you sign that release we discussed in order to include you in my next paper."

I have no memory of such a discussion. I bet I know who does.

"Are you aware of switching?" Dr. Montgomery asks me.

"Not in advance. But I know when it's happened. When it's over and I've switched back."

I don't know how to talk to him about this. The only thing that reassures me is knowing it was my decision to come here, *my* idea, not Pär's, to come and be cured, if that's even possible.

"So, when you dissociate," says Dr. Montgomery, "you're aware of Pär taking over?"

I write, *"I'm not aware of dissociating. How could I be?"* Am I, though? *"I've been aware of fading out. Not of him taking over. Not until coming here at least."*

I suspect Pär is teasing him, letting me share this much. I can see Dr. Montgomery's eyes widen with excitement. I am—*we are*—an exceptional specimen for his research. He asks me more, about my childhood, our past. Was there abuse of some kind? Neglect? A separation from a caregiver or loved one?

I scour my memory for anything that might fill the bill, offering up the divorce. But I was this way beforehand. Pär, I think, has always been here. I write, *"I came this way."*

"Of course! The adoption." Dr. Montgomery scribbles in his notebook.

In my own, I write, *"But my mom and dad adopted me when I was a week old. There was no trauma."* I shake the pad at him until he looks up and reads it.

"Perhaps there was no neglectful orphanage or abusive circumstances," says the doctor, "but recent studies suggest that infant brains are deeply affected by the early separation from the biological mother. Relinquishment trauma." He writes another note, then nods in approval of his own insights. "What I'd like, Eddie—it's still Eddie? Yes? What I'd like, then, is for you to continue the independent journaling to see if something more comes up to inform this assessment."

Now he calls for Dwight.

"Tell me more about relinquishment trauma." But Pär slaps the pen out of my hand and laughs aloud, taunting me: "Butterfingers!"

❦

Another day. Dr. Montgomery raises the subject before I can. "We were talking about relinquishment trauma. You had written that the separation from your birth mother couldn't have been traumatic because you were too young to have thoughts."

My heart starts pounding at this point, palms growing warm. It's Pär's anxiety rising, not mine.

"Primitive memories precede language." The doctor shares some of the research, explaining that even adoptees with stable, loving families may show signs of trauma. "In cases of domestic violence during pregnancy, for example. There's also the impact of in utero rejection, when a birth mother who is ambivalent about parenting secretes chemicals that reach her unborn child. And of course, the loss of connection to the body who has hosted the developing infant for nine months."

Pär squirms wildly inside. He doesn't want me to hear the science, the possibilities. He's looking for a way to break in before I can get any answers.

"So I lose time because my birth mother gave me up?"

"I'd need to know more about your history to answer that."

"But something bad happened that I can't remember? I'm not just naturally psycho?"

"Dissociation often results from trauma. There are a variety of treatments available which have yielded some success in such cases. Hypnosis, for one. Electroshock, though that can backfire and lead to memory loss, which wouldn't do."

"Electroshock?" Will they hook us up to some torture device to purge us of one another?

"Never without your consent." Dr. Montgomery responds to the horror on my face, though there's something appealing about the idea of being zapped into normalcy. He continues, "There are other ways. Things I'm experimenting with on my own. For example, something I call Direct Targeted Exposure, where we go back in time to locate and undo the trauma, as it were. You would agree beforehand to participate in my research project. DTE would require finding your birth mother if possible and, simply put, reimprinting your brain."

"By giving me back to her?"

"In a manner of speaking. Connecting you to either biological parent might be helpful. It's still a theory in its early stages."

I write that I'd have no way of finding my birth mother, that my birth father—Kenyan, Ethiopian, or Somali—is a big question mark.

"Your interracial background is another aspect for us to explore," he says. "We know that there is some trauma inherent in that."

"In being mixed?"

"Not in being mixed per se. It's more about being *of* two races yet belonging to neither."

"Is that usually traumatic?" I've known for some time that being the only Black person in my family's circle contributed to my sense of oddness. Not only did we have no Black family friends, I was told to avoid "dangerous" Black people, discouraged from making Black friends. How could I, looking as I did, not feel odd? But trauma is more than that. I write, *"Isn't trauma when something awful happens that scars you for life? Like combat veterans?"*

"That's acute trauma. There are all different kinds." Dr. Montgomery looks down at my pages again, digging for more revelations. "Was your birth mother a substance abuser?"

"Not that I'm aware of. I, on the other hand, partake quite a bit."

Dr. Montgomery looks unfazed. "Yes, we did blood and urine tests when you arrived and identified significant levels of cannabis."

That would be the special joint my neighbor Sasha gave me. It hit like something more than weed. *"Was there anything else? A hallucinogen or something?"*

"We're still waiting for the full analysis. You were distraught, certainly, which is why you dissociated. Your trauma response was activated somehow, prefrontal cortex was shut off, amygdala went into high gear. And I'm guessing that's when Pär took over."

6.

PÄR

It did go a bit like that. Montgomery is right about some, though not all of it. We were not always at odds, Eddie and I. You must know this before we go any further. Long before we arrived at the Hudson Valley Psychiatric Hospital, long before we had any inkling of Lucy, or even Robert, Eddie and I were one in the most primitive cellular sense. I came to be inside the womb along with him, then took my current form when he was just a few hours old, at the end of the surgery, when things were being tidily stitched up. And once Eddie was left behind, left alone at the mercy of harried, rough-handed nurses, I nestled into the wound itself, believing I could help him heal.

And so, while I didn't *arise* like a "dissociative identity," Montgomery is correct that protecting Eddie, curating what he absorbed of life, was once my primary function. From the beginning, whatever I didn't think Eddie could handle, I edited out, which is why his memory is so full of holes. Mine, by contrast, is excellent. I can tell you nearly everything that brought us to this point, to this hospital. For those few matters I'm unsure of, I'll extrapolate and embellish based on the facts I have.

Like the story of our conception, which begins in June of 1965, in a comfortable hotel suite in midtown Manhattan. I like to imagine the Waldorf. Here is Britta, a gawky sixteen-year-old Swedish girl, in

America for the very first time. She's tall, strong shouldered, and fair in a typically Swedish way that Americans go for. Watching a beautiful boy admire her, Britta's sense of adventure takes over. He is staggeringly handsome, with deep, dark skin like no one Britta has ever seen in her home village of Boliden. Such novelty is exactly what Britta came for.

On the whole, Swedes are polite, reserved, not given to excess, never boastful. Britta wants the opposite of all that. She wants to personify excess like Americans, to meet an American boy, to be adored as the next Ann-Margret.

The beautiful boy has to repeat himself twice before she is able to understand his English, which is halting, unsure.

"I like very much the Beatles, and you?"

Britta takes a risk and smiles. "Yes. And Elvis Presley."

This boy is not the American boy Britta hoped to meet—not cocky and self-assured like Elvis Presley himself, with thick, shiny hair and a slow, easy grin. But this boy—with his tightly coiled hair and black skin (not brown-black but *black*-black, ever and ever *so* black!), his high cheekbones and hooded, mysterious eyes—fascinates Britta. Beautiful and brave, he's the only boy who has dared to speak with her, though all the others are staring. Tomorrow, they will meet their American host families, but tonight there is an informal gathering, a "mixer" for the foreign exchange students, who represent nineteen different countries.

The music changes and the boy extends his hand, inviting her to dance. Britta follows him without so much as a backward glance at the other two girls from her country, who giggle together, trying out the idiomatic English phrases they've learned. Britta dances, changing already. The night is as young as she is, the scent of possibility more intoxicating than alcohol. And the music, the *music* . . .

That is my story of how Britta, our birth mother, met our birth father. Highly plausible, I think, given the facts I have.

There's more. Around this time, in a classic six prewar on West Eighty-Sixth Street, an awkward, chunky three-year-old boy named Robert Daniel Asher is riding his tricycle. Around and around go the wheels. He is thinking of motion and speed, not of the babies his mother waits for, singing to her belly. They come and go. The babies go without coming.

∽

Some months have passed—we're at a bus depot, somewhere in rural New Hampshire. There is a mirror in the bathroom. Britta sets down her small suitcase, steadies herself, and takes in her image, so changed from the day she arrived in this country. Her hair, grown long—wild from the wind and rain—frames a face more drawn, older than her now seventeen years. Under the heavy American men's raincoat, her body swells incongruously. She's hidden the pregnancy from her host family, but soon it will be apparent to everyone. Britta means to hide somewhere, somehow, until the baby is just about to come, then go to a hospital and—*what?* Leave it there for the nurses to sort out? Britta never thinks beyond the arrival at the hospital, never thinks of the pregnancy as a baby—a living, breathing soul that might cry and need . . . her. Only her. Mamma. She thinks of her own mother, not herself. She cannot be Mamma to anyone.

The remaining pieces of the narrative: Britta's arrival in New York, where she searched for the baby's father, found him, but opted not to share her condition; later, the childbirth; Britta's surprise to see that the baby is not the Pär of her dreams—no lake-blue eyes or sunshine hair; her simultaneous regret and relief that he is not. But the important part is that the baby—formerly Pär—will grow up to be Edward Benjamin Asher, whom you know as Eddie.

I kept the name Pär, as you know, and accepted that I was along for the ride. I'd cast in my lot with Eddie. He needed me, and that was that. I kept quiet most of the time at first. I watched, I studied, I waited. It was not until he was six years old that I came forward.

I remember the afternoon of Eddie's first memory lapse like it was yesterday. He was small for his age—as he would remain until puberty—and roughhousing with Robert, who was then a robust ten-year-old, tall, given to plumpness. Robert had not intended to hurt Eddie but, due to the size differential, had done so. It was the pain, the crack of our head against the radiator, that summoned me to action. Eddie experienced it as blacking out, then awakening to learn that he'd attacked his brother—lunged at him like a mad dog, sunken his teeth into Robert's hand, drawn blood. Eddie had no recollection of having done such a thing, though clearly it had been done. From where Eddie sat, in Joanne's well-upholstered lap, he could see Robert, cowering in the corner, washcloth wrapped around his hand.

"What the hell happened?" their father demanded upon entering the boys' room. (They'd have had their own rooms if not for Eddie's fear of the dark. As it was, he wound up in Robert's bed every night, wedged against the older boy.) Dave was flummoxed. Eddie was the fragile brother, the crier. For Robert to be the one in tears didn't compute.

"He went nuts," Robert blubbered. "We were playing and one second, he was—you know—Eddie. And then he was like this *beast*."

It was the first such episode of many. One minute Eddie would be *Eddie*—meek, sweet, if a bit nervous, as teachers characterized him on report cards—then suddenly he would turn volatile, hell-bent on destruction. To Eddie, it was a fast-forward to the near future, having no idea of how he'd gotten there.

To outsiders, meaning to anyone who was not Eddie, the lapses came out of the blue. In truth, they were brought on by the threat of physical or mental annihilation—such as being landed on by a brother who was more than double his size. An exaggerated activation of the amygdala, if you will. And why did it start then? Why at six and not sooner? Well, I was just six myself; it hadn't occurred to me to try it before.

After the third or fourth incident, a colleague of Dave's referred the family to a child psychiatrist, Dr. Glenda Lloyd, who would soon change the trajectory of the Asher family dynamic in more ways than one. Eddie liked her immediately. He called her "Glinda" after the Good Witch in *The Wizard of Oz*—a horror film, from Eddie's perspective, to which he was once exposed by a babysitter. Dr. Lloyd did bear a slight resemblance to Billie Burke—tall, with cascading waves of blond hair. Eddie believed she *was* a good witch, his young mind endowing her with great benevolent powers. He fantasized that an hour spent with his Glinda would yield the same magic as the kiss her eponym used to protect Dorothy.

Eddie dreamt about her too—dreams he'd never share in therapy or anywhere. In the dreams, Dr. Lloyd *was* Glinda the Good Witch, decked out in the same big, pink satin dress and towering tiara. Eddie was with her in Oz, along with the munchkins and the flying monkeys. She didn't speak much and neither did Eddie, but there was always a seat for him beside her throne. With Glinda's arm around him, Eddie could feel her magic.

In therapy sessions, Eddie would stare at her: the composite image of Glinda the Good Witch and his birth mother, about whom Eddie had been told very little. He knew her name, Britta, that she was Swedish, very tall, very blond, and that she was too young to be a mother. In any event, Dr. Lloyd was the grande dame of Eddie's semiconscious.

7.

EDDIE

On my first full day free from restraints, Dwight, whose title is orderly but whose responsibilities seem to include security, shows me around. The room I'll be sharing with another patient is bigger than the exam room with the recliner but smaller than Dr. Montgomery's office. My bed is neat, with tightly drawn white sheets and a scratchy standard-issue gray blanket. The other bed is in disarray thanks to my roommate, who's elsewhere now.

"Gilooley is a character" is all Dwight says about him at this point. He calls me "blood" right away, noting that I am the only Black patient in the ward, the first one since the start of his employment a year ago.

"Catchment area's not what you'd call diverse," Dwight tells me.

The bedrooms are located on the second and third floors of the main building. Gloom prevails, not only in the beige of the furniture and the patients' clothing, the gray of the blinds on the windows, the white of the walls, the sheets, the uniforms worn by nurses and orderlies. I can feel the grimness in the other patients we pass on the stairs and in the hallways. Some are solo, others accompanied by staff members. Men and women alike, unkempt, deflated silos brimming with secret torment. I feel no different, slouching beside Dwight, taking in his monologue. But as we're crossing the gymnasium—with its buckling wood panels, indoor track overhead, and lopsided basketball hoop—he tells me it's not just my race that makes me unique. I'm the only patient he knows of who rode a Greyhound to get here and checked himself in voluntarily.

"I know you don't talk," he says. "But one day maybe you'll let me know why you chose to come here. I mean, people get *sent* here, man. You know that, right?"

The main floor houses offices, examination rooms, an auditorium, a dining room, and a rec room with pinball machines, card tables, two shabby beige sofas, and equally drab chairs. The room is sparsely populated when Dwight brings me by: just a handful of residents reading, staring into space, or playing cards as light streams through an incongruously grand gothic window that looks out on the property. We're high on a hill full of trees, bark laid bare for winter, the pines a deep January green, their needles shuddering in the chill.

The dining room has a wall full of sepia-toned photos from the hospital's heyday.

"Back then," says Dwight, "this building here was for white patients only. One wing for men, another for women." He points to posed group photographs from each constituency. "The Negro ward"—Dwight makes finger quotes—"was down the hill in the annex, along with the 'Locked Ward for Criminal Deviants.'

"They lost the annex to a fire in the '70s," says Dwight. "Today everyone's under one roof. Men, women, Black, white, harmless, deviant."

"Now that roommate of yours, Ray Gilooley," Dwight says as we move past the dining room gallery, "he would have been in that locked ward for damn sure."

Since I have no paper, I wait for him to expand.

"Yeah, dude doesn't weigh more than a buck twenty, but watch out when he's pissed off." Dwight whistles, ushering me back to the hallway. "We got you rooming with Ray because of how you flipped out on me and the nurses, but he can be—what's the word?" He leaves his own question hanging. "I mean, he's okay if you don't provoke him. You don't seem like the provoking type."

I nod, because *I'm* not. Pär is a different story. But Dwight has already moved on with the rules. "Security's high. There are monitors in every room and a whole system of coded whistles in case of power outages. We have plenty of those. Opossums get at the wires. Follow the rules and you'll be just fine."

I feel as safe from external forces as I need to be. Just not from Pär.

8.

PÄR

They've started Eddie on a new pharmaceutical regimen that has yet to take effect, but it will soon, no doubt. I have no love for psychotropic medication. You would think that after so many years, trials, starts, stops, and pivots, I would have learned to dodge the impact—perhaps by ducking into an unaffected center of the brain and letting the chemicals slip past me. Believe me, I have tried. The first time was at the hands of Dr. Glenda Lloyd, though psychopharmacology was only a small part of their sessions. It seemed to be an afterthought, which was part of her formidable stealth.

Glenda was gentle when she spoke to Eddie, who was not yet seven when they began treatment, usually asking questions that she made clear he was under no obligation to answer.

"Has it been a good week?" or "A fun week?" Her smile a toothy hammock above her narrow chin. "What was the most interesting thing that happened this week?" "Can we talk about the fears today?"

Eddie's response was, more often than not, a shrug. He wanted Dr. Lloyd to like him and feared saying something dumb that would disappoint her. As he didn't know what would or would not disappoint her, he kept mum to the best of his ability. She gave him puzzles to do, markers and paper to draw with, though Eddie had no artistic talent.

It was very difficult not to grab the markers and try my own hand, suspecting as I did that I was the superior illustrator. But I was also curious about what Dr. Lloyd would think of Eddie in his natural state.

Of the pills, there were two—a tiny round pink one and a larger white one—each with a split down the middle. Eddie hated swallowing pills, so Joanne embedded them in a bit of cookie dough, which went down nicely. Initially we started with half of each pill and worked our way up to three-fourths and finally a whole. It took us two weeks to advance to a full dose, and I noticed nothing at all until the third week, at which point colors began to come in more vividly than before. Things that had been flat, like the walls and floor, gained bizarre dimension, bowing, rising, and sinking with no predictability. Joanne's lipstick created a violent crimson gash across her face, the yellow kitchen was now a blinding rotating sun. Sounds were sharper and louder—Dave's chewing, Robert's snoring, Joanne's laughter, all of it an assault to my psychic equilibrium. I could not think straight, was powerless to guide and monitor Eddie, unable to switch in.

On the other hand, Eddie himself seemed unaffected by the psychosensory assault. As paintings and light fixtures swung out from their spots and looped around the room randomly, he passed through these obstacles as if there were nothing amiss.

Whereas I normally considered myself the driver of the apparatus that was Eddie's body, glad to relinquish the wheel to him as I saw fit, now I was an invisible, unwilling passenger, with no seat belt, no safety hatch, no intercom with which to request exit. It was as though we'd exchanged roles, Eddie and I. The difference being that when I was in charge, I was nonetheless hyperconscious of him, focused on him, incapable of acting without considering the impact on him. I had not a single thought that was independent of Eddie and his well-being. But with our positions reversed, he was no more aware of me than he had ever been. I had no more significance than the crescent moon–shaped scar I called home. Oh, the humiliation!

Yet the pills kept coming. Joanne created fresh cookie dough each night for the morning pills (which she and Robert would help themselves to as the day wore on). Eddie kept swallowing.

To report on the impact, Joanne would join Eddie at the end of each session with Dr. Lloyd.

"He seems less bothered by things," Joanne said on one occasion. "Isn't that right, Eddie?"

"Kind of." A verbal shrug.

"Kind of?" Dr. Lloyd's method—employed by every subsequent shrink, we'd find—was to repeat the last thing Eddie had said with a question in her voice, leaving him a blank to fill.

"I kind of, um"—Eddie fumbled half-heartedly for words, distracted by the puzzle—"don't really notice when things don't bother me." Then, holding aloft a lily-shaped piece: "Mommy?"

Joanne got down on the floor to help Eddie with the puzzle. It was a jungle scene: giraffes, elephants, monkeys, trees with giant leaves, colors swirling and psychedelic (it being 1973), exaggerated in shape and shade, utterly dizzying to me. As Joanne moved the pieces around, I lost my hold on consciousness.

"—half the time he doesn't!" Joanne was saying when I tuned back in. Whatever the complete rejoinder had been led Dr. Lloyd and Joanne to have a good, girlish giggle together. Even Eddie looked up, and I felt his cheeks crease in mirth. I did notice, and I doubt that Eddie did, that Dr. Lloyd never quite met Joanne's eyes.

In any case, the conclusion was that Eddie's new medication was a success. The erratic behavior, the turning on a dime from placid to ferocious, had ceased. Things still frightened Eddie as much as ever—cats, spiders, watermelon seeds, turtlenecks—but his crying about it had diminished, which made him much easier for others to live with. As for me, all I could do was retreat, too disoriented to act. I was frantic with worry. I did not believe Eddie could function without my influence. Who would dull the pain of living for him? What might he stumble upon that he was not prepared to understand? You can't imagine how helpless I felt.

There were reprieves here and there. Occasionally, Eddie would develop a reaction to the medication, a rash or a new tic that could be traced back to one or another of his pills. Or else they would stop working, and Dr. Lloyd would make an adjustment either in dose or substance. During these periods, I would awaken and enjoy a modicum of vitality before being relegated to view-only status.

But let the record stand: I was the first to mistrust Dr. Glenda Lloyd.

⟋⟍

Eddie had been seeing her for almost three years when Robert joined his first family session. Dr. Lloyd wore her customary uniform of a Mexican peasant top with faded blue jeans, her long blond hair falling free. The contrast was stark between the psychiatrist and Joanne, who— in addition to being short and squat—had neat, cropped brown hair and wore red lipstick, which she must have left on her bedside table, because the boys had never seen her without it (not even when Eddie had fits at night).

Later, over a game of Battleship, Robert confided to Eddie that he thought Dr. Lloyd was "pretty in a folk-singing sort of way."

Eddie mulled this over. "What sort of pretty is Mom, then?"

"Mom's not pretty." Robert's tone was indignant. "She's our mom!"

Eddie surmised that "pretty" was beneath their mother, undignified, un-mom-like.

"What other kinds of pretty are there?" he asked. "Besides folk-singing?"

"I don't know. I made that up. There are all kinds."

"What kinds, though?" Eddie, almost nine, was building a mental portfolio of information about girls, regarding whom his brother seemed deeply knowledgeable.

"Shut up," Robert said. "I don't want to talk about this with you."

The only person Robert did want to talk about girls with was his best friend Bruce Fishman, who lived on the fourteenth floor of their building, two flights below the Ashers. On weekends, Robert and Bruce were allowed to visit each other as they pleased. When Robert was feeling especially charitable, he'd bring Eddie, who had no best friend in the building or anywhere else.

There was some good-natured hazing, to be sure, some forcing of Eddie into Bruce's old toy cabinet so Robert and Bruce could pore over Bruce's older brother's girlie magazines without the intrusion of Eddie's questions. The toy cabinet had a loose flap through which Eddie could spy, however. He was nearly as familiar with the basic layout of a naked woman as were Bruce and Robert.

One such Saturday afternoon, when Robert and Bruce, just months from their respective bar mitzvot, had secured Eddie in the cabinet to enjoy said magazines, Bruce's mother knocked on the door to announce that it was time for Bruce to go visit his grandmother and for Robert and Eddie to return home. Robert had his own key and let them into the apartment, which the boys assumed was vacant. It was not. Walking down the hall to their bedroom, the boys found themselves facing— coincidence of coincidences—a naked woman, who had just emerged from the bathroom. Robert instinctively grabbed Eddie, covering the smaller boy's eyes, turning him away. The woman hastened to cover her privates with a hand, her breasts with a hank of her long blond hair, which was loose and wild. She did not think to cover her face, which would have been prudent, since hers was a face Robert had been to enough family therapy sessions to identify in a lineup.

Dr. Lloyd was speechless, as was Robert, who hustled Eddie past her into their room.

"Who was that?" Eddie said when Robert released him. Eddie really had not registered her face. (I had.)

"That," said Robert, "was no one. It didn't happen, understand? If you say anything about what we just saw, if you so much as think about it, I will have to hit you very hard, okay?"

"Okay."

"What did we just see, Eddie?"

"Nothing." He really did not know.

"Good boy."

~~~

Robert opted against blowing the whistle on his father and Dr. Lloyd, biding his time for the better part of a year. The secret finally came out on a day that holds a significance for me far beyond the fate of the Ashers' marriage. It was a day that changed me, heightened my understanding of my own existence. For the day that Dave Asher and Glenda Lloyd got sloppy and hence, caught, was the same day—the same moment, frankly—that I became separated from Eddie.

Joanne was hauling fourteen-year-old Robert (with ten-year-old Eddie in tow) to a pediatric diet doctor who rented office space in the same building that housed Dr. Lloyd's practice. It was not the first such doctor she'd brought him to, which made the day feel quite ordinary. Walking from the bus stop, Joanne and the boys chatted about ordinary things like school and the reasons they could not have a dog. Turning onto Lexington, Robert asked for the third time if this appointment was really necessary.

"I'm fine as I am. Everyone likes me like this. Even girls." He winked at Eddie, who knew the statement to be true. At Robert's bar mitzvah, giggling, flirting girls in newly minted high-heeled shoes had been in abundance. Though Bruce Fishman and the other boys had hung back against the wall, Robert had been king of the dance floor, rotating through an unending line of colt-legged, tin-grinning partners.

"You'll thank me," said Joanne nonetheless. "I only want you to be happy."

"How will a diet doctor make me happy?" said Robert.

"He will make you thin."

Robert was pondering a rejoinder when Eddie piped up. "But, Mom, *you're* fat. Aren't you happy?"

Joanne used their arrival as an excuse to evade the question, darting into the revolving doors ahead of the boys. Another family was already in the vestibule awaiting the elevator: a tall, elegantly dressed mother with a plump girl about Robert's age and girth, and a boy about Eddie's age, similarly slight, head down. I began to feel inexplicably on edge. Eddie's hand went to his right shoulder almost as if to reassure me.

Before the children could size one another up, the elevator doors opened, presenting a tightly embracing couple that revealed itself to be Dave and Dr. Glenda Lloyd.

The ensuing chaos—the gasps, denials, accusations, tears, embarrassment, confusion—obfuscated what might have been an even more momentous encounter. (Only I would become aware of the potential, as I would soon be the most impacted by it.)

Dave shouted, "Jo! *Jo!* This isn't what it looks like!" as Joanne and the boys stood briefly frozen.

The elegant woman huffed. "Children, let's not gawk." She grabbed her daughter's hand, then Eddie's, and pulled both onto the elevator.

In turn, Joanne shouted, "Boys!" yanking Robert and the remaining boy onto the elevator as well. Only when the doors closed (on a contrite Dave and a miserable-looking Dr. Lloyd) did Joanne and the elegant woman recognize their errors and exchange boys.

As this occurred, I experienced the most curious sensation. It was I who felt it, not Eddie, of this I am certain. It was an electric shock where I experienced myself as an entire independent being: limbs, a heart, a nervous system . . . the works. Then I saw Eddie, *all of Eddie!* From a distance of just under a yard. I was looking *at* him as I'd only been able to do heretofore with a mirror. Without a mirror, the most I'd seen of him prior to this was the right side of his neck, an earlobe, his chin and what have you, but not this. Eddie was indeed a handsome boy, I'll tell you that much. *Stunning.* But I digress.

There I was, apart from him for the first time since I'd nestled in and then—

All at once I was rooted again. My perch was a lump rather than a groove, but I was stuck fast nevertheless. I felt giddier than I had with Eddie, my heart lighter, my feet unable to resist moving, tapping in a side-to-side jig. The elegant mother placed a hand on my arm, delivered a look that spoke without words: *Be still. We're in an elevator. In public.* But stillness was a challenge for this body, which needed to move. The girl winked at me as if she knew who I was, how I was, and sensed what a struggle it was for me not to dance. I glanced from Eddie—from whom I was still detached—to the numbers that lit up above us. The boy to whom I now adhered counted the elevator's rhythmic bumps, anticipating. Would there be a long hallway down which he would be able to leap? He could leap very high, I felt that in these new legs. The muscles in this body were coiled and primed for flight.

Then, while being this other boy, I caught Eddie's eye and gave him a grin, aware that we (meaning Eddie and the new boy) had been mistaken for one another. I wanted to laugh out loud that the two silly mothers had confused us. But I was silent, mindful of the elegant woman's firm hand on me. No giggling or dancing until the elevator doors opened and I hopped out, ahead of the girl and the mother, into a hall that was indeed long and carpeted and ripe for a big running leap, which I did. I say "I." Of course, it was not "I" but this other boy whose body wore me. It was different from my connection to Eddie in that every motion, every pulse and breath came as a complete surprise. I was a guest rather than a coinhabitant. And this body was more way station than host. I rode along aboard my buoyant new vessel, watching his life with borrowed eyes. He stopped leaping (though, dear lord, it was fun!) and turned toward the sound of his name (which was neither Eddie nor Pär).

The elegant mother, daughter at her side, stood waiting for me with her arms neatly folded. The elevator doors were closed now. Joanne and her boys were nowhere in sight. Which meant that Eddie was gone.

Gone from me. The bouncing joy I'd felt a moment earlier was replaced by surging panic—not for myself, but for Eddie, who, I thought, could not survive without me any more than he could without a heart or brain stem! Had he collapsed in the elevator? Was he now gasping for his last breath? How could I return to him? What was the formula? I was overcome with worry, but there was nothing, *nothing* to do. I was, for the first time since our birth, absolutely Eddie-less. I was so rattled, thinking about Eddie, the boy I'd lost, that I delayed in considering why I had landed on *this* boy and not some other boy.

And now the new boy had returned to the mother and daughter. The former looked stern; the latter nudged him and quipped, "No home training." A phrase with which I was unfamiliar.

"Well," said the mother. "That is going to change, isn't it? You're not living in the woods any longer." Why had I, he, we, been in the woods? The mother gave the shoulder upon which I was situated an affectionate squeeze, which bathed me in a scent that was rich and heavy with floral notes. Joanne's scent had been crisp and lemony.

As I lacked the wherewithal to contemplate the meaning of *home training*, *change*, or *the woods*, I could only glide along for what turned out to be a dentist appointment for both the girl and the boy whose body I belonged to. It was unlike Eddie's dentist appointments, which he faced with terror and tears but had never involved such vigorous digging and prodding with sharp metal instruments. The boy's body flinched with each scrape. I overheard the mother say to the dentist (of whom I could see nothing but sky-blue gloves and matching mask):

"He's only just come to live with us. I suspect he hasn't had much dental care prior to this."

Then there was a needle. A scream from this new throat raced past me. Things went blank.

9.

EDDIE

Still no voice. Keeping on with Dr. Montgomery's assignment, I write anything that feels relevant, either to my memory lapses or my relationships with Robert and, of course, Lucy. The doctor thinks it'll be cathartic even if it scares me—the memories as well as the holes. It would help if I had some weed to get me past the dread. I'm not allowed to smoke here, though Dwight sometimes takes pity on me and sneaks me outside, where we'll share a joint. A red side door in the gymnasium opens directly onto a path into the woods. The cold and our lack of coats—along with the fact that patients need special clearances for walks on the grounds—keep Dwight from taking me far. We shiver together, concealed by a pair of white oaks, smoking. No medication can compete with the restorative pairing of weed and mountain air. At the moment, however, the best I can do is take deep breaths, as Dr. Montgomery recommends, tuning into my memories.

What pops into my head right now is a day when Mom had dragged me along to Robert's appointment with some diet doctor whose office was in the same building as Dr. Lloyd's. That was a big thing for Mom and Robert—fights about food and weight. She was always trying new diets and putting my brother on the same ones. Robert would enlist me to sneak him cookies when she wasn't looking.

He'd say, "Do me a solid, Eddie."

And I'd zoom off for the kitchen, surreptitiously climbing on counters and scaling cabinets to find where Mom had squirreled away the treats.

When I returned with the bounty, Robert would beam and rough up my hair, telling me what a wizard I was.

"Our secret, right?" I'd say, just to hear him say it back.

"Our secret, Eddie." It's hard to express how much I loved being in cahoots with my brother.

So, there we were in the diet doctor's lobby, waiting for the elevator, when the doors opened and there was my dad and, of all people, my psychiatrist, Dr. Glenda Lloyd, making out. Which was one of the most disorienting things that had happened to me at that point. All I could think of was that anything that was going to happen between my parents would be my fault. And I knew that Glenda, whom I thought of as Glinda the Good Witch, was never going to be my shrink again. I didn't yet guess that she'd soon be my stepmother, but still, it was bad.

Sure enough, that afternoon, after Robert's appointment (his first and last with the diet doctor, since no one ever wanted to go back to that building again), my mom went looking through all my dad's stuff—papers and bills—and turned up restaurant and hotel receipts. The whole time, she was cursing Glenda's name. When Dad got home, he came clean, but then went off on Mom, listing all her shortcomings, insisting that it was her fault he'd strayed. But each time they referred to Glenda, it was "Eddie's psychiatrist" or "Eddie's doctor" or "Eddie's something," meaning that each of them saw me at least indirectly as the thing that had driven a wedge between them.

Things got worse between my parents before they fell entirely off the rails.

Robert and I got home from school one day, surprised to find Dad home, already in the middle of a fight with Mom. They were shouting:

Dad: "You're taking him out of therapy because of this? You're punishing our son?"

Mom: "I'll get him a new psychiatrist! A real one who doesn't tear families apart!"

Dave: "He's connected to Glenda!"

Mom: "Don't you say her name in my house. I spit when you say that sick woman's name!"

My brother and I hid out in the vestibule: Robert with a protective arm around me, while I leaned into him—as if our physical closeness might keep the family together. We kept still, listening until something expensive—glass or porcelain—was thrown and shattered. Then the screaming stopped, followed by stomping feet and slamming doors. When we stepped out into the open field of aftermath, there were the remnants of my mother's favorite ceramic fruit bowl. I looked to Robert for comfort, but he turned on me. We were brothers, so we'd scuffled before, play-wrestled, always with Robert going pretty easy on me because I was littler. But I'd never seen his face look like that before: raw and terrifying and full of rage. I didn't know Robert could hate me, but he clearly did then. Maybe he had before, only I'd never seen it. I'd made my parents stop loving one another; had I made Robert stop loving me? Was I cursed? My eyes grew hot, but I fought back the tears. If I cried I'd lose him for sure.

"What kid needs a psychiatrist for four years?" Robert said, shoving me. When I fell to the floor, he took hold of my collar, one fist raised. I held my breath. He was not going to spare me this time. "What psychiatrist can't fix the kid in four years?" Robert held me another beat, then let go and plodded off into his room, leaving me lonelier than I'd felt in my whole life.

♋

Looking back, I know now that I wasn't responsible for the new wedge between my brother and me. Even if you put aside the tension in the household over Dad's affair—arguably, indirectly my fault—ten and fourteen are natural ages for brothers to grow apart, especially if the younger one is a needy little pill. Robert was pubescent. Moody, changing—physically and mentally—hostile with everyone in the family. But anytime he brought his friends around—and there was always a good-size group: Bruce Fishman, a handful of other guys, and a few girls too—Robert seemed gregarious and full of joy, his voice and laughter booming above the others'.

There were times when I'd catch him staring at himself in the mirror, sometimes turning sideways, sucking in his gut, checking the progress of his new facial hair. I had this notion that he was imagining who and how he would be if he had no brother—or if one of the babies Mom lost would have survived so he wouldn't have *me* for a brother.

The next part I should put down is how Robert saved my life. Before I get into that, I feel like I should acknowledge that Dr. Montgomery is getting conflicting information from Pär—who he's still calling my "alter." I'm the "primary," Dr. Montgomery says, the one who "presented for treatment." In any case, whatever the reason for my mutism, whether my unconscious or some other part of my brain is responsible, please accept these as a record of my own true thoughts and memories.

I was ten and Robert was fourteen when my brother saved my life. This was how I knew he still loved me. Dad had just moved out, so things were calmer in the house. Mom was still sad, though, and Robert was still acting testy with me since I had pretty much doomed our parents' marriage.

My brother was probably trying to get at the mirror to check on some new physical development, which he did about a dozen times a day. He knocked and knocked on the bathroom door and finally burst in to find me immersed, face down in the tub like I was trying to float. I don't remember how I got that way; I did so much weird shit as a kid.

But right before Robert got there, I'd had an experience I've never been able to make sense of. Nor have I told anyone until now. Like I said, I don't know how I came to be face down in the water, but there I was. Sounds came in muffled, thick, and dull: the ticking of the clock, the crash of each drop from the faucet. Suddenly I was aware that I was paralyzed that way. I could feel the weight of the water behind me, the air just an inch behind my head. I couldn't arch my neck to break the surface for oxygen. Soon, as it became a fight to keep my lungs closed, I panicked.

But then—and this is the crazy part—the base of the bathtub fell away, opening onto a vast, dark underwater place: a lake or pool with no end. And I split in two.

I know it makes no sense, but I swear I did. There was me, regular Eddie, and then there was another Eddie. It couldn't have been a reflection, as I was underwater already. He was a whole other kid, identical to me as far as I could tell.

I'd stopped fighting for air by then. I wasn't even scared. He took my hand, and we swam together, the two of us, side by side in this cavernous trench. It was beautiful, really, being down there with him. I had such a good, warm feeling, a sense of absolute, utter acceptance. I'd never felt that way before, and I've never felt it since.

The other me swam like a fish, free and easy. He'd power ahead for a bit, then circle back, trying to get me to follow. I couldn't swim fast enough. The fish-boy-me waited as long as he could. Then I heard him say, "I'll come find you," before disappearing into the depths.

The next thing I knew, the bathtub was our regular bathtub again and Robert was there, pulling me out. He wrapped me in a towel, and I could see tears on his cheeks. Our mother ran in and grabbed me from him. While I tried to catch my breath, they chastised me, both of them demanding to know what I was doing, why I had chosen to take a bath in the middle of the day. I had no answers. All I could do was wonder how and if I was ever going to find the Fish-boy again.

I was grateful to have Robert's love back, which made me less lonely than I'd been since I'd stopped seeing Dr. Lloyd. I'd run out of pills by then, so the nerves were as bad as ever, but I still had water as a balm for them.

Mom said no when I asked for swimming lessons. After the incident, I wasn't even allowed baths, only showers. She didn't trust me in an entire pool. So I did what divorced kids do and asked my dad, who didn't know about the bathtub snafu (Robert and I were sworn to secrecy, as Mom feared Dad would blame her). Dad thought swimming lessons were a great idea, anything to give me confidence. He even consulted Glenda, who claimed the physical activity would aid my anxiety.

Mom backed down. Now, at last, like Robert had school and his friends, I had my haven. I would have swum every day if I could have. When we took vacations, there was always the sea, a lake, or a swimming pool in the vicinity. I liked holding my breath, diving far underwater to explore, to see as much as I could see. Fish and other underwater life-forms didn't scare me anymore; I found nothing terrifying in sea- or lake-weed.

Robert would ask, "What do you do under there for so long?" Though he knew I wouldn't answer beyond a shrug.

I dreamt of water, of having gills that let me swim endlessly, deep down under. I was searching for the other Eddie down there, but always woke up before I found him.

10.

EDDIE

"I have some questions about this bathtub incident," Dr. Montgomery says, reading. "You have literally written here about splitting apart. This is fascinating."

"You want to know about the Fish-boy. You think he's Pär, don't you?"

"I know that the Fish-boy is *not* Pär. But it's my hunch that each of these identities—Pär, the Fish-boy, possibly others—emerged as a result of traumas."

"But there was no trauma."

"None that you recall. But there's a discrepancy between what you've written and Pär's account. Look, Eddie . . ." He holds the notebook open to a page where I've described Robert's rescuing me. "Here you say that your brother found you. He pushed open the door?"

"He must have."

"And your mother came in afterward? She didn't hear him knocking and knocking?"

"No one heard us. No one was there but me." My head is pounding now, vision going blurry, confusion setting in.

"No one was there but you and your brother, you mean?"

"No. He came in when he heard me."

"But you were face down in the water. What did he hear?"

"Splashing, I guess." This pen is running out of ink. *"How should I know?"*

"Is it possible that Robert was there longer than you're saying?"

I set down the pen, shut my eyes. I won't write any more about this memory. There's nothing more to say.

11.

PÄR

Reading over Eddie's shoulder as he writes is helpful to me, filling in a bit of what had transpired during my first absence from Eddie's life. (How different the bathtub incident was for me.) Meanwhile, the new boy onto whose body I was now grafted was not the son of the elegant mother. He had recently come to live with the family in an apartment building on the Upper West Side of Manhattan, slightly south and a few blocks east of the Ashers. As far as I could glean from overheard snatches of conversation, the boy was nearly as new to this life as I was.

"Has just come to live with us" was a common refrain from the elegant woman. She mentioned this to the uniformed doormen and elevator men, to neighbors, to people she spoke with on the phone. The "us" was a family brimming with girls, not just the sister of the dentist appointment but three others, as well as an infinitesimal dachshund called Foxtrot who was frequently underfoot and therefore at constant risk of demise. The girls stood in descending height, making stairsteps down from their elegant mother, whose name was as elegant as she was: Dominique LaFontaine. Though the boy was told to call her Mrs. Wynter, he would soon graduate to "Dominique." The sisters' names matched in rhythm: Regina, Sophia (my companion from the dentist appointment), Althea—all but one, who was called Lucy.

Lucy neither rhymed nor matched the others. She stood out for being slighter of build and of a lighter brown complexion than the others. Lucy's mother, I learned from snippets of hushed discussion, was not the elegant woman. I would also learn that Lucy's mother was dead.

The father of the girls was named Tyrone, though the boy called him Mr. Wynter. He belonged to all four girls, even to Lucy. It was Tyrone who interested me the most. Unlike Dave Asher, Tyrone was a Black father: tall, with a musical stride, a booming voice, and a laugh that rang out like the brass horn his name brought to mind.

The apartment, a penthouse atop a building called The Majestic, was sprawling and light filled, overlooking Central Park. It was a veritable art gallery inside, most walls adorned with enormous canvases of oil paintings and woodcuts and charcoal drawings depicting Black people, either posed alone or else captured in motion, at work, in prayer, in song, dancing, grieving. Even the portraits told stories in the intricacies of each face, showing mood, expression, hinting at lives lived. In addition to the canvases, there were wooden masks, as well as stone sculptures, wooden figurines, and drums and tools on display, all, I learned, from West Africa.

The Ashers' art consisted mostly of landscapes, abstract splashes of color, and family portraits, but nothing like this. I wanted to stare and stare, as did the boy, I was fortunate to discover. He was, I was, we were, surrounded for the first time by Black splendor.

"You love those, don't you?" said Tyrone, coming up behind the boy, one hand on the shoulder I now called home. "They belong to your history, you know. Just as you belong to them." Tyrone's palm was strong, with long, nimble fingers. What radiated from them into me could only be described as a love like nothing Eddie or I had ever known.

I sensed that this boy's body was also new to such a touch. I was gaining the ability to scan him for what was and was not familiar. For coded in his cells were images, sounds, flavors, and scents that I soon recognized as his memories: things I would need to learn if I was going to live as him rather than pine for Eddie, whom I expected never to see again. I hadn't had any control over leaving Eddie. I could not work out how I'd possibly return to him. All I knew was that I was now *here*—on Central Park West between Seventy-First and Seventy-Second Streets—with the Wynter family, rather than *there*—on Eighty-Sixth between Broadway and West End Avenue—with the Ashers. So I studied these remembrances, flashes of this boy's *before time* that ran parallel to Eddie's past, which I knew by heart. And now, this boy was learning more about himself, and I was learning alongside him. He was now a "ward" of this family. He belonged to these works of art, this light, this view, this park. But where did he belong prior? I ached to learn of those "woods" Dominique had referenced just as he ached to leap again.

"It's okay," said Tyrone, though I had not heard the boy utter a word. "I understand how that goes. When you have a gift like yours, being still hurts, doesn't it?" He led the way across the apartment, past an ivory-colored grand piano, to a spot in the living room where the rug ended and the floorboards gleamed in the light. There was a mirror along one wall with a freestanding white barre. A dance studio, the boy's mind translated for me, a bona fide dance studio, right inside the apartment. "Here you go." He directed the boy forward. "Knock yourself out."

The heart leapt before the legs could begin. The boy may have been new to the family and the apartment, but I could tell that this corner was already known to him. In the mirror I could see that he had on tights, was dressed and ready to dance. But oh, the mirror. The mirror! Before I could make sense of what, *who*, I was seeing—not Eddie, of *course* this boy wasn't Eddie, not exactly—my gaze was drawn to another figure not far behind Tyrone. It was the girl who did not rhyme. Lucy. She wore a black leotard, pink tights, and an indignant frown, arms akimbo.

On another occasion, Lucy sets the boy straight about the barre. The boy is playing on the balcony with Althea, the second-smallest girl, who has been teaching him a clap hands game.

"Daddy installed that barre for me," Lucy says, joining them outside, shutting the french doors behind her. "It's important that I practice ballet every chance I get." She glances at Althea, then back at the boy. "I'm the best at dancing. Daddy says I'm going to make it as a professional."

"I might make it too," Althea pipes up, though she sounds less sure. "We're too young to know."

"Your arches are too low," Lucy tells her. "Sophia is too fat, and Regina is too tall to do anything but sing." Lucy slips back inside, but not before looking down her nose at the boy, making him wonder if she considers him low-arched, fat, or useless.

"Lucy is mean," Althea tells him. "I love her because I have to. We play and stuff, but she's mean to me and everyone else. It's not her fault. She acts like that because she has problems. *Bad* problems."

"How do you know?"

"*Please.*" Althea waves her hand, intimating. "When you're the youngest, you learn to listen in on conversations, and you find out all the secrets people don't want you to know."

To be taken into a confidence thrills the boy. "There are secrets?"

"So many secrets," says Althea. "Just trust me. Lucy's fun, but watch out. She'll get you. If she says things to hurt your feelings, tell me or Sophia and we will fix her."

As much as he likes this new intimacy with Althea, the boy feels sorry to learn that the first other mixed child he has met, the one who could be a real sister to him, is mean and has problems. "What kind of problems does she have?"

Althea lifts her chin, then makes a key out of her thumb and forefinger, miming locking her lips. The boy will have to wait and learn.

12.

EDDIE

"—can help me understand," Dr. Montgomery is saying as I return to myself. "So let's unpack that, shall we?"

I raise my hand. *"Unpack what?"* I write to show that it's me and not Pär. Dr. Montgomery has asked me to confirm when a switch happens. I think Pär prefers to catch him unawares.

"Eddie!" The doctor greets me with exaggerated geniality. "We were just discussing your history with Lucy. I hope it's all right that we continue?"

My anxiety notches up, but I nod yes. If Pär has been talking about Lucy, I need to know what he's shared.

"So, based on Pär's story, she was someone you met as a child?"

"Lucy? No! What are you talking about?" I shove the pad at him.

"Interesting. A discrepancy."

"I met her three years ago. I was 24 and she had just moved in with my brother. I visited them in Seattle."

Montgomery reads what I've written, reiterating, "Interesting." Now he does his usual thing and scribbles some notes of his own that I won't get to see.

I write, *"It's a crock of shit. He's lying to make me look crazy."*

"And why would Pär do that, do you think?" Dr. Montgomery tilts his head as if he knows the answer. He'll wait while I puzzle it out. But I'm in no mood for puzzles.

"I have no fucking idea why he does anything he does!" Writing the f-bomb is nowhere near as cathartic as shouting it would be. *"Fucking Pär!"* Marking the umlaut with such force it tears the paper. I rip out the page, ball it up, and toss it away.

Later on, uncertainty gnaws at me. Like, wait—could it possibly be true? What a whopper of a lapse that would have been. To have missed years and years of Lucy? No way. Robert would have known her too. He'd have mentioned it when he first told me they were dating. "You'll never guess who I'm banging!" is just how my brother would have put it.

And wouldn't Lucy have remembered meeting me before? I think back to camp, school, swimming lessons, Hebrew school. Lucy would have been a grade ahead of me but—maybe? I press my hands into my eyes and try to get a picture of what she'd even looked like as a kid. But it's absurd.

Unless they both lied to me. About everything. And everyone else was in on it too: Robert and Lucy, but also my parents—step, adoptive, biological, everyone. And wait again: Did anyone else know Pär as Pär? And if so, why did no one tell me about him? Is fucking everyone laughing at me?

13.

PÄR

Sowing doubt is my new preferred way of using my influence. Rather than blocking him, curtailing his awareness, since the medication is hampering my ability to do that, I've had to adapt. And the past—when I lived apart from Eddie—it's the perfect tool, reinforcing Montgomery's hypotheses, his working diagnosis. Of course a true "dissociative identity" cannot skip to a second host like I can.

My initial days with the Wynter family—with the boy who had become their ward—were consumed with thoughts of Eddie and his survival. But soon, I fell in love with the new life. It was summer by this time, and dancing was the center of our days. I say "our" because the new boy and I were joined in the way of horse and rider (even if this rider had no reins as I did with Eddie). The family rose early to a bustling breakfast full of rich aromas and sizzling sounds, then set off for Lincoln Center, the location of Juilliard, where Mrs. Wynter, Dominique, taught opera singing, which the daughters, Regina, Sophia, and Althea, studied. One block north was the site of Tyrone's own dance academy, where Lucy and the boy (and I, of course) attended classes all day.

Though the boy had studied dance in the mountain town, his training had been rudimentary at best, serving only to reveal that he had a great gift. I overheard Tyrone say this to a ballet teacher called Madame, who was fond of smacking wayward feet with her cane. It was Madame who invented the nickname *Mountain boy*.

It didn't take long for the Mountain boy to think of the academy, the Wynter family, and their penthouse overlooking the park as his own. He loved New York City and gushed to Tyrone, Dominique, and the girls about the vastness of the buildings, the fascinating ways people dressed, appeared, and behaved. The noises, the lights, the energy of New York—things Eddie took for granted—fascinated the boy. I loved seeing it all through his fresh eyes.

Over a dinner, as the boy raved about what he'd seen that day—a film crew shooting a commercial on the steps of the natural history museum, an elderly woman roller-skating by in a bikini—Tyrone beamed while Dominique tilted her head, covering a smile with her well-manicured hand. The boy understood that she was working to maintain her dignity, careful not to show how much she enjoyed him. Regina, Sophia, and Althea clapped their hands and laughed at his dramatization. Lucy remained unmoved. No matter what he said or did, she watched the boy with a slight twist of the lip, a roll of the eyes. Yet it was Lucy for whom he inflected his voice when he came to the most extraordinary parts of his reflections.

"We live together because my father lets you," she confided later that night, after teeth were brushed, pajamas on. "But I am not your friend, okay?"

"Okay," the Mountain boy said.

He was nonetheless determined to win her over. The boy thrilled whenever people asked if she was his sister. Every so often, when the boy dared, he would catch Lucy's eye in the dance studio mirror, certain she would feel their partnership, their oneness in flight, as they performed their *grande allegros* full of *glissades, jetés,* and *saut de chat.* But Lucy's love was always out of reach. I yearned for it too.

One night I dreamt of Eddie. We were separate but together, out on the penthouse balcony overlooking the park. There were four of us, each with independent bodies: Eddie, the Mountain boy, Lucy, and me. We weren't speaking or playing, just standing there watching the birds. I did not know I could dream before this. When the Mountain boy awoke, he remembered the dream. He went to the balcony to stand alone. We saw wild geese forming a V over the city.

"I was the only Black person at my school in Massachusetts," he once told Althea, who clicked her tongue sympathetically. "And in my family."

As the Mountain boy said this, my loneliness for Eddie burned again. Eddie had this in common with him. Of course, Eddie was isolated from his family, his peers, by more than his color. But would his fears, awkwardness, twitchiness have abated if someone had taught him a sense of belonging outside of Hebrew school, where his brownness made him stand out all the more?

"I'm going to show you something," said Althea, who brought him to the living room and took out Tyrone's and Dominique's family albums. She showed the Mountain boy page after page of Black and Creole relatives as the boy studied them in awe, drinking in all the different shades of black and brown and beige. He loved that he himself could fit seamlessly into the Afro-inclusive color wheel.

Althea pointed out one of her uncles, Tyrone's brother Lou, insisting he looked like the Mountain boy. He knew it wasn't true, but the lie made him feel more at home than ever. Lucy watched them from across the living room, standing at the ballet barre. Her lip wasn't twisted in its customary sneer. There was no eye roll. The boy could see only sadness in her expression. He would have gotten up to hug her if she hadn't scared him so.

"Well, of course she's sad," Althea told him later on. "Her mother died, and no one ever talks about it because of—you *know*."

The boy didn't know. "I feel so sorry for her," he said.

"Don't. She doesn't want us to."

14.

EDDIE

"What's happening right now?" says Montgomery. "I'm seeing such torment in your eyes."

I write on the clean page, *"Is it possible that I met her as a kid and forgot?"*

"It is not only possible, but likely, given your history. Especially if there was coinciding trauma."

"Again with the trauma."

Dr. Montgomery caps his pen and studies my face. "What if we set aside the word 'trauma' for now. There are significant events in our lives, or significant ongoing circumstances that cause cumulative distress, even if we don't notice it in the same way we might a house fire or the sudden death of a parent." Another shrink-y tool that I know too well: the lead-in, couching his new line of inquiry in long, pretty words so as not to "dysregulate" me. He shifts in his seat. "We haven't talked about your race at all, you and I. Pär brings it up with me, but you don't."

"This feels off base to me. Like race has anything to do with my lapses, or with Lucy. She was mixed too. Did you know that? If anything, Lucy's being mixed canceled out the question of race. I mean race had nothing to do with—" I stop, beginning to sweat, though it's cold in here, always

a bit too cold. My whole body feels like a lie. Instead of protesting, I write, *"What does Pär have to say about it?"*

"Pär told me that you grew up Black in a white, Jewish family. He told me that you grew up in settings where everyone close to you was white. There were no Black family friends or neighbors or extended family. That your race was only talked about in passing. I can't help but wonder what that must have been like: appearing so starkly different from everyone else in your world and yet no one gave you the language to discuss it."

I write, *"My mother never let me say Black. She always reminded me that I was only part Black and that my birth father was African, not American Black. That was what my birth mother had written in the note she left with me along with my name. He was an African exchange student, but she never said which country he was from. I think my mom thought saying 'African' was supposed to make me think that I was above other Black people. It made it worse. Like I couldn't even have anything in common with the Black kids."*

"It sounds as if that was lonely."

"It was. I didn't have any real Black friends until I went to college. As a kid, I was even afraid of Black people since I had never really known any."

"Even growing up in New York City?"

"I went to private school then. When we moved to Long Island, the public school was pretty divided up."

He waits for me to write more. Weren't we going to talk about Lucy and when I actually met her? But now that we're talking about race, it occurs to me that Lucy was the first person I met who felt like me: mixed and Jewish and lost. Maybe the concentration of ingredients was different, but she was still those things. She believed that her value was being beautiful in one very specific way, so she clung to it, used it, relied on its impact. But like me, Lucy bit her nails down to the quick, destroying the small parts of herself that no one could see unless they really looked. The commonalities meant everything to me. But when did she really make her entrance? What am I blocking? How could I have put her aside?

I am off-balance, as usual, doubting what I think I know about my own life. If Lucy had been there earlier, sooner, wouldn't I have felt less alone?

Montgomery suggests that I stop beating myself up for not being able to remember. "Continue journaling. Let the words flow without judgment to see what you recover."

Later, in the rec room, I bring my notepad to a quiet corner with a round table and a single chair. I am supposed to write about my race—races. At the top of the page I write "Being Black as Eddie B. Asher." Not "Being Mixed." My very first Black college friend, Stephen Bradley, who was from Baltimore, used to tell me that calling myself "mixed" or "biracial" was a way to avoid being Black, which was how the world saw me. This confused me, but I accepted whatever Stephen said because I reasoned that he knew better. He'd been Black all his life and understood what that meant. Now I stare at the word "Black" as an exercise to see what comes. I glance up at Dwight, who's on duty, keeping an eye on all of us. He gives me a nod, which I return. This is where I'll start my entry. When I interact with Dwight and Xavier, another orderly, we use the handshakes I learned from Stephen and my other Black friends in college. I switch into the rudimentary Black slang I learned from these same friends who tolerated my ignorance of the culture and laughed at me with affection because I wanted to learn so badly. I was away from home for the first time, at Rutgers-Newark. I wanted to become a new version of myself that included my Black side.

My friends surprised me in their forgiveness, blaming my parents instead. "It was criminal for them to adopt you," said a girl named CeCe, who would become my first real girlfriend. We would sit together in BOS meetings. Leaning into one another in lounges around campus, she would correct the misinformation about Black people gleaned over a lifetime. She would tell me which Africana Studies classes to take, with which professors.

I did not speak to Stephen or CeCe or anyone else about being Jewish, about the fact that I felt I had more in common with the Jewish students than I had with the Black students. This also made my body feel like a lie.

Back when I was a little kid, discussions about race in my family had always been minimal, usually limited to my meager questions and my parents' perfunctory answers. Being brown in my family meant that I was at risk of being separated from them, at the very least visually, since I did not match.

To compensate, my mother was much more demonstrative with me in public than she ever was with Robert, holding my hand even when we weren't crossing the street, stroking my head when we sat side by side on the bus. I once asked her why. I was probably seven or so, old enough to notice other mothers with seven-year-olds didn't seem to touch quite as much.

"I want people to know you're mine," she told me. "People can't see it the way they can with your brother." In other words, her every gesture was meant to claim me, to challenge others to try, just *try* to question our bond.

"Because I'm Black and you're white?"

"To strangers that's what we are. But in real life, you are not Black and I'm not white. We're just people, a boy and his mother who love each other." She closed her mouth and nodded, meaning that the conversation was over. Then, more likely than not, my mother hugged me tightly. The kind of hug that used to cut the breath out of me but that I tolerated because the love was worth it.

I lost this from her in the months after she'd discovered Dad's affair. My mother would have denied it if asked, but I knew she blamed me as much as she did Dad and Glenda. Mom's gratuitous holding and stroking of me ceased. Her rare embraces felt cavernous and cold. Her fond gazes were replaced by perfunctory glances. This brought on a brand-new state of existential crisis for an adoptee like me, but also came with a silver lining.

The loneliness forced me to adapt. I needed friends and would take them however they came to me, which happened, ironically, to be through Blackness, what made me stand out. I was in fifth grade by then. White classmates would come to school quoting pithy lines from *Good Times* and *The Jeffersons*, asking me if I could "do J.J." Disappointed when my "*Dyn-o-mite!*" came out anemic and tentative, they moved on to the other two Black kids in the class, Charlie, who was also adopted by white parents, and Maya, who was also biracial and lived only with her white mother. Still, a degree of unearned cool was ascribed to me by virtue of my skin tone. I was, all of a sudden, as likely as Robert to get my hand slapped five upon my arrival at school. For the first time ever, boys befriended me and girls passed me suggestive notes. I had what passed for a social life.

(Here is where I probe around for Lucy now. At Riverview Prep we would line up single file to navigate the brightly painted halls and stairways down to the gym or the art and science rooms. We'd pass classes of kids from other grades. Siblings would catch glimpses of siblings and risk a poke or a bop on the head. Camp friends would spot camp friends and squeal and slap each other's hands. I slow down those images as I write, scanning for her, aging her backward, adding pigtails, braces, chubby cheeks, knobby knees. Lucy? *Lucy?* There were other mixed-looking kids in other grades, but my mind's eye cannot find her among them.)

Robert's esteem for me grew around this time too, now that I was less of an embarrassment. He was learning to take Mom and Dad's fights in stride, maintaining his cool, his sense of humor in the face of my agitation. He'd distract me by taking me to the arcade on Eighty-Eighth off Amsterdam to play pinball or Pac-Man, or else to the movies we were now old enough to go see alone. During one particularly brutal parental skirmish, Robert found me hiding under his bed, dragged me out, and held me like I was his kid.

"We're going to make it through this, buddy," Robert said. "You and me."

There was nothing like being part of a *we*. I would always fall for that. It's what drew me to Lucy, who called me her "fellow freak" the day we met. That's why I doubt that she was there any earlier than I remember. If I'd had a fellow freak all along, wouldn't things have been different?

15.

Eddie

Last night, once I'd drowned out my roommate's snoring with my head under a pillow, I dreamt of Lucy, way back before I actually remember meeting her. She didn't have a starring role in the dream, but she was part of the crowd at West Harbor Junior High in the schoolyard.

I was about to get my ass kicked by Elliot Blumenthal, who had me up against a wall, one fist that was about the size of my head poised for release. Over his shoulder I could see the masses of kids. Lucy was there, staring right at me, lips moving as if in prayer or, more likely, telling me what a dumbass I was to get into this fix in the first place. In any case, seeing her there gave me hope and strength. I broke free and wailed on Elliot—which actually happened—but, in the dream as in real life, I was outside my own body by then.

Awake now, I try to bring back the real fight with Elliot, thinking that maybe, if I search the crowd, she'll be there—Lucy as she would have been back then.

⌢

I was twelve when we moved to West Harbor, entering seventh grade. I was promised, by my stepdad Michael, by my mother, by the parent who'd given us a tour, that the school was a welcoming "melting pot," with white kids, Hispanic kids, Black kids, Asian kids all thrown in together: a big, happy multicolored family. This was not reassuring to me. I knew that few kids were eager to embrace new kids of any color unless there was a bribe attached.

On the first day of school, over a breakfast of pancakes that I was too anxious to eat, my mother warned me to steer clear of the Black kids. She didn't say the *other* Black kids.

"They are dangerous. All of them." It wasn't their fault, my mother explained. It was because of the poverty. But wasn't I part of the "they"? Would I be dangerous without our money? I did not ask.

Michael said I had nothing to fear from the Black kids. "It's the Italians you want to watch out for. Don't even make eye contact. You don't know whose family is associated with *you know what.*" (I didn't.)

I could really trust only the Jewish kids, they said, though I wasn't sure how I'd identify them. Certainly no one could tell I was Jewish just by looking. Mom's and Michael's missives only added to my stress.

Before the doors opened, all the kids stood around in factions. White girls stood with white girls, flipping their hair, preening in jeans that were easily identifiable by the labels: Jordache, Calvin Klein, Chemin de Fer, and Sasson. White boys stood with white boys. And then I noticed some swarthier white boys and girls standing together and wondered if these might be "the Italians." The Hispanic, Black, and Asian kids (though I saw only three of the latter) also stood apart, each sect closed to the others, surrounded by its own ethno-religious-economic force field.

(*Lucy?* I think a kindred mixed face in the crowd would have anchored me. But where would she have stood? Would she have tried to catch my gaze, or would she have avoided it?)

While there was no explicit fighting that first morning, there was palpable tension, looks of hostility cast from group to group. Observing, I stood less than a yard from the driveway where Michael had dropped me off on his way to work. When the bell rang, the mob blustered by.

I remained frozen on the lawn until the principal shouted at me to get to class.

When attendance was taken, the teacher shrilled my name, which was first on the roster. Twenty-five quizzical faces turned around as whispers ensued.

The questions began immediately that first lunch period:

"What are you? Why's your name Asher?"

"Are you Black? Why don't you talk like the Black kids?" (From white kids.)

"How come you talk like a white kid?" (From Black kids.)

"Are you Ethiopian Jewish?" (From Jewish kids.)

"Are you adopted?"

"Are you American?"

"Do you speak Spanish? Swahili? Hebrew?"

This continued through recess, resumed after school, and started up again before school the following morning. It was like spinning in a centrifuge machine. Each time it stopped, I'd regain what I could of my balance only to have another query fired my way.

(*Lucy?*)

I answered whatever questions I could, but my voice quavered, my explanations too long and eye-roll inducing. On day two, I got croaky. On the third day, my selective mutism from early childhood returned, begging a new question: "What's the matter with you?"

Elliot Blumenthal was in my homeroom. His size and his mustache had led me to mistake him for the teacher on the first day. Elliot was legendary, I learned from other kids, for having hit puberty in fifth grade, rapidly advancing to a burly six foot two. Elliot was wealthy and always had the right sneakers and jackets, often setting the trends himself. He played tennis and was well ranked for his age. His family belonged to the West Harbor Yacht Club, and his older brother was a quarterback for the West Harbor High football team. Elliot enjoyed the power of bullies, meaning most of his bullying—the intimidation and rounding up of victims, if not the actual physical assaults—was done by henchmen, a handful of boys who feared him as much as anyone else did but were fortunate enough to be his neighbors or his father's business partners' sons.

I was Elliot's ideal victim: a new kid, a small kid, a nervous and nervous-looking kid, a kid with no connections. But when the henchmen seized me and handed me over, my right foot shot out and kicked Elliot in the shin. A hush spread over the whole schoolyard. No one had ever kicked Elliot Blumenthal. Still gripping me by the collar, Elliot sucked in his breath, eyes wide with rage. He spat a litany of curses and slurs. Prominently featured was the N-word, which drew the attention of the Black kids, who pushed to the front of the crowd gathering around us. (Lucy is nowhere in the recollection; I can't identify any faces behind my captor.) Elliot pulled back his fist, which is the last thing I can tell you about our fight.

I came to in a cot in the nurse's office, an ice pack in my hand that I seemed to be applying alternately to my lip and one eye. In a cot against the opposite wall was a large human being, also icing his face: Elliot Blumenthal, who was whimpering softly.

When our mothers arrived, we were escorted to meet them in the principal's office, at which point we were each suspended, I for one day, Elliot for three, owing to his use of a racial slur—which someone had reported along with Elliot's being the first punch thrown.

"Fighting, Eddie?" my mother had harangued in the car ride home. "How could you think of fighting at school?" She waited until we were stopped at a light to turn toward me, leaning close, lowering her voice as if there were others in the car. "Of all people, *you* cannot get away with being violent." She tapped my arm. It took a moment to register that she was referring to my color. It was the first and only lesson my mother would teach me about race as it concerned me, as opposed to abstract, anonymous "Black kids." If I were violent, I'd be one of them, at least in my mother's eyes. The notion hurt and frightened me, addling my mind more than Elliot's blows. I wanted clarity but couldn't harness my words into a question. And by now the light had changed. Mom returned her focus to the road, adding, "And fighting such a boy? He could have really hurt you."

Miraculously, Elliot hadn't. My bruises healed. I returned to school (two days before Elliot) to an enthusiastic reception by my peers. I had conquered the beast. The other Jewish kids were impressed; the Italian, Asian, and Hispanic kids were impressed. Even Elliot's henchmen were impressed. I remembered nothing, not even when other kids filled in details, like how I'd laid into Elliot like an unhinged maniac, a rabid David, pummeling Goliath with my small, brown fists. As for the Black kids, they gave me occasional respectful nods when we passed in the hallway. They didn't befriend me or seem to view me as one of them, but I made sure to nod back. My mother knew nothing about any of them.

16.

EDDIE

My roommate, Ray Gilooley, is somewhere out of sight, but I hear him breathing as Nurse Sylvana enters with our medication. Sylvana is in her forties, with a large-bodied sexiness she owns unequivocally. It's in her walk, the way she allows her shoulders and hips to command space. A light chuckle comes from under Gilooley's bed, from whence he's trying to see up her skirt.

"Get up, Ray." Sylvana is all business. "Or I call security."

He slides himself out, and she gives us both our meds. I take one pill, then the other; I could never swallow more than one at a time. When Sylvana exits, Ray clicks his tongue. He pulls two pills from his beard and drops them down a hole in his metal bed frame.

"I warned you about swallowing."

He did. It's one of the only things I remember from my first day here.

"Watch out for the pills" was how he first greeted me, crouched on his bed a few feet from mine. "They hand you them little white cups with the pills clicking and whispering inside. You swallow now, Mr. Asshole, like a good boy. They'll keep 'em coming until the day you get the fuck out of here, which is two ways only." He jerked his chin toward the window. "Out there—'cause there's ways to get the bars off. Dudes done it before, man, I could show you. Or . . ." With his one full arm, he lifted his pillow, smothered his face for a second, then treated me to a big, yellow grin.

Gilooley has tried to teach me all the ways in which he tricks the staff, how he hides the pills in the gaps between his back teeth, behind his massive ears, or in the depths of his wild facial hair. I lack his physical crevices and rebellious will.

Since I got here I've been swallowing diligently, twice a day, maybe more (I'm fuzzy on the passage of time). And since I *do* swallow, I know better than Gilooley how the pills work. They're supposed to tame your symptoms, dull your sensitivity, but on me they have the opposite impact. I'm more aware of Pär, not less. But Gilooley says the pills murder your soul, and without soul, you're good as dead.

"Though in your case . . ." Gilooley twists his mouth to one side. "Huh. God must love the hell outta you, 'cause you've got two! *Two* goddamn souls! Who'd ya screw to get more than one soul?" Cackling.

"What makes you think I have 2 souls?" I hold up my journal for him to read. He squints one eye to do it.

"What do you think? I've met 'em both! You and the one who talks. Apple. Peach. What the hell's his name?"

"Pär?"

"Yeah," says Ray. "Pear. You spelled it wrong. Anyway, if you got two souls, there's a good reason. You hang on to both of them, sonny. Never know when you'll need a spare."

Gilooley says he guards *his* soul with a vengeance, which I admire, though it meant the sacrifice of his arm. "Ironic," he says. "An arm for art's sake. You know me, though, don't ya?" He strikes a theatrical pose. "Yep, I'm *that* Ray Gilooley. *The* Ray Gilooley."

The name means nothing to me, but I try to look impressed.

"I know you've read about me. You've seen my stuff, for sure." Ray intimates that his sketches are banned from most venues, the images considered too brutal for popular consumption. "But my sculptures are everywhere. You've seen them. Probably sat and ate your lunch on one.

"What I do is experiment with different media—stone, brick, wood, plaster, petrified cat food, dog shit (swear to God), and even human bone, when I can get my hands on it." His pale eyes glow beneath the chaos of his brows. I think of Dwight's mention of the old deviant ward.

I wonder for the first time about my own safety once Gilooley offers the details behind his first admission to Hudson Valley Psych. A girl he'd spent the night with was found in his apartment, lying in a lake of her own blood. The dirty drawstring bag containing Gilooley's sculpting tools lay beside her body, which he'd been inspired to carve into "something outta sight." The cops easily located Ray himself, squatting in a dark corner of the basement laundry room, in the buff, smoking a joint. The coroner determined that the girl had died of a heroin overdose two hours before Ray had begun his chiseling.

As he speaks, I do remember reading about this, being sickened by the story. All I could think of was the poor girl, who had been someone's daughter, someone's sister. I'm now rooming with the person who did it. But who am I to judge? Lucy was once someone's daughter too—a sister, lover, former fiancée.

Though I don't ask, Gilooley tells me he lost his arm as a result of a similar incident. He'd been out of inpatient about a year when he was inspired to carve his own left arm into the shape of a bathing nude. Homeless at this point, Gilooley worked out in the open before an audience of his "fellow vagrants." It took a while for the implications of his stunt to dawn on anyone. One guy finally slipped off and called 911, but the caller was too high to identify Gilooley's precise whereabouts. By the time the paramedics found him and got him to a hospital, gangrene was already setting in. Gilooley was recommitted at Hudson after the amputation had healed. Now there's just a touch of redness around the scar on the end of his stump.

"Spick and span," he says, showing it off. "Less of a '*cumbrance* this way." Gilooley rubs his chin, eyeing me. "You got what it takes, Pretty Boy. I like you more'n the other one. Bastard thinks he's better than me, wants to one-up me all the time."

"*The other one, meaning Pär?*"

"Apple Pear, Peachy Pie. He's too damn full of himself. If it weren't for you, Pretty Boy, I'd have done him in by now."

I write, *"Why? What does he tell you about me?"* I shove the notebook in his face, but he pushes it away with his good arm and laughs and laughs.

17.

EDDIE

I've been tracking the history of my lapses, creating a timeline, as requested by Dr. Montgomery. He looked it over and wanted to know why my mother and Michael hadn't put me back in therapy after the Elliot Blumenthal fight, since that lapse stood out at the time as my most glaring. The reason is that I never told them I'd blacked out. Only Robert knew, and he'd instructed me not to tell our parents. My brother was afraid I'd be sent away or locked up somewhere and didn't want to lose me. He'd joined the West Harbor High wrestling team by then, which had earned him social currency along with increased muscle tone. But he wasn't popular like he'd been in the city. For the first time ever, Robert saw me as a companion.

"You're not as weird as you used to be. We can actually hang now."

He meant now that I had respect at school as a result of kicking Elliot's ass. I wasn't cool, but I was cooler, less of a burden for him. Another thing: the closer Robert and I were, the less frequently I tended to lapse. Of course, I was swimming a lot then, and on new medication. (If I remember correctly, it was one that got taken off the market after being linked to narcolepsy.)

When it was time for him to go to college, Robert turned down Stanford, his first choice, in favor of Columbia so he could stay relatively close and help me survive high school (though by then I was on the swim team and was okay during the winter months). Robert went to med school at NYU, close enough for us to see each other on weekends, seeing as I was in Newark, just across the Hudson.

When he was applying to residencies in thoracic surgery—this was in '88, my senior year at Rutgers—I assumed he'd be staying in New York and suggested we find a place together after I graduated. I'd be starting at Cardozo Law School, where Michael—who had steered me toward law and coached me for the LSAT—was teaching at that point. I told my brother we could probably afford something modest together in Brooklyn.

"No," Robert said. I was not accustomed to hearing that word from him.

"No—what?"

"No, I'm not staying in New York. I've matched at UDub."

"UDub?"

"The University of Washington."

"DC?"

"Washington State, idiot. In Seattle. I need to go, Eddie. And you're ready to be on your own."

No matter how shamelessly I begged him to stay east, Robert insisted that the separation would be good for us both, meaning good for him. I'd be living with Mom and Michael in West Harbor.

"I wouldn't be doing this," he said, "if I didn't know you could handle it."

༺༻

I held it together through the summer and for a few months into my first year at Cardozo. But the abandonment weighed on me, and by November of that year, the blackouts were back. I'd be riding the train to Manhattan, where I was teaching swimming lessons on weekends, when all of a sudden I'd find myself somewhere else, like a bar in Jersey

City, drinking a gin and tonic, which I hate. One time I went out to the deli for coffee, blinked, and found myself waist deep in rough seawater at Rockaway Beach. It was January.

Along with my bodily agency, I lost any pretense of keeping up with my studies. Law had been an arbitrary choice to satisfy my mother, encouraged by Michael, who had been initially delighted to mentor me. When Cardozo suggested that I take a leave before the spring semester in 1989, my relief was tempered by my parents' disappointment. They'd been supporting me while I was a student. I could still live in West Harbor, they said, if I outlined a plan to return to school. I didn't, but my mother was willing to let it be until my dad weighed in from California. Dad accused Mom of babying me, letting me live rent-free. He insisted I'd do better if I lived on my own and had to fend (more or less) for myself. Mom and Michael kicked me out with a soft landing, paying my deposit plus first and last month's rent on the tiny studio in Brooklyn. I made ends meet by supplementing my now full-time swimming instruction with my parents' continued charity.

I spiraled sometimes, got too scared, too lonely, too high. Missing Robert, desperate for connection, I welcomed the advances I drew from women. Sex eased my loneliness, but only until the act itself resulted in a lapse. Funny how I still think of them as "lapses," though now they have a name. To think that it was Pär all along.

I remember how it happened with one particularly pretty girl I'd met at the laundromat who had invited herself back to my apartment.

When I woke up, the sun was just coming out. The girl—tattooed, pierced, with chin-length braids—was sitting against the wall, crying.

"Are you okay?" I said.

"I am more than okay," she replied.

"Why are you crying?"

"Because no one has ever made me feel that powerful before."

She looked at me, but her gaze was not welcoming. It was not a look we shared, but a look of which I was the object. I did not know what she meant, or what to do. I offered to bring her water.

"Why would I want water?" She laughed at me through her tears. "What happened between us was already perfect. I felt whole. I felt real. If you touch me again, or give me water, it will spoil fucking everything."

I tried unartfully to find out what had happened that was so damn perfect. My awkwardness disgusted her.

"No questions," she said, hand raised. "Please. Just let me leave before you ruin the memory, okay?" She dressed hurriedly, snapped in her lip ring, and was gone.

I panicked, feeling that she had stolen something from my body that we should have cherished together—or each kept half of. I wanted to feel as real as I had made her feel. Didn't I deserve that too? I started to go after her, but of course I couldn't risk ruining everything she'd left with. Everything she had left me without. This way, one of us was whole. What was wrong with me? Where had I gone? How did I not know?

At the time, I just thought I was crazy. I mean, now I know I am. But back then I didn't understand the parameters of my craziness. In any case, these circumstances, or similar ones—a woman, an evening full of time, of drink, of sex, then me, excised from an encounter that the woman would recall and relish—would repeat themselves again and again. Leaving me utterly bewildered.

I'm still sitting by the window in the Hudson Valley Psych rec room, thinking about this girl, thinking about Lucy of course, when Gilooley lands in the chair opposite me, looking even more wild-eyed than usual.

"Hey there, Pretty Boy," he says, spittle flying. "You ain't so pretty inside! You lying sonovabitch you!"

I grab a pad and write. *What did I lie about?*

"What do you think?" Face up close to mine, halitosis hitting hard. "You ain't got but one soul now, Pretty Boy, and I seen it! And know what I'm going to do? I'm gonna draw you, Pretty Boy. Now, before it's too late."

I stare back at him. He wants to draw me before it's too late? What comes to mind is *The Picture of Dorian Gray*, which I read in college. This guy unwittingly sells his soul so his portrait will age and reflect his rotten treatment of people, while he stays young and flawless. The guy leads a life of total debauchery, hanging out in opium dens, screwing anything that moves, murdering his enemies. Causing the death of the one girl he actually loved. That's not me. Not me. Shit. Gilooley's eyes are so intense right now. What is he really asking and why?

"Come on, Pretty Boy." Gilooley pounds his one fist on the table, arousing the attention of Dwight and another orderly—the white one who's either Jim or John. Gilooley lowers his voice and leans closer. "Just lemme draw your soul while there's still some left. Before he takes it all."

He? *Pär*. Before *Pär* takes it all. *What* all? This body? My soul? And what would that even look like? I turn the page of my notepad and write, *"Okay."* Gilooley howls in glee.

18.

PÄR

Taking it all. Body and soul. How I like the ring of it! Such a prophet is Ray Gilooley. Though if you'd have asked me back in '88, when Robert broke the news about his UDub residency, a coup wasn't even on my radar. I had been dormant due to Eddie's rigorous swimming workouts, combined with his cannabis habit and anxiety medication he'd been prescribed. (By dormant, I mean elsewhere, though I won't go into that just yet.)

But Robert's revelation and subsequent cross-country move over-rode all Eddie's remedies. Unmoored without his brother, Eddie unraveled, dropped out of law school after just a few months. The lapses, sponsored by yours truly, returned in force. By this time, having lived another life besides Eddie's, I was envisioning an existence of my own. If I am being honest with myself, this is where the notion of taking over permanently began to bud.

Which brings me to the evening with the "lady friend" who would give Eddie Dr. Montgomery's book. This night, late in the winter of 1989, is notable for being the last before Eddie heard Lucy's name. I think of him that night as *Eddie Before*, Eddie still pure of what was coming.

He had no real sense of me yet. But I was hovering close by as he watched the woman sip her vodka gimlet. Her lipstick left no trace on the glass.

"You're very exotic," she told him.

It occurred to Eddie that the woman had done this before, that she was practiced at covering her tracks. For the first time since accepting her invitation, Eddie was intrigued by her.

He said, "Thank you," though "exotic" was not a compliment. Eddie knew he should have said something next to put the spotlight on her, but he came up blank.

"You're not," he said, and immediately felt like a heel. He wished he could suck the words back inside. He was losing the here and now, possibly feeling the threat of me. Eddie imagined anxiety as a thin rope between *a few minutes ago* and *soon*: a frayed zip line from which he was hanging, unable to control his direction. But then the woman laughed—a benign, very rich, very white, Upper East Side married woman's laugh—a laugh that said, *It is impossible to offend me. For all my privilege, the things I can buy, the places I can ski, the things I can say with impunity, I deserve a little ribbing, don't I?*

Eddie had grown up, not rich, but *fine*, as in "Why are you asking about money? We're *fine*." As in a big Manhattan prewar on the Upper West Side, but one his grandparents had purchased when people didn't have to be rich to own such things. At this point in his life, Eddie was a law school dropout turned swimming instructor, one month behind on his rent.

The woman had wanted to go to a "seedy bar," completely removed from her world. The Brooklyn Tavern was the best Eddie could do. The interior was dark and dusty: stools, walls, pool table, jukebox. "Suite: Judy Blue Eyes" came on. Most everyone in the place was Eddie's generation: midtwenties, born in the '60s. The hits available on the jukebox tended to be from the '60s or '70s, giving patrons a sense of nostalgia for an era they had barely been old enough to register: Vietnam, love-ins,

Afros, and bell-bottoms. Meanwhile they sat, drank, and laughed with what they imagined was ageless gravitas.

Across the bar, Eddie saw some people he knew but didn't hang out with. A crowd of grad students who played Ultimate Frisbee in Prospect Park, a guy Eddie had gone to law school with until he dropped out, the guy's performance-artist girlfriend and her sister, who did some kind of readings for people. If they saw Eddie, they didn't nod or wave.

The rich woman took Eddie's hand, repeated that he was exotic, and, of course, asked *what he was* and why he had such *spectacular* coloring.

Eddie answered dutifully: "Half Swedish, half..." It shamed Eddie that he had no idea where, within the vast African continent, his birth father had come from. Tonight Eddie chose: "Somali."

The woman volunteered that she was of Norwegian descent and confirmed that Eddie had a Scandinavian jaw. She meant it as a compliment, like when people said his features were *so* European looking, despite the brown of his skin, the tightness of his curls. When they were done discussing his appearance, the woman commanded Eddie to take her back to his apartment, which was a few blocks away on the Cobble Hill–Carroll Gardens border. She wouldn't be the first of his swim students' mothers to come home with him.

Eddie didn't initiate these trysts. The women offered themselves—some more forcefully than others. He could never come up with the words to deny them.

On Thursday afternoons, during Eddie's Guppy Level I swim class at the Sutton Place Racquet Club, the mothers sat on their side of the viewing mirror, presumably watching their offspring swim, really watching Eddie. When they moved close enough to the glass, he could see them whip out their compacts, check themselves, and reapply lipstick as needed, plotting ambush. After the class, they waited—some innocent question on their lips along with the crimson gloss—as Eddie, clad only in dripping blue swim shorts, ushered their children out of the pool. What the women saw was the body and face Eddie was blessed with, not the fears, not the rituals he needed to stay safe. Of course, they met him in and around the water. Be it a pool, lake, ocean, or bathtub, water put Eddie most at ease.

Whatever the lascivious mothers asked or suggested or implied with their eyes, Eddie was compelled to say yes. He knew the rendezvous might lead to another lapse, but Eddie was agreeable to a fault.

Earlier that day, as this particular woman's boys had gathered towels and flip-flops, she had asked when, in Eddie's estimation, Connor and Pierce might be considered for Guppy Level II. When Eddie said he didn't know the testing date offhand, she'd stepped closer. As Eddie crossed the threshold into her lavishly perfumed bubble, she handed him a business card, suggesting he call when he had a better sense. On her way out, she'd squeezed his elbow and reiterated that he *must* call.

That night, Eddie followed her up the stairs to his apartment, giving her enough of a lead to admire the *tilt, switch, tilt* of her ass—that classic flat ass that trails so many upper-class white women—in fitted black capris. Beneath her broad, square hips was a pair of jarringly thin thighs, set so far apart that Eddie had to marvel at the space between them.

When they arrived upstairs, the woman asked if Eddie had any weed, which he did. They sat on his green-and-yellow-plaid sofa—a stoop-sale acquisition like most of his furniture—and smoked. This part Eddie would remember. Also, watching her stand before him, removing the white top and black pants, revealing a pink bra and thong. He would remember thinking that bubblegum lace undergarments were years too young for her. He'd remember focusing again on the wide gap between her thighs, daring to reach up and pass his hand through without touching either side. He'd remember the beginnings of the fear, despite the weed—not the fear of intimacy, as his last shrink posited, but the fear of disappearing, of where he disappeared to when the lapses happened. Eddie would remember actually touching the woman—or rather, watching his hand cup her right breast. He would remember the weight of her body on top of his. After that, he would only remember fading out quickly. At that point I took the helm.

In the morning, Eddie awoke on his back, in his bed, the woman asleep beside him. She was face down, hair fanned out, arms splayed, pink thumb-shaped blotches all over her back. *Oh God,* Eddie thought for a minute, *she's dead.* He held his breath until he saw her back rise, then fall.

Eddie pulled down the sheet to study the rest of her, hoping in vain to jog his memory. Next, he got up and checked the mirror, seeing only himself, no answers (no *me*). He spotted the remnants of a blunt in the ashtray but knew it wasn't the weed that made him slip away, not the weed that squeezed him out of whatever happened. Eddie was just as likely to be high on those occasions when the lapses didn't occur. It was all a riddle to him. (*I* was a riddle. Which was how I liked it back then, how I maintained influence even when I wasn't in the driver's seat.)

The woman stirred, rolled over, and gazed at him, lazy smile taking shape. It was her confidence that impressed Eddie most of all. Wherever this woman was, she was home. He admired that, wished it for himself.

"My God," she said, voice huskier than Eddie recalled from the night before. "Where on *earth* did you learn that?" She sat up, allowing the sheet to fall where it would. "No, don't answer that. I want to imagine that it was all inspired by me!" Playfully she clutched a pillow, bit her lower lip, and batted her green eyes at Eddie. The effect she achieved, despite her age, was coquettish.

Eddie rubbed his hot cheek, pulled on his ear. "What was—I mean specifically, what was it that you were most—when you say, 'Where on earth did you learn that?'—what was the *that* that you meant?"

The woman laughed and told Eddie he was too delicious. She rose, gathered her clothing, and strode to the bathroom, pausing to pinch his ass on the way. She emerged clothed, cleansed, and fresh looking.

"You really are confused, aren't you?" The woman sat on the bed beside Eddie, stroked his cheek in a manner that suited their age gap, then ran her finger along the line of his "Scandinavian" jaw. "I can tell. You changed last night when we made love. Your confidence surprised me."

I felt Eddie's eagerness in our pulse. I held back his words, *Please say more.*

"I hope I'm not overstepping." Concern dented the space between the woman's well-tended eyebrows. "Are you familiar with the work of Dr. Richard Montgomery?"

Eddie was not. Nor was I.

"He's a brilliant psychiatrist. An innovator. I probably wouldn't have heard of him either, but he's my brother-in-law. He has a book out that you might find interesting." She mentioned the title. "I'll send it to you."

The woman called a car service and kissed Eddie goodbye after extracting a promise of absolute discretion when they met next at the racquet club. When the book arrived, I didn't allow Eddie to give it more than a glance before tucking it away on his bookcase between a mass of unread literature assigned by his law professors. He would forget about the book almost immediately, about the name Montgomery too.

So we have the woman, the vodka gimlet woman of Norwegian descent, to thank for our presence here. And Gilooley? Ray Gilooley is yet another human catalyst. I cannot wait to see the sketch he comes up with based on the crumbs I've fed him about Eddie's torment. I hope it will work. In sharing details with Gilooley—as opposed to Dr. Montgomery—my goal is to spin Eddie into the perfect psychic whirlpool. I have high hopes for the one-armed artisan.

19.

EDDIE

Gilooley is granted paper, charcoal, and permission to sketch me in the sunniest corner of the rec room. I don't have to do anything besides sit here and stare out the window, through the bars that keep us all from jumping (though, as Ray says, there are *indeed* ways of getting past them).

Hudson Valley Psychiatric Hospital is nestled high in the rolling hills of Dutchess County, New York, partly buried by trees, though the spires of the main building peek out for an intriguing view from the road. I have memories of trips I took with my parents, driving up to ski in the Berkshires, crossing the Rip Van Winkle Bridge over the northern part of the Hudson. Robert and I would scan the hills for what we thought was a real castle rising through the green. We'd ask about it, though my parents had no idea what it was. My brother and I wanted to see it, climb what there was to climb. "Can't we go up close one day?" I remember asking. Life's ironies.

As Gilooley sketches me, I look down at these same trees, completely bare now, wondering vaguely if I'll still be here when spring breaks out and green spreads to fill the whole canvas. I look down at the bridge, see all the cars full of families on their way upstate to ski and ice-fish. *Hey, Mama, what's that castle doing there?* The children in the cars are too far away to see the bars of this place, or the residents, plotting away inside, grooving to the songs of our own personal tambourine men.

Gilooley mutters as he works. I'm getting used to his monologues. A few other residents are in the room at the time: Bill Who Thinks He's Jesus and his sometime-nemesis Kendra at their card game—playing peacefully thus far, no accusations or threats. Molly, in the corner writing to her late husband. Seth, sitting in a chair, staring at his hands, following doctor's orders to "be around people" and "avoid isolation." Dwight stays near the doorway, eyes on Gilooley's back, chatting with Jim/John, the white orderly who's got *his* eyes on Bill/Jesus. All is peaceful so far.

Molly finishes her letter and begins strolling around the room, smiling suggestively, first at Dwight and Jim/John, then at Bill/Jesus. She's shaken her tunic off one freckled shoulder; I'm trying hard not to look. My anxiety rises as she approaches our corner. It's me she's staring at, massaging her single long red braid, licking her lips. Compelled to take in the spectacle of her, I finally look. Molly was probably a stunner once, but time, madness, and substances have eroded all that.

Molly raises a hand in the direction of Gilooley's neck, but stops herself. She knows better than to touch another resident—especially a volatile one like Ray—with the orderlies standing by. Instead she clasps her hands in front of her and looks down at Gilooley's paper. Her face contorts in horror, and a scream rattles the glass window-panes along with all our nerves. Seth flies across the room, grabbing for Molly's neck, as everyone decompensates in our personal ways, some up and hollering, others quaking in fear. Dwight jumps in to separate Molly from Seth. Jim/John blows his whistle and presses the buzzer for backup. Within seconds, three nurses and another orderly arrive on the scene, restraining everyone who needs it. Sylvana trots in waving a syringe, followed by Dr. Montgomery, who's got one too. Soon, order is restored. We're escorted to our rooms.

When Ray and I are finally alone and I've got access to a pad, I write, *"What was it? What'd you draw?"*

He grins at me. "I drew your soul, sonny boy. Your goddamn immortal fucking soul."

~~⑤~~

The following morning, though I plead with Dr. Montgomery, he's ambivalent about letting me see the drawing. It triggered an episode for Molly, and she wasn't even the subject.

"I'm afraid of retraumatizing you."

"So Gilooley drew a traumatizing picture of my immortal soul? If I don't see what it looks like, I'll go crazy wondering."

"I understand. And I empathize." Dr. Montgomery taps his pen, considering. "But you must know: Ray says that the picture is based on things he learned from Pär."

"Then I need to see it."

"It just might jog your memory of things." At last the doctor agrees on the condition that we first secure the environment. Only when Dwight, Xavier, and Nurse Sylvana—equipped with a full syringe—are in place, each in a corner of Dr. Montgomery's office, does he unfurl Ray Gilooley's latest work of art.

The degree of precision astonishes me, considering Gilooley couldn't have been working for more than half an hour before we were interrupted. I don't see my likeness anywhere on the page. Instead it's a woman with wild, curly hair and a high, domed forehead: Lucy—no question about it—standing in front of a darkened tunnel, a halo of light surrounding her. The details Pär must have given Gilooley! Lucy wears her vintage black coat with the sash and shoulder pads. In one hand, she holds her flapper hat, which is missing most of its feathers. The other hand grips the handle of her weekend bag. But her feet are bare and bound with rope to the train tracks on which she stands. Her wide eyes stare out at me from the page. Longing? Frightened? Accusing? My brain makes her three-dimensional; the light around her vibrates. Now there's sound to the image, the rumble of an approaching train.

"Eddie." Dr. Montgomery's voice is far, far away, drowned out by the roar of the engine and the wind. "Eddie, can you hear me?"

The eyes of Gilooley's Lucy feel like her real eyes. I could swear they widen in terror. I could swear her lips part, ready to scream. Her hair blows in the wind from the tunnel. The halo behind her brightens and brightens as the train barrels toward us. I feel the vibration in my own body, the wind on my skin.

Lucy drops her hat and the case, twists around to see the light, then doubles over, pulling in vain desperation at the ropes on her feet. She faces me now, pleading, but I'm paralyzed, rooted just as she is. Lucy screams my name until she's silenced by the screech of brakes, her last words stinging my ears: *Eddie, Eddie, what did you do?*

PART II

20.

PÄR

This is the point! And here we go! I can feel remembrance's rope, the backward pull of time. It's a tangible suction-force, driving in reverse— from the train platform, to the intensity between them, to the glow of attraction, to the first time he saw her, back, back, to the time before they met—through the tunnel of our memories: Eddie's and my own running parallel. Present is past; past is present.

See? There's Eddie, back in his Brooklyn apartment—not as it was when he left it last, but a few years before that. It's the morning after the night with the vodka gimlet woman. She's just departed for the Upper East Side, and Eddie is left deciding what to do with himself and what to make of the latest of his memory lapses.

He counters the disorientation, the fear of disappearing again, by inserting himself directly into the cool morning mist. Eddie's neighborhood lies midway between the Gowanus Canal and Atlantic Avenue. On breezy summer mornings, rank droplets from the former mingle with incense and spices from the shops on the latter. It's something to smell. Eddie inhales deeply, drawing the mixed-up air into his lungs. He feels the wind on his cheeks, the muscles in his legs as they propel him forth toward the deli.

When he returns home with his coffee, he pours it from the soggy paper cup into an aged, chipped mug that belonged to his parents before the divorce. Eddie sits by the window, looking out at the brown-stone across the courtyard, thinking of the night, feeling jealous of the missing memory. He watches the gray Brooklyn morning sky, waiting until it's late enough to call Seattle.

"It happened again," Eddie says when his brother picks up.

"Shit. The lapse thing?" Robert's voice, though sleep craggy, soothes Eddie enough to tell the story coherently.

Robert admits that it's weird. "But weird is your normal, Eddie." A weak, if accurate, attempt at humor. "Those lapses sound like the ones you used to have when we were kids. What does your therapist say?"

"It's not that kind of therapy. It's more chants, herbs. Some other stuff."

"How does that constitute therapy?"

"It helps me to stay in the here and now. We're working on my phobias and anxiety by being present."

"Have you told the guy that you can't remember sex?"

Before Eddie can answer, he hears a stifled giggle in the background. A woman is over, which shouldn't be a shock. Eddie has suspected for a while that his brother is dating someone. Robert has been too distracted lately, too happy. But Eddie feels betrayed by the fact that the girl is right there, right now of all times.

"Is someone else there?"

The sound is muffled briefly. Eddie's face grows hot with the recognition that Robert is laughing along with the girl, laughing at Eddie himself—trying unsuccessfully to hide it, a deeper betrayal. Eddie slams down the phone, having no idea who the girl is.

(I, on the other hand, recognized her laugh.)

∽

Robert calls that afternoon to apologize for failing to tell Eddie he'd had company earlier. "It wasn't cool."

Eddie remains quiet, chewing the bed of his thumbnail. He knows Robert is going to tell him about the girl next.

"Eddie, you there?"

"Yes."

"Dude, there's someone I've been—"

"What's her name?"

"Lucy." Robert pronounces her name like it's something delicious. Eddie waits for more while I marvel at how life comes full circle, how things spill into one another. "Lucy Rivkin. She's a dancer."

So, Lucy goes by "Rivkin" now, not Wynter? Is that for Robert's benefit? Posing as a nice Jewish girl? I lie low, clamp down on my thoughts, keeping Eddie in the dark. I'll let him learn who she is, what she is, on his own.

He asks Robert, "How long?" Eddie is already flipping out over the thought of sharing his brother.

Robert says, "About a year." Waits a beat. "We're looking for a place together."

"A year?" Eddie jams his fingers into his dense black curls. "Are you fucking kidding me?"

"This was what I was afraid of," Robert says.

"What was?"

"Anytime I have a serious relationship you freak out."

"I'm freaking out because you kept it from me."

"You should be happy that I'm in love."

"You're in love and didn't happen to mention it to your only brother."

"You should be happy that I'm happy."

Robert correctly takes Eddie's silence for continued pouting. Eddie hears his brother inhale before blurting, "Dude. It's *unnatural* for you to be jealous of my girlfriends."

"Fuck you," Eddie tells him. "Fuck the *shit* out of you." And slams down the phone once again.

Robert should have known better. Never call an adoptee "unnatural." Maybe it wasn't calculated, just careless, but Robert should have remembered what people used to say when the Asher boys were little.

At gatherings and parties and places where adults talked over their heads with impunity:

"Such a shame that Dave and Joanne couldn't have any more natural children after Robert."

Robert was the *natural* child; Eddie was the *unnatural*.

To his credit, Robert calls back immediately this time. "I shouldn't have said that."

"Uh-huh."

"But I know you can handle my having a serious girlfriend. You're tougher than you think." Robertese for *Get over it*. Robert goes on. "Dude, you always do better when Mom and I stop coddling you. You got your job without my help, didn't you?" A foolish reference that hardly speaks to Eddie's independence. Being immersed in water, as you know, neutralizes Eddie's neuroses. Still, Robert keeps talking, trying to build Eddie up to distract him from the pain of being replaced.

"I don't like this apology," says Eddie.

"It's not an apology. It's a challenge. I want you to come visit me. I want you to meet Lucy."

"Visit you in Seattle?" Air travel being the most stubborn of Eddie's phobias.

"I wouldn't ask this of you if—"

"If I couldn't handle it?" Eddie resists the impulse to hang up on him yet again. For the truth is, Eddie wants to go. He wants to get on a plane, see his brother, meet this girl. Like the normal guy he's always aspired to be.

"We're going to make this happen," says Robert. "Trust me. Do you trust me?"

"It's not you I don't trust, it's my brain."

Robert chuckles, though humor is far from Eddie's intent. "Your brain will be fine. It's survived worse. Just promise you'll come."

Eddie promises. He'll go. He cannot fathom just how much is about to change. Despite his terror of airplanes, he allows Robert to book his flight.

21.

PÄR

Over the course of several phone calls, Eddie learns more about Robert and Lucy's courtship. They actually met in New York City five years ago and dated until Lucy returned to her ex, an Italian dancer by the name of Carlo, who was a soloist in her father's dance company.

"Her father has a dance company?" Eddie says.

"Her dad is Tyrone Wynter."

"Should that ring a bell?"

Robert gives a laugh that's just this side of pompous. "Ever heard of WynterDance?"

Being a New Yorker, Eddie has indeed heard of the company. Enormous WynterDance ads adorn full pages of newspapers, the sides of buses, and subway walls, depicting either the full face of a smiling, bearded older Black man—Tyrone himself—or a diverse quintet of regal-looking men and women in red unitards, all mid-split leap.

"So her dad is the WynterDance guy."

"And Lucy's mixed like you," Robert shares at this point. "Her mom was white and Jewish. After she died, Lucy's dad and stepmom took her in."

Learning that the girl is "mixed like him" doesn't make Eddie feel kinship with her, as Robert was probably hoping it would. If anything, it makes Eddie feel more replaced.

"Lucy and I ran into each other at the Pike Place Market right after I moved out here," Robert goes on. "She was dancing in the corps of the Pacific Northwest Ballet by then. She seemed so happy to see me, so eager to catch up, I put aside any reservations I had left about the Italian guy. We jumped back in, and here we are.

"At her core," Robert adds, "Lucy's a nice Jewish girl from the Upper West Side of Manhattan, destined to marry a nice Jewish boy from same."

"And a doctor," Eddie says, biting down on his sarcasm. "Deal closed."

Robert laughs, and Eddie hates them both.

In June, a month before Eddie's trip, Lucy moves into Robert's apartment just off the UDub campus, a one bedroom with a fold-out sofa in their living room on which Eddie would be sleeping when he visits, if not for his phobia of cats and the fact that Lucy has one. Fortunately, Robert agrees to spring for a room at a hotel near their place.

◦◦

Robert meets Eddie at Sea-Tac airport and brings him straight to a little Mexican place in Seattle Center near the theater where Lucy will soon appear among a bevy of titular birds in the evening's performance of *Swan Lake*.

While they wait for a table, Eddie catches a glimpse of himself in the window beside Robert. He can't always, but on this night, Eddie can see the handsomeness in himself that others remark on before they register his neuroses. Eddie resolves to use this and masquerade as a cool guy—the laid-back brother Robert has always wanted. He knows it's working when the blond hostess seats them, meets Eddie's gaze, and blushes. He can feel it each time Robert calls him "dude," the way he's addressed his guy friends ever since high school. Eddie calls Robert "dude" back and can tell Robert likes it. *Normal,* Eddie thinks, *this is normal.* They're two brothers, reunited, out on the town, shooting the shit.

Over margaritas, Robert gushes again about how awesome Lucy is.

"And she's hot, right?" Eddie says, sticking to the dude script.

"Are you kidding?"

Eddie has been to the ballet before and is always amazed by how beautiful the women are, but also how perfectly identical.

"How will I know which one she is?"

"I'll point her out. Besides, even with the stage lights, you can see she's darker than anyone else."

Robert takes a photograph out of his wallet and sets it on the table. Eddie absorbs the image of the couple standing together on a beach somewhere, Robert and Lucy. The impact of her image is intense for us both. For Eddie, it strikes with a bolt of déjà vu like nothing he's experienced before. He cannot know this woman, but he recognizes her nevertheless—from the mass of dark, coiling hair to the high, broad forehead to the eyebrows that arch, giving her a look at once amused and judgmental.

It isn't like the familiarity of someone whose face he remembers from camp or high school. The woman in the photograph—Lucy, Robert's girlfriend—strikes him as someone closer than that. I can hear her voice in my mind, and through me, so can Eddie. For the first time, Eddie thinks he believes in past lives.

Robert notes Eddie's fascination with the photograph and clears his throat. Embarrassed, Eddie changes the subject and asks about his hotel.

"About that." Robert takes a drink. "*Ix-nay* on the *otel-hay.* You're staying with us. Lucy knows how close we are. A hotel would seem too weird."

"I *am* weird," Eddie says, stress level climbing. He'll not only be sleeping under the same roof as this female stranger with whom he feels disturbingly intimate. He'll also be bunking with a cat. "I thought you told her about me."

"I said you have anxiety issues. I thought we'd give her some time before we get into specifics." Robert gives him a patronizing smile. "The cat, Feather. She's small, old, and not particularly frisky. Besides, isn't exposure therapy something they do now?"

"This is you not coddling me."

"That's the idea. From now on, no more coddling. It'll make you stronger."

"Or kill me." Eddie takes a gulp of margarita. When the lime slice lodges in our throat, I take right over to do the coughing. Lacking any faith in Eddie's efficacy, I hack and hack, fighting the citrus wedge like Heracles against the Hydra, but refrain from grabbing Robert's arm for support like Eddie would do. Robert, oblivious, continues to admire the photograph of himself and Lucy. By the time he notices our plight, I'm clutching our throat with one hand, the table with the other, eyes wide, tearing. Robert laughs. He *laughs*.

"Eddie, dude. You're making a scene." He glances over his shoulder, then back at us. In his eyes I see what Eddie never sees. He doesn't think Robert would let us die, but I know otherwise.

Robert takes another sip of his drink, then hauls us up and performs a half-assed but effective Heimlich maneuver. The lime slice goes sailing through the air and lands somewhere behind the bar, a tequila-logged dragonfly. I'm still incensed, still at the helm, glaring into Robert's smug face as we retake our seats.

"I think you're trying to set me up." This is me talking, not Eddie. "What?"

"The bullshit about the hotel room. My cat phobia." It is wonderful to lash out, albeit *as* Eddie. "You've always been jealous because I'm better looking than you, thinner, stronger, in better shape. You're threatened. You want to make me look like a freak in front of Lucy so she won't want to fuck me."

Something new and interesting happens at this point. I feel Eddie observing us, as I so often do with him. He knows *he* didn't say those words, but he experienced them being said by a force (me, whom he does not yet know) that usurped the physical apparatus of his mouth. And bang—I slip back inside and pull the meaning of the words I just spoke along with me.

Robert squints at Eddie. "Where the *fuck* did that come from?"

"Where did what come from?" Eddie seems mystified, but is he really?

Robert looks exasperated. "What you just said about Lucy wanting to fuck you."

"*What?*"

Robert repeats the whole of what I said.

"When did I say that?"

"Just now. What the fuck, Eddie? It's like that shit you used to pull when we were kids."

It's like a dream coming back for Eddie. He *did* hear someone say those words; he didn't know how or why, but it could have only been him. Eddie tells his brother he's sorry, that he didn't mean it.

Robert, whose drink is now empty, takes up Eddie's and downs what's left. He studies Eddie's face, perhaps with some regret that he pushed so hard for him to visit.

"You're not stronger than me, you know," Robert says.

22.
PÄR

About a third of the way into act 2, the residual stress of the lime slice incident drops from Eddie's shoulders. He delights at the sight of twenty-four stunning women in white tutus tearing around under smoky-blue lights, arms rising and falling to create the illusion of wings, of *flight*. His brother's whisper comes through as just another roll of the snare drum.

"That one's Lucy." Robert points. "Front row, third one in."

Eddie takes his word for it, but the girls keep moving, switching places. There's no one who even vaguely resembles the bikini girl from Robert's photograph. He tries again to zero in on Lucy when she performs a quick little number, arms crossed with three other girls. The cygnets get big cheers, but Eddie still cannot distinguish her features.

After the show, Robert and Eddie wait for Lucy outside the stage door, watching the dancers trickle out in pairs and trios, chatting, laughing, a few pausing to light cigarettes. Now and then, one will step out alone and fall into the arms of a waiting significant other bearing flowers. Robert, Eddie notes, is empty-handed.

"I see her dance three or four times a week," Robert says. "She doesn't expect flowers every time."

Which underscores how serious they are. Lucy is among the last to emerge, walking with the well-muscled arm of a tall, blond danseur linked through hers. He is clearly in the throes of an irreverent yarn; Lucy snickers girlishly behind one hand, completely engrossed. Only when her friend pauses to run his fingers through his hair does she spot Robert and Eddie. She pulls her friend toward them.

"Hey, Kenny." Robert shoulders Lucy's bag as she stands on tiptoe to kiss him.

"Hello, Dr. Asher," Kenny addresses Robert before turning a flirtatious pout on Eddie. "Lo and behold!" He uses one finger to give Eddie a playful shove in the chest. "Has Andy Lindberg returned from hiding at last? *Mon Dieu!*"

"Has *who* returned from what?" Robert is as perplexed as Eddie.

"Oh!" Kenny says. "I thought you were someone else."

"This is *Eddie*," Lucy explains over Robert's arm. "From New York." But she's barely given Eddie a glance. He thinks she's even prettier when she speaks—her face still luminescent from the effort of performing, hair free and wild, a few stray pins left in it. It's a fight for him to keep from looking at his feet.

"Of course," says Kenny, eyes performing a full scan. "Eddie. Perhaps we'll meet again."

As Kenny leaves them, Lucy shakes Robert off and takes Eddie by the chin. "Holy shit." She turns his face to study one side, then the other. "Well, I was going to be obnoxious and say, 'All of us mixies look alike,' but Kenny's right. You do look like Andy." She tilts her head in a manner Eddie cannot read. Is looking like Andy a good thing or not?

"Your foster brother?" Robert clarifies.

"That's not what Andy was." Lucy leaves it at that.

It's eleven, but no one has eaten. Lucy says it's too nice a night to be indoors, so they pick up a pizza and a bottle of red wine and find a bench by the Puget Sound. Even this late at night, Eddie observes, the western sky is full of swirling colors: purples and blues and grays, as if the sun isn't convinced it's really quitting time. Between its leftover glow, that of the crescent moon, and the city lights, Eddie can make out the monstrous snowcapped peak of what Robert identifies as Mount Rainier over to their left.

"The San Juan Islands are that way." Robert points in the opposite direction. "Keep going and you'll hit Vancouver."

"Watch the water," says Lucy. "Far in the distance: out there."

"She's obsessed with whales," Robert says with affectionate tolerance, putting an arm around her.

"They're out there. Keep looking."

Eddie looks out at the dark water, straining to see what she wants him to see, distracted by her touch. He wants to take her out in a boat right now. He wants to see her see a whale. Most of all, Eddie wants to light up the joint he has in his pocket, but he knows that Robert, who's officially given it up, would disapprove.

Robert's pager goes off just after midnight.

"This might be an emergency." Robert walks off down the boardwalk to where he parked his car, which has a phone. About halfway to the car, he stops and looks back at Eddie and Lucy. Robert's too far away for Eddie to see his face, but he knows Robert well enough to read the hesitation in his posture. Robert is reluctant to leave them alone, more likely than not, wondering what crazy thing Eddie might do to offend Lucy and scare her away from the whole Asher family. Or maybe it's Lucy he doesn't trust. Whatever Robert's misgivings, he shakes them off and trudges on.

Lucy turns to Eddie. "So, how was your flight?"

"Fine."

"Bullshit." She laughs. "Robert told me why you never fly. How did you deal?"

Eddie relaxes just a notch. "Seriously? The friend who drove me to the airport let me get high in her car before I went in."

"Ah."

"And I took a Valium."

"So you were nice and sedated."

"Not enough. The flight attendants still had to take care of me."

"Did they?"

"They let me sit with them and—" Eddie's heart rate picks up. "This is so embarrassing, Lucy. I wanted to make a good impression."

"You're making an *awesome* impression, Eddie." She nudges him. "You're going to be fun to have around this week. Robert told me you had a way with women."

"Oh God. What did he really say?"

"That you appeal to their maternal sides."

Which Eddie admits is true. Next he says, "You have a cat, right?"

Lucy catches the tremor in his voice. "They freak you out too? I can't believe Robert didn't tell me. I would have had a friend take Feather for the week."

"Robert would call that coddling me," Eddie says. "It's okay. Really, it's not like my flying thing."

Lucy glances from Eddie's right eye to his left, a tic reminiscent of the Sutton Place Racquet Club mothers. He takes it for attraction, thrills inside, then tamps it down, forcing himself to remain in the moment. He's certain there was a past life between them that wasn't so pure. There is an enticing wayward part of Lucy that complements Eddie's internal mayhem.

"As long as I know where the cat *is*," Eddie says, growing braver. "Like, let me know if she's nearby or warn me—"

"If she's going to pop out at you or something?" Lucy giggles, and Eddie laughs along, grateful for her casual teasing. There is an ease to the two of them that Eddie can't remember experiencing with anyone before. He glances down the walkway, finding no sign of his brother.

"Robert told me to keep quiet about this," Eddie says. "He didn't want you to know what a freak I was. Yet."

"Well, he's an idiot, because he knows *I'm* a freak. Here—toast." Lucy touches her plastic cup of wine to Eddie's. "Fellow freaks?"

"Fellow freaks." They drink.

"Anyway," she says, "you don't have much to fear from Feather. She's tiny and sweet and old and actually kind of frail. She can't even jump up on things."

"Right."

"Okay, fellow freak. I'll keep her in our room the whole time."

"I hate to be a pain in the ass."

"Eddie." She reaches for the wine bottle and tops off both their cups. "We're beyond that now." They toast again.

"Do I really look like your foster brother?" Eddie asks her. "What was his name?"

"Andy?" She faces him, inching closer, eyes roaming over his face again. "You totally do. Andy's a little lighter skinned than we are, but you could seriously be brothers. No, not brothers: stand-ins. You could play each other in the movie versions of your lives!" She makes a dramatic flourish with her hand, cracking herself up. Eddie laughs along. There's a spell he's falling under, Robert be damned. *Oh God,* Eddie thinks.

Lucy reaches up and pats the top of his head. "Andy's hair wasn't as tight as yours, but you have the same smile. Almost the same face."

"My father took both of us in when we were kids. I'd lost my mom, and Andy's let him move in with us so he could train at my father's dance school in New York. People thought we were related because he was mixed too." Another sip. "Andy was gay, though. You're not—right?"

"Right."

"Obviously not." Eddie doesn't ask what's so obvious. Lucy adds, "Not that being gay changes what you look like. But with Andy it kind of did. He hated the word 'flamboyant,' but he was—in terms of how he dressed and his mannerisms. His hair was never the same color for more than a month." Lucy looks wistful.

"You're using the past tense. So, Andy died?"

"Let's just say I'm dead to him. For reasons that I don't know you well enough to get into." She gazes back out at the sound.

"I'm sorry," Eddie says, unsure of what he's apologizing for.

Lucy shakes her head and finishes her wine. Eddie doesn't expect her to turn her face to his right now, eyes glistening. Nor does he expect her to lean so close, to kiss him, softly, swiftly, just beside his lips, not on them. An ambiguous yet still illicit kiss. Eddie can't breathe for a second.

"I don't know why I just did that." Lucy uses a thumb to wipe her lip gloss off his face. "I just wanted to."

"It's okay," Eddie says as Robert's footfalls become audible.

Lucy turns. "You're back, babe!"

Eddie watches her jump up, run, and leap into his brother's open arms. If Robert saw the kiss, he doesn't acknowledge it. In any event, Lucy's mouth is now on Robert's, legs around his waist. Eddie remains on the bench, watching them thus entwined. Robert sets Lucy back on her feet but, on second thought, goes in for another kiss, hands in her hair. When they come apart, Eddie observes by the light of a streetlamp that their faces are both glowing, united beneath the electric halo. Eddie concedes with sinking shoulders that this is what it really means to be kissed by Lucy. What happened to him just a moment ago was nothing more than an affectionate, spontaneous hiccup of the lips.

Now the whispered words that pass between Robert and Lucy—something like, *What was that for? For you; I missed you. I was only gone for five minutes. Your point?*—their soft laughter, underscores their oneness. Eddie is merely the shamefaced interloper.

Robert says his patient is stable; he doesn't have to go to the hospital tonight.

"Still, we ought to be getting back," he says. "I have to be there bright and early in the morning."

Lucy has the next day's matinee off and doesn't need to be at the theater until 3:00 p.m. She says she'll give Eddie the full tour of the town in the morning. Eddie anticipates this with equal parts joy and angst.

23.

PÄR

It's one in the morning when they get to Robert and Lucy's apartment. Lucy darts in ahead of the Asher boys, meaning to get Feather the cat out of the way before the creature can offend Eddie's delicate sensibilities.

"Feather? Sweetie?" she calls as lights switch on in one room after another.

All at once, Eddie and Robert hear a piercing scream, followed by a moan.

"*Oh* . . . my sweet baby!"

Benign little Feather expired while they were out eating pizza and scanning the horizon for whales. Lucy is beside herself. As she howls, fists to her eyes, Robert tries to embrace her, but she pushes away from him, runs and closes herself in their bedroom, from which Eddie and Robert can hear her weeping.

"Let's give her space." Robert directs Eddie to the living room, into which Eddie could fit his entire Brooklyn apartment. The sofa they sink into is black leather, as is a matching armchair—clearly not from a stoop sale. There's also a glass coffee table, a broad-based lamp, and some decorative baskets. Posh by Eddie's standards, but every inch of the place has at least a few telltale white cat hairs.

"That cat came with Lucy's first Seattle apartment," Robert tells Eddie while they wait. "Feather's original owner died of a heart attack, and the landlord included Feather along with the other amenities when she listed the apartment. The cat was sick from neglect, but Lucy nursed her back to health."

Now Lucy emerges from the bedroom and tumbles into Robert's arms, one leg pressed against Eddie, who first tries to make room for her by flattening himself against the arm of the sofa, finally exiling himself to the armchair.

"She was my best friend." Lucy's voice comes out muffled against Robert's chest. "I told her everything, *everything*. She knew me better than *you*, Robert. She knew me better than I know myself."

Lucy sobs, chastising herself about signs she should have seen, precautions she should have taken. Robert holds and strokes and rocks her. As she grows calmer, Eddie notices Robert glancing past her to the oversize square clock on the wall.

In a motion that extends from the rhythm of his stroking, Robert takes Lucy by the shoulders. "Babe, I am so sorry. So sorry." He pushes some hair off her face. "But we're going to have to get some rest soon. I have to be at the hospital at seven." She stares at him, eyes red, leaking, and wounded. Robert is bringing up the practical in her time of grief. "I mean I'll be in surgery, so . . . Look—why don't we wrap her in something, and then tomorrow we'll figure out what to do with, you know, her body."

Either the suggestion of sleep or the reference to a "body" devastates Lucy, who rages at him. "Tomorrow? I'm not waiting until tomorrow! I'm not going to wrap Feather in something and then go to sleep as if she was nothing!"

As Lucy pounds his chest, Robert first defends himself, then apologizes, then defends himself again. Eddie keeps quiet but sides with Lucy. How can Robert be so callous and insensitive? How can he not see that what Lucy needs is not sleep but resolution for her beloved Feather?

"It's kind of life or death, Luc," says Robert. "I have patients who need me to be—"

"Fine!" Lucy says. "Go to bed!"

"Babe, it's not that I don't want—"

"It's okay," Eddie says. "I'll help. I'll help you figure out what to do with . . ." He stumbles, momentarily forgetting the cat's name, loath to make his brother's mistake and call her a "body."

Robert and Lucy turn to him, each face marked by its own brand of gratitude.

"Really?" says Lucy.

"Sure."

"Thank you." Robert presses his hands together and nods at Eddie. He kisses Lucy, then hugs her for good measure, relieved, it seems to Eddie, to relinquish both Lucy and her dead cat for the night. Robert heads off to sleep in service to the patients who will be counting on his steady hand in a few hours.

Eddie offers to collect Feather, a sweet-faced Persian mix with a long white coat, now lying on her back under the kitchen table. She's wet, possibly due to the release of bodily fluids. Eddie does not so much as flinch when he touches her, cat phobia neutralized by the feline's insentience. He slides Feather into the open and, under Lucy's tearful direction, wraps the cat in a pink towel and places her in an old backpack of Robert's. With Feather squared away for now, the floor cleaned (by Eddie, heroically, though he owns no mop and has never, come to think of it, used one), the two of them sit at this same kitchen table, chairs pulled catty-corner, yellow pages open before them.

As Lucy scans listings with her finger, Eddie matches the rhythm of her breath, the tension and tautness of her body. She is closer than she was an hour earlier when they sat on the bench by the sound, though Eddie imagines he is the last thing on her mind. This fact frees him to study her unabashedly. She's gathered her mass of hair and twisted it into a quick, masterful knot, enabling him to drink in her profile, neck, shoulders, learning her on his own terms.

There is something in Lucy, on Lucy, about Lucy, that makes room for Eddie to—he does not know what. He notices her left hand, which lies on the table beside his right. He notices that the hands are the same shade of brown. He notices too that Lucy's nails are stubs like his own, bitten to the quick, which surprises Eddie—that this beautiful, seemingly self-possessed woman engages in the very habit that shames him. The hands are also similarly large in proportion to their wrists, the delicacy of which has also shamed Eddie all his life (especially when contrasted with Robert's pale bulk). It's Lucy's mixed-ness, her girl-version-of-Eddie-ness that fortifies. Sitting beside this woman, Eddie is the opposite of exotic. This is nothing short of exhilarating when topped off by the fact that, in Robert's absence, Lucy *needs* him. Eddie Asher, who needs so much comfort, reassurance, propping up—from his brother, his parents—but has never been needed.

Eddie grows in Lucy's presence, taking up more space. By contrast, I retreat into Eddie, deeper into the moon-shaped atrophic scar I call home, then I retreat *from* Eddie, back to a memory of Lucy that is not his.

She's perched on the railing of a balcony many stories above Central Park, her arms spread in anticipation of flight. Terrified for her, I creep up silently, stealthily, so as not to startle her. As smoothly as I can, I grab her by the hips, pulling her into me like in pas de deux class, falling back with her onto the concrete. I am bruised, injured, but I hold her as she sobs, waiting for her to speak, to tell me the story of why she set out to fly. She lets me hold her. Lets me offer myself. *She needs me,* I thought. *Lucy needs me.* To be needed by Lucy was and is a heady thing.

Of course, she didn't know *me,* not as myself, not as Pär. In that body, the body that belonged to the Mountain boy—or to Andy, as you now know him—I had less space, no atrophic scar, hence less grip, no impact. Only surveillance and empathy. Still, I loved her. That was possible.

But now, it's Eddie she needs. Or so he believes. What an experience it is to see Lucy through Eddie's eyes, to feel what he feels for her in the body we share. This is brand new, this odd, squirmy sensation. Is it desire, or a different kind of sensory yearning altogether? It alarms me to feel this way for her yet not be in control. I can only watch and wait.

They begin by leaving messages for every animal shelter and emergency veterinary facility in a ten-mile radius. It's two in the morning and no one is answering their phones, a fact Lucy meets with fresh tears.

"We'll figure this out." Eddie swells into his role. He touches her hand, then squeezes it, admiring again how the hands match, how strong his own voice sounds. "I promise we will."

Eddie takes over the phone book and starts in on the white pages. Under *S*, he turns up a listing for Stella and Al's 24-hour Pet Mortuary and Farewell Rituals.

"That's it," says Lucy. "I want a farewell ritual for Feather."

To Eddie's surprise, a woman with a soothing voice answers. "This is Stella. Tell me about your animal."

Eddie gives the phone to Lucy, who, presumably prompted by Stella, shares the entire story of her relationship with the cat, a weepy confessional spiked with the occasional laugh. Lucy stands as she speaks, doing some ballet stretches, foot in her free hand, now twisting and untwisting herself around in the phone cord as she chats. Eddie is spellbound, watching, listening, a guilty recipient of these unearned pieces of his brother's girlfriend.

"Seriously, Stella, I know she was a cat, but to me she was family."

Feather, Lucy explains, was a salve for the loneliness that haunted her when she'd arrived in Seattle, heartbroken over her ex, who had used her, cheated on her with her closest guy friend. (The story is familiar to me, but I know it a different way.) Eddie is rapt. *Rapt.* He should give her privacy but fears calling attention to himself by leaving the room. Lucy goes on to share how furious she was with her father, who forced her to audition for other dance companies just to get her away from Carlo, when she wanted to stay in New York, in hopes of winning him back. Feather, though frail and sick, returned Lucy to emotional health with her sweet demands for chin rubs and head scratches. At a certain point, she understood that Feather was more than a cat. "I've never believed in reincarnation but . . . Oh, Stella! This is going to sound insane."

Now Lucy is silent, listening. Then: "Thank you. Okay, well, I always felt like Feather was my mom, sent to look out for me." Listening some more. "Yes. When I was ten. It was pretty awful." (Eddie can only guess, filling in the gaps, but I know the story.)

Fighting tears of his own, longing to take the motherless, now cat-less Lucy into his arms, Eddie busies himself with the phone book. He's counting the number of heating and plumbing specialists who offer free consultations when Lucy jostles his arm, motioning toward the counter, where Eddie finds pen and paper to take down directions. Al and Stella are willing to do a farewell ritual for Feather tonight, Lucy tells him when she hangs up.

"They're getting everything ready now."

After a brief search for Feather's favorite toy—a stuffed squeaky fish, which will feature in the ritual—they head out and walk two blocks to the lot where Lucy's electric-blue Corolla is parked.

Eddie offers to drive, but Lucy says no.

"I don't want to feel helpless. If I drive, I'll feel like I'm doing something for Feather."

Perhaps encouraged by the session with Stella, Lucy keeps chatting as she drives. First it's small talk about New York, their shared home-town, comparing notes about favorite bars and stores. Then she pulls onto 520 and changes the subject.

"Well, you just got an earful about my life," she says. "Your turn to share." Here, a conspiratorial glance. "We're free of Robert now, so you have to give me the real scoop on the Asher family. Like, details."

"The real scoop?" Goose bumps rise on Eddie's forearms, a signal of looming distress. "What do you want to know?"

"Robert gave me some background. But you know him. He's so unflappable and stoic when he talks about things like the divorce and the move to Long Island. I want to know how it all *felt*. I mean, jeez,

Eddie, your dad left your mom for your shrink? How did you—I don't even know what to think about that!"

"It was strange," Eddie says. "It's still strange. She's my step-mother now."

"I know. *Jeez.*"

"So the divorce was basically my fault."

"Don't say that." Lucy pats his knee. "Divorce is never a kid's fault. Besides, you were in therapy as a kid for a good reason. I mean, Robert told me you had those episodes, where you'd like wig out and change into this crazy version of yourself and—"

"He told you about that?" Eddie grows hot with the shame of being so exposed to a woman he barely knows—to this woman. He releases the car door handle to cover his face. "Thanks, Robert. Fucking thanks."

"Hey." Her hand on his leg again. "Eddie, I'm sorry. I shouldn't have mentioned that. I shouldn't have said it that way. Please don't be embarrassed."

"I'm not embarrassed. I'm fucking mortified."

"You shouldn't be. It's my fault. I shouldn't have said 'wig out' or 'crazy.' My therapist says being flippant like that is a defense."

Eddie peers at her from the side of his left hand. Lucy's eyes are on him. "Please just watch the road. *Please.*"

"We're like the only car, Eddie." Lucy returns her eyes to the road but keeps her hand where it is. "My therapist calls it deflection. I deflect big feelings with inappropriate humor."

"It's okay," Eddie says, though it isn't. He wants her to move her hand off his knee. He wants her to keep her hand on his knee forever. It burns, tingles, confuses—for me too; my nerves are Eddie's nerves, after all. But my sense of Lucy is my own: shaped by Andy's memories, textured by Eddie's longing.

"Anyway, I have issues too," she says. "You heard me on the phone just now. And I'm sure Robert told you things."

"No."

"Well, I'm damaged too."

Lucy moves her hand and Eddie drops his own from his face, feeling cold as a new shame sets in. Lucy gave him an opening to ask how and why she's damaged. He should ask her, tend to her, seeing as it's her dead cat in a bag in the back seat, not his. Instead, Eddie turns away. The face reflected in the passenger-side window of Lucy's Corolla looks like his but somehow isn't.

"Shit! That's our exit." Without checking the rearview, Lucy jerks the wheel, wrenching the car across four lanes. Someone with a deep horn honks long and hard as Eddie grips the door again. Having narrowly avoided another disaster, navigation corrected, Lucy glances at him again. "Sorry. You okay?"

"As okay as I get. You?"

Lucy's laugh jars Eddie's nerves as much as the abrupt lane change. "I'm as okay as I get too."

24.
PÄR

In a sleepy residential area full of well-maintained houses with exquisite landscaping, they pull up in front of a center-hall colonial distinguishable by its wild, overgrown lawn.

As they ascend the walk, Lucy cradles Feather's backpack like a sleeping child. Eddie—conscious of filling Robert's shoes—shakes off the humiliation from the car ride and places his arm around her. The doorbell treats them to a few bars of "Casey Jones," which makes them smile despite their purpose. A large, fleshy guy of about fifty, joint between his lips, greets them at the door along with a waft of weed. Eddie's connoisseur nose deems the latter to be pretty high quality.

"Al Jones." Who transfers the joint to one hand, extending the other for Eddie to shake, then nods respectfully at Lucy and her bundle. "Welcome." His relaxed undone-ness puts Eddie at ease.

"I'm Eddie. She's Lucy."

When Al gives them another once-over, Eddie decides he's taken them for a couple. They follow their host into a living room that boasts a set of overstuffed psychedelic-print furniture. A green-and-purple spiral-glass bong sits filled and ready on the coffee table, which cheers Eddie. He's less pleased to discover a mottled gray cat of enormous proportions covering a third of the sofa.

"That's Boonie," says Al. "He's harmless."

Which Eddie finds less than comforting. When Al tells them to sit, Eddie hesitates, unwilling to join Boonie on the sofa. The only chair is piled high with yarn and an accompanying knitting project, and the love seat seems inappropriate. But Lucy pulls him down upon it, with an eye on Boonie. That Lucy is thinking of him and his phobias, now of all times, makes Eddie reel with tenderness for her. He'll be fine as long as Lucy stays close, and the cat stays right where he is.

"You get high?" Al raises the bong. "I grow my own stuff."

When Eddie responds enthusiastically, Al places the bong and lighter in his hands as Stella, a tall, powerfully built woman with long gray hair, sweeps in.

"Welcome to both of you." She seats herself beside Boonie and nods at the backpack in Lucy's lap. "And this must be Feather."

To clear a space for himself, Al shoves Boonie off the sofa, the big cat's legs bowing outward with the burden of his mass. Boonie glances at Lucy but chooses Eddie, lurching forward to sit at his feet, wriggling close and rubbing against him. Eddie holds the bong like a life raft. He's terrified but knows that any evasive action will draw attention he doesn't deserve. He's there to support Lucy, not make a scene among strangers. Instead Eddie lights the bong, takes a hit, sweet and smooth, and feels himself chill a bit.

"Boonie can always spot a kindred spirit," Stella says. "He was a lost soul too when we got him."

"Is it that obvious?" Eddie tries to quip into the smoke as he hands the bong to Lucy.

"Not obvious," says Stella. "I just have a sense of these things."

There's something grand about Stella's presence that makes Eddie think of Dr. Glenda Lloyd before she became his stepmother. Stella's very presence comforts, inspiring faith that her intuitive powers will turn lost souls like Eddie and Boonie into found ones. When it's Stella's turn with the bong, she shuts her eyes and utters something Eddie can't make out. He bows his head out of respect.

"You getting something, babe?" Al says.

"Just a presence." Stella opens her eyes and takes in Eddie's and Lucy's curious faces. "My grandmother was a shaman who specialized in death and dying. She was biracial—as you two are, yes?" Both Lucy and Eddie nod. "Nana was Black on her father's side but had both Irish and Tillamook heritage on her mother's. She communicated with the spirits of animals as well as humans as they were passing.

"Nana taught my sisters and me all she could, pulling from ancient Celtic and Native traditions. I haven't studied near enough to call myself a shaman, but I have sight and I can tell you that Feather's spirit is waiting for us to see her off on her journey to the hereafter."

Accepting the bong, Al adds, "I first met Stella right after my dog Jerry had died. A buddy of mine sent me to her for a farewell ritual where I learned Jerry had forgiven me for having to put him down. We think Jerry sent us Boonie in a gesture of gratitude."

For the farewell ritual itself, Stella and Al bring Eddie and Lucy out back to a gazebo covered in flowers, the door to which Al opens after lifting a mass of vines. Inside, Stella lights candles—sending spiders scattering for the corners, which would unnerve Eddie were he not quite as high. Next, Stella sets fire to some herbs contained in a small stone bowl. Al's job is to extinguish the flame but keep the bowl smoldering with a feather, representing, Eddie supposes, Feather the cat, whose body Stella removes from the backpack and places in Lucy's arms.

Stella hands Eddie a rattle and instructs him to shake it in four directions, bringing to mind the lulav and etrog of Sukkot. Eddie sees the relief on Lucy's face as she clutches her bundle. For the first time, he feels the purpose of faith. Eddie grips the rattle and shakes it for all it's worth, trying his spiritual best.

"Eddie." Stella motions for him to tone it down a bit, then begins chanting something beautiful and lyrical that Eddie feels deep in his chest. He rattles in rhythm, but softly now, keeping his place. Next, Stella dips her hand into Al's stone bowl and smudges a bit of the soot on each of their foreheads, saving Feather for last.

"At this point," Stella tells Lucy, "the bereaved often gives their beloved a silent message of farewell."

Lucy nods and holds Feather close, Stella placing one hand on Lucy's shoulder, the other on Feather's head. The last part of the ceremony involves a meditation during which Stella encourages everyone to let their minds wander.

Eddie's mind is suddenly drawn to his right shoulder, which tickles, then itches, then itches more intensely. Scratching doesn't help but leads to a burning sensation in the spot, the pain of which soon consumes him. The gazebo fades, as do Al, Stella, and Lucy. Eddie is in another place entirely, an unfamiliar room that looks out onto a city: buildings with flickering windows, the impression of bustling energy, people, and traffic down below. He's standing at the window, a houseplant to his left, a steaming cup of tea to his right. The moon shines brightly over a skyline that belongs neither to New York nor Seattle. His shoulder burns dreadfully. When he rubs it with his left hand, the spot is hot to the touch.

As for me, I am aghast, thinking that this cannot be possible. How can it be? Given the influence to which I am accustomed? I'm thoroughly stumped. I yank down the curtain of Eddie's consciousness to the best of my ability and pray for the vision's erasure.

The next thing Eddie knows, he's back in the gazebo, holding hands with the others in a circle around Feather's body. Where did he just go? Did anyone notice? Stella is humming softly. Al and Lucy still have their eyes closed.

When it's all over, Stella gives Lucy a pouch with a stone by which to remember Feather, while Al places the cat's body in a container for cremation.

Crossing the yard again, Stella pulls Eddie aside, taking both his hands.

"Are you all right?"

Eddie replies, "Yes." Though he isn't certain.

Stella keeps hold of his hands, tilting her head as she gazes at him. She looks magnificent in the moonlight, Eddie thinks, as a breeze tousles, then settles her silver hair. "And did you see him?"

"Did I see who?"

"I don't know, Eddie. You tell me." Then Stella kisses both his cheeks and follows Lucy and Al into the house. Eddie stands rooted for a moment, remembering that he did see something just now. A plant, a teacup, a skyline. No *him*, though, whoever Stella meant. Eddie touches his shoulder, which seems perfectly fine now.

By this time, it's four thirty in the morning. Exhausted and still high, neither Lucy nor Eddie is in any kind of condition to drive back to Seattle. Stella and Al insist they stay for what's left of the night and open up a sofa bed, no questions asked. When the older couple leaves them, Eddie offers to sleep on the floor, but Lucy tells him not to be ridiculous.

"We're practically family, Eddie. Besides, Boonie might be prowling around down there."

So they get into bed together, still stoned but fully clothed.

Eddie has just begun to doze off when Lucy shakes him gently.

"Hey." By the light of the moon coming through the open curtains, he can see that she's lying on her belly, leaning on her elbows, chin resting in her hands. Her face is just inches from his. "You were my hero tonight, you know?"

"Well," he stammers. "I mean—"

"Shh." She covers his lips with her finger briefly. "Just—thank you. I know Robert couldn't come. It wasn't his fault, but I think it was better to have you here."

"Really?"

"Just because he's so practical. I can't imagine him going for Stella's ritual, can you?"

Eddie admits he can't.

"But you were into it, weren't you? I could tell by how lost in thought you seemed afterward." Lucy shifts to her side, still so close. "Can I tell you something?"

Eddie can hear his own heart. "Of course."

"When Stella was chanting, I saw my mother. Did I tell you about her?"

"You said she died." Eddie can't remember when he learned this. From Robert? On the bench by the sound? Eavesdropping on Lucy's phone call with Stella?

"I was just a kid," says Lucy. Before Eddie can ask how she died, Lucy adds, "I don't like to talk about it."

She's looking hard at his face now, and Eddie wonders what she sees. The moon is on Lucy herself. Can she tell his eyes are as wide as small moons themselves? Eddie thinks he should say how sorry he is about her mother, or that her memory should be a blessing, which would get them past the awkwardness of such a profound intimacy. But he's tongue-tied.

Lucy continues, "I don't mean I had an image of her, like a normal memory, because I have those all the time. What I mean is that I saw her. Like I opened my eyes and there was Stella and Al and you, and there was my mom right there in the gazebo with us. And she was just looking at me. Not sad or mad, like she usually was, but more curious, like she showed up to see how I turned out and she was okay with it. Or that she really was Feather all that time and she was saying goodbye to me again." Lucy flops down on her back and covers her eyes. "God, that sounds so cheesy."

Eddie finds his voice. "It's not cheesy. I think it's kind of beautiful."

She turns her head toward him again, eyes moist in the moonlight. "Robert would have thought it was cheesy. He would have made a joke and we'd have laughed about it."

Eddie holds her gaze, resisting the urge to throw his absent brother any further under the bus. He gloats inside over Lucy's preference for him tonight, a prize easily squandered. Eddie longs for words. He wants to say just the right thing, at the very least, to savor the crumbs she's offered him. He wants to know and be known by her. Should he share what he saw during the ritual: the tea, the skyline? But it wasn't anything concrete that he can name—not like Lucy's vision of her mother.

Eddie wishes she would ask what he saw, though it's a relief that she doesn't. The decision to share or not share is made for him. He does not know what he saw, especially since it's already grown fuzzy. (I'm doing what I can to erase it.) Mentally Eddie thumbs through an array of assurances.

"It was a hard night." He's grappling for more to say when he hears that Lucy's breathing has gone slow and rhythmic. Eddie is truly exhausted himself. Before dozing, he allows his thoughts to drift to his brother again, thinking jealously of the fact that Robert lies beside Lucy every night. The warmth of her, the sounds and scents of her—these belong to Robert, are Eddie's on loan to cherish maybe for the next few hours. Of course he dreams of her.

Eddie dreams of Lucy climbing on top of him, kissing him before he can open his mouth to protest. He dreams of succumbing, of joining her passion as they tear off each other's tops, fumble with belts and undergarments. He dreams of weed-fogged, frenzied lovemaking with his brother's girlfriend. Eddie marvels at how their proportions match, how their bodies mesh, melt, flow together. They are at sea in the dream, on a raft surrounded on all sides by breaching whales. He knows somehow that the whales are dream-whales, that the raft and the sea are a dream-raft and a dream-sea, but his singular connection to Lucy is real. Of this he is as sure as he's ever been of anything. Eddie does not lapse in the dream. He's present for every kiss, every maneuver, every moan. Lucy fills his soul.

Soon, Eddie's open eyes register gray light coming through the windows. The smell of weed—now mingled with mildew and wet earth—still hangs in the air. There's the patter of light rain falling on vegetation, birds singing, the garbled discourse of small children in a neighboring yard. Lucy's breathing gives form to the symphony; the backbeat is Eddie's own galloping pulse.

Early panic strikes, as Eddie fights to distinguish his dreaming and conscious selves. Has he just betrayed the one person who has always been his anchor in the world? Has he set himself completely adrift in a single foolish hour? Was the dream-raft a metaphor or truth? Now Lucy stirs, sighs, then sits up with the sheet against her chest, skin soft and inviting, except for the places where her thinness pulls it too taut against the bone. She brushes some hair off her face and turns to Eddie with an ambiguous smile.

"Oh God, Eddie," she says, then yawns as if nothing is amiss, or as if they've been lovers for ages. There's no, *What have we done?* But simply: "What time is it?"

And now that he's really looking at her, studying her face and eyes and hair, Eddie sees that she is a different Lucy from the one in his dream. As real as it felt, this Lucy was never in his arms, against his naked body, rolling and writhing with him on a sofa bed turned raft. The intimacy of her gaze comes only from the intensity of a night full of sorrow, strangeness, and newness. Not love. That part was only on Eddie's side. He turns away from her, hot-faced, making a grand show of searching for his watch. He's still wearing it, more evidence that theirs had been a sex-free bed share. Eddie normally removes his watch during lovemaking. (As far as he can remember.)

He tells her, "Ten twenty-five." But dares not meet her eyes.

25.
PÄR

"You're quiet," Lucy says on the car ride back to Seattle. Eddie is driving since Lucy doesn't trust herself behind the wheel without any coffee in her system.

Eddie keeps his eyes on the road, lacking the words to mask his embarrassment.

"Are you okay?" she says.

"I should be asking you that." Eddie tries to sound casual, but Lucy's gaze distracts him. He glances at her.

"*What?*"

"Nothing." Lucy gives a laugh he wishes weren't so sexy. He heard that laugh in his dream. She adds, "Well, *something.*"

"What 'something'?" Trying to focus on the road, on safety. Unlike the night before, there's moderate traffic on 520.

"You can't tell Robert, okay?" she says.

"Okay."

"No, seriously. I don't know if you guys are close like that, if you say you won't tell each other things and then get drunk and tell each other anyway. My half sisters are like that. Not the drunk part, but they refuse to keep secrets from each other."

"Okay."

"So, promise not to tell him."

"I promise."

"I dreamt about you last night, Eddie. We were messing around."

Eddie nearly crashes into the tiny white Fiat in front of them.

"Um," he says. "Okay. Wow."

"Careful!" Lucy laughs again, turning to watch his face. "So, wow? What do you mean, 'wow'?"

"I mean, wow. Like, what am I supposed to say? My brother's girlfriend dreamt about messing around with me?" Eddie knows he sounds flustered—angry, even—the opposite of cool. Pressured speech is what one former therapist would call this. His heart gallops.

"Shit," says Lucy, still laughing. "I'm embarrassing you, aren't I?"

"Kind of."

"*Kind of?* Think you're too dark to blush, my fellow mixie? You're not."

He drives, wearing her gaze like a lead coat.

"Oh my God! Ha!" There's triumph in her tone. "You dreamt the same thing, didn't you?"

"Shut up," says Eddie, changing lanes. "Please give it a rest."

"Oh my God, you did! That's hilarious! That's awesome. Now we really can't tell him."

To Eddie, there is nothing hilarious, nothing awesome, only humiliation. The parking lot Lucy directs him back to is blessedly dark, concealing whatever blush is still on his face, but she sees through it.

"Eddie, are you crying?"

He wipes his face, looking out the driver's side window at a cinder-block wall. Lucy unstraps her belt and moves closer, draping an arm over him.

"Oh, honey, you *are* crying. I shouldn't have teased. I'm just like that. Ask Robert. My sense of humor is—"

At the mention of his brother's name, Eddie shakes her off and steps out of the car. She respects his silence until they arrive at the apartment.

"We did nothing wrong, you know," Lucy tells him outside their door, keys poised. "We were asleep. They were only dreams, okay?"

"Okay."

"For what it's worth, I do think you're hot—but like, *objectively* speaking. Besides, I would never cheat on Robert."

"I know," Eddie says, swimming in her words. She thinks he's hot. Objectively. He stuffs it away.

"Your brother is hot too, of course," Lucy says. "In his way. Anyway, he's my absolute rock. I know he's yours too."

"He is."

"Hey." She stands on tiptoe and kisses Eddie's cheek. "We didn't do anything. We love Robert, and we're good people."

Robert isn't home, having gone off to the hospital hours earlier. Lucy and Eddie take turns showering and decide to get breakfast somewhere, since Lucy has plenty of time to kill before warm-up. Over lattes and croissants in a café near their apartment, Eddie catches himself staring again at the ripe, full mouth he was dreaming of kissing just hours ago. Her eyes—dark brown pools—look dangerous this morning.

"You won't be able to get away with staring at me like that this week," she says, and Eddie remembers that she's a conscious being.

"I'm not staring."

"Yes you are. Just think of us as friends. Brother and sister. Sister-in-law. Try that."

It hurts him to think that. "Okay."

"If you can't manage it, I might have to do something to hurt your feelings."

"Like what?"

She shrugs. "It would be spontaneous. I can't plan. Just know that I can be super cruel if I need to be."

"I don't believe that."

"Oh, believe it." Lucy takes a bite of croissant and chews thoughtfully. "I've done a lot of things that would probably seem mean and kind of crazy to a regular guy like you."

"I'm not a regular guy."

"Right, I forgot. Still, I've had a complicated life, Eddie. I've learned things I shouldn't have."

"Such as?"

Lucy looks past him. "Some day when I've known you longer, and I've had a drink or two, I'll tell you my story."

"Have you told my brother?" Eddie tries not to sound jealous.

"He knows almost everything."

How he hates Robert for that.

"Just remember," Lucy says, face hardening a shade, "I can't afford to lose Robert. I know you can't either." This frightens Eddie.

"Okay," he says.

After breakfast, the two of them roam the city, from the Space Needle to the Pike Place Market. Standing on the walkway by the Puget Sound again, Eddie leans against the railing, looking out.

"So," he says. "Whales." He can picture them now. Lucy would have liked that part of his dream, he thinks, the breaching whales.

"They're out there," Lucy says, leaning next to him. Eddie detects relief in her voice, that maybe he's not pining for her after all.

From this point on, things seem easier between them. There are no more discussions about dreams, or the implications of their mutual attraction, or anything that happened at Al and Stella's. At two thirty, Eddie drops Lucy off at the theater and walks off on his own.

It's grown overcast, threatening the rain Seattle is known for. As he wanders, thunder cracks somewhere up in the clouds overhead and the sky opens. Grateful for the downpour (cleansing, absolving), Eddie wends his way up and down the city's hills. Every time he looks up, there's Mount Rainier watching him—observant, protective, judgmental. *Fuck you and your pretty snowcap,* he thinks, and feels a bit better for the inner outburst. Eventually, Eddie locates the apartment, where he dries off and crashes on a couch thick with the white hairs of dead little Feather.

☙

A strange week follows for Eddie. While he expects to feel remorseful, unable to look his brother in the eye, he's surprisingly at ease around Robert. Any awkwardness he experiences is with Lucy, for whom he still aches. For her part, Lucy behaves toward Eddie as if nothing out of the ordinary has transpired, and when Eddie is honest with himself, it hasn't. He is suddenly hyperaware of how affectionate Lucy is toward Robert, touching him, kissing him, leaning into him any chance she gets. Eddie yearns for that closeness with Lucy, believing he knows from the dream just what he is missing.

Eddie runs out of weed by the end of the trip. All he has for the plane ride home is his last half Valium, hardly enough to stave off a panic attack. Yet he falls asleep before the aircraft has even reached full altitude, dreaming of Al's weed and Lucy's company.

∽

A week after Eddie arrives home from the trip, Robert calls to say he and Lucy are engaged.

"Mazel tov," says Eddie, after catching his breath. "Give Lucy my best."

"Give it to her yourself," says Robert. "She's right here."

Now Lucy gets on. "Hey, fellow freak."

Eddie presses his eyes shut. "Hey."

He can tell by the sound of Lucy's voice that she's smiling, that she can't stop smiling.

"Mazel tov," he tells her, pledging to himself that he will get past the dream, get over himself, and be happy for them.

26.

PÄR

Eddie discovers that love makes Robert uncharacteristically, maddeningly chatty. He calls Eddie at least twice a week to talk about the wedding and to share more Lucy stories.

"You'll never guess what she did this time," he'll say, fondly recounting his latest Lucy adventure while Eddie bites his lip or picks at the skin around his fingernail beds until they bleed. It's Eddie's job, as best man, to listen.

One day Robert sounds unusually sober.

"Lucy's father is dying. Prostate cancer. It's metastasized, so they're not going to do surgery."

"I'm sorry."

"Lucy's beside herself. We're thinking of moving the wedding date up to make sure he can be there."

The word "wedding" shakes Eddie each time Robert mentions it. The notion of it happening sooner than planned is frankly more devastating to Eddie than the thought of Lucy losing her father.

"Her sister is throwing us an engagement party in December."

"I didn't know she had a sister."

"She has three, actually."

And now Eddie remembers Lucy's mention of the half sisters who "tell each other everything." Robert goes on. "Althea—the youngest one who's hosting the party—is the only one who talks to her. The older two resent Lucy for a bunch of reasons, but Althea's kind of the family's golden child. Lucy says Althea has no cause to resent anyone."

So Eddie will be meeting Althea and Tyrone, possibly other members of the family. How will I feel? Seeing them again, only through Eddie's eyes? I imagine I'll feel much as I do now, hearing from Robert's lips—Robert's! Of all the lips in the world—about the Wynter family dirt. With no small degree of my own resentment, I take in the story (which I know far better) of Lucy's parents.

"Tyrone has been married to Dominique LaFontaine, the opera singer, for decades," says Robert. "They're solid, but back in the '60s, Tyrone had lots of affairs, including one with a girl in his company, Ruth Rivkin, one of the few white dancers at the time. Ruth was twenty-two when she told Tyrone that she was having his baby, whom she intended to keep."

"That baby was Lucy," Eddie says.

"Bingo. It was a scandal. Dominique—Mrs. Wynter—was also pregnant at the time, with her third child, who would be Althea."

Ruth left the company of her own will, Robert explains, but was paid to keep quiet. (The first part is false, the second part true.) She taught dance to make ends meet, bestowing the gift of her talent on Lucy. They had no connection to Ruth's family, who were both aware and disapproving of the baby.

"Was it because Lucy was Black?" Eddie asks.

"I don't know," says Robert. (Of course it was.) "Anyway, Lucy says there was a history of illness—physical and mental—in her maternal family, which complicated things. Ruth killed herself when Lucy was about ten. I'm not sure how. I think pills. Lucy doesn't talk about it."

"That's horrible." Eddie didn't even think to ask how her mother died. "Poor Lucy."

Eddie can't help tallying and comparing what Robert knows of Lucy with what he himself knows of her. Did Lucy share with Robert what she saw during Stella's ritual? Or anything about that evening? Eddie hopes not, imagining that he holds something of her that is out of Robert's reach.

"After that," Robert continues, "Lucy went to live with her father, Dominique, and her half sisters, who were told initially that Lucy was Tyrone's niece, though Dominique knew better and resented her, especially since Lucy was just three months older than Althea. It was all pretty messy.

"Still, Lucy and her dad have always been close. The cancer thing is hitting her pretty hard."

The engagement party, Tyrone's chance to unofficially give Lucy away, is scheduled for early January, Robert says. "We'll fly out right after Lucy's last *Nutcracker* performance."

Which gives Eddie, and me, plenty of time for reconnaissance.

27.
PÄR

The first thing Eddie does is buy a ticket to see WynterDance. The company is performing at City Center in mid-October. When the day arrives, Eddie sits alone in the mezzanine and opens his program to the full-page biography of artistic director Tyrone Wynter. The accompanying photograph, dated 1973, shows a handsome Black man with a high Afro in a white dashiki. Tyrone looks to be in his late thirties or early forties. Eddie studies his face, searching for Lucy. Tyrone has her forehead and her elaborate mouth, which turns up slightly at the corners, though his is adorned in a thick chevron mustache. Eddie can see Lucy's expression in his eyes, *something I have never noticed myself. I've never concerned myself with resemblances. It's a bitter topic for me, not being able to participate in such things. To look like someone else, one must have a physical self all one's own.*

Eddie turns the page to find a group shot of the whole company, taken recently. Tyrone is sitting in a chair at the center—much changed from the earlier photo, the cancer having accelerated his aging. He's bearded and gray-haired now; gaunt, lanky, but still striking.

Eddie had no idea when he bought the ticket that tonight was a special performance, but as the house fills up, he hears snippets of excited conversation about a new ballet, *My Father's House*, fourth and last on the program, set to spirituals and gospel music. The subject matter, according to the program notes, is "the survival of the Black American spirit against all odds." The description makes Eddie feel awkward and respectful, his usual state in the face of anything pertaining to Black culture, despite his exposure and study in college. He has never been able to shake his adoptee's impostership. The man to his right, also Black, leans close to Eddie.

"What a treat: Dominique LaFontaine is singing live tonight."

Another program photograph reveals Dominique herself along with her three daughters, Regina, Sophia, and Althea. Through Eddie's eyes, I take them in. This is the first he's seen of them. A poised, lovely woman of a certain age in a cream-colored silk pantsuit, along with three younger renditions who have reaped the gifts of both Dominique's and Tyrone's genes. The daughters, Eddie reads, will be singing as well. He stares at the images of Lucy's half sisters, who have their father's and therefore Lucy's forehead. I remember how much I miss them, and Eddie feels it too. He cannot make sense of why he yearns to be near them, why his emotions are in a jumble. He chalks it up to Lucy. Dear lord, he's obsessed. Dom and her girls smile out at the camera with love, as if they're smiling at me. Though it was never me they saw.

As the houselights dim, Eddie picks up an intensity of whispers in the row behind him, diagonally to his right.

"It is *too*! It's totally him."

"Shush. It's not. His hair wasn't like that."

"That's from all the peroxide and dyes."

"It's *not* him. He wouldn't dare show his face without calling me. He just fucking wouldn't."

"Ivan, *shh*."

And the curtain rises.

During intermission, Eddie follows the crowd up the aisle to the restroom. While washing his hands, someone clears his throat theatrically. Eddie looks up at the mirror to see two men standing behind him, one Black, one white, about his own age. Danseurs both, judging from their elegant posture and dress. They are staring at him with indignant familiarity.

"You little bitch," says the white one.

Hands still wet, Eddie turns to face them. "I'm sorry. I think you have me confused with—"

"See, Ivan?" The Black guy touches his friend's arm. "It's not Andy."

As the white guy gapes, Eddie ducks past them, drying his hands on his pants, as embarrassed as if he were the one mistaking a stranger for a friend.

As the houselights fade, Eddie is conscious of Ivan's eyes on him. This marks the second time Eddie has been mistaken for Andy—Lucy's not-exactly foster brother. At the second intermission, he's too shy to turn around and grill this Ivan about Andy, his look-alike. Eddie suppresses his curiosity and keeps his head down, reading and rereading the program notes.

For the last piece, Dominique LaFontaine and her three daughters stride across the stage in front of the curtain and take their places on a platform. There they are. I have not seen them since . . . I maintain my distance, my calm. I observe through the virgin eyes of Eddie. The music begins, a solo piano in the orchestra pit, and the women begin to sing in unison, then harmonies. The beauty and richness of their voices, the poignance of the notes, stir Eddie to his core. He cannot understand why he feels it so deeply. For him, it is like being in water. Like the purest, deepest love.

It all comes back to me: their embraces, the joy it was to be Black, to belong unequivocally to the Wynter-LaFontaine women. I abandon decorum and move into place. Of all people, *I* deserve to hear them perform far more than he does. My tears roll down Eddie's cheeks.

28.

PÄR

A few hours before Robert and Lucy's engagement party, Eddie is standing before his bathroom mirror. I watch him staring at himself, trying to conjure a fortitude he suspects is close by, just on the other side of the glass. He had it only once before: on the day of the bathtub episode—when Robert saved his life (if you are to believe Eddie) or tried to drown him (if you accept my own summary of the event).

Eddie remembers what he felt in the presence of the other version of himself—the sensation of absolute belonging. If only he could recapture that energy. If I could whisper in his ear—which I will learn to do in time but haven't just yet—I would tell him, *We've always been here, we've been here all along.* But I can't, so Eddie shakes it off, telling himself he's crazy. But something sticks; he's a degree better than normal.

Once he's thrown on his secondhand parka and shouldered his backpack—containing a bottle of wine, a gift (a book of cheeky cartoons about the first year of marriage)—Eddie monitors himself, as his current therapist strongly encourages. He "checks in with his body," "notices his responses," and counters his anxiety by "grounding himself in the present." Riding along, I will admit that on this evening, I need Eddie as much as he needs me.

As Eddie plods through the bitter January wind toward the subway, his heart pounds to the rhythm of his footfalls. He continues checking in, noticing, grounding. Surroundings: restaurant, bookstore, baby clothes store, restaurant, laundromat, restaurant, deli. People: neighbor, stranger, stranger, cop, cop, neighbor, stranger.

The subway platform is cold and stinks of fresh urine. The train itself is packed with bodies. Two teenage girls and one silver-haired man send flirtatious glances Eddie's way. He tries to keep his eyes on the floor until the train arrives at his stop: 125th and Broadway.

In keeping with Joanne Asher's admonishments about the "Black kids" in West Harbor, Eddie was taught as a child to fear Harlem, along with the outer boroughs, except for select neighborhoods in Brooklyn where Dave and Joanne had distant cousins. Eddie and Robert were cautioned to avoid places in the city to which Joanne referred as "high crime." But on the Upper West Side where the Ashers lived, even on Eighty-Sixth Street, both boys could tell that there was plenty of crime, plenty of people who seemed unhinged and dangerous, including a woman notorious for wearing a plastic bag over her head and swinging a hatchet. If Robert and Eddie saw her, they knew what to do: cross the street and keep moving. But Hatchet Woman, as far as Eddie could tell, was white. And on some level, he understood that it wasn't the geography or the potential for crime that made neighborhoods like Harlem "risky" but the fact that most of the inhabitants were Black. They were threatening just by looking the way they did—which was, ironically, a lot like Eddie.

These days, in a subtle rebellion against his upbringing, Eddie has an affinity for Harlem, which is strong as he emerges from the station, heading toward Althea Wynter's address. He blends in unnoticed, unremarkable, following the flow of pedestrian traffic. Althea lives on an upscale block, nicer than the one where Eddie lives in Brooklyn. Althea's is a prewar building of red brick with an ornate entryway, topped off by a crystal chandelier and wrought iron fixtures. A dog barks from inside an apartment when Eddie rings for the elevator, which hiccups pleasantly as it passes each floor between the ground level and Althea's: five.

Althea opens the door and stares at Eddie with incredulity. He's had women look at him with varying degrees of intensity, but it's not sexual interest he's picking up from Althea tonight. She shakes her head slightly, smiling. When she embraces him, they cling with a mutuality that surprises Eddie. He chalks up the sense of reunion to his yearning for Black affinity.

She holds him away from her now, then covers her mouth with both hands. "Oh my God. You're not—" Althea composes herself. "You're Eddie."

He nods, taken mildly aback.

"Hello, Eddie."

Hello feels distant to him, especially in light of the embrace they've just shared. *Hello* is formal and mature compared with the *hi* he would have offered. Eddie feels instantly underdressed, as if Althea's changed his invitation and made *Hello* the attire for the evening. *Hello* is poised and in control, which makes him look up to Althea right away. Eddie's seen her on the stage, but up close, she is even more striking: posture-perfect and statuesque, hair in long, abundant braids that curl slightly at the tips. Eddie remembers Robert describing Althea as "the golden child" and wonders whether her simple navy shift dress is a conscious choice aimed at not overshadowing the bride-to-be.

"You're early," she tells him. The party is called for seven, which Eddie somehow didn't register from the invitation. It's now six, and he is mortified, tongue-tied, until Althea escorts him inside and hands him a sweet, fizzy, golden drink.

"Thank you."

Eddie works on grounding himself again. Bookshelves: well stocked. Paintings: modern, abstract. Sculpture: African. Plants: philodendron (his least favorite fauna; the long vines always seem animate, sentient). Pets: none, to Eddie's relief. Music: '70s funk.

"I won't ask why you're so jumpy." Althea observes his eyes darting about. "I'm going to have to give you a job to ease those nerves."

She takes Eddie by the wrist—he notes her refined, unchewed, plum-colored nails—and leads him to the kitchen. "It's going to be fine."

"How do you know I'm afraid things *won't* be fine?" Eddie ventures. "Is it that obvious?" He relaxes ever so slightly when she laughs.

"It *is* that obvious, sorry to say."

Althea puts Eddie to work squeezing lemon on fish, chopping crudités, placing napkins in napkin rings, setting out serving platters, serving forks, and spoons. She gives him an approving nod, tops off his drink, and, without warning, calls out, "Clark!" Explaining that her boyfriend is in the bedroom with Tyrone, who's been resting. It's time for the men—presumably Clark and Eddie himself—to move furniture.

Our heart quickens with curiosity and excitement as Eddie cranes our neck in the direction of the hallway. Tyrone is here! And Althea has a boyfriend, a real one, I surmise.

"Clark!" she calls again. I hold Eddie's breath. Who gets to be my sweet Althea's boyfriend?

Enter Clark. Tall, Black, powerfully built, bespectacled—and gnawingly familiar to us both. Eddie scans his memory. Did they ever coach swimming together, he wonders? Attend the same gym? Eddie is certain he's seen the guy half-dressed. Clark registers the fumbling look on Eddie's face, removes his glasses, and raises one eyebrow, at which point Eddie recognizes the "Fortissimo Guy," the burly, shirtless spokesman for the popular men's aftershave. At the end of each television commercial— whether he's been lifting weights, riding a horse, or poolside, enjoying the company of a beautiful woman—the Fortissimo Guy pulls down his sunglasses, winks, and says, "Because strong can be sensual."

"You're—" is all Eddie gets out before Clark acknowledges, "That's me."

I choke off Eddie's urge to repeat the commercial slogan because I want Clark to like us. (Althea's good graces are no small prize.) Only when the moment passes, and Eddie is no longer at risk of blurting anything embarrassing, do I cede control.

Clark is now looking askance at Eddie. "Wait. *You're* Lucy's fiancé's brother? I thought he was—"

"White," supplies Althea, passing them on her way out of the room with a tablecloth in her arms. "This is stained. Yeah, Robert's white; Eddie's adopted."

"Oh, okay." Clark extends his hand, which devours Eddie's as they shake. Althea returns and spreads a fresh tablecloth on a sideboard, sweeps her braids behind her back, and claps her hands, calling Clark and Eddie to attention.

"We need to create the illusion of space and luxury." She hops up on a stool to preside over the men, directing: "Move the sofa here . . . No wait—there . . . Now, put these chairs together . . . No, in a semicircle. And space them apart more . . . Yeah, like that . . ."

Clark and Eddie toil away, working up a sweat, sharing an occasional amused glance behind their commander's back, the camaraderie relaxing Eddie further. When Althea deems their work complete, he abandons his fizzy drink to share a beer with Clark. The two of them kick back in two chairs they have placed flanking a fichus tree.

"By the way, the answer is no," Clark says.

"No what?"

"No, I do not wear Fortissimo. Shit reeks like turpentine."

Eddie laughs. "I wasn't going to ask. But hey, if it pays the bills."

"It does that," Clark says. "And it's also the thing that got Ty and Dom to give their blessings."

Eddie translates: Tyrone and Dominique. Whom he holds in esteem too high for such abbreviations. That evening at City Center, when Dominique was finished singing, Tyrone joined her onstage for curtain calls. Together they radiated a godlike energy, Eddie thought then. "Ty and Dom" humanizes them.

Clark glances toward the room where Tyrone is still concealed, then lowers his voice, intimating, "They had higher hopes for Althea than a starving actor." He sips his beer as Eddie muses to himself that Clark looks far from starving. "Naturally they respect the performing arts, which is their world after all, but they also know they are the exception to the rule. Black artistic aristocracy and all that. Althea should pursue her dreams, but for her, uh—intended? They were hoping for someone with more career stability."

"Promoting Fortissimo seems pretty stable."

"It's a lucrative stepping stone for now."

Clark shares that his real passion is straight theater. He dreams of performing something by August Wilson or Adrienne Kennedy on Broadway. As he talks—which he seems to enjoy—he conveys an artistic sensibility, using his body like a performer rather than the athlete he could easily pass for. Clark *projects*, even when he speaks softly. His gestures—including the maneuver he uses to reach for and embrace Althea as she passes through the room once again—seem to have an audience in mind. This reminds Eddie of Lucy. Also like Lucy, Clark shares more than he asks, which suits Eddie.

"So you guys are engaged?" I let Eddie ask. The word "intended" did not escape either of our notices.

Clark looks around, again theatrically, making sure Althea is out of earshot. "It's complicated." An echo of Lucy and Robert's characterization of the Wynter family.

"We've been together four years," he says. "I've proposed as many times."

"And you have her parents' blessing?"

"I do."

"But not Althea's?"

"She's skittish about marriage." Clark takes a drink. "I don't know how much you know about the Wynters."

"I know they're 'complicated.'"

Clark chuckles. "Lucy and Althea are three months apart. Which tells you all you need to know about Tyrone's views on fidelity. I mean—I love the guy, I really do. But his old ways have done me no favors.

"I have proven in every way imaginable that I am not a player like Ty. I come from a long line of faithful, monogamous Black men. But Althea says her father told her mother the same thing." Clark shrugs. "One of these days I'll wear her down. Maybe Lucy getting married will convince her. The two of them haven't got much in common, but Althea gets a kick out of Lucy and her antics. They're pretty close these days. The engagement could work in my favor."

Eddie is stuck on the phrase "Lucy getting married." He tries to douse the pain with beer, but Clark picks right up on it.

"What?" he says, raising the famous eyebrow. "Robert and Lucy don't have *your* blessing?"

"No!" Eddie says. "I mean, yes. Of course they do. I mean—"

"*Ohhh.*" Clark touches his beer to Eddie's. "I see." They both drink while Clark watches Eddie's eyes.

"Have you met her?" Eddie says.

"Lucy? A few times. It was enough."

Before Eddie can ask him to elaborate, Althea joins them, settling in Clark's lap. She whispers something in his ear that makes Clark grin and kiss her. How naturally they fit together, Eddie observes, how clearly they belong to one another. Eddie has seen that kind of love before—not between Lucy and Robert, but in both his parents' second marriages. Dave and Glenda, Joanne and Michael. Like Clark and Althea, they exude joy and ease in each other's company. Eddie has only ever felt that way in the water, where he's whole, never awkward, never alone. To have a love like water, Eddie thinks, that would be something.

By seven fifteen the party is in full swing. As Robert forecasted, it's a modest gathering, with just a few representatives from each relevant constituency. A coming together of worlds, including a handful of dancers—WynterDance members who are friends of Lucy's; Bruce Fishman, Robert's best friend and former downstairs neighbor; a few of Robert's friends from Riverview Prep and Columbia; Althea, Clark,

Tyrone, and Eddie. Intimidated by the elegant, self-possessed dancers, Robert's friends greet Eddie with startling enthusiasm, glad to find a familiar soul whose awkwardness they all remember as surpassing their own.

Guests mill from the front room, where Clark and Eddie set up the bar to the living room, where Tyrone—in an elegant white suit—now sits like royalty. Lacking the courage to ask for an introduction, Eddie regards the older man over the shoulders of Robert's friends. A wing-back chair upholstered in green paisley serves as Tyrone's throne. As admirers approach to greet him and chat, Tyrone shakes hands, throws back his head in an occasional laugh, but does not once get up.

At around seven thirty, Eddie's attention is usurped by his mother. Joanne looks smart in her best beige pantsuit and matching size 5 pumps, Michael at her side. They've recently sold the house on the Island and bought a two-bedroom condo on East Eighty-Ninth Street, planning ahead for their dotage, when they'll want to live on one level, have easy access to Manhattan doctors, and increase the potential for visits from adult children and grandchildren, of which Michael already has two.

Dave and Glenda will not attend this evening, but they've assured Eddie and Robert that they will come with the girls for a "good long stay" around the wedding itself. Other notable absences from the engagement party are Dominique and her eldest daughters, Regina and Sophia, who have never come around to the point of fully embracing Lucy.

"We're worried about you, Eddie," Joanne tells him, which is nothing new. What is new is the revelation that she and Michael have broken a decade-plus-long freeze and reached out to Dave and Glenda. "We all think you should go back to law school. We'll support you in any way we can." Everyone, Eddie learns, is on board with this cross-country intervention: parents, stepparents—even Robert was consulted. The swim coaching is a dead end, everyone has agreed, far beneath Eddie's potential. "And you don't look well," Joanne adds. "Is it drugs, honey?"

She touches Eddie's face, which he allows, calculating that pushing her hand away will only lead to further misgivings about his health and lifestyle.

"No, Mom."

"Are you going to therapy?"

"Yes, Mom."

"Making progress?"

"Joanne, that's his business." Michael gives Eddie a wink, in keeping with his assumed role of the easygoing one who respects his privacy—which Eddie recognizes as unadulterated bullshit. Joanne does all their active prying but shares everything with Michael, who then reinforces her worst fears about Eddie's dereliction. Doing drugs, sleeping with strange women, coaching swimming—a clear path to ruin.

"If it's money you need," puts in Michael gently, according to custom, "that's no problem. And your mother and I talked about it. Our offer stands." Eddie is welcome to give up his apartment and move in with them if he'll only return to law school. Though Eddie cannot imagine a scenario that appeals to him less—Joanne's nagging, Michael's condescension, having each aspect of his day scrutinized, the absence of weed—he tells them he'll consider it.

❧

Now Eddie means to join Clark and Bruce Fishman, who have met and appear to be getting on well, but Althea intercepts him.

"You haven't met my father yet, have you?"

"No." Eddie's pulse quickens as she takes his hand. Why is he so reluctant—terrified, even? He lets Althea pull him into the living room but lurks in the doorway.

"Daddy," Althea says, parting the group of dancers encircling Tyrone's chair.

"Andy!" Tyrone's voice is a gravelly bellow that Eddie and I both feel deep within our bones. "Andy Lindberg! You stand in the foyer expecting me to come to you? Where are your manners, boy?" Eddie glances behind him but is undoubtedly the one Tyrone is reaching for. The old man guffaws. "Get your skinny Black behind over here!"

Eddie's skinny Black behind sees no alternative but to comply.

"Andy." Up close, Eddie experiences Tyrone's voice like a cello. "*Andy Lindberg.* It's good to see you, son. You look good, still dancing." (This is not a question.) "Got some color, I see. Pull up that chair. I never forgave you for leaving, you know." But his smile tells Eddie that he—Andy—is off the hook. "Now, I know I was no saint. Dominique and I could have handled things differently. But did we not make amends? We did, man, we *did*." (*Amends for what?* Eddie wonders.) "What was so great about Hubbard Street?" (Which, Eddie won't learn till later, is a rival dance company in Chicago.)

As Andy, Eddie shrugs, nods, and smiles at everything Tyrone says—the way you do with the charismatic old and infirm. Eddie feels stronger now that he can think of himself as Andy, the renegade dancer, the prodigal son. He remembers Lucy's description of Andy: remarkably like Eddie, same face, same smile, but slightly lighter skinned with looser curls. Gay. A brilliant dancer. As Eddie tries to envision himself into the role, I help with the posture, fine-tune the laugh, which I remember coming more easily, melodically than Eddie's. It feels much better to be Andy, or at least not-Eddie, a lonely law school dropout mooning over his brother's fiancée. As Andy—or as a convincing imposter—I catch the eye of Clark, rippling pectorals in his tight oxford, starting another beer. Eddie doesn't feel this the way I do. In any case, he's hardly brave enough to raise his own beer more than a fraction of an inch at Clark (even in character as Andy). Still, Clark notices, raises the Fortissimo eyebrow.

For me—as I imagine it is for Eddie—things are becoming confusing as we stretch to cover Andy-ness. I go with it, riding along. Eddie goes with it too. I cannot help wondering, wherever he is, does the real Andy feel a shift? Is his shoulder burning at the very least?

My mind is crowded with the conflation of too many thoughts, the body with too many souls. And, cognizant of the other dancers and friends around, their eyes on us, I cannot fathom how to guide Eddie. From my perch, I can see that the Maestro's eyes are the same as ever. I cannot lead this reunion, cannot summon Andy's essence to Eddie's body. (The last time I tried anything remotely like that, I almost killed us all.) No, this cannot *be* a reunion. It's too much, too hard. I hold my position, cling to the scar. Just watch, Pär, just stay back and watch them together.

Tyrone leans forward with some effort. "Between you and me, Andy, Lucy's choice astonished me. Don't get me wrong: I am thrilled. I like this Robert very, very much. I love the fact that he's out of the dance world, that he's boring"—Tyrone chuckles—"that he's stable, hardworking. A doctor, of all things. He'll take care of her, you got me? And boy, how she dodged a bullet. You know who I'm talking about, Andy."

What is this? What is Tyrone doing, exactly? The way he emphasizes Andy's name—uttering it too often, chin lowered, gaze fixed on Eddie's—raises a flag. He's performing, pretending. The other dancers, their audience, seem fully absorbed.

"I do know," says Eddie (playing Andy, of course), hoping to learn what he claims to know.

And Tyrone (playing a confused version of Tyrone, one who believes that this perplexed young man is his beloved Andy) says, "I thought for sure she was going to go back to Carlo." The observing dancers murmur their agreement. Everyone knows about Carlo, Eddie gleans.

Eddie-as-Andy nods along (while Eddie-as-Eddie vaguely remembers Lucy mentioning this Carlo and needs to hear more). I watch Eddie piece it together from Tyrone's discourse: how Carlo was Lucy's first true love, that Tyrone had hired Carlo away from La Scala Theatre Ballet when Lucy was a teenager, taking him on as a soloist at WynterDance. How Lucy and Carlo had dated stormily for several years until Lucy took her broken heart to Seattle and the Pacific Northwest Ballet.

"You and I both knew he was bad for her all along, Andy. If it hadn't been for you consoling her, she'd have died of a broken heart from all his messing around."

He treated her like dirt. Eddie nearly blurts out my words, but I catch him just in time, holding his tongue. Stay back, Pär, stay back.

"Daddy," Althea interjects, "this is Eddie. Not Andy. Eddie is Robert's brother."

I watch Tyrone look Eddie up and down, absorbing—I cannot tell what. "Of course he is. Of course." He nods theatrically toward the dancers. "As y'all can see, Robert's brother is, in fact, a *brother*."

There is awkward acknowledgment in the room. Althea laughs, patting Tyrone's arm. "And we know having a Black brother raises Robert's approval rating from Daddy."

"Nonsense." But Tyrone's wide grin says otherwise. He repeats, "Eddie." And before anyone can stop him, Tyrone, with some effort, lifts himself out of his chair. He says it again. "*Eddie.*" And moves toward him, hands out. "My *man*." Tyrone clasps bewildered Eddie by the shoulders, using him for support, as an array of emotions crosses the old man's face. The dancers float discreetly from the room, sensing the need for a private reckoning.

Althea stays. "Daddy, are you okay?"

"Never better."

"Daddy, you're crushing him. Sit down."

When Tyrone releases Eddie, Althea helps him back to his chair.

"Thea, baby," Tyrone says, eyes still on Eddie's, "go see if we have any tomato juice."

She hesitates another second, then leaves them alone.

"Have a seat, Eddie. Pull up that chair."

The Maestro leans forward, clasps one of Eddie's hands between his two frail ones. Eddie notices the range of brown between them, the similarity between the shapes of their long fingers, marred only by Eddie's gnawed-off nubs of nail.

"Tell me about yourself, son," says Tyrone.

Eddie stammers initially, as is his way. He does not know where to begin, but begins. He talks. Tyrone listens, probes, nods. It's too much for me to bear. I have been Andy, rested upon Andy. I am not Andy. I therefore don't remember all the details, but I do know the feeling: what it is to love and lose Tyrone Wynter, to fight him, to leave him, to break inside when he lets you go. Eddie has no access to those memories. Tyrone was never Eddie's father figure; he was mine. As is this hand clasping his, this heart breaking. To be cast out while Eddie is allowed to touch, be touched, and blend into this man! It's unfair. How is it that the more I see, the less I become, whereas the opposite is true of Eddie? It hurts out here. It's too much to try to share the stage. If only I could retreat and watch without a stake. Or else . . . What if it were *me* living this body's life, *me* being touched and missed and loved? *Me* loving in return, *me* experiencing, laughing, shouting, swimming, dancing, being. For all my conscious life, I've resisted the idea, reasoning that it was better to affect but not commit, to have partial access to two separate bodies rather than full possession of one. But I have never envied Eddie the way I do at this moment, never been so clear that I want what is his. Can I even do it? What would the consequences be for me? No matter: I've opened my mind and won't turn back. Tonight is where it starts.

Presently there comes a crescendo of voices from the direction of the front room. Hearing Robert's laugh followed by the ring of Lucy's, Eddie waits as Tyrone lets go of his hand, calling out, "Is that my girl? Is it my Lucy-bell?"

In an instant, the living room is glittering with the essence of her: excitement, enthusiasm, energy. Champagne and a new crush of guests follow Lucy and Robert into the room as glasses, kisses, and embraces go around. Robert's hand claps Eddie's back.

"You made it, dude."

"You too."

Lucy kisses her father's cheek, perches on the arm of his chair before realizing that it's Eddie sitting opposite him, at which point he's treated to a squeal of delight. Lucy almost spills her champagne as she hands it off to throw her arms around Eddie, her brother-in-law-to-be, planting a kiss of warm, wet breath on his cheek.

"Eddie! Eddie!" Lucy's eyes tear up. "I'm so glad you're here!" She adds, "My partner in crime!"

"Hi, Lucy." It's all Eddie can get out. Partner in crime? A joke, meaningless. Meaning less. And while there was no actual crime committed that night in Al and Stella's sofa bed, they each dreamt of one, which—for Eddie—aroused nearly as much guilt. Today, however, Eddie can tell he has not crossed Lucy's mind since July. Robert meets his gaze now, beaming, full of appreciation for the gift of this girl, his girl. Robert and Lucy's beautiful life together is beginning in earnest. *All the best to you both,* people say, over and over. *All the best.*

When the numbers thin out, Joanne and Michael take their leave. (But not before Michael slips Eddie a twenty and the business card of an attorney friend whose son also dropped out of law school, then returned with a new outlook and passed the bar with flying colors. "He might have advice.")

Eddie seeks out Althea in the kitchen, where she and Clark are in the early stages of cleaning up. Althea hands Eddie a towel, nodding toward a platter in the dish drainer. As before, Eddie settles, almost comfortably, into the job and the company of these two. He feels the itch of longing, longing to belong.

Drying, he asks Althea, "Can you tell me about Andy Lindberg?"

"Andy lived in my house from the time we were ten and eleven until I left for school. What do you want to know?"

"Do I really look like him?"

She faces him. "Eerily so, yeah. I kind of freaked out when you got off the elevator."

"Only he's lighter?"

"A little bit." She squints, then laughs. "It's more like someone took Andy, cranked up the Black genes half a degree, made him a little prettier, and got you."

"Wait—who's prettier?" There's a note of jealousy in Clark's tone as he takes the platter from Eddie.

"Eddie is." Althea tilts her head flirtatiously at him, resemblance to Lucy briefly surfacing. "And there's something else. You have a similar, I don't know—bearing. He was a sweet guy, Andy. Too sweet. He got taken advantage of a lot, if you ask me."

Eddie wants to learn all he can about Andy, whom everyone talks about in the past tense, whom even strangers mistake him for. "Think he'll come to the wedding?"

"Not a chance," Althea says. "He and Lucy haven't spoken in years. Very bad blood between them." She won't elaborate further. "Not my place. Not my story. But my dad loved him like a son. He looked at you the same way. Even when I told him you weren't Andy." Now Althea dries her hands off and stands, arms akimbo. "What did you talk to Daddy about when I left the room?"

"He just asked me about myself. What I did for a living, why I dropped out of law school, what I was doing there in the first place. Also, about my and Robert's childhood. Stuff like that."

"He took a real liking to you, then," says Clark. "I don't think he ever asked me that much to my face."

"Well, you know Daddy," says Althea. Without elaborating, she goes to answer the phone that is ringing in the other room.

"It's a tough family to break into," Clark says, and takes another platter from Eddie.

"Clark." Althea pokes her head back into the kitchen, holding a hand over the phone. "Regina's busy tomorrow and can't take Daddy to pain management. Can you?"

"I have an audition."

Althea says she can't either—nor can Lucy or Sophia or even Dominique.

"I'll do it!" Eddie says, surprising himself. "I'm free."

Clark catches his eye. "Brownnoser." And swats him with a dish towel.

Althea checks with Tyrone and returns to the kitchen.

"Daddy is thrilled to have you take him, Eddie," she says. "He said you're his first choice."

Clark shakes his head. "Well, everything goes best when you give Tyrone Wynter what he wants."

"And we all do, don't we," Althea says. "We're all in his thrall. The same goes for Lucy. But you already knew that, didn't you, Eddie?" Althea drawls out his name, making doe eyes.

"I don't know what you mean," says Eddie, convincing no one.

"Like hell you don't," Althea says. "I saw the way you looked at her. How she kissed you and called you her *partner in crime*." She nudges Eddie in a way I remember her playing with me when I was Andy. What fun we had. *It's me,* I am thinking, hoping Althea senses *me*. How I wish I could fall back in, be Althea's almost-brother, the Wynter family's ward, to belong, to be loved and have a place.

"Althea, leave him alone," says Clark.

"I'm just letting him know I understand. My sister is charming and adorable and mysterious and all those things that lead to trouble."

As if on cue, another one of Lucy's delighted, shrieking laughs reaches them from the living room.

"She's my brother's fiancée," Eddie says helplessly.

"Very true," says Althea. "And even if she were not, I would warn you about her. Because she clearly thinks you're cute too."

"Stop messing with him," Clark says.

"I'm not. I just want him to be careful. Be careful, okay, Eddie?"

But he won't. Misconstruing his own heart's pull toward Lucy, Eddie believes he's fallen at least halfway in love. I have no solid plan, but this must be the key. Eddie's ambiguous, liquid love for Lucy is where I will enter and expand my control, to—ultimately, with hope and a little luck—flip the switch irrevocably.

29.
PÄR

On the day after the engagement party, Eddie exits the subway at Seventy-Second in front of the Dakota and drinks in the towering cream-and-orange-concrete building directly across the street, atop which the Wynters' penthouse sits. Eddie has glimpsed The Majestic hundreds of times, either walking to the park or else riding the number 10 bus along Central Park West. He's been inside once too, visiting friends of Joanne's who lived on the ground floor, but he was so young he barely remembers that. The Majestic lives up to its name. And Eddie, in old brown cords and a parka from a secondhand shop on Schermerhorn Street, feels way too underdressed to pass the scrutiny of a doorman. But the uniformed, mustachioed guy at the door breaks into a smile when Eddie presents himself.

"I thought it was you! Been a while." The doorman calls up to the Wynters and then points the way to the elevator, the operator of which has a similar reception for Eddie.

"Where've you been, my friend? Dancing all over the globe?"

"Um. Kind of." To correct and disabuse and explain feels to Eddie more complicated than playing along. He's never lied so easily before. Never with such aplomb. Being perceived as an entirely different person makes him feel at ease. Clearly Andy was liked by everyone.

Eddie is anxious about meeting Dominique LaFontaine, however. He's seen her only in program photos and onstage, dressed like a queen, voice like an otherworldly being.

"She's a force," Clark told him the night before. "Everyone cowers in her presence at first; I mean, I still do. But Dom is kind and genuine. Grace personified."

"Just don't call her Dom to her face," Althea cautioned. "And do not mention Lucy if you can help it. That business will always be a sore point. But you're a sweet guy. You'll be okay."

Dominique stands waiting as the elevator doors open, dressed in a navy suit. She finishes fastening a silver earring in place, greets the elevator man, then pulls Eddie into the foyer.

"Goodness," she says. "I had a moment. Jacques said it was Andy when he called up, but I knew it wasn't. Althea warned me that you resemble him. She and Clark both like you very much, by the way. Tyrone does too. So. Eddie . . ." She pushes back the parka hood and takes him by the shoulders. "Let me look at you."

Eddie stands for inspection, unaware of what it is for me to be this close to her again. How strange to remember so much that is brand new to Eddie: her perfume, the small mole on her left cheek, the shape of her smile. I remember her sternness, her "home training," the gift of her hard-won approval. Eddie has only this moment.

"I do see it," Dominique says. "But when someone you've just met looks like someone you loved and miss, it makes the stranger somehow—*more* strange." Eddie nods, feeling apologetic. Leading the way past the open living room, Dominique adds, "I hope I didn't offend you. Tyrone and I both loved Andy and have many regrets about what happened. Anyway," brightening, "I am so grateful you were able to come today." She directs him toward the master bedroom and excuses herself. She has an interview to do.

Tyrone is dressed, seated in a rust-colored leather chair that dwarfs his slight form. When the Maestro squeezes his hand and calls him "son," Eddie helps him into his wheelchair, feeling both useful and grateful.

When Althea calls after the appointment to thank him, Eddie says, as casually as he can, that he'd be happy to help out anytime.

"Don't offer unless you mean it," she says. "We are all busy, and we will take you up on it."

Eddie means it. He never really felt needed before meeting Lucy and the Wynters. Coddled, accommodated, yes, but needed? Never. Soon it's weekly, then twice a week. Eddie arrives and takes Tyrone to his appointments, either chemotherapy, pain management, acupuncture, physical therapy, or occupational therapy. Eddie pushes the wheelchair while Tyrone lectures him about the music and poetry that has inspired his choreography. The older man tells stories about his youth too, the fiery days when he was in his dancing prime, long before he settled down with Dominique. Mostly Tyrone talks and Eddie listens, but sometimes Tyrone asks the questions.

"Are you sure they never put you in dance classes, Eddie? Growing up here in New York? Looking like you look? Really? Come on."

But Eddie insists. "Really. Never."

"Damn shame," says Tyrone. "You'd have been a natural. Andy was a natural."

No matter how at home Eddie feels with Tyrone, how accepted and welcomed, there is always some mention of Andy. As if Eddie doesn't exist independently for the family.

"I'm like Andy's stand-in," Eddie mopes to Althea, remembering that Lucy declared as much on the night they met.

"Not his stand-in," Althea says. "More like a chance at redemption for whatever happened between Daddy and Andy."

"What did happen?"

"I don't really know, to be honest. Andy was like a kid brother to my sisters and me. Things didn't go wrong until I'd left for college. It had to do with Lucy and Carlo. A lot of drama that led to Andy leaving WynterDance. Daddy never got over losing him. I think your being here helps in some way."

It surprises me that I know so much more about it than Althea: the rumor concocted by Lucy herself that Tyrone was so quick to believe; the ease with which he and Dominique turned their backs on Andy as if he'd never belonged to them.

"What if the real Andy comes back?" Eddie says.

"He won't," Althea replies, though how can she possibly be sure?

Eddie doesn't press. He is curious about Andy, though, with half a mind to look him up in Chicago. But if he did, and it led Andy to reconcile with the Wynters, would Eddie be expected to step aside? He will not take that chance.

On their walks and excursions, Eddie often finds himself lulled by the rhythm of Tyrone's speech, soothed by his company. Wheeling his chair past the Strawberry Fields memorial at the Seventy-Second Street entrance to Central Park, Eddie knows that strangers take them for father and son. This is exhilarating for Eddie, whose racial loneliness is beginning to lift. He can see through the thin film of gauze separating the life he has from one that might have been. Eddie is really Black with Tyrone, less of an imposter.

During these same monologues of Tyrone's, Eddie's mind drifts with the sense that these are stories he's heard before. Eddie wonders, is it that he wants to belong to Tyrone so badly? Or is it that somewhere, in some version of the universe, he once did?

In any case, though Eddie relishes the role, thankful for Andy's continued absence, his curiosity grows. He looks his apparent doppelgänger up in Chicago to find no listing for an Andy Lindberg, nor Andrew nor Andreas nor anything similar. Next, he reaches out to Hubbard Street Dance. Alas, the secretary there tells him: Andy Lindberg has recently ended his employment there. She is unfortunately not at liberty to share where he's gone. Eddie is welcome to leave his name and address, however, and she'll forward it to Andy. Eddie declines, embarrassed. After all, who is he to Andy? A stranger who looks like him. Stalking him. To what end?

30.
PÄR

In the meantime, Eddie has become known at the cancer center on York Avenue. He is greeted by the security guards, who no longer need to check his visitor's identification bracelet as he wheels Tyrone past the gate. The girls at the desk call him by name: Eddie, not Andy. Tyrone, they address as Mr. Wynter or "sir." Even the ones who have never seen a dance performance understand that Tyrone is a man to be revered.

During the hours-long chemo days, unless Tyrone is dozing, Eddie stays, sits, and chats, or else fetches things like tea or coconut-flavored Italian ices. The antinausea medication will eventually knock Tyrone out, but in the transitional moments between stupor and lucidity, he often talks. Pieces of stories come through, some more coherent than others. "Daddy's mutterings," Althea calls them. "Half the time, he wakes up thinking I'm his mother." Mostly, while Tyrone sleeps, Eddie watches over him. And when Eddie gets drowsy, I take over.

On one such visit in late February, Eddie, who was out late the night before, nods off in his chair almost before Tyrone does the same. I sit vigil, observing the Maestro sleeping, twitching here and there as the fluid drips from the bag into his port. It seems impossible that this is the same man with the booming voice and confident stride who we all looked up to. *We.* Of course, the "we" didn't include me, but no one can claim I didn't love him too. And now here I sit, watching for hours through our lowered eyelids until the nurse shakes Eddie awake.

"We're nearly done. About twenty more minutes for the fluids to run through, and you can take him home." Whispering, which is how Eddie knows Tyrone is still unconscious. But when the nurse leaves, Tyrone starts talking.

"Hey, are you there?" The old man's eyes are still closed, his voice thick with sleep.

"Of course." Eddie wonders who Tyrone imagines he's talking to.

"I never told you about my boys, did I?"

"Your boys?" Eddie straightens up. "Like—*sons*? I didn't know you had any."

"I sure do. Or I did." Head rolling toward Eddie's side of the room. "They never knew about me. Did you know that? Their mother—she wouldn't let—" Tyrone breaks off. He winces, face strained, like he's aching for words. "I tried, you know? I did try. But she just took—" He goes quiet again, lost to a dream, breath light but even.

Eddie and I are both hyperalert in this body now, both feet on the floor. Is it true? Or a drug-induced hallucination? How did no one in the family—neither Dominique nor any of the sisters, not even Lucy—ever mention that there were Wynter boys? Tyrone murmurs something else, then jolts himself wide awake, eyes landing on our face.

"Where are they now?" Eddie demands, directness courtesy of me. I am learning to shape his words, to speak using his voice.

"Where are who?"

"The boys. Your sons?"

"What? How'd you know about them?"

"I didn't. But you were just—"

"*Hmph.*" Tyrone shuts his eyes again. "Didn't know I said it out loud. But I tell you, I've been thinking about them quite a bit lately. Quite a bit." He sinks lower into the hospital bed. "You won't say anything about it to Dom, will you?"

"Of course not," Eddie promises, bewildered. I'm no better off. All along I've believed that Lucy was the only issue from her father's affairs.

"Good man." Tyrone fades out again.

Eddie entertains the idea of asking Althea, or even Lucy, about the "boys"—their brothers—but decides against it. Maybe Eddie knows all he wants to know. It's enough that he and Tyrone have a secret between them. On the next visit, we'll both learn more.

But Tyrone never mentions his sons again, and neither Eddie nor I can find another opening to ask about them. Still, we brood over the subject, replaying the scant phrases Tyrone uttered that day in his drugged state. Perhaps the Maestro was dreaming or simply remembering a film he'd seen—and there were no "boys" after all.

31.

PÄR

It's mid-April when Lucy phones to tell Eddie that she's coming east for five days to spend time with her dad. Robert can't get away; she's coming alone and will be staying with Clark and Althea. Eddie dares to ask if he'll see her.

"Don't be an idiot," she says. "Of course."

On Wednesday night, she calls from a pay phone near The Majestic to demand Eddie's presence in an hour at Dublin House, an Upper West Side bar. She needs to drink.

Eddie panics. He's going to see her, without Robert as a buffer. What if he becomes a drooling, stammering, nail-bitten pile of madness in her presence? His heart races, hands shake, body sweats. *Stop,* he admonishes himself. *Calm the fuck down. It was a dream, a dream.* But Lucy dreamt the same thing. And between them there was an admission of mutual attraction. Or something like it. Objectively hot, Lucy had called him, which was not the same as attraction exactly. And whatever it was—the energy between them—they had agreed it would remain forever dormant. But it burns inside Eddie still. I can feel it. I want to use it. Eddie senses something—senses *me*—fearing an oncoming lapse. *No!* Eddie smacks himself in the face, grounding himself in the pain.

What comes to him now is a memory from junior high school, in West Harbor, standing alone in the yard, watching the Black boys and Black girls together, playing, chasing, taunting each other. The exchange of insults, which might have sounded cruel in other contexts, drew great hoots of laughter from even the targets. The Black kids' rapport was louder, rougher, more intimate than what Eddie saw between the white boys and girls. He remembers how one Black girl saw him staring and bellowed in his direction:

"Whatchoo looking at, boy?" to the resounding mirth of her friends. Eddie had run off in shame at the time, but he remembers longing to stay. To meet the girl's challenge with a clever rejoinder that would have earned him membership. How he'd wanted to join them, to play and chase and bathe in the camaraderie.

Is that what Lucy stirs in him? Not desire? Not lust? What cheap, plebeian words! They belong in Robert's realm, far beneath what Eddie imagines he and Lucy can have. (With just a small push from me, Eddie's thoughts congeal into an uncharacteristic hubris. A fascinating shift!) Eddie wants to be *of* Lucy more than *with* her. The memory of her touch when she nudged him and called him "fellow mixie" or "fellow freak" with playful affection makes him reel a bit. (Is he lapsing? He's not, but smacks himself again to be sure.)

Next, Eddie looks at himself in his bathroom mirror, spotted with toothpaste and shaving cream residue. The image could be clearer, but it suits me fine, and I do it. I show him, not himself as he expects, but me. And I wait, breathless.

Eddie studies the face, which is his own face, yes, mark for mark, cell for cell, but he recognizes somehow that it is not him.

He digs his fingers into the front of his curls (I do the same, of course), puffs them up so they stand at attention over his head, then pats them into place again. He smiles widely, then frowns (as do I). He blinks. Again. And again. He can't lose me in these physical tests, but it's something in the eyes. The way I direct them isn't the same, he thinks.

I let him see this, let him know I am here—this alternative version of him. For now, I let him make of it what he will.

He keeps his eyes on mine, messing with his hair again, observing his chin line as if checking for an unshaved patch or a blemish. He can see, objectively, what others see when they remark on his beauty. It doesn't embarrass him to register this because it's me, not him, that he's seeing.

Outside, there's a film of ice on the ground, making people walk like toddlers to keep from skidding. Blustery wind rips at Eddie's ears, winter hanging on with fierce teeth despite it being a few weeks into spring. In his vintage leather jacket, Eddie regrets having left the sec-ondhand parka home. But his shivering has little to do with the weather. *Lucy,* he's thinking. *You're going to see Lucy.* The notion warms him from the inside out. *Lucy, Lucy.* The *c* taking over: the hissing of a serpent guarding something precious. But wait—what if it's changed? What if the spark between them has dimmed? Eddie strikes bright red blood on the cuticle of his left thumb. He didn't realize he was gnawing it. Shit. Blood freezes like water, only more slowly. Sharks are attracted to blood in the water. On the subway, will it draw rats? It's I who feed him this joke, summoning a laugh from the throat, which makes a passing woman stare. Eddie suspects he's out of control.

His feet solve the problem, taking him to the East River Gym, the only place in the area with a public indoor pool. In Eddie's locker there's one pair of trunks and one towel, both still wet from earlier that day. Changing, he catches a strong whiff of mildew. No matter.

Eddie plunges in, begins his freestyle laps, leaving the jitters—over what? He can't remember—in his wake. So he's going to see Lucy. Big deal. It'll be fine. They'll drink, talk, hang. And they'll be what they are. In-laws-to-be. Awesome. She'll marry Robert, Eddie thinks, and he'll live through it, live with it, as long as he can see her and be near her long enough to sustain himself. Long enough to live a normal life—long enough to meet some other Lucy. A girl who cares about him, who's patient enough to tell him what happens when he disappears. A girl who won't recoil from his Eddie-ness, who makes him feel as easy as he does here in this pool.

A Lucy of my own, he thinks. A Lucy to call home. And being in the aura of Robert's Lucy will tide him over in the meantime. It's okay, Eddie tells himself. All okay.

When he passes the locker room mirrors, Eddie looks for me, then sees me, or thinks he does: The Other Eddie. He stops and steps closer to check himself, myself, out again. He regards me as cooler, tougher, his fantasy self. It gives him a charge. He imagines me thinking that Lucy will have a hard time staying faithful to Robert.

"Not my problem," Eddie says aloud, trying to impersonate me. He does this well, loving how it feels to inhabit the psyche of someone (Mirror Eddie) who does not give a fuck.

Next, Eddie—as me, or his imagined version of me—rides the subway uptown to Seventy-Ninth Street, unafraid to make eye contact with strangers. On his way up the stairs, he sees an elderly woman ahead of him struggling with the wind. She has a cane and what looks like a heavy bag. Eddie bounds up the stairs to catch up.

"Ma'am?" He offers his arm gallantly, a Black Cary Grant, or Billy Dee Williams in *Lady Sings the Blues.* He carries her cane and bag up the stairs as she leans on him. He helps her cross the street and she thanks him, tears in her eyes from emotion and the wind.

"What a nice young man you are," she says, "a dying breed. Handsome, chivalrous, and kind."

"The pleasure is mine," he tells her. The woman gives a girlish laugh when Eddie surrenders her things, taking his leave with a bow.

Lucy has arrived at the bar first. In a purple sleeveless top with a decorative scarf around her neck, she smiles when she sees him, raising a glass half-full of red wine. Eddie feels himself, as his actual self—as Eddie proper—but as Mirror Eddie all at once. He is himself; he is me. Around Lucy, he doesn't care which.

"Hi, Lucy." Eddie can smile, really, naturally, despite everything, the confusion between selves, between what he is to Lucy and what he wishes to be. (And what is that, exactly? Neither of us knows for sure.)

"Hey, Eddie." The first thing she does, after hugging him, is reach up to touch his hair, which is frozen.

"I was swimming," he says.

"Just now? Since we talked on the phone?" She laughs. "You're so weird, Eddie. That's what I like about you."

I feel the surge of joy coming up through Eddie's core, along with his awareness of the hard rules floating in the space around them.

- RULE #1: Expect nothing. We're brother-in-law-to-be and sister-in-law-to-be, close but by no means sexual. Never. Of course not.
- RULE #2: Don't be sad/bitter about Rule #1.
- RULE #3: Take all cues for how we should act toward one another from Lucy herself.

Despite the rules—maybe because of the rules, which provide structure, guidelines, alleviating anxiety—Eddie's joy persists with laughter on its heels. As KISS screams—"I Love It Loud"—from the jukebox, Eddie wants to touch her, grab her waist, and pull her closer. He stops himself, signaling to the bartender for a beer. Lucy helps herself to one of Eddie's cigarettes.

"Don't tell Robert."

It takes a second before Eddie comprehends that she's talking about the cigarette.

Lucy smokes, tossing back her head to exhale, and the story of why she needs this drink comes out. "My stepmother, Dominique. Who's not really my stepmother. It's complicated. She's—"

"I know Dominique," Eddie says, then feels sorry. He is welcome at The Majestic penthouse while he knows Lucy isn't these days. "Althea explained how it was between you and her mom."

"Right. I forgot you're all tight with Althea and Clark now." In her voice, Eddie detects just a shade of bitterness. Lucy takes a drag of her cigarette. "And you hang out at the penthouse." Eddie can't think of the words to defuse her jealousy. She goes on. "Dominique's a mess right now. Tyrone is the love of her life, and I understand: he's dying. She's devastated. But she won't let me in her apartment to see him. The pain over his affairs, especially with my mom, is coming back to her, apparently. Althea says it's all mixed in with her grief or whatever. Dominique never got over his infidelity. All I am is a reminder of it.

"No one gives a fuck that he's my dad too, that he's my only parent. Like—I'm fucking devastated too."

Eddie is listening, but mostly he's watching her speak. Her hand on the cigarette, her lips forming words, her finger tracing the rim of her wineglass. How he aches for her, aches on her behalf!

"Dominique's mostly been so good to me, gracious when there was never a reason for her to be. She never even blamed my mom for the affair. According to my sister, when Dom found out, she called my mother a naive little twenty-two-year-old white girl, and what did she know? Dom only blamed Tyrone. She held her head high, gave him an ultimatum about cheating again, and forgave him. When my mother died—Althea and I were ten—Dominique took me in. Can you imagine what kind of strength that took?

"But now, all of a sudden"—Lucy drinks, then licks the droplets of wine off her lower lip—"Dom says that I was the one who stole her life. And *'Get out!'* she tells me. Before I can see my own father!"

Her wide, kohl-embellished eyes well up. Eddie is finished. "That's so awful." A weak offering.

"It is awful," Lucy says. "It's understandable, though. I didn't live with them until I was ten, but they knew about me all along. They had more of Daddy's money, more of his time, but I shared with him the most important thing: dance. My mother really had been a fling, meaningless to him except for me. By the time she died, she was nothing but a bank debt to him. But then I became the daughter he brought everywhere. A year or so after I moved in with them, Andy showed up and became the son my dad never had. Andy had never had a father—he'd barely even met an adult who wasn't white, if you can believe that—so the two of them were kind of in heaven together, at first.

"My half sisters were talented musicians and singers and won all kinds of awards, but Andy and I were the dancers and the ones Daddy liked to show off. My sisters didn't mind it so much with Andy because he was a boy and not actually Tyrone's kid. But with me, it cut deep. I was Daddy's pretty little ballerina. With light skin, and all the baggage that goes with that."

Having grown up as the only brown Asher, Eddie has never dealt with such baggage. He nods nonetheless.

"If my mother had been Black, I bet they'd just have felt sorry for me. But I represent something political for everyone. Regina and Sophia used to call me Dad's 'little white princess.'"

"But none of this is your fault," Eddie says, eager to defend her. "You've never done anything to them."

"You don't know me that well." Lucy laughs and takes another drag of her cigarette. "I've said and done things I shouldn't have. I told you I can be cruel, Eddie."

"Oh."

"Really, I can. The truth is, I was way more jealous of my sisters than they were of me. They not only had a living mom, but a fabulous, famous one. I mean, God, can you imagine Dominique LaFontaine being your mother?"

"No," Eddie lies. He can.

"Anyway, my sisters had money their whole lives. I had only what my mom could scrape together and what Daddy gave her to supplement it. I know what it's like when the landlord turns off your heat in the winter and you have to wear all your clothes just to go to sleep.

"And my sisters knew we lived like that. The first time I showed up at their apartment, I was wearing Regina's hand-me-down dress. They all recognized it. I will never forget how they looked down on me. So, if Daddy treated me like a princess, I may have rubbed their noses in it, just a bit.

"Althea is the only one who has never held any of it against me."

"Why doesn't she?" Eddie says.

"For one thing, she's three months younger than me. Daddy could have been over his affair when she was conceived, right?" Lucy snubs out the cigarette but eyes the pack for a second. "Althea never had a reason to resent me. Also, you know Althea. She's like Dom: stunning and *magnifique* and all that. No one's a threat to her.

"Anyway, thanks to Althea, who begged her sisters to go along with the plan, I'll get to see Daddy this week."

For the next two days, while Lucy's in town, either Sophia or Regina will take Dominique out for lunch or dinner or a movie, allowing their younger half sister time alone with Tyrone.

"To Althea." Lucy raises her glass, drains it, and wipes her eyes. Eddie echoes the toast and Lucy adds, "I'd be lost without her, just like you'd be without Robert."

At this, Eddie becomes so overwrought, he senses himself fading, but I stay back and observe. He grips the bar with one hand, the stool he's on with the other. *Stay,* he bids himself.

Lucy intuits his unease and nods toward his beer bottle. "Want another of those?"

"Sure." He resists the urge to drop his eyes. "Lucy?"

"Yes?"

He blurts, "Does Robert know you called me?"

She twists on her stool, facing him with her whole body, then lifts his chin with one finger. "We need to have a rule, Eddie."

Rule #4.

"We don't speak about Robert like that when we're together, okay? Whatever we—I don't know—confessed to each other in Seattle? That never happened."

"I know."

"You don't know. This is going to be super hard. I mean, you're beautiful, Eddie. You're so fucking hot—even with your, whatever, *eccentricities*—but that's not what I'm talking about. I can't explain what it is about you. It's almost as if—"

Eddie dares then—Eddie proper, not me, not the mirror version—to touch her face. Lucy swats his hand away.

"Don't do that. That's not what this is. There's something between us, and it's very, very big, Eddie—like a magnet, I swear. I know you feel it too." Her eyes watch his: left, then right.

Eddie's hand reaches for her again. "I do. I really do." Oh, how he feels it! His own thoughts articulated by Lucy's soft, full lips.

"No shit." She swats him again. "I don't even know if it's sexual—it's bigger than that, I think, deeper. But we'll never have a chance to figure it out, understand? We'll have to—stop it, Eddie!"

"Sorry." Both his hands are on the beer bottle now. He doesn't know what he's apologizing for, what she wants him to stop. Staring? Longing? Maybe their bond dictates that she can feel his insides, his racing pulse. *She understands,* he thinks. *We defy terminology. We are everything.*

Lucy smokes, exhales toward the ceiling. "When I met you, I knew you already. Part of it was because you look like Andy, but mostly I felt like you *saw* me, and I made sense—which I've never felt with anyone."

"I felt that too."

"Well—" Lucy balances the cigarette on the edge of an ashtray and places both hands firmly on the bar. "It's all we have. Robert is my plan and you're not. I'm going to marry him, which means that this 'us' thing—we're going to live with it for the rest of our lives."

"How?"

"We'll be best friends. I don't have a lot of friends."

"Me neither."

"Jeez, Eddie! Don't look at me like that."

"Like what?"

"Like *that*. It's dangerous."

They're sitting so close together, Eddie feels the draw of her like he did in Seattle. If I weren't holding him back, they'd melt into one another. Their second drink fills the space between them. They talk. About Eddie's apartment, such as it is. Eddie's job. Lucy's job. She confides that her chronic Achilles tendonitis is worsening, that the culprit—there's no denying it after all these years—is pointe work, along with overstretching her arches and insteps to match the ballet ideal.

"It's breaking my heart," Lucy says, "but I'll be leaving Pacific Northwest Ballet when my contract ends. I'll go back to contemporary, maybe even to WynterDance again. Robert is begging me to move back east, anyway. He'll be doing the second half of his residency at Mount Sinai."

Which is news to Eddie. "In New York?"

Lucy nods, helping herself to a drag of the cigarette Eddie has just lit. "I don't want you to think I'm giving up ballet to follow your brother around the country."

"Of course not."

"It's really time to give my feet the life they deserve. Besides, Seattle's cute, but it's no New York." She adds, "I mean, I'll miss Mount Rainier and the Space Needle."

"And the whales," Eddie puts in. "You and your beloved whales."

She brightens, as if relishing being known by him.

"Yes, my beloved whales."

"But New York has rats and roaches going for it," Eddie jokes.

"Yes. Here's to the rats and roaches."

Lucy raises her wineglass to Eddie's beer as a staring silence unites them. To calm the current, they discuss Tyrone: Lucy's plans to see him the following day. "You should come with me."

But the thought of hanging out with her too soon, too often, scares Eddie. He declines.

"I'm substitute coaching the JV swim team at Mitford Academy," referring to the Upper East Side girls' school.

"We'll go afterward," says Lucy. "I don't want to go to that apartment alone. Dom will be out with Regina, but Sophia will be there and maybe other relatives I don't want to face by myself."

"Can't Althea go?"

"She'll be working. I'm begging you, Eddie."

It occurs to him that he was Lucy's companion when she put Feather the cat to rest. Now he has a chance to be on hand at her father's deathbed. Lucy needs him again. What a sucker Eddie is for that.

"Fine," he says. "I'll come."

They visit Tyrone together each day that Lucy is in town. Eddie discovers he can belong to the Wynters even in Lucy's presence. He is physically strong enough to help Tyrone into his beloved paisley chair and, on occasions when the home health-care aide is not present, to the bathroom. He has a relationship with Tyrone, with Althea and Clark too, apart from Lucy, which gives him license to laugh and share and be a part of things. How natural he feels. Ironic, seeing as he does not know the ease comes in part from my own memories of living as Andy the Mountain boy.

I have been here. I know the family's rhythms, the smoothness and dips in the floors of the penthouse, the squeaks of every cabinet, the precise way to angle your hands to avoid the catch in the french doors to the balcony. Eddie doesn't know how he knows these things. He simply accepts them, feeling a total, blissful entitlement to Andy's former domain. This provides him with the freedom to do and say things he wouldn't otherwise. And here's what I'm afraid of: the more time Eddie spends filling Andy's discarded shell, the less Eddie will need me. Thus, I fear I am running out of time. I must take action before I am rendered obsolete. I look to Lucy, who at once centers and destabilizes Eddie, orients and disorients him, puffs up his confidence while weakening his defenses.

After the visits with Tyrone, Eddie and Lucy hang out. They walk around the city together; she goes with him to work, watches him teach, takes in his sleek form in a Speedo.

It's from this vantage point that Lucy notices what she's never had occasion to notice before, not even when she and Eddie were side by side on Al and Stella's sofa bed: the scar on his right shoulder. Later, she asks him about it.

"I was born with an extra piece of skin there," Eddie responds. "They removed it when I was a few hours old."

I notice Lucy's frown, though she says no more. Eddie doesn't know she's familiar with the scar's position and shape, if not its dimension.

At night, they go out to clubs with Clark and Althea. Once, in the thrall of "Ooops Up" by Snap! and under the influence of a lot of weed and alcohol, they nearly kiss under the neon lights. When a group of wild college kids bumps them off-balance, the moment passes. Lucy and Eddie fall against one another, laughing with embarrassed relief.

Eddie has never been skilled on the dance floor but takes a risk and tries to mimic Lucy's expert steps. The music stirs us both, but the muscle memory is all mine, taking me back to the Village gay bars I frequented on Andy's shoulder, the sweat, the lights, the pounding rhythms. I remember spinning, my shirt off, all eyes on me and my partner, his chest against my back, his arms on my shoulders. I can feel him, smell his cologne: my prince, my beautiful, ever-attentive—

"Damn, Eddie!" Clark says, grooving over with Althea at his side. "My man's got *moves*."

Oh no he doesn't. But *I* do. I craft Eddie a sly smile. "I'm full of surprises."

But Lucy has stopped dancing. She's staring. At me. No really: I think she sees *me*, not Eddie. *Holy shit,* I think, *I'm doing it.* Taking over, really. Maybe?

But Lucy leans in. "You know who you dance like, right?"

Eddie doesn't. I hold my tongue, letting him back in his body.

"What? Who?" Eddie has lapsed without even knowing it. But when he and Lucy dance again, Eddie finds to his delight that he's able to keep up. She teaches him some bits; he follows with aplomb.

When the song ends, Lucy yanks up the front of Eddie's shirt in a playful, big-sisterly gesture. "You're a natural."

For the next song they freestyle, getting creative, playing off each other. Lucy gets silly with Eddie. He relaxes around her; his sense of humor emerges. Even I like this version of Eddie. If I succeed, I wonder: Will I miss him?

꩜

Cue multicolored clouds speeding overhead, the sky blackening, brightening rapidly in turn, to indicate the passage of time.

꩜

Tyrone gets sicker but hangs on. The engagement party notwithstanding, Robert and Lucy have yet to set a date. At first, they considered speeding things up so Tyrone could make it to the wedding. That meant appearing before a crowd in a wheelchair, deflated—circumstances Tyrone had too much pride to face. By May, he can't tolerate being out of bed for more than an hour. Attending a wedding, let alone giving the bride away, is out of the question. So Lucy and Robert decide to push the big event back until six months after Tyrone's death, the date of which is anyone's guess, of course. For on he lives.

Robert and Lucy move back to New York City in June of 1991 and get a place on West Seventy-Third Street. Lucy and Eddie pick up their friendship right where they'd left off in April: as very, very close friends.

Robert starts at Mount Sinai in July. Lucy returns to WynterDance, teaching at the academy, training with the company, performing occasionally as a guest artist. In September, she begins a social work master's program at NYU. Eddie gets hired as a full-time coach for the middle school girls' team at Mitford Academy and in no time begins getting anonymous, often graphic, love letters from thirteen-year-olds.

By this time, Tyrone's cancer has spread further. He elects to stop receiving chemotherapy, which is only ruining what quality of life he has. His pain waxes and wanes but is soon constant. Managing it becomes everyone's primary goal. The acupuncturist and physical therapist, old friends who work with the WynterDance company, bring their services to the penthouse. A visiting nurse and in-home hospice care are arranged. Eddie—along with myriad others who come to pay their respects—is a welcome visitor but no longer needed.

32.
PÄR

In the wee hours of an October morning in 1991, Tyrone dies in the penthouse, in the presence of Dominique and the visiting nurse. It's just after six when Althea calls Eddie to give him the news. As expected as it is, he and I share a moment of profound, overwhelming loneliness. From Eddie's window, we can see clouds going from indigo to lavender, with the odd orange streak. Eddie's fingertips graze the scar on his bare right shoulder, and together we wait for the sun to rise on a world without Tyrone Wynter. Eddie's next thought is of Lucy; it's a fleeting one. Did Althea call him first?

There is no question that Eddie will attend the funeral, to be held at Riverside Church, in support of his brother's family-to-be, but also for himself. As the grateful, newest family member—the stand-in-would-be son—Eddie wonders about the real surrogate. Does Andy know Tyrone is dead? Will he attend the service? And will Eddie meet him at last? (My guess is no, but the thought unnerves me. What stance should *I* have toward such a meeting?) Eddie imagines identifying Andy amid the crowd of mourners, spotting a face like his own across the nave. Andy will recognize him too. Someone has surely told him about Eddie. And doubtless it's happened to Andy once or twice: someone stopping him on the street to continue a conversation they'd begun with Eddie.

In any case, they'll find each other if Andy comes. They'll hug like long-lost brothers, Eddie thinks, share a laugh about their similarities—which will no doubt seem insubstantial to them.

On the morning of the funeral, Eddie meets Robert and Lucy outside the church. Lucy is so deep in grief, it feels selfish and inappropriate to ask if she thinks Andy will show, but Eddie cannot stop himself.

"No" is her emphatic response. Lucy glares through her tears, and Eddie can't tell whether she's annoyed with him for raising the subject or at Andy for being absent. Either way, Eddie dares not ask how she's so sure.

The place is full of regal, sinewy dancers of all ethnicities, doughier ex-dancers, artists and theater people, others who looked like they could be family—either Tyrone's or Dominique's. All is elegance, well-chosen fashion, deliberate greetings, intimacies, gestures. *Hello, baby . . . Hey there, girl . . . Hello, darling . . . How long has it been? Wish the circumstances were different.* All manner of declarations are made about Tyrone, some scripted, some candid. *There was and will be no one like him, a character till the end, a force, so strong. Cancer met its match when it picked the Maestro. Sometimes I thought he was the devil incarnate, other times . . . I know, baby, I know.*

As Lucy greets people, accepting hugs, sliding around the crowd, mindful to avoid Dominique, Eddie goes to stand near the back of the church between Robert and Clark, both of whom stand out. They're among the largest men present, each well over six feet, Robert's fleshiness and Clark's gym-bound bulk straining the seams of their dark suits. Eddie, a lean five eleven, is thankful to fit in easily with the crowd. Women and men alike, even those who have never heard of Andy, kiss Eddie on both cheeks, whispering snatches of dancer code, assuming he is one of them. And part of him, of course, is. Feeling merciful, I share my understanding with Eddie, along with my memories of some of the mourners. Just enough so that he does not need to pretend, especially when he is mistaken for Andy. I feed him the correct responses to the best of my capability. Today is not a day for confusion.

Eddie sees no one who could pass for him and settles into his disappointment. For my part, I sense no disturbance that would indicate Andy's presence. He is not here, will not be coming.

Eddie sits with Clark and Robert, while Lucy is many pews ahead, surrounded by a crush of dancer friends. Tyrone's brother Lou, a minister, gives the service, which is followed by several addresses by friends and family, along with performances by some of Tyrone's dancers. Dominique sings "Amazing Grace" as everyone weeps, Eddie included. Dominique cannot get through the song alone, so Sophia, Regina, and Althea join her to finish the last verses. There is light, respectful applause and then total silence for about two minutes as Reverend Lou encourages everyone to pray and reflect independently. To Eddie's right, Robert shifts, arms folded over his belly, eyes closed for what Eddie suspects is more nap than contemplation. To his left, Clark's lips move rapidly, now and again emitting a whispered *Loving Jesus* or *Father guide me*. Eddie's eyes find the back of Lucy's head, freshly straightened hair twisted into a topknot with a few tendrils dangling about her shoulders. She turns back, and Eddie sees that her eyes are red, spilling over. She will not be going up onstage today—neither to speak nor dance. Lucy, the favorite daughter, will keep a low profile. How Eddie wishes he could go up and comfort her!

Lucy smiles at him faintly, and without thinking, he blows her a kiss. Lucy's eyes dart toward Robert, who Eddie knows is asleep. Does she blow his kiss back, or does Eddie wish for it so hard that his brain concocts this? Lucy's kiss—real or imagined—sails Eddie's way across the congregation, landing on his lips, spreading throughout his body. Eddie closes his eyes and joins in the group reflection. As do I. Flooded with emotion—frustration, loss, yearning to have been known by Tyrone, whom I once loved and hated—I command the body.

For Eddie, time shifts, as it has not done for months. He next comes to awareness to find he is standing in the church vestibule, amid a chatting crowd. People are saying goodbye. They clasp and unclasp one another's hands, making sure, inexplicably, to stop and thank Eddie, to nod at him, to touch and occasionally embrace him.

A small woman whom Eddie estimates to be in her nineties grips his wrist.

"I don't know who you are, but you did what I thought no one could do for that man."

That man, meaning Tyrone.

"What a speech you made. All those people, the ones who loved him in spite of himself, in spite of each other. You found the words to bring everyone together. Thank you, my dear." She pulls his shoulders down toward her level, and Eddie lets her brush a dry kiss against his cheek. He stares after her. Others continue to pay their respects—to Eddie. But why? Dominique, Sophia, and Regina surround him, full of sorrow, grace, and delicately mingling perfume. Each hugs him, nodding thanks. Dominique squeezes Eddie's hand.

"Thank you, Eddie," she says. "Your words were a gift today, just like you've been to Tyrone and the family these past few months." She holds him tightly.

She has no awareness that it's me she's holding, not Eddie, not Andy, but me. The part called Pär, whom no one knows. (Whom no one *will* know for another two years when Eddie introduces us to one Dr. Richard Quentin Montgomery.) However painful it is to lose Tyrone, the worst part is that I cannot share the loss with Dominique or the girls, who know nothing of me. Only Andy. And now Eddie. The brutal unfairness of it all.

Dominique brushes away a tear and invites Eddie—not me—to the penthouse, where people will be gathering.

Outside the church a few minutes later, Eddie is searching the crowd for Robert, Lucy, Clark, and Althea, hoping to learn what he said during his earth-shattering speech, when he feels another hand grab his elbow.

"Ciao, Andy!"

A man in an exquisitely tailored black silk suit is holding a cigarette aloft so as not to burn either of them. He pulls Eddie in for a hug, then kisses him on both cheeks.

"Andy, Andy, Andy. Back from the Windy City." Good God. His Italian accent is undiminished: *the Weendy Ceety.* "I am moved by what you say about Maestro. We all were. It was beautiful."

I leave off, letting Eddie figure this one out on his own. Some hasty processing jogs Eddie's recollection of Tyrone's story about Lucy's first love, the Italian name, which escapes him, though it matches the accent. Adding weight to his suspicion is the guy's suave bearing, coupled with the belief (shared by quite a few others today) that Eddie is Andy Lindberg. For a brief moment, uncertainty invades the man's expression, as it seems to occur to him that maybe this isn't Andy after all. His face prepares an apology; he's about to take his leave. Then Eddie remembers his name.

"Carlo Giannini," Eddie says. "What a surprise." This is his first time deliberately impersonating Andy, desperate to learn everything he can about Lucy's past, Andy's role. I am fascinated and intrigued. Can he pull it off with no further assist from me? I stand by.

The broad, beautiful Mediterranean grin I remember so well spreads itself over Carlo's face. Eddie is embraced once again, cigarette closer to his ear than before.

"Beautiful Andy. Andy, Andrea, Andreas. You have been taking in sun somewhere, no?"

I beat back the old stirring inside me and force myself to study Carlo through Eddie's eyes. The two are of similar heights, but Carlo is broader in the shoulders. Carlo is older. Eddie estimates at least thirty-five (he's close). His features are large and irregular, neither classically nor exotically beautiful, though he has that thing—confidence times mystique—that many European men have, making them irresistible to women and others. Carlo keeps the slightly apologetic angle in his brow, and—without any intervention from me—Eddie grasps the piece of the story that Tyrone omitted.

Andy loved Carlo too. Together, Carlo and Lucy had broken Andy's heart. This insight helps enormously with Eddie's current deception.

Carlo offers Eddie a cigarette, and they walk halfway down the block together in the bright sunshine. Carlo, unaware that he's talking to a total stranger, speaks with candor.

"I almost didn't come, Andy," he says. "But in the end, I could not stay away. I needed to see Lucy one last time.

"I still feel for her. Deeply, *deeply*." He catches Eddie's eye. "My friend, you cannot imagine what it is to be powerless at the touch of a woman. You are fortunate."

Then he flushes, as if remembering that "Andy" is no more fortunate than he. "When I heard of her engagement, do you know what my first thought was?"

Eddie does not.

"I can tell you this, because you were there with us when our hearts were one. You remember. I thought: Carlo, it is not too late. You can win her back, you can lure her away from this . . . this Robert, the doctor."

They cross the street, entering the park, selecting a bench from which to look out at the Hudson River. Carlo snuffs out his cigarette and lights a new one. *This Robert, the doctor.* He says it again with contempt, turning to smile at Eddie, a tear forming. Eddie can see what Andy saw in him, the beauty of his deep feeling.

"I should not speak of this on a day like today," Carlo goes on. "Maestro's funeral. But I can't help it. She is all I think about."

Eddie does what he imagines Andy would do: places a gentle hand on Carlo's shoulder. He offers a smile, wistful and full of empathy. Eddie wonders how Carlo is so easily duped. How can he not tell the difference between a stranger and a past love? Carlo touches his cheek.

"I am sorry for the way I treated you, my friend. It was the way she treated me, I suppose. But I was so cruel, it makes me ashamed. You did not deserve that."

Eddie thanks him for saying so. He looks into Carlo's dark eyes and remembers vicariously the truth of what he's saying. Eddie imagines he can feel Andy's memories by now—maybe not the substance, but the sentiments. He understands that wherever Andy is—the Windy City or elsewhere—his heart is still broken, not just by Carlo, but by Lucy and Tyrone too. By this whole group of people. Why else would he stay so reliably away? And here comes rage on Andy's behalf.

"None of you had any right." Eddie allows Carlo to light his next cigarette. A consolation for breaking Andy's heart. Before Eddie can address the apology, Lucy and Robert are upon them. Looking across the street, Eddie sees that the flow of mourners from the church is thinning. Those who were lingering on the steps have crossed to the park as well, presumably to walk and commune with their thoughts of the deceased.

"There you are," Lucy says before she realizes who Eddie's companion is. Then: "Oh my God." No *hello*. No kisses on both cheeks. Just *Oh my God*. Eddie sees Lucy tighten her grip on Robert's hand as she gapes at Carlo, her first love. She says, "Eddie, we have to go. Meet us later at Althea's."

As she pulls Robert away, Carlo and Eddie watch from the bench, smoking in the bright autumn sun.

"Who is Eddie?" Carlo asks. Eddie drags on his cigarette, then exhales with a mystified shrug.

33.

PÄR

I know what you're wondering at this point: Where is he, anyway? The real Andy Lindberg? That, I'll tell you. While I am addressing Tyrone's mourners at Riverside Church—essentially using Eddie's body to utter Andy's thoughts—the corporeal Andy is on an acupuncture table in Chicago, getting treatment for his chronic lumbar pain.

And indeed, he does know that today is Tyrone's send-off at Riverside Church. Althea notified him, aware that he'd probably decline. Andy told her he had no intention of going. (The conflicted grief rising in his chest called me away from Eddie at once. As Althea spoke, I settled astride Andy's shoulder.) Andy said he had no wish to see anyone in the family or anyone else who might be at the funeral.

"Ivan will be there," she told him. "And Rudy too. They miss you. Come for them if not for us."

"Ivan's not speaking to me. He thinks I snubbed him at the debut of *My Father's House*. Which I didn't even attend."

"Andy, please—"

"I'm so sorry about your dad, Althea. But I have to go now."

When he hung up, Andy let himself collapse on his bedroom floor, weeping. He was due to meet his dancers in the studio in an hour—he'd be setting a ballet of his own, his first full-length piece of original choreography—but he knew, between his back and the news about Tyrone, that his focus would be shit.

After work, instead of taking the L, Andy walked the long way home, taking Hubbard Street east, wending his way to the Lakefront Trail, turning north. He meandered, mind brimming with words there was no one to tell. When he got home to his place on Cornelia Avenue, Andy popped in an old jazz cassette: Coltrane, Davis, Parker—Tyrone's favorites. Choreography journal open on his desk, Andy wrote to the music, his best and worst memories of Tyrone, the man he loved like a father, who'd cast him out for fear of an illness the Maestro didn't understand. When Andy was done, he read what he'd written, tore it from the notebook, and tossed it away, feeling lighter, purged. He said to himself, "Someday I'll make a ballet for him." And went to bed.

But his ode stayed with me, every last word. At the funeral, with Eddie as a vehicle, this same treatise fills the nave of Riverside Church.

Andy doesn't know exactly what's happening, that there's an imposter claiming his place in New York City. But for the hour of the service, his right shoulder throbs with pain—not like the good ache from the acupuncture needles, but a hollow, gnawing pain. The mysterious way rain exacerbates an aged wound. I drift from Eddie briefly to find myself in Andy's body as it languishes like a porcupine on the table.

"You know what might ease the pain?" the acupuncturist is saying to Andy. "Swimming. You really ought to take up swimming."

Which amuses me to no end.

34.
PÄR

Eddie does not go to Dominique's. Instead he leaves Carlo—kisses on both cheeks, of course—and catches up to Robert and Lucy, who are walking east toward Althea's. Lucy doesn't speak to Eddie, as if seeing him alongside Carlo has changed things between them. The trio walks in silence. Robert isn't speaking to him either, and Eddie wonders if it's because of what happened at the funeral—the *lapse*—which may have embarrassed him. By the time they get into the elevator together, Eddie is feeling despondent, guilty, *hated* by them both. In the short ride up to the fifth floor, he manages to gnaw away a small section of his right middle cuticle. A drop of blood lands on the sleeve of his white oxford.

At Althea's gathering, Robert and Lucy continue giving Eddie the silent treatment. He begins to believe he deserves it, even if he cannot pinpoint why. People drink, talk, laugh, and cry, all the while playing videos of Tyrone dancing—clips from a documentary made about him several years earlier. Clark comes up and hands Eddie a drink.

"It was a beautiful speech you made."

"About that," Eddie says, staring at Lucy's back, on the verge of tears, "please, *please* tell me what I said."

"You really don't know?"

Which is obvious, so Clark explains. Everyone who was asked to speak had spoken. Reverend Lou then asked if there was anyone else. Some people who didn't know the family story looked at Lucy, assuming that the favorite child would have something to say. Lucy was flustered, knew she couldn't stand up or her sisters would have her head.

"So, you got up and saved the day," says Clark. "I didn't realize you knew Tyrone that well. I guess it's all that time you've been spending with him since the engagement party." The look he gives Eddie is almost suspicious, like he's either hiding something or completely unhinged. "You were up there talking about the Maestro's career, his inspiration, influences, favorite music, poetry. Then you went ahead and quoted his favorite Langston Hughes and Lucille Clifton poems. Man, it was beautiful."

Eddie absorbs this, baffled by himself. He thought that nothing could shock him about what he did during those temporary exits.

"Did I introduce myself?" Eddie asks him. "When I got up there, did I tell people what my name was?"

Before Clark can respond, Althea pounces on Eddie and draws him into a corner. Her eyes are swollen and wild.

"Tell me what your game is, Eddie or whoever the hell you're claiming to be."

"I have no game." Hands raised in surrender. "I'm only Eddie."

"Yeah, I know you're Eddie." She shakes her head. "But you're lying to us. You've said you didn't know Andy, but clearly he wrote that speech you just gave."

"I swear I don't even know what that was," Eddie says. "I didn't make that speech. I mean, I did but . . . I have these things that happen to me, like episodes and . . ." His words fade into one another. Then, glimpsing Robert over Althea's shoulder: "Ask my brother. He'll tell you it's been happening all my life."

"What has?"

"Those lapses. Me, losing time, acting a certain way, doing things I don't remember."

Althea looks skeptical.

"I think he's on the level," says Clark. "I've heard of that happening. You dissociate. You know, like *Sybil*."

Oh, Clark, I think from the inside, *such a blow. Sybil, indeed.* But it seems to work for Althea, so Eddie goes with it, panicked by the thought of losing her love and trust, the connection he has with the Wynter family. Especially with Tyrone gone and Lucy giving him the cold shoulder.

"Have you seen anybody for it?" says Althea. "Like a shrink?"

"Dozens," Eddie says. "No one's been able to figure it out."

Althea softens. "It's really creepy, Eddie. But whatever. It worked for everyone today."

So I can stay, Eddie thinks. *At least until Andy comes back.*

Robert, it turns out, isn't mad at Eddie after all, just confused by his latest antics.

"Jeez, Eddie," he says. "I was just thinking I was done having to worry about what the fuck you might do next." The brothers are off to the side of Althea's living room, out of earshot of Lucy and the rest. "How were you able to talk about Lucy's dad like you were family or something?"

"I've been his go-to guy for almost a year now." The explanation eases its way out of Eddie fully formed. It's mostly true. "Dominique says I took the place of that guy—you know, Andy. Like I was redeeming Tyrone for whatever he did to him. I don't know why, but he spent the last months of his life confiding in me."

Robert shakes his head, smiling. "You are a freak in the best sense of the word, little bro." He clinks his beer against Eddie's. "I love you for that."

Eddie can see how exhausted his brother is. Everything is taking its toll. Work, caring for Lucy during this time of grief, putting off Joanne's questions and skepticism about the wedding and when—if—it will ever happen. On top of everything, he's on call tonight.

By the time Robert's pager goes off, the friends are dwindling. Althea and Lucy sit holding each other, watching the documentary about Tyrone one more time. A tissue box on the floor before them, they speak in hushed sisterly intimacies, bawling on and off but laughing too.

"Lucy," Robert has to say three times before she looks up and notices that he has his backpack on.

"Oh no," she says. "Not tonight."

"I'm so sorry, Luc. I told you, though; I said I was on call. There's nothing—"

"Fine. *Go.*"

"—I can do."

"Whatever. I said, *go.*"

"I'm sorry." He begs her forgiveness. It's unclear whether she gives it to him, but Robert goes.

Two hours later, it's just Eddie, Lucy, Althea, and Clark. They're crowded onto the couch, watching a movie by this time. It's an old one with Fred Astaire and Rita Hayworth on American Movie Classics: *You Were Never Lovelier*. Lucy still hasn't spoken to Eddie. When the film ends, Eddie says he's leaving, hoping the announcement will shake Lucy into acknowledging him. He's the only one left to escort her home. Eddie gets as far as the door before Lucy shouts for him to wait.

"I can't crash here. I don't have anything with me." Lucy doesn't want to go home alone either.

Althea purses her lips in disapproval, but Clark calls them a car service, explaining that you can't hail a yellow cab this late at night, this far uptown. Eddie and Lucy agree to ride together down to Seventy-Third and then Eddie will take the train back to Brooklyn.

"You're mad at me," Eddie says to Lucy in the car heading south. She turns to stare at him, tears in her eyes—from grieving, from being wronged by Robert, presumably by Eddie as well. He can't calculate the layers of her look. "Street Hassle" comes on the car radio, scratchy, staticky.

"What did you talk to him about?" Lucy says.

"Who?"

"Fuck you. You know who."

Eddie stares back because he doesn't know who. Then he does. "Oh. Carlo."

All at once, screaming sirens drown out the potential for conversation. A stopped ambulance and police activity near the Twenty-Fourth Precinct at One-Hundredth Street force the driver to take a detour. By the time they're past the hubbub, Lou Reed has gotten quiet, the beat persisting, the backup girls wailing through the Springsteen cameo between parts 1 and 2.

"So, Carlo was your first love." Eddie doesn't share how he knows this. Lucy doesn't ask. Instead, she repeats herself.

"What did you talk to him about?"

"Nothing. He talked to me. He thought I was Andy."

"Of course he did. Jeez, Eddie, today you *were* Andy. Really—the way you got up there—I don't know how you did it. It made everyone happy, though—all the poetry. I'll never know how you knew my father's favorite poetry. But that's just what Andy always did: figured out how to make everyone but himself happy."

For once Eddie doesn't want to hear about Andy. When she moves to touch his hand, he shakes her off, barking, "Stop it! I am not Andy!"

The driver glances at him in the rearview mirror, and Lucy shushes him, adding, "I didn't mean anything bad."

"Can you tell me about Carlo?"

"No." She looks out the window.

"Do you still love him?"

"Don't be stupid."

"That doesn't answer my question. You never told me about him."

"Why would I? I've never even told Robert much about him. Carlo's part of my past. Nothing more."

Eddie disregards the casual mention of Robert and presses, "If it was nothing more, you wouldn't have bothered saying 'nothing more.'"

She turns back. "Don't be jealous of Carlo, Eddie."

"No? I should just be jealous of Robert?"

"We're not supposed to talk about your brother, remember?"

"I didn't know we still needed rules." Eddie's heart leaps at the thought that they might.

"We do." Lucy shoves the curls off his forehead. From the pressure of her touch, Eddie can tell that they're okay again. "You're the weirdest fucking guy ever."

Eddie knows that in another world, in another universe, he might draw her close and kiss her, if only to see if she'd stop him.

"You like me weird," he tells her.

"I *love* you weird," she says.

"I love you weird too."

It's cramped in the car. Besides, there's the driver. When they arrive at her building, Lucy invites Eddie up to her apartment, as though it's clear what there is between them. But once inside, they stand in the vestibule, staring at each other's matching brown eyes. Lucy laughs, an unnatural burst of sound.

"Now what?" says Eddie.

"I don't know," says Lucy. "Do you want me?"

Eddie: "I think so."

Lucy: "I think I want you too."

Eddie: "What's stopping us?"

Lucy: "Not Robert."

Eddie: "Something else."

Lucy: "Right. But what else?"

Eddie: "It doesn't feel normal."

Lucy: "*We're* not normal. We're freaks, right?" She's grinning by this time and so is he, as if there's nothing in the world but the two of them. Lucy and Eddie; Eddie and Lucy. So, why don't they? Neither can answer.

Eddie: "Hi, fellow freak." He reaches for her, believing it should be him who reaches first. Lucy moves closer, takes his face into her hands. But when their lips meet, the electric force is one of repulsion. Like two protons, Lucy and Eddie jump apart, eyes wide, short of breath.

"What was that?"

"I don't know."

They reach again, hands for hands, holding on amid the weirdness. "Then it's not for us, is it? I mean—sex."

Lucy shakes her head. "No. But I still love you."

"I know." Eddie has never been more certain of anything. He can say it aloud. "I love you, Lucy."

"It's a different way from the way I love Robert," she says.

"I know," Eddie repeats. "But I think about you." It's a relief to admit it. "I think about you without realizing it. I'm always thinking about you."

"Me too!" she says. "I think about you so much! Like, what would Eddie say right now? Half the time, I'm thinking about you when I'm with Robert. Is that awful of me? You and I would laugh so much at some of the things he says and does. You're the only one who gets it."

"It's not awful. Lucy, you're the only one who gets *me*."

And now that they have said the things aloud, weathered the ill-conceived kiss, there is no reason not to hold each other close. He inhales her, and it smells like the entire world. He is fearless. She is freedom. They are water.

35.
PÄR

"We're not in *love*," Lucy states once again for the record, as she's stated several times in the weeks since the night of Tyrone's funeral. "We're *enmeshed*. There is a difference."

Enmeshment is one of the concepts Lucy is learning about in her graduate program. "It usually means a lack of boundaries between family members," she explains over cappuccino at Cafe Lalo, one of their meeting places. Lucy and Eddie hang out almost daily, usually when Robert is at the hospital. "Unhealthy emotional interdependence. It's not a good thing, generally speaking, but it seems fine for us. Like, we're not romantically involved, but I think I might be insanely jealous if you had a girlfriend."

"You would?" With faux indignation, Eddie disperses a patch of cinnamon with his spoon. "But you have Robert!"

"Well, so do you," says Lucy. "I'm serious, though. If you had a girlfriend, I think I'd try to sabotage it."

"You would, wouldn't you?"

"I'm selfish like that." Lucy wrinkles her nose comically. "Would you sabotage me and Robert?"

"I wouldn't if I could." Eddie doesn't say why, though: that he now sees Robert as his guarantor of keeping Lucy in his life.

"You're an angel, Eddie." Lucy eyes him, stirring the dregs in her cup. "And you know what else? If I ever cheated on Robert—"

"It would be with me?"

"Of course not," she says. "But you would be the one person I'd tell."

"*Why* would you cheat on Robert?"

"I wouldn't. But if I did, I'd tell you."

It's a peculiar thing to say, even for Lucy. Even for the things Lucy and Eddie say to one another. But Eddie feels reassured of his place.

Robert wouldn't understand their growing closeness, Eddie and Lucy agree. Though there's nothing illicit about their meetups, Lucy and Eddie keep them secret—easy to do, given the flexibility of their schedules versus the strict demands of Robert's.

"Robert is more important to either of us than we are to one another," Lucy declares as they relax on Eddie's secondhand sofa, sharing a joint one afternoon. "He's more important than either of us is to our own selves, Eddie. Which is exactly why we can do this kind of thing." Referring to the time together, the leisure, the weed.

Lucy is the one learning about human behavior and the psyche in her graduate social work program. Who is Eddie to argue with her?

"Anyway, spending time like this has nothing to do with Robert," she promises him, pulling his head into her lap. "This is about you and me and our deficiencies." She takes a toke. "We're healing each other."

"Okay." Eddie takes the joint.

"No, I mean it. In both our lifetimes we've lost connecting parts of ourselves—my mom, now my dad, your whole biological family. We can use each other to practice being whole again. This way, we don't have to drive Robert crazy with our neediness." All of this rings true.

Meanwhile, Lucy and Robert's wedding date remains a moving target. The venue will be the Tribeca loft that Dave and Glenda still own but currently rent out as a photography studio, so there's flexibility there. Lucy wants to be a spring bride, with her eye on late May or early June, when it will be warm. The issue is that Althea, her maid of honor, is scheduled to be on tour in Europe for all of May and June of 1992. In July and August, the loft is to be in use for a film, which brings things to September, when Althea will be performing in Montreal.

Lucy decides that they'll have to push the date to May of '93—nearly a year and a half away—which seems to Robert a ridiculous amount of time to wait. The delay suits Eddie. He would like for things to continue as they are.

Fall turns to winter; 1991 turns to 1992; winter turns to spring.

Summer 1992. On steamy days that threaten rain, Lucy and Eddie meet in Central Park. While other people spot the clouds and scurry home, Eddie and Lucy are unfazed. The sky cracks wide open, sending down torrents as they run for shelter by the band shell or the Delacorte Theater. Thunder crashes, lightning fires away. Lucy always says, "It can't do this for long," but, more often than not, it does. Pressed up close together, Eddie's arm around her, Lucy's warm breath on his neck, everything evaporates but their closeness—the smells of one another, magnified by the humidity. They stare up through the torrents, laughing at nature's wrath, feeling invincible together.

Other times, if the rain holds off, they walk farther. Lucy will take Eddie's hand. He'll glance nervously around, and she'll laugh.

"If you don't act guilty, you're *not* guilty. What's wrong with holding your sister-in-law's hand in public?"

Eddie will relax 25 percent of the way, the best he can do.

"We're doing nothing wrong." Which has become Lucy's mantra. Regardless, Eddie can't stand to be away from her for long. He has ceased dating altogether. Robert or no Robert, Eddie is addicted to Lucy. If she were to ask him to do without her, he doesn't know how he'd handle it.

Lucy and Robert will wed as planned, have a family, a little country house someplace, and all the trappings of a wonderful life together. Eddie will be the dutiful brother-in-law and uncle. Good old Eddie, the sideman, around for laughs, like Howard on *The Bob Newhart Show*, consumer of life's runoff.

Lucy torments Eddie from time to time by predicting that he'll "meet some nice girl and settle down one day," acquiring as much as possible of whatever Lucy and Robert have.

"But what if you get jealous?" He wants to hear her say it.

"Sabotage," says Lucy, giving him a squeeze. "Sometimes I think that you were the Asher brother I was supposed to meet first—the one fate meant me to have." She then kisses his cheek to make up for what comes next. "But I met Robert first. And that's done. Besides, how could I ever reject all he has to offer?"

For this, Eddie has no rebuttal. But the point is, he and Lucy are secretly committed. For fate, for always.

And where does that leave me? In Eddie's whole adult life, he's glimpsed me only twice, resisted me perhaps once, but the potential is there. Eddie's will is growing, fortified by his love for Lucy, his exposure to the Wynter family, and occasional guise of Andy Lindberg. I find fewer and fewer opportunities to usurp. Unnerved by the threat to my influence, my dream of a rout, I panic and breach my personal code of conduct. Remaining illusory is critical to my survival, but arrogance gets the best of me.

There comes a day in late September. Lucy and Eddie have arranged to meet in the park near the boathouse for a picnic lunch and then a walk before each has to work. Eddie arrives and waits for her. He waits and waits, watching tourists walk by with noses in their maps, stroller brigades of nannies and their charges, young couples ditching work, strolling hand in hand. The waiting becomes endless. Eddie panics, and

I stretch my metaphoric limbs. He can feel me—just as if I were standing to the right of him, breathing on his neck. He turns as if expecting to see me. Of course he can't, but he knows I'm here. There's no mirror to blame, and yet I, Mirror Eddie, am here.

"She's not coming," I tell him.

Eddie whips his head around, unsettled but not exactly shocked. He knows it's me.

Being a dick, leaning into my advantage, I say, "She's forgotten you."

"Shut up." He whispers it, aware of passersby.

"She's got a good reason." I know nothing for certain, but I need to capitalize on his vulnerability.

Eddie plants his feet. Folds his arms. "We're on speaking terms, now? But you're me, right? You're me and I'm crazy. Is that it?"

"Not crazy," I tell him. "Not entirely. Think it over. Scan your dreams. You know who I am."

Our body jolts as we're almost leveled by a trio of runners. Eddie checks his watch. More than an hour has passed; he needs to leave for work. Plagued by thoughts of Lucy and her duplicity, Eddie goes to catch a bus bound for the Upper East Side and Mitford Academy.

After work, he calls Robert and Lucy's apartment from a pay phone.

"Hey," he says when Robert answers.

"Dude. You sound weird. What's going on?"

"Can I talk to Lucy for a sec?"

Shuffling, music in the background.

She gets on: "Hey, freak, what's up?" Cheerfully, like nothing is wrong.

"Where were you? Today. I waited an hour."

"Yeah? Well, I guess that didn't work out," she replies. Eddie understands that Robert is still within earshot. "Hey, if you're not in Brooklyn already, you should come over; we're ordering in and renting a movie."

Eddie fights his rage and changes direction in favor of the crosstown bus, which will drop him a block from their place.

As soon as he walks in, Eddie senses a shift in Lucy's demeanor toward him. She kisses him lightly on the cheek without any eye contact. She sits between Robert and Eddie on the couch as they watch *Flatliners*, but her hip remains clear of Eddie's.

A week passes, then another week, without a word from her. Previously, Eddie's answering machine was swamped with Lucy's messages: "Eddie, it's me. I miss you so much I can't stand it." "Eddie, it's me. Just bored, doing coursework, dreaming about you in your little Speedo." "Eddie, it's me. Again . . ." He was always deleting her messages to make room for more. Now he wishes he'd kept them to rewind and use to console himself, proving her love was real. The words of Mirror Eddie—whom he now calls "The Other"—are true. Whatever the reason, Lucy has forgotten him.

36.

PÄR

And then one night, Eddie sees them. He's in the Village because the swim team had a meet downtown. Eddie is walking east on Bleeker and spots them sitting by the window inside a little espresso place. They both have tiny cups before them. A cigarette—Carlo's, no doubt—burns on an ashtray in the center of the table, smoke rising, blending with the dark atmosphere in the place.

Lucy and Carlo don't notice Eddie, though by now he's crossed the street and is standing right outside, not a foot from where they sit, holding hands, fingers woven, gazing into each other's eyes, perfectly still. Burnished into Eddie's eye: a perfect snapshot of a perfect love—outside of which floats a true, solitary freak. Eddie can feel me again—The Other—holding him back, refusing to let him smash through the window of the café and destroy whatever there is for all three of them.

Into Eddie's ear, I hiss, "You knew better than to believe she'd tell you if she cheated on Robert. Why would she tell *you*? You believe she cares about you? *Please.* Walk away. Don't let her know you know. Have some fucking pride." I force Eddie to take a deep breath. He lets me take him into hand. "She's not yours, anyway," I add, pulling Eddie back toward the street, back toward Sixth Avenue, where he can catch a train. "She was never yours. All that business about 'I love you weird' and 'enmeshed' and 'you're the only one'? It wasn't real. I let you get close to her. The point was just for you to borrow what's his, to use her, to fuck with him."

"Fuck with who?"

"Who do you think?" I let him hear my exasperation. "Oh, Eddie. It's time you remembered." And, with no intro, no fanfare, this is where I let loose with memories I've squirreled away from him. There, on the southbound 4 train, I take him back.

Let us rewind further still.

⟋❧

1978. The old place on West Eighty-Sixth. Dave has moved out. It's just the boys and Joanne. The latter has baked an enormous batch of the sumptuous rum-raisin rugelach she only ever makes to soften bad news. She carries a platter to the dining room table and calls the boys. Just the sight of the pastries—along with an unusually beatific smile from their mother—raises both boys' hackles.

"Sit," Joanne says, and waits. Eddie sits; Robert takes his time. During the pause, Eddie's knee begins to dance. His brother grabs two rugelach, pops one into his mouth whole, and finally plunks himself down opposite Eddie. Joanne gives each boy a gracious nod. "There are going to be some changes in our lives." Eddie begins to freak, though there are no outward signs of this as yet, beyond the knee bouncing away under the table.

Joanne continues. Said changes will include:

- A wedding—Joanne and Michael's.
- Some dietary adjustments, seeing as Michael keeps kosher and Joanne has always (news to the boys) felt drawn to kashrut. (Robert grabs five rugelach, on which he chomps violently.)
- A move, since this apartment holds so many painful memories. (This brings on a vocal protest from Robert, early

strains of a panic attack for Eddie.) They will be moving into Michael's beautiful colonial home in West Harbor on Long Island. Which will necessitate:

- A transfer from the boys' beloved Riverview Prep (where everyone knows and accepts Eddie, eccentricities and all) to West Harbor Junior High for Eddie and West Harbor High for Robert. Michael's children, who are older, in and out of college—Ivy League universities—all loved the schools.
- There will be a new synagogue, where Eddie will join a new bar mitzvah class—since he's already preparing so nicely. (Cantor Zev, Joanne assures Eddie, will reach out to the new rabbi.)

Here, Robert, in a cloud of rugelach crumbs, rises to his full height, enunciating something to the effect of "Fuck that shit! No fucking way!" as Joanne pleads, "Honey, language," but Eddie couldn't say for sure because his mind is now a whirring, faulty instrument, unable to process anything accurately. (I am on hand, ready to step in if needed.)

Joanne persuades Robert to stop swearing and sit. Robert sits, seethes, and devours the last of the rugelach as their mother reaches out to squeeze both boys' hands.

"A fresh start," she says, "will be good for all of us. You'll see. And I'm happy with Michael. So happy." Tacking on the Jewish mother's most powerful tool of persuasion: "I ask very little."

Neither boy can argue, in part because they have not had time to prepare a thorough defense. The phone rings.

"It's Michael." Their mother, blushing—*blushing*—flies like a giddy schoolgirl to answer.

By now, Eddie is visibly consumed by panic: rocking, reciting racing thoughts aloud.

Robert, tabling his own angst—minimized by the rugelach—focuses on his brother, slipping into Joanne's chair to shake him, murmuring, "Easy, easy, buddy. We'll figure this out, okay?" over and over until Eddie's body stills. Robert adds, "I've got a plan."

Robert's plan involves Dave—who believes that the burbs are the root of all evil, followed closely by organized religion. Dave had grudgingly joined a reform synagogue when Robert was old enough for Hebrew school, and only then because Joanne told him he wasn't actually expected to show up except for the boys' bar mitzvah days. Robert predicts Dave will threaten to take full custody unless Joanne and Michael *Fucking* Stern (as Robert refers to him) change their tune.

But Dave has news of his own. "Bad timing," he tells Robert and Eddie two days later when they are over for their weekend visit. "Glen and I—"

("Glen," Eddie infers, is Glenda, his own erstwhile shrink.)

"—just closed on a house in Berkeley."

"As in, California?" Robert's voice cracks.

"We'll move in June, which will give us plenty of time to nest."

"Why the fuck do you need to *nest?*" Robert says as Eddie sits saucer-eyed.

"Hey, language, buddy," stalls Dave. But a moment later he discloses that Glenda's baby (baby!) is due in August. The Berkeley house will accommodate Dave, Glenda, their new baby (baby!), but also Robert and Eddie, anytime they want to come visit. They're welcome to "hop over for the summers, school breaks. Seriously, anytime."

That's right, they can *visit.* But Joanne will maintain primary custody. According to the divorce agreement, if either parent moves across state lines, he or she loses their part of the joint custody. Nor can Robert and Eddie skip town with their father just to avoid the new rules at Joanne and Michael's. Like it or not, they're going to Long Island.

When the boys leave Dave's Tribeca loft Sunday evening, their heads are spinning with new revelations. On its descent, the elevator—an enormous apparatus with a hand crank, covered in mirrors on three sides—gets stuck between floors. From every angle, Eddie can see twenty-five, fifty—hundreds and hundreds of pairs of Asher boys: Eddie and Robert,

Eddie and Robert, Eddie and Robert, and so on. The Eddie brigade loses its shit completely, sobbing, muttering about how life is now going to suck in every way. The Roberts try to make the Eddies get a grip, hugging them, shaking them, finally slapping them—as with women deemed hysterical in old films. These approaches fail. (Here, I will fill in the hole I created in Eddie's memory at the time, when I'd slipped in for the purpose of absorbing Robert's blows.) Robert strikes Eddie harder. Then again. Which feels quite nice for Robert, I imagine. Exhilarating, to unleash his fury on the brother who has caused all the trouble, the brother who should not be his brother at all. The Roberts hit the Eddies again and again, awash (I can only guess) with pleasure, guilt, relief! It is quite some time before the elevator gets moving again.

That same night, once Robert has cleaned, iced, and bandaged his brother's wounds, Eddie has the birth mother fantasy dream again—starring Glenda as Glinda/Britta the Swedish good witch. She wears jeans and an embroidered peasant top and carries a wand.

"Pär," she says—using our actual name, "come sit."

Eddie obeys. (In dreams like this, he understands that he was Pär before he was Eddie.)

"Here," Glenda/Glinda/Britta says. She taps his shoulder with her wand. "Now you're safe no matter what." But Eddie doesn't buy it. He needs her to kiss his forehead; he knows that's how she protected Dorothy.

"You know I can't do that." Her smile is tinged with sadness, and Eddie understands that it's because of his Kenyan-or-Somali-or-Ethiopian hair, the brown of his skin.

"Please," he says, "can't I just have the shoes?"

∾

When I conclude the memory for him, 1992 Eddie cries on the Brooklyn-bound 4 train, as he cried in the Tribeca loft elevator in 1978. But back then he cried in the arms of his brother. Here, since I can't physically embrace him, and I doubt I would if I could, he sobs alone, thinking, *No, no, no. It is not, cannot be true.* So I keep on sharing, all the past Roberts and Eddies and elevators and cookies and bathtubs and stepparents and bloody, crusted-over cuticles that Eddie has ground into his own flesh.

(No, I don't share everything. Not the letter Eddie stumbled upon that one time in '75, addressed to Joanne, with a man's block lettering, the only part he registers:

> *... but I would just like to meet him. To learn what he is like. Besides, he might have questions. I think he should at least know something about ...*

... before I swoop in to block—to erase, even—his certainty that Eddie himself is the "he" being discussed. But this I won't share.)

It's all at once familiar and unrecognizable to Eddie, who watches the mind-movie in horror. *Who am I?* he wonders. Who is The Other, who can twist the truth of his past into horrific images with no connection to reality?

Eddie begs me to stop, but I persist with what he tells himself are false memories of Robert—who loved him, who cared for him when no one else was able to, who explained how to act around other kids, how to deal with girls. Robert, who adored Eddie and taught him everything!

Sure, they fought some, Eddie rationalizes. But Robert never beat him, locked him in a closet, held him down while his friends force-fed him a live earthworm. Robert never tried to drown him in the bathtub, never slammed him against the mirrors in the elevator at Dave's loft in Tribeca. Never, never, never! How The Other can come up with such things is beyond comprehension. Because Eddie swears he remembers how his brother really was, is.

"He *never* hurt me," Eddie says aloud to the sleeping man sitting beside him as the train hurtles along under the East River. "Not on purpose, anyway."

37.

PÄR

On the day that Eddie spies Lucy and Carlo at Zabar's, handling cheeses, he remembers that these are the same cheeses Joanne used to force him to touch—at Glenda's urging—hoping to cure one of his phobias. (Hanging-cheese exposure therapy was quite enjoyable to me, frankly.) Carlo tells Lucy something—about cheese, presumably—that makes her whoop with glee, then cover her mouth, glancing around in giddy embarrassment.

After this, Eddie withdraws. From Lucy and Robert. From everyone.

One day, not shockingly, Eddie is dismissed from his job at Mitford Academy. There has been a claim made against him by one of the girls, one of the three Samanthas on the middle school team. Eddie flirted with her, Samantha W. reports to her parents. Her parents subsequently share this with the head of school. Young Miss W. claims that Eddie also asked her to do certain things. The allegation is false, of course. Preposterous, really. Eddie can't even flirt properly with women his own age. In any case, he could never, ever proposition a child. But Eddie is not offered an opportunity to defend himself. Someone gets the idea of searching his locker and discovers a small sack of cocaine. (No one planted this. The blow is Eddie's, fair and square.) The whole affair is kept out of the news, discretion being top priority at the school. In any case, Eddie is sacked.

⁓

At this point, Eddie begins to wander. With no Lucy, no Robert, no job, he wanders the streets like a crazy person—no longer searching for Lucy and Carlo, just wandering solo, marinating in his own misery. His income, besides his parents' increasingly grudging charity, comes from the occasional swim class at the McBurney YMCA. No kids' classes, just small group or individual lessons for adults. But mostly he wanders. Mostly high, blacking out frequently, coming to in places he isn't expecting. Coney Island, on the beach. In the lobby of Joanne and Michael's new apartment building on East Eighty-Ninth Street. A bench in Tompkins Square Park, gazing up at a lifeless maple tree. The place he wanders most is Prospect Park, which is enough like Central Park to remind him of Lucy, but not too much.

It feels like years since the two of them walked hand in hand, waiting for the rain. Eddie is sure he's spent more time with Lucy than Robert ever has—not counting the years they lived together in Seattle. Eddie made it a point to always be available when she called. To be as lighthearted as he could be, to talk only about what Lucy wanted to talk about, to keep his anxiety, his phobias out of the discussion unless it was Lucy's choice to analyze him (which she sometimes enjoyed). Eddie was as close to normal with Lucy as he's been with anyone.

He can still feel the pressure, the texture of her hand in his, on what he did not realize was their last Central Park sojourn. It was mid-September, and a thin rain was starting up. Lucy opened her umbrella, which was a defiant sunshine yellow. Eddie held it over them as they huddled close, pressed together as they walked. Few people were in the park because of the weather and the fact that night was falling quickly.

"Eddie," she said, her pace slowing. "You've never asked what happened to my mother."

"I know."

"Haven't you wondered?"

"I know she died. I never wanted to ask. I was afraid I'd upset you."

"She is dead, yes." Lucy stopped walking. "But *died*—that's too passive."

Eddie waited. Beside him, he felt Lucy's presence shrink down to fragile, childlike proportions. He shifted the umbrella and put his arm around her, but not too tightly. Eddie had a fleeting notion about how Robert did not know his own strength, how he often crushed her with his embraces, causing her to yelp. Eddie's lean body and more modest height were better suited for holding Lucy, his instincts always sound with her. He was always able to be just what she needed, a loving vessel of trust. She spoke then.

"It was here—somewhere right around here that I last saw my mother. I was ten. The park, as long as the weather was nice, was our usual place to meet my father when I was going to spend the weekend with him. My mother never wanted to go near The Majestic and risk being seen by Dominique and the girls. She never said it, but I knew she felt so much guilt and shame about the whole thing—about *me*. So we'd meet in the park."

"You went to him every weekend?"

"Every other weekend, starting when I was about seven or so. Dominique didn't seem to mind me then, and my sisters still thought I was his niece—a lie which didn't last long. Anyway"—Lucy pulled on Eddie, getting them to walk again—"one weekend we met my father here as usual. I was angry at her that day. My mother wouldn't let me wear what I wanted to wear or something. She made me dress nicely for my father and Dominique—no T-shirts with slogans or anything, nothing with Mick Jagger's tongue on it, which was all I wanted to wear. I kissed her goodbye—all sullen, like kids get—and walked away with him. But something—this weird feeling—came over me, and I turned to see her standing at the edge of the park watching us go. I waved at her, feeling sorry I'd yelled, not angry anymore. And she blew me a kiss, which wasn't something my mother normally did. She wasn't ever a kiss blower. But that day she did. It was the last I saw of her."

Lucy described for Eddie what she discovered upon arriving home after the weekend. At ten, she had her own key and entered her mother's apartment alone. It was far quieter than it should have been. Her mother often had the television on to keep her company, but not this afternoon. On the dining room table there was an empty liquor bottle on its side, and next to that, an empty prescription bottle. Lucy understood right away that her mother had swallowed pills with alcohol—which she knew you were not supposed to do. Ruth had done it once before but had only wound up sleeping for a day and waking up with a terrible headache. Lucy left the dining room and rounded a bend, where she stopped short and stood staring for a long, long time. When Lucy was very small, a neighbor had installed a swing in the doorway to her bedroom. The tension rod that had secured the swing remained in place. But now, the thing swinging from it was Ruth. Lucy stared and stared because what she was seeing did not make sense, could not be real. She did not scream, call for help, or so much as cry. Lucy certainly did not call her father, which would have gone against their agreement. She was not to call the Wynter home except to say if she was running late for a visit.

Ruth was a small woman, but Lucy was far smaller. It took great effort and some danger to Lucy's own body to climb up on a ladder and cut the nylon necktie her mother had used. It was a man's necktie, one Lucy did not recognize. When Ruth fell, Lucy dragged her body to bed and got in beside her. After several hours, she got up to go to the bathroom, at which point she found the note her mother had written for her.

Dearest Lucy, I love you, but we are better off without each other.

At that point Lucy did cry. She did not agree that she was better off without her mother but understood that it was Ruth's choice to be rid of her. Lucy was hurt and deeply ashamed. Then she became frightened that someone else—like her father—might read the note and learn the truth: Lucy wasn't worth sticking around for. She lit a candle, burned the note in the kitchen sink, and returned to her mother's side.

Eddie remembers he stopped to hold her then, letting the umbrella list to one side, still covering her but not him. He remembers that he cried because he sensed that Lucy couldn't. Ten years old and her mother hangs herself for Lucy to find. And the note. No one knew how depressed Ruth was, what she'd been through, but Lucy would take the scars with her to her own grave.

Why did Lucy choose that day, their last day, to tell Eddie about her mother? Was it her way of explaining how she could let go of love with such fluidity? What she'd said to Eddie in Seattle, after the night at Al and Stella's: *For me, a lot of things are possible.* Was this what she meant? That because of her mother, no attachment could be indelible?

38.

PÄR

The holidays happen without Eddie. Red and green lights and Santas everywhere. The music they haul out each year squeaks from aged speakers at the Key Food on Atlantic Avenue. Eddie sees a few menorahs in shop windows: a nod toward *his* holiday. A vague, sad memory hits him. Long, long ago, an aunt who'd married into the Asher family but hadn't converted—she was Episcopalian, Eddie recalls—brought Eddie a Christmas gift. Aware of his Swedish heritage, this aunt-by-marriage gave him a book about seven Swedish farm children preparing for Christmas. *Christmas in Noisy Village*, that was it. The author was Astrid Lindgren, who penned the Pippi Longstocking books. Eddie remembers that the artwork was strange and stylized; the cheerful faces of the children were dark, almost Latin. Almost mixed. One of the boys had dark hair and eyes and looked just like Eddie. *Olaf.* His name was Olaf—how does he remember that? *Olaf*—not Pär. But still, Eddie felt sure that Olaf was him, the self he would have been if his birth mother had raised him. The book was confiscated by Joanne, who disliked the aunt in question. Joanne did not want Eddie to be confused by the goyish offering.

"His life is complicated enough, thank you," she said.

The Brooklyn Christmastime comes to a head and then bursts into a collective mania over people's upcoming New Year's celebrations.

Eddie detects a peculiar fatalism in the air at this time each year. As if everyone is on the verge of learning that the world was flat after all. Time is cruising fast toward the edge of 1992, about to fall into the abyss of 1993. *Well,* Eddie thinks, *I'm not afraid. I already live in an abyss all my own.*

As the year drains away, he walks the city in a spiral pattern. Gazing into the frozen Gowanus Canal, he sees a version of himself beneath the trash, beneath the surface ice layer. Eddie is sure that this isn't The Other—who loves to provoke him—lying still amid the flotsam. Is it the Fish-boy, after all these years? Is he trapped there? Or is the Fish-boy the free one, gazing up at Prisoner Eddie on this side of the frosty barrier?

When Eddie arrives home, there is a message from Lucy. She's been trying to reach him for two months. Which is possible, in theory. Eddie hasn't been answering any calls, has given up opening his mail too. Since losing his job, he has redirected bills and important mail to Joanne and Michael's home. (Maybe Robert stopped coddling him a few years ago, but he can still count on Joanne.)

Eddie is about to play Lucy's message over, hoping to tease out clues as to her real meaning, when the phone rings. Caught off guard, he answers.

"Eddie?" Lucy's surprised voice. "It's really you? Where the fuck have you been?"

He can't see her face, of course. Is she glad it's really him or annoyed she couldn't leave a message and slip quietly away?

Eddie says, "Around."

"Did you get my invitation?"

"No."

Lucy tells him that she and Robert are having a party two nights later, a belated New Year's gathering—nothing huge, just an intimate group of their nearest and dearest friends. And Eddie. He must come, Lucy says. He has to. If only to see Robert.

"I don't know if you're mad at me or what, Eddie. But what matters is you and Robert. You're brothers, and you need each other."

"We need each other? Now that you're done with us both?"

"I don't know what you're talking about."

"Fuck you, Lucy. You fucking bitch."

"Eddie—"

He hangs up, then throws the phone at the wall and watches it smash to the floor. It cracks, batteries rolling.

"Fuck you!" Eddie says to the phone. Lucy is probably trying to call him back, for damage control. *Shit*, he imagines her thinking, *how much does Eddie know? Has he told Robert?*

"Fuck her!" he says aloud. Let Lucy figure out what he meant by "done with us both."

Let Lucy figure out that he knows what she's been doing. Or *who*: Carlo Fucking Giannini. Now Lucy can neither assess nor control the damage because she can't reach him on the broken phone. Eddie has a split second of self-satisfied glee, which vanishes as quickly as it arrived, replaced by a hollow, resounding dread.

Eddie is alone at the bottom of a dry well with no one to pull him up. If he calls out to Robert, he'll just drag his brother down with him. And Dave has Glenda and their girls to deal with. Joanne has Michael. Michael, Eddie guesses, has God. But there at the bottom of the well, Eddie finds an escape hatch. Resting in a brown sea-glass ashtray is a joint—a gift from his neighbor Sasha, for taking in his plants while he was away. Sasha is a rep for a pharmaceutical company, also a bass player who often tours with his brothers' Russian punk band. Eddie and Sasha aren't exactly friends, but they get high together. Sasha has heard Eddie bawl about Lucy.

"Is good weed," Sasha had said with a sideways grin when he handed Eddie the joint. "Special. For what ails you."

Eddie crams it into his coat pocket and leaves for the Borough Hall subway station, full of determination but lacking any sort of plan. All he knows is that Robert is likely out, based on Lucy's statement about them

being "brothers" who "need each other." She'd never have said it, probably wouldn't have called him if Robert were around. Once Eddie might
have taken advantage of his brother's absence and called Lucy to come
and meet him. Better yet, he'd have surprised her, which would have
been outrageous and unpredictable and just how they were together.
But now there's Carlo to slip inside anytime Robert steps out. If Carlo
is with Lucy now, so much the better. Ridiculously, Eddie thinks, *Then
I'll have it out with them both.* When the train arrives, Eddie is already
shaking. He takes deep breaths and fingers the joint in his pocket.

39.
PÄR

It's never pretty watching Eddie when he gets like this—I could choke on the shit he's eaten for months, served by Lucy, by the powers that be at Mitford Academy. But the rage, when he allows it, feels good, warms my figurative spine. The people on the train stare at him and for once he stares back. He gets out at Seventy-Second Street and Broadway, then walks east to their apartment building on Seventy-Third between Amsterdam and Columbus, planting himself on the steps of the brownstone across the street, eyes on the front door.

Eddie lights the joint and smokes to pass the time, waiting for the chill and the calm that never come. Instead, it's Lucy who comes out alone, pulling her weekend bag, waist cinched by the sash of her long, narrow black coat. Her hat is green felt—a retro flapperish affair with a pinned-on feather arrangement. As she strides west, Eddie snuffs out the joint, carefully returns it to its pouch, and follows her, giving her a quarter of a block's berth. She's heading for the subway station Eddie's just come from. Turns left on Broadway, crossing to where the oversize IRT canopy looms. We won't call out; we'll take her by surprise. And what a surprise we'll be. When we're close enough, down on the southbound platform, I'm the one who grabs her forearm and turns her around, not gently.

"Eddie! Where did you come from—*ow!* Let go!"

He obeys. Even in his pain and fury, Eddie cannot harm her.

"Eddie."

He means to stare her down, to make his voice deep and full of hate. He prepares the accusation: four . . . three . . . two . . . one: "How could you do it?" But his voice catches, rolls up the scale, squeaking like a mouse. Eddie repeats, *"How?"* Lets her go, weakening progressively, prideless: Eddie Pathetic. I can only stand back—float on the ether around his stupid head as he tries not to sob in the middle of the platform.

"Jesus, Eddie," she says. Eddie snivels while I choke on vitriol—Andy's from the old days, Eddie's now. I glance at the tracks, thinking that perhaps, for the first time since we met, there will be action taken.

"I've seen you two together," Eddie says. "You and Carlo Giannini."

Caught before she can lie, Lucy needs a moment to work out her next move. Will she choose the truth? Or find some way to protect Eddie's heart and her own ass?

Her eyes drop, then lift, imploring. "Please understand."

And he tries, as she talks, to understand. He swallows his pain. He tries posing as Andy once again. Andy, who—Eddie believes—listened to and understood everything with respect to Lucy and Carlo. Eddie wears his Andy disguise. I stay present but impersonate Eddie. We are matryoshka dolls: one inside the other inside the other.

Now, across the tracks on the northbound side, motion distracts me. A pair of lovers play, chasing each other, falling together, kissing. When they part again, I see her. It *is* her, but how can it be? She gazes upon me, oblivious to the roar of the oncoming train. And, as myself—Pär, not Eddie—I act.

Together, Eddie and I hear the screech of the train, screams of would-be riders, chaos. Through Eddie's eyes I watch it unfold. This is the turning point for us, for me. I have heretofore been his observer and protector, occasionally entertaining myself by meddling, but never with malice—only to advocate for Eddie or to push him toward actions he would otherwise shy from.

This was not premeditated. By now you know me well enough to recognize that I prefer kismet to planning. Nor was it my intent to make Eddie believe he is a monster, capable of murdering a woman he loves. But serendipity smiles on me tonight. I seal off the facts from Eddie's memory, leaving him with nothing but the feathers of Lucy's hat that remain clutched in his fist. *How did they get there, Eddie? Where is the rest of her? What did you do?* I'll use his doubt and panic to my advantage. The more vulnerable Eddie is, the more accessible the body is to me. *What did you do, Eddie? What did you do?* I can manipulate him into anything with that. I am nothing if not a survivor.

But I can't stop myself from taking in the sight of her one last time, with a sorrow and anger that is all my own. Andy got so much, so much more of her.

"Why?" I say aloud, in spite of myself. "Why couldn't you have chosen *me*?"

PART III

40.

EDDIE

I'm dreaming of the Fish-boy, who is now a man like me. We're swimming together, somewhere deep and blue and beautiful—just us, in sync. I can't see his face, but his body shimmers in the light filtering through the water. He is not Pär. Unlike Pär, the Fish-boy is benign, loving. This I know in my bones. His movements are smoother than mine, like a real fish. I can see he doesn't have to think to coordinate himself, doesn't need to calculate strokes or speed or distance. He just is. One with himself, with the water, with me—as our hands, arms, shoulders, graze each other. I am jealous, the way I get when I wake from lapses. How I would like to be him. Imagine it, trusting yourself to belong wherever you are. Never doubting. If I cannot be him, I can imagine and keep imagining. Pretend. The way I do with . . . I cannot remember his name in the dream. I want to call out to him before he swims away, but his name sticks to the tip of my tongue.

All at once, bright lights pierce my vision; my skin prickles ice cold, then burning hot. I feel needles sticking into me all over, everywhere, machines screeching. What is happening to me? Hands restrain my thrashing body. I am strapped down. A sharp, searing pain in my arm, and now a hum, magnetic and vibrating through my body. I am still, staring as faces come into focus. Who are these people? What is this place?

"Eddie?" someone says. "Eddie, are you with us again? Eddie?"

Eddie is not the name I was trying to remember. Eddie is not what it was. Eddy is a word that means something other than a name. It is a current of water, swirling around, disturbing the water from my dream, where the Fish-boy can be found.

"Eddie."

Eddie is a name. Eddie is *me*. I am Eddie. I stop thrashing and stare at this man, whom I think I recognize. He is Black. The woman beside him is white. My parents, my birth parents. Have they come for me? Now they're speaking, to one another, not me.

"I can't tell if he's even in there."

"He is. He's coming back, I can tell. Just give him a minute."

"Eddie, man. You're here with us, okay?"

"You're at the Hudson Valley Psychiatric Hospital."

The Black man is not my father, the white woman is not my mother.

"What else?" says the man. "Okay. Eddie, it's 1993. Um. February."

"Bill Clinton is president."

"The new president. Eddie, nod if you hear us."

Dwight. That's his name. The woman is the nurse. Her name is—I can't remember. Still. I nod.

"He's back!"

Applause rocks the room, which is full of men and women: doctors, nurses, and others. I have in some way given them reason to celebrate. It's too much, too much to take in. Nurse Sylvana—that's her name!—senses my distress, administers another injection, and soon I'm fading into a true sleep.

41.

EDDIE

"Welcome back, Eddie," says Dr. Montgomery. "What a ride we've had these past few days."

Apparently, I was in a trance of some kind. The last thing I remember is seeing Gilooley's drawing.

"Ray's art seems to have triggered all your memories of Lucy. I was able to record everything you said while you believed you were back in that period of your life."

But I am still without a voice. I pick up the pad and pen. *"I spoke while I was out of it? Aloud?"*

"Quite clearly. Between you and Pär, I was able to get a fairly detailed picture of what brought you to the confrontation on the subway platform."

"What did happen on the platform?" I'm still a little sedated, detached from my panic. I cannot write the questions: Did I push her? Did I kill her?

"I'm sorry, Eddie. That part of the story was confusing. You and Lucy argued. You were distraught and left."

"But what happened to Lucy? Is she dead?"

"Dead? Neither you nor Pär mentioned anything about that. What makes you think she might be dead?"

Neither of us mentioned it? How is that possible? *"In the drawing she was tied to the train tracks. And I remember for certain that I saw her fly."*

"Ray's drawing was a metaphor, Eddie. Gilooley interpreted something he learned from you or from Pär and did what artists do. He created a visual image of your emotions."

"But I saw her fly." All I can do is rewrite this. My vision swims over the words.

"I have an idea, Eddie." Dr. Montgomery leans forward in his chair and extends both hands toward me. "Would you try something for me now?"

He tells me to close my eyes, to breathe slowly in and out, and try to bring up any images from the night I arrived. I close my eyes. I breathe slowly. Dr. Montgomery squeezes my hands one at a time in rhythm, like the pulsing of a heart—right-left, right-left, right-left—distracting me from the here and now. I am on the platform. She's there with me. There is a streak of silver, flashing lights, a deafening engine roar, and the shriek of steel. Pär is quick; he darts in, cutting the memory short, forcing me back to this office. I jolt free of Dr. Montgomery's hands and take up my notepad again.

"There's nothing," I write. But of course there's more to tell him. More than I know. I'm as scared of remembering the full truth of what Pär—or *I*—did to her as I am of the consequences. The ink in this fresh pen waits to share that I am a murderer. Instead I cap it, setting it down.

42.

EDDIE

Ray Gilooley is in the corner, fashioning a rope out of his bedsheet—a daily ritual, meant more for provoking the staff than attempting to end his life. It's a fascinating procedure, the way he grips the base of the sheet between his feet, then uses his arm and chin to twist and weave and tie. He was equally resourceful the day he drew me, sketching with his arm, shading and blending with his stump.

It surprises me that we're still roommates, frankly, given that my interactions with Gilooley, or his with Pär, and the resulting art project triggered what Dr. Montgomery is calling my catatonic fugue. But I have access to Ray, cameras or no. I write:

"Did you draw what you drew because I pushed Lucy onto the train tracks? Did Pär tell you that?"

I read it over while Gilooley works on his rope. Is this what I really want to ask him? Gilooley's grip on reality is so fleeting, I don't want to squander it. Of course he drew the picture based on Pär's input. Of course Pär would be cagey with Ray, leading him to draw something devastating to me. I cross out the question and replace it, holding out the notebook as I move close and crouch down to Ray's level. He looks up to read aloud.

"'Did I push her or did Pär?'" Gilooley lets the sheet fall while he rubs his face. "Did *you* push her? Or was it Peachy Pie Pear that done it?" His eyes dart around the room like he's looking for an answer in the air. "Did you or did he? Right. Right, right. Trying to remember what he said." More darting and rubbing. "Right. Nope. He didn't tell me that. Told me he wanted the credit for pushing her. Told me he wanted you to think you did it. But nope. Didn't say just how it went down." He picks up the sheet and resumes his labor.

I write. *"Then why did you draw Lucy and call it my soul?"*

Ray ignores the notebook. When I put it right up to his face, he slaps it out of my hand so it slides across the room. I scoot after it, then sit on the floor beside it and regroup. I am ready for real answers, not the collaborative riddles of Pär and Ray.

For my own eyes, not Ray's, I write:

"If I did it, why has no one come for me? The police? The FBI? My brother?"

I'd been on the verge of asking Dr. Montgomery these questions long before Ray drew me. But dread—of hearing the truth aloud, of facing the police, a trial, then *prison!*—stopped me. My picture should be everywhere, shouldn't it? Surely there was a surveillance camera in the subway station, more of them in Port Authority, where I apparently bought a ticket and boarded a bus for Hudson. It doesn't add up.

I flip the page and creep closer to Ray again, staring until he looks up at me.

"Now what do you want?"

"Around when I came here, was there anything in the news about a woman getting pushed onto the subway tracks in the city?"

Ray squints at me as a grin distorts his beard. "Hoo-hoo! Hot *damn*. I knew it! It was you after all."

"But did you hear anything about it before Pär told you?"

"I ain't hear nothing," still chuckling. "You know they don't let us watch the news. But you did it, didn't you. I'm looking into those big brown eyes of yours, Pretty Boy. I can see it now: you pushed her!"

The words slam against the wall of my resistance, tension flooding my body.

"You li'l scoundrel! Hoo-*hoo*!"

Flinging my notebook at his face, I roll on the floor, beating my head, flogging myself with both fists, as if I could fend it all off. But the shadow memory patches through. I hear the train, see my hands, my own hands.

Ray guffaws. "Threw the li'l bitch on the goddamn tracks! Get a *load* of you, sonny—"

I fly at him, meaning to make him shut his fucking psycho mouth. Then Pär takes over.

～੭

When I wake up, I know I'm not in our room due to the absence of Ray Gilooley's mildewed-onion bouquet. I'm back in the medical recliner, arms fastened in straps above my head this time. Nurse Sylvana looms like a thick, white obelisk, lips pursed, hands on hips. Whatever she's injected me with dims my brain.

"He's awake." She says this to someone over her shoulder.

"Eddie." Dr. Montgomery steps out from her sheltering form. There's no question in his tone. How can he tell it's me, not Pär, just by making eye contact? Are our expressions so different now? There's a key in his hand and one of my notepads under his arm. "Nurse, I trust he'll be fine. You can leave us."

Sylvana complies with a snort as Dr. Montgomery removes my constraints.

"You know each room is monitored. I saw and heard what happened between you and Ray Gilooley."

The doctor pulls up a chair to sit, then hands me the pad and pen. "Was it you or Pär who attacked him?"

I shrug. *"Ray provoked me. I don't remember hurting him."*

I feel Pär around my shoulders, monitoring what I write. He doesn't trust me any more than I trust him. *"Is Ray all right?"*

"He will be." Dr. Montgomery jots down a note. "What I'm curious about, Eddie, is your interest in the news story. That's what Gilooley said you were discussing: the woman killed on the subway tracks."

"So there really was a news story?"

"I read about it in the Metropolitan section of the *New York Times* a few days after you arrived here. That weekend, a woman either fell, jumped, or was pushed in front of an oncoming subway train in New York City. I've been following the story in light of your own confusion over the events that brought you here. Apparently the authorities are still trying to figure out whether it was a suicide, homicide, or accident."

My heart is pounding again, hands sweating, breath short. *"It was Lucy. I did it. I pushed her. Or Pär did."*

The doctor leans forward. "You believe this was the result of your confrontation on the platform?"

"Yes."

"Ah, but do you remember pushing her?"

"I saw my own hands. I saw the train. I killed her. You just said as much."

"I didn't say Lucy was killed on the tracks. I said a woman either fell or was pushed to her death." I can tell by his knit brow that he's not sure either. "Is it possible that extreme distress made you conflate the argument with Lucy and a terrible, coinciding, but unrelated event?"

Sure it's possible, I think but don't write. Dr. Montgomery knows it's possible, but he suspects me now. He didn't before, but now his money is on me having pushed and killed her. It must be what he's writing in his notebook.

"Eddie," he says, "is pushing Lucy a true memory? Or is it one Pär invented for you?"

What I remember for certain is the rage, the determination to rid myself, my brother, and the whole world of her. It does not occur to me to ask Dr. Montgomery if the woman's photograph was in the paper.

Nor does he mention it. A deliberate omission to study my response to uncertainty?

"Think hard, Eddie." He reiterates, "Is it a true memory?"

My head is fogging up again. *"How would I know that?"* I'm fading, falling—either sleep takes me or Pär does.

43.

EDDIE

In light of the assault—mine or Pär's upon Gilooley—I've been moved to a small single room on the third floor. The window is larger, but still barred, and there are two cameras instead of one. There is no one to talk to here. Only Pär.

"What happened?" I implore him all day, every day. "I need to know."

But he stays quiet. Taunting me occasionally by moving a chill around my body.

"Please." I don't need a voice to address him. I know he can hear even if he ignores me.

Dwight unlocks my door to escort me to the showers, which are down the hall from my new room. There are no bathtubs at Hudson Valley Psych. The nurses provide the orderlies with the toilet articles we are to be trusted with—toothbrushes but no razors—towels and flip-flops to prevent the spread of fungi. Anyone who desires a shave can ask for a staff member to do it. Few take advantage of this service, evidenced by the appearances of Gilooley, Bill/Jesus, and others. Dwight has secured a pick for my hair, though it is not explicitly approved, there having been no prior need at Hudson to regulate such an item.

Dwight allows me to draw the curtain while I shower. The water hits like ice at first, matching the outside temperature, then turns instantly scalding. For no reason, Lucy's scent engulfs me, coats me inside and out. How did I wind up holding just those feathers?

"Pär, are you here? I'm ready for the truth."

"No you're not," comes his disembodied voice.

"Tell me anyway. I need to know." How pathetic am I? Begging for access to my own mind.

"So, you trust me, then?" says Pär.

"No. But you're all I have." I brace myself against the sides of the shower stall and allow him to bring me back to that night, from the moment I saw Lucy exit her apartment building, pulling her weekend bag. As she turns the corner, I snuff out Sasha's joint, carefully returning it to its pouch. I catch up with Lucy and grab her sleeve as she heads down the subway steps.

She starts, frightened. "Eddie! Where did you come from—*ow!* Let go!" Then takes in the desperation in my eyes. "Jesus, Eddie." Alarm fading to annoyance, like even my stalking of her is deadly predictable. Just *Jesus, Eddie*, and keeps going. On the platform, I grab at her again, securing her hand, smooth and brown, bones light as a bird's. I squeeze it.

"Eddie, stop."

I tell her I know all about Carlo, the other guy. Laughable: we are not lovers, but *I'm* supposed to be the other guy. She says it again: "Jesus, Eddie." Full of pity. Lucy explains what she thinks I need to know, the unbreakable hold Carlo has on her heart, the depth of their "forever" love. "Not even you, Eddie, not even *Robert*," emphasis suggesting my brother's second-place status to my third, "can come between me and Carlo." As a consolation, she lets me hold her, her back to my front. I feel our bodies mesh for the last time.

I pull her close, her head nestled under my chin, narrow back embedded in my chest. Once, when I held her like this, she asked if I could feel her melting into me. "We're one person now," she said then.

This evening I look over her head, across the tracks, where a couple—our age, midtwenties—is laughing together, encased in their love, sealed off from the rest of humanity. The girl wears a red coat and a pink scarf with hearts, though Valentine's Day is more than a month away. Lucy strains against my hold. I imagine our hearts pounding in rhythm, but it's only the vibration of an approaching train.

Pär takes over the moment the train's headlights become visible. I am incapable of what comes next, so it must be his doing. My arms extend a split second before the train rushes past. A glimpse of Lucy flying away sears my mind. Next come screeching wheels, the screams of other would-be riders. *What's happened? Was that a person?* I can't see through the gathering crowd. Is she there? Is she alive? What's my imagination, Pär's trickery, the truth? I don't trust him or myself. I stare at my hands, the right one white-knuckled, clutching the feathers from Lucy's hat.

Both the north- and southbound number 1 trains have stopped halfway into the station, doors shut, the platform buzzing with frenetic motion, the blur of blue police uniforms, a voice over a loudspeaker. Panicked, I stash the crumpled feathers into my pocket and flee.

"Eddie, wrap it up, man," Dwight breaks through the vision. "Time to finish and head back to your room." He hands me a towel. I am shaking as he guides me up the corridor, a different Eddie altogether than what I knew myself to be. Pär is the scaffolding of my mind, but I am the monster. I did it. I did it. And I'll never be free of her scent.

Following this, I withdraw, unable to interact with anyone or even write on my notepad in sessions. To write, I would need some hope that I could be helped, that I could become better. I sit across from Dr. Montgomery without responding to his questions. I don't even look him in the eye. To address this new bout of depression, he adds to my medication: an oblong yellow pill, a second white one.

Sedated as I am, Dwight often brings me to sit by the picture window in the rec room, with its expansive view of mountains and sky. I am riding a hot-air balloon in the clouds. Cottony white, they pass before me like marshmallows. Now my eye wanders the grounds and locates the path that leads to the reservoir on the southern side of the property. Weeks ago, I asked Dwight if I might swim there if it got warm enough, or at least walk around the perimeter. He told me anything like that would be impossible without Dr. Montgomery's approval.

Now I try out a meditation like one my old therapist taught me: breathing slowly and evenly—in through my nose, out through my mouth. I envision myself on the bank of the reservoir, with sun beating down on my shoulders. Still breathing slowly, I can smell a bit of pleasantly rotting vegetation near the edge. I wiggle my toes closer so they just graze the lapping water. Breathe, in and out again. I am allowing myself to relax. I am aware of Pär close by, but at this level of meds, I think he too is muted, possibly even impotent. Maybe this is the best I can hope for.

44.

EDDIE

Dwight looks out for me. I bet he suggested that I visit the reservoir, though it's Dr. Montgomery who surprises me with the idea. Declaring that exercise might improve my mood, the doctor arranges for me to join a small, supervised group for a walk around the grounds and a visit to look at the small body of water up close.

It's a balmy day for late February, sporadically threatening rain since morning. The cloud cover is mottled and pretty, with small patches of sun peeking through. Besides me, there is Bill/Jesus, a young kid with tracks on his arms, and a few others from outpatient. Jim/John and Dwight accompany us as chaperones with Jim/John up at the front, Dwight trailing us, at least at the outset.

My breath eases, deepening as the reservoir comes into view. I think if I could get closer, close enough to sneak my feet into the mud at the edge, peer into the depths, I'd find some solace, maybe the Fish-boy, maybe the rest of myself. But Dwight catches me getting too close and grips my arm.

"The doctor said you could look at the water, not go in it. Besides, it's too cold for wading, man."

I don't push it yet, just enjoy the view while my mind continues to wander over the gullies and cliffs of memories. Another one comes back now, an earlier one that Pär didn't curate: Lucy and me, in the bed in the butler's pantry.

Lucy said, "Do you ever wonder about him?"

I thought she meant Robert, though she had already made the rule that we wouldn't bring him up when we were together.

"I mean your birth father," she said. "What do you know about him besides that he was from somewhere in Africa?"

"Nothing. Just that he didn't know I existed." Then I told her about a Kenyan friend I'd had in college who'd told me that no one in his culture gives up a baby. "So my birth father's family would have taken me if they were Kenyan. Think about it: if he had learned about the pregnancy, we wouldn't be having this conversation. We'd never have met."

"We might have anyway." Lucy rolled onto her side to look at me. "One way or another, we were destined to meet."

I loved her more than ever when she said things like this. Gently she shoved me over onto my front, straddled me on her knees. She began my massage.

"Tyrone didn't have much to do with me at first," she said. "I mean, he knew about me. He gave my mom money. But we didn't meet face-to-face until I was four."

This was when she'd first explained about her parents' affair. It was like Lucy to ask something personal, then use my disclosure as a vehicle to talk about herself. I didn't mind; I would rather have heard about her life than talk about mine.

Now a fat raindrop lands on my eyelid, another on my nose. Thunder—an intro to the storm. Dwight steers me around.

"Time to head back, Eddie," he says. But we're at such a pretty spot, with cattails along the banks, crowded among stones, orange and green fish swimming not too far beneath the surface. A second clap of thunder makes Dwight pull me along. He doesn't like it; storms freak him out, I can tell. My own heart rate quickens, though I'm not afraid, just exhilarated. I wonder if it's raining in the city.

There is a commotion up ahead. Jim/John is unable to control the kid with the arm tracks, who is fighting him, panicked, convinced that a nemesis is hiding in the trees. Dwight, who is stronger and steadier of nature than Jim/John, offers to take over and switch posts. Jim/John, relieved, surrenders the kid to Dwight and moves to the back of the procession.

Meanwhile, the reservoir calls to me, glimmering silver-white and full of hope. I wait until Jim/John is distracted, helping someone with a wayward shoelace. Then I break off from the group unnoticed. Stripped down, I feel warmer than bundled up—warmer still when I step into the water and go with the urge to dive in, swimming out to the center. I feel the chill, but only in a distant sort of way, like a light, cool breeze inside and outside, just grazing my skin, filling my belly. The chill tickles, like Lucy's fingers walking all over me, tracing little circles. Laughing out loud, I let myself sink down under, where it's dark, colder, but not unbearable. It's difficult to make out his silhouette in the murky water, but when the Fish-boy touches my hand, I know to join him. He swims alongside me, laughing—at me? With me? I am thinking that it's okay to stay. What else, who else do I need? Down here I can imagine that there is no Lucy, no Robert or Carlo. I can forget what happened on the subway platform. I can be the Eddie I've always wanted to be. Not a killer, not a monster, not a freak. I can go back, back to a time before all that. When I was Pär and Pär was me and that was all. I don't feel the cold anymore. My lungs don't need the air. I can imagine a peace like I haven't felt since that time. We are just the two of us, surrounded by water.

I wake up in the recliner, covered in a heated blanket, though my arms are free. Dr. Montgomery, a pad and pen in his hands, tells me I almost drowned and am suffering from hypothermia. Dwight has been let go. Awash in guilt, I reach for the pen and paper for the first time in days to protest, writing that Dwight was helping the arm-track kid when I broke away; he changed places with Jim/John, who was in charge of me at the time.

"It's the only way I could have done it. Dwight would have never let me get away."

"I understand," Dr. Montgomery tells me. "Dwight was your friend. Of course you want to defend him, stick together." Montgomery gives me a patronizing smile as the implication about race settles between us. I'd lie to protect a brother and throw Jim/John under the bus.

"Dwight wasn't responsible for me."

Nothing I say will change his mind. I was in Dwight's caseload, not Jim/John's. There are rules, after all, and safety concerns. Dwight had confided once that he was paying his way through college, meaning to become a psychiatrist like Dr. Montgomery.

45.

EDDIE

"Eddie."

Hours, days, or weeks may have passed. A man is standing next to Dr. Montgomery. He is also white, roughly Montgomery's age but not wearing it as well. He's a big dude, barrel chested, with a large, square head. A gun is holstered over his beige button-down shirt, the significance of which takes a moment to sink in.

"Eddie, this is a friend of mine, Detective Tom Donaldson of the New York Police Department."

Waking up face-to-face with law enforcement should spike my anxiety. Instead I'm relieved. After all the doubt and confusion, I can write a confession and be done with it. Let the law deal with me as it will. But Pär is waiting to crowd me out, I can feel him.

"Mr. Asher, I'd like to ask you a few questions." The detective's voice is higher in pitch than I'd expect from a man of his size, which jars me more than the gun. "Rich here tells me you know Lucy Rivkin?"

Deducing that "Rich" is Dr. Richard Montgomery, I nod.

"Lucy is your brother Robert Asher's fiancée, is that right?"

Another nod. Donaldson looks annoyed until Dr. Montgomery hands me a notepad.

"You may not be aware that the NYPD has been looking for you and Lucy since the night of January 2."

I write on the pad. *"How can they be looking for Lucy? The train hit her."*

Donaldson looks over what I've written. "Rich said you'd say that. You and Lucy Rivkin both disappeared the same night a woman was killed by a subway train at the Seventy-Second Street IRT station, but the Jane Doe's description doesn't match Miss Rivkin's.

"Lucy's doorman reported he saw her leave her building with a suitcase at seven fifteen p.m. He saw you follow her and seemed to be gaining on her as you turned the corner. Sound familiar?" He waits for me to write a response, looking impatient.

"Is Lucy all right?"

"We're thinking you would know the answer to that. You're the last one to be seen with her. Until the doctor here reached out to me, the NYPD was operating under the assumption that you and Lucy were together somewhere."

"How could we be?"

Donaldson sets his feet apart, folds his arms. "See, that's what confuses me, Mr. Asher. Are you saying that you and Lucy had something to do with the woman on the subway tracks?"

His last words echo in my ears—*subway tracks, tracks, tracks*—as Pär rewinds the memory and runs it again: train roars, lights flash, my arms push, Lucy flies, lights, steel, screeching wheels, screams, feathers, dread, run.

Donaldson is still talking, shifting slightly from side to side, but Pär muffles the sound so I cannot make out his words. My skin stretches, then contracts. I've never felt the switching this way before. Pär forces me out, but enough of me remains to bear witness. Donaldson looks at Montgomery again. "Does he understand?"

"Eddie," says Montgomery. "Is it you, or—"

"Eddie's done. He's out."

"Now you're talking?" Donaldson humphs. "What's that mean: Eddie's done?"

"Tom," says Dr. Montgomery. "This is Pär. He's Eddie's alter."

"Eddie can't take this kind of shit," Pär tells the detective. "Too anxious. Ask me anything."

"All right. *Pear.* Like the fruit?" With a slight smile.

"P-Ä-R," he clarifies. "I'm Swedish."

Donaldson's eyebrows work together now, checking us out like, *We both know there's no way you're Swedish, pal.*

"You were on the northbound platform?" he says. "Waiting for the uptown train?"

"Downtown. Southbound."

"Southbound?"

"Southbound."

"Are you sure?"

"Never more so," Pär says. "Southbound. Or wait—perhaps it *was* the northbound. So hard to distinguish."

Donaldson exhales hard. "Wiseass. And you were there with Lucy?"

"Eddie was."

From the inside, I take in this exchange, trying to put facts together. Hope pries open the door to my consciousness a crack. The rest of the interrogation is like a dream for me, as Detective Donaldson presses and probes, attempting to find out the whereabouts of Lucy Rivkin, last seen by Edward B. Asher. *Has* she a whereabouts? Hope waxes, wanes, waxes again as Pär plays with them both. Though I don't understand the game, it sets me to thinking: Is there a chance that I am not a murderer but simply a fucking idiot? If Lucy was on the southbound platform when—

"What happened next?" Donaldson says after jotting down a note.

Pär winks at him, singing, "A peanut sat on the railroad track."

"Pär." Caution in Montgomery's tone.

"Her heart was all a flutter."

"We'd like to speak to Eddie again, if possible."

For effect, Pär shakes the arm straps. "The six-oh-nine came roaring in!"

"Pär—"

"*Toot toot!* Peanut butter!"

Pär adds verses, singing into my ears, drowning out Montgomery. The doctor's voice is just a hum at first, thin lips playing a backbeat to Pär's senseless solo. At last Montgomery hits his limit.

"Eddie!" he says. "Eddie Asher! Please come out and address us! *Eddie!*"

He startles Pär, who blinks. My eyes open.

"Eddie?"

I did it. I overrode him. Victorious, despite the circumstances, I write, *"Yes."*

Now Donaldson holds up a photograph.

"Eddie, do you recognize this woman?"

I shake my head no. She's white, older; midforties, maybe. Blond.

"Are you sure, Eddie?" says Montgomery.

Donaldson shares with me that this is a photograph of the woman who died on the northbound IRT tracks the night Lucy and I disappeared.

"Is she at all familiar?"

I shake my head no, certain that she's not. Then he places the photo in my hands, at which point I take a closer look. There is something about her face that I know: her unmistakable Scandinavian jaw.

46.
PÄR

I remember that Scandinavian jaw when it was taut with the spring of youth. She was seventeen by the time she delivered two tiny boys.

Turn back your lens, now open it wide inside the Saint Vincent's maternity ward on the sixteenth of March in 1966. There they were, Britta's twins, in matching caps and blankets, lying side by side in their plastic basinet. Their wounds were dressed in sterile gauze. They'd grow up knowing nothing about their scars, how they'd once been connected by a hunk of organic tissue. (I have no medical training per se, but my personal theory is that the aforesaid tissue was all that remained of a third embryo that had expired early in gestation, linking the two who lived. Though my body would never grow to be sustainable, my consciousness persevered, observing, opining, ultimately developing the capacity to drift at will from one twin to the other.) The doctor who separated the twins was so skilled that she was able to sever, cauterize, and seal things off in just over two hours, all the while chatting to her team about the extreme rarity of these twins.

Britta's boys were likely semi-identical, the obstetrician surmised, based on the fact that they shared a placenta, shared an amniotic sac, but differed physically. Semi-identical twins, the doctor told the nurses, the assisting resident, and the interns in her tutelage, occurred when one egg was fertilized by two sperm. The egg split, as with normal identical twins, prior to the twelfth day of gestation but grew into a pair with identical DNA from the mother and fraternal DNA from the father. (While there is some skepticism among the obstetrics research community as to whether this phenomenon was even possible, I assure you that it is.) Britta was asked to sign papers giving permission to study her boys as they grew. She declined.

In the meantime, the boys lay together, tiny fingers intertwined, faces touching, pink cheek against brown. That's right. One of the twins was a bit smaller, darker. He did not favor our tall, raw-boned Nordic mother. Nor did the paler one, but it was too early for Britta to see that. All our mother could see was that one of the boys was as pink as her own breast, the other brown.

"Amazing how different they look," murmured the nurses. "Amazing how they cling to one another."

If one of them was picked up, the other fussed until his twin was returned. Only together were they perfectly at peace. But Britta, young, alone, and frightened, made a desperate choice. She gave both twins strong, proud Swedish names: Anders and Pär Lindberg. Then Britta signed a paper provided by a social worker and left the hospital with Anders only.

Pär was alone at this point—not yet Eddie, the name the Ashers would give him, but Pär, the name Britta provided, the one I would keep for myself. When Britta and Anders exited the scene, I hid out at the site of Eddie's wound. He was failing to thrive by this time. The confiscation of one twin from the other, the amputation of half the self, compounds the shock of birth, which left their souls cracked apart and bleeding. I was glad, at the time, that I'd remained with him.

About Anders, I can only tell you what I know, beginning in the lobby of the pediatric diet doctor and the dentist whose offices were under the same roof as Dr. Glenda Lloyd's. Dave and Glenda's indecent exposure led to the chaos in which Dominique and Joanne each grabbed the wrong twin. Anders (whom the Wynters liked to call "Andy") took little interest in the kissing couple but certainly did notice the other boy when the women had exchanged them once again. (Here I'd made my jump, as you recall.) Eddie's build and face were familiar, similar to the image Anders saw each day in the mirror. He noticed too that the boy was brown whereas his mother and brother were not, suggesting adoption. Anders who, at this point did not know he had a twin, nevertheless smiled at the other boy. Eddie—né Pär—did not smile back or appear to notice Anders at all. Before Anders could give the boy another thought, the middle Wynter sister, Sophia, squeezed his hand, reminding him where they were going: the dentist. Anders usually went to see doctors and dentists in Sweden, where the health care was excellent and free for children, but it had been some time since he'd visited his mother's country. There might be drilling, Sophia warned him. And the other boy, Eddie, slipped from Anders's radar.

By the end of that first summer with the Wynter family, it was clear that Anders's talent was worthy of a full-year scholarship at the WynterDance academy. Britta had given permission for the Wynters to enroll him at the Lincoln Schoolhouse, a "K to 12" school for child performers, where his tuition was covered by a Pell Grant and an anonymous benefactress who had observed him in dance classes.

Though Britta managed to attend the end-of-summer recital, she had declined a job offer from Tyrone and Dominique, which would have allowed her to move to the city and live in a decent rent-controlled apartment with her son.

Then Anders learned that Britta planned to return to Sweden—the place I'd seen in Anders's memory, with the blue-and-yellow house, the crystal lake, and curious women.

"Of course you will visit," Britta promised him over the phone. She had called the Wynters to finalize arrangements. "On holidays. And for midsommar. But you will get to live with the Wynters and dance to your heart's content." Anders could imagine the shape her lips and chin made when decisions were final, protest futile.

"How fortunate you are, Anders," Britta told him, "to have found a place where you belong so well. It is best for everyone."

Anders handed the phone back to Dominique. He would not let his mother hear him cry.

Before her departure, Britta summoned him back to the mountain house to spend a week together before the start of his school year. This visit would change Anders forever, while also returning me to Eddie.

Britta had left him alone in the mountain house one evening. One of her several jobs was as a waitress at a local tavern. Being alone in the dark did not frighten Anders as it would have Eddie. Anders was accustomed to the mountain house and the way it creaked, echoing the snapping of twigs and swaying of branches in the wind outside. On this night, in a mood to explore, Anders let himself into his mother's closet and pulled out a trunk where she kept old clothes and trinkets from her past. Here he found a collection of news clippings detailing the circumstances of his birth, including the existence of a twin brother who was left behind. He had a brother! A twin brother, who was someplace in the world without him. Anders was deeply shaken but also, in some small way, relieved. The absence of his twin explained the persistent loneliness that went beyond his lifelong wish for a father.

"I have a brother," Anders said aloud to himself. "A twin brother. Who is my twin brother? Where is my twin brother?" He studied how his mouth felt when he said, *My twin brother*, emphasizing *my* as he claimed the anonymous other boy as his own. They belonged together, but Britta had left Anders's twin. How could she have done it? How could she have left her own baby? How could she have deprived Anders of his twin?

With his face moist with tears, Anders drew a bath for himself and stripped off his clothes. It was all he could think of to undo the anger, confusion, and longing: to be immersed naked, in a warm bath.

As he lowered himself into the tub, sinking down beneath the surface, Anders shut his eyes. He challenged himself to return to a time so long ago that he could not possibly remember it. But I remembered. Anders pressed and pressed on his eyes until his inner vision spun with sparkling colored lights. Through these, I could see what he wanted to see. It came back slowly, the feeling of a second heart beating in rhythm with mine, the sense of being whole. And when Anders opened his eyes, which were my eyes now, we both saw another face gazing down at him. I knew just who it was even if Anders didn't know his name: *Eddie!* Anders's twin was none other than Eddie Asher. I'd grasped it on a preconscious level—the reason I had landed on Anders of all the other boys in the world—but that was the moment I knew for certain. Had I not been immersed, I might have cried tears of relief and joy. Eddie, my Eddie!

We blinked again, all of us, Anders, Eddie, and I. In perfect tandem. And when our eyes opened, I was looking down, not up. I was back with Eddie. Home, but not safe, far from it. Robert's hands were on him, holding him beneath the surface. Eddie had already released the bubbles and needed air by now. He struggled. Then I, regaining some authority, struggled too. We splashed and kicked until we couldn't any longer. We were losing the fight to keep our lungs closed when Joanne must have burst into the bathroom. Her scream was muffled by the water. Robert pulled us out, played it off like he'd caught Eddie doing something crazy again. Joanne hugged both her boys and thanked God that Robert had heard the splashing in time to save his little brother. Eddie was never the wiser. I didn't want him to be.

But as I returned to Eddie, I could hear Britta's voice back in the mountain house: "Anders! What are you doing?"

I couldn't hear Anders's response, but I imagine he confronted Britta about his lost twin. I believe that she confessed only what she wanted him to know.

47.

PÄR

Once he'd learned about Eddie, Anders felt his brother's absence in some small part of every breath. Anders, always empathetic by nature, bestowed upon others—the Wynter family, Lucy, his friends Ivan and Rudy—the overspill of love he could not share with his missing twin.

Did it hurt me, you might wonder, that neither boy ever gave a thought to the missing triplet? Or so much as learned that there *was* a missing triplet? Absolutely it did! How could it not hurt? I'm human, for the most part. Jealousy, resentment, frustration—these emotions have always been my lifeblood, fueling my interventions when I couldn't tolerate plain old observation. While Eddie, as you know, was my primary vessel, in time I learned I had access to Anders as well. Curiosity regularly drew me to him.

I recognized that I breathed more easily when my brothers maintained their distance from one another. My nemesis was New York City, a place where each twin could blend in with the crowds and noise and traffic, but where strangers were thrown together in all manner of places. Where twins who did not know each other could wind up face-to-face without warning.

And did the Ashers ever cross paths with the Wynters again after the incident in that fateful office lobby? Oh, certainly they did! There must have been dozens of occasions where Eddie and Anders *almost* noticed one another but for a hasty maneuver on my part, when I turned one twin's head away or gave the other a sense that he'd forgotten something he needed to return home for. There was the time at the Hayden Planetarium, where Anders and Eddie were three rows apart viewing the sky show. When a particularly grand meteor hurtled toward the audience, Eddie screamed as if he were being stabbed, kept screaming until his mortified father hustled him out. Everyone in the auditorium, including Tyrone, who had brought Anders, Lucy, and Althea, turned to stare. In the darkness the culprit's features were impossible to make out.

There was the day when Althea and Sophia, along with Anders, had appointments with an ophthalmologist at around the same time as the Asher boys. The older children, Sophia and Robert, were taken first, leaving Althea, Anders, and Eddie behind in the waiting area. The twins, without so much as glancing at one another, sat side by side, wordlessly sharing the only children's magazine on the rack—a dog-eared copy of *Ranger Rick*. (Neither twin was a quick reader, each boy's lagging impulse to turn the page in sync with the other's.)

I wonder if you can imagine how thrilling yet how taxing and painful these near misses were for me. The pull between the twins was more powerful than I. But while I had no body of my own, no independent existence, I did have agency.

After the bathtub incident, when I returned to Eddie following our first separation, I possessed new insights and a brand-new skill: twin-hopping. During periods of relative calm for Eddie, when I could afford to take respite with Anders, I did not literally hop—being physically unequipped—but only *wished*—very, very hard, with all my heart. (See, once again, *The Wizard of Oz*. Like Dorothy, I'd always had the power, I just had to learn it for myself.)

As I gained knowledge of Anders, I understood that things weren't always easy for him. Despite his talent and *joie de vivre*, he was as haunted by the severance as Eddie was. And now that he understood the source of his loneliness, it became his mission to cure it by molding himself to fit wherever he was. He did this in Sweden under the gaze of the initially skeptical Mormor, whose heart he won. He did it with the Wynter family, whose rules, customs, and banter he learned quickly, whose Blackness he absorbed and made his own.

Anders's methods worked, as noted, on everyone but Lucy, who alternately ignored, taunted, and abused him at first. None of it dimmed his adoration for her. The feeling was not romantic. He had known for a while that girls didn't, and wouldn't, interest him in that way. But he could sense Lucy's pain to the point where it became another mission of his to heal her. Anders longed to become her brother, her confidant, her truest friend.

One evening when they were teenagers, Anders succeeded. He stepped out onto the terrace to take in a glorious twilit Central Park, only to find Lucy perched on the railing, arms spread in anticipation of flight. Terrified, Anders crept up behind her, silently, stealthily, so as not to startle her. He grabbed her hips, pulling her into him like in pas de deux class, falling back with her onto the concrete of the terrace. He held her as she sobbed. Then finally she spoke, telling Anders what had happened five years earlier, how she'd found her mother's hanging body, along with a note that broke poor Lucy's soul. Anders listened and, when Lucy allowed it—and she did allow it this once—he rocked her as his mother used to hold and rock him (as Eddie would hold and rock Lucy many years later when she'd tell him the same story). Anders told Lucy that she was good and worthy and that her mother had made a big, horrible, abominable mistake. Lucy allowed herself to be comforted. And finally, she did love and trust Anders, who, by then, knew her best.

It occurred to Anders that sharing a confidence of his own, the story of his missing brother, might be the ace in the hole that would seal his bond with Lucy. So, the following Saturday morning as they walked together to the dance studios, Anders allowed his own story to come forth.

"I have a secret too," he told Lucy.

She glanced at him, then rolled her eyes. "Everyone already knows."

"They do?"

"You're gay. Duh."

Anders stopped walking, digesting this. He didn't know everyone knew he was gay. Nor did he know how to feel just then, though it seemed that most of the boys in the level above his at WynterDance were gay and out. WynterDance, Anders knew, was a safe place to be out, though the rest of the world was anything but. It wasn't just that people called you names on the street, not just the threatening looks from certain men on the subway trains, but also the illness that was circulating, the blame and fear that followed it.

"That's not my secret," Anders said.

"Good," said Lucy, taking his arm and leading them onward so as not to be late. "Because it's not a secret." There was a bite to her tone, begrudging tolerance to cover her disgust. Anders felt it and was briefly ashamed. Hastening to keep up with Lucy's near-trot, he felt the story of his lost twin burning hotter than ever. As if sharing it would erase Lucy's disdain and win her esteem.

"There's another secret," he said. "A real one."

She was really trotting by then, interested only in getting to class— regular ballet technique that morning, which Lucy favored over modern and jazz.

"Lucy, I'm trying to tell you something!" Anders was panting, getting angry now. He didn't expect her—or anyone—to care the way he cared, but he did hope for some reciprocity.

"I don't want you to," she said. "Obviously."

Anders stopped, shocked, letting Lucy race ahead while he plodded after her. *Why not?* He didn't get to ask her this until later, when they were walking home together. She'd tried to dodge him, to leave on her own, but Anders had dressed quickly, barely wiping the sweat from his back before putting on his dry sweatshirt. He'd dashed out of the boys' dressing room to lie in wait for Lucy in the vestibule. She slipped out, then sighed with irritation as she registered his footfalls beside her.

"What?" she said.

"Why don't you want me to tell you my secret? You told me about your mother. Let me tell you about—"

"No!" Lucy's petulant stance shifted to one of pleading, her shoulders sagging slightly. "If you tell me, it will ruin everything."

"What will it ruin?"

She placed one hand over her heart as if to hold herself together. "The other day I was such a mess. I needed to tell someone about my mom, about finding her, about the note. It was tearing me up, like . . . *eating* at me.

"Andy, when you cried too, I knew it was okay, that the secret was out of me and you could share the pain."

"I wanted to," he said. "That's what friends do."

"I know," she said. "And now I can be free of it, at least sometimes, because you know it too."

"You can do the same thing for me." As Anders said this, it dawned on him: a friendship with Lucy went one way only. The friend did what friends do, and Lucy got that thing done for her.

"No I can't," Lucy told him. "I'm too messed up to deal with anyone else's pain."

Anders could see the truth of this in her eyes, which had a deadness to them, less shine in the brown than other people's. They were like shark eyes. Unblinking, flat, despite their wide, lovely shape. Anders felt what he'd felt the other day when he pulled her from the railing: a vacancy to Lucy. She faked it well, but her soul, he thought, was missing.

"Besides," she said, removing the hand from her chest, taking his so that they could walk again. "You have a mother who is alive."

Anders did not see how this was relevant but didn't argue.

Lucy said, "You have a whole other country you belong to. You even speak Swedish."

As if that absolved him of need. The story of his brother faded back inside him. Anders held his tongue, held her hand, and allowed himself to be pulled across Broadway.

So you see that I had certain bricks and blocks of Anders's history, just as Eddie had of his own. For me, the whole experience was a bit of a pendulum ride. While I largely controlled my own hops from twin to twin, I was often indecisive and made poor choices. If Eddie was having a reasonably tranquil period, as in high school, I might drift to Anders. But as Anders experienced distress, my heart—which was technically the heart in Eddie's chest—would ache for Anders yet manifest for Eddie as an inexplicable sorrow or worry. I would then be drawn back to Eddie and subsequently would miss the next crucial event in Anders's life.

It was difficult to keep track of both twins, which I knew I'd need to do in order to control when, whence, and whether they were to reunite.

48.

PÄR

In the fall of 1984, the twins and I were eighteen. I was residing with Eddie, who was away from home for the first time, enrolled at Rutgers-Newark, attempting to reinvent himself, determined to make Black friends. With access to a swimming pool and a powerful new anxiety drug (which would later be recalled due to patients experiencing disorientation), Eddie was remarkably stable, given the circumstances. I was hence ripe for exploration.

It was late September when I detected an odd but not unpleasant stirring that came neither from myself nor from Eddie. Though each twin had experienced a number of unrequited crushes, both were late bloomers in terms of dating and sex. Therefore, I could not name the sensation "sexual desire," though I would soon know to define it as such. In any case, curiosity enticed me away to Anders.

Anders and Lucy—who was then nineteen—were both full-time ensemble members of the WynterDance company. Anders received his diploma from Lincoln Schoolhouse in June and deferred college. Lucy was enrolled in a correspondence program at Barnard that allowed professional dancers to matriculate without having to miss rehearsals. Carlo himself was twenty-four, which made him seem worldly to Lucy and

Anders, along with the fact that he was Italian and referred to the two of them collectively as *bambini*.

Lucy and Anders were far from the only company members smitten. No one was immune, not even, Anders suspected, Tyrone himself. Carlo did not have a handsome face exactly, but his bearing was romantic, inviting Anders's eyes to linger on his prominent chin and strong neck, his sloping shoulders and powerful arms. With the intimate tenor of his laugh, the casual flick of his cigarettes, the easy way he would sweep a lock of hair, either his own or that of a companion, behind an ear, Carlo represented for Anders (and me as well) the magical enterprise of love. On those rare occasions where he was the object of Carlo's attention, Anders wanted both to soar along with his heart and to hide before he could say or do anything dumb.

Carlo's hair was long and golden brown like his skin. He wore stud earrings in both his ears—glyphs to be interpreted. According to current lore, one in the right ear meant you were straight, one in the left meant gay. Two meant you were toying with everyone who might be interested. But one older dancer suggested that the earring rules were different in Europe, that they meant the reverse of what they meant here in the United States. Someone else argued that there was no stigma at all about earrings or sexuality in Europe, that everyone was bi and cool about it. There was a continuum, and earrings had nothing to do with who you were into.

Regardless. The earrings, the cigarettes, the way Carlo was not fastidious like Americans when it came to grooming, the way he allowed his unfettered natural scent to permeate the nostrils of others, the confidence he had in his presence—it was all one big aphrodisiac to Anders, to his friends, to Lucy.

Anders doubted that anyone saw or knew the real Carlo Giannini. Maybe the other dancers ascribed romantic traits to him based on foreign films they'd seen, based on their stereotypes of European men who danced and smoked and gazed romantically with heads tilted to the side. But Anders believed that there was more to Carlo.

On a walk home to The Majestic, Anders mused to Lucy, taking a risk, "Everyone's in love with the idea of Carlo, but I want to know the real guy." Showing his cards, trusting her with his heart, a risk which usually came back to bite him.

"Please, Andy," Lucy said with a suggestive laugh. "*I* already know the real guy. Intimately."

Lucy was winning, like usual, leaving Anders to wonder what she had experienced of Carlo—*with* Carlo—that he had not. Somehow it got back to Carlo, news of the dualling affections of Lucy and Anders—the *bambini*. The Italian dancer was flattered, amused, ultimately enticed. Then his living arrangement, at an artist's residence, fell through because of a lie someone told—that there were just three people living in the two-bedroom apartment rather than six, Carlo being one of those excised due to his lack of citizenship. Tyrone invited Carlo, who did have an artists' visa, to live in the penthouse on Central Park West. Regina and Sophia had grown up and vacated their rooms by then. Dominique and Althea were living temporarily in Paris, where the former was guest teaching and the latter was studying. Both Lucy and Anders were delighted by the new arrival, though each secretly feared Carlo preferred the other.

How could Anders win against an opponent as fearsome as Lucy? Her heart seemed encapsulated in a shell resistant to breaks beyond the one it had already suffered. But the main reason she would win is that ballet was on her side. The WynterDance repertoire still included some classical pieces at the time. These all seemed to feature gallant young men and fragile young women, the "gentlemen" supporting the "ladies" like ornamental poles and shimmering flags. A girl standing alone on pointe drew a cavalier to her side to proffer a shoulder to balance on, strong arms to lift her skyward, showing her off, embellishing her decorative femininity. What could Anders possibly do to compete? Absolutely nothing, unless you counted standing against the barre, looking bitter and forlorn as he watched them dance—Lucy, his rival, and Carlo, his desired—eyes never leaving one another's faces. The fact that it was part of the choreography made it sting no less. Add the most indulgent strains of Tchaikovsky and Prokofiev, buoying their lifts and dips, their pirouettes and promenades. Anders had lost. To save his heart from breaking entirely, he did what he was best at and took on the role of devoted ally to each party.

Until one night when Lucy had a late rehearsal for a piece that a delightful new feminist choreographer was setting on all the women of WynterDance. Anders was invited by Carlo and some of the other guys to a bar they knew in the Village. Anders was underage because New York's drinking laws had just switched to twenty-one, but no one checked. The group ordered drinks with confidence, so Anders did too. Upstairs, the place was a dive with a rundown billiards table, but down-stairs, if you were admitted—which of course the dancers were—there was dancing and cocaine, if you knew who to ask. Anders was too scared to partake of the latter, but he drank and danced, enjoying the attention of the older company members, including Carlo. As the other patrons recognized the talent in their midst, they cleared the floor, becoming an audience to take in the virtuosity, the aesthetic glory, of the professional dancers, some of whom were shirtless by then, displaying their enviable physiques.

Despite the strict—dare I say flagrant?—hetero vibe he exuded around Lucy and the other women of WynterDance, Carlo was clearly, just as easily, in his element here. He was performing for everyone but—Was it true? Could it possibly be?—the Italian dancer's eyes kept landing on Anders. Anders allowed the alcohol to embolden him and flirted—not with Carlo, but with everyone else, calling attention to himself, presenting himself as unavailable only to the one he'd set his sights on.

Nothing transpired between them at the bar, but they went home together. Of course they did. They *lived* together, a fact that had cheered Anders throughout the evening. On the subway ride home they engaged in drunken, giggling flirtation. Laughing at the looks they got from other passengers, laughing at themselves, at one another. They leaned in close when they spoke, alcohol blurring any boundaries left between them. Only one sober moment struck Anders on the journey. A man stepped onto their car at Fiftieth Street, looking impossibly pale and impossibly thin—not muscular-dancer thin, but an eerie, unwell thin, characteristic of the disease. The man's body crumpled into a seat as people nearby cowered, giving him the widest of berths despite his taking up so little physical space. There were lesions on his exposed white arm, purple, some yawning. There was one on the side of his neck. Anders shuddered, heart racing, feeling Carlo's breath again, close, so close.

Anders had read that you could not catch it from breathing the same air. You could not catch it by touch, by sharing a seat, or by rubbing past someone on the subway. Only by the exchange of bodily fluids. But people feared for themselves irrationally. Anders did too. When the ailing man's eyes met his, Anders looked away. He felt the dread in his heart. But then Carlo elbowed him gently. Anders remembered how precious the older dancer's attention was, how rare were their moments together free of Lucy.

When they arrived back at the penthouse, it was after two in the morning. The place was dark but for the lights out on the balcony. Lucy's and Tyrone's bedroom doors were shut, no light glimmering from beneath. Even the now-aged dachshund Foxtrot was nowhere to be seen. Anders and Carlo fell together onto the sectional sofa opposite the mirrored wall of the Wynters' makeshift dance studio. Anders floated on a cloud made of love and booze, tingling at Carlo's every touch, relishing his weight, his smells, the way his eyes drank him in. Anders could not pinpoint what it was about how Carlo looked at him. Was it gratitude? The older dancer's gaze made Anders feel special and central, like a gift Carlo was accepting. It was a heady, heart-racing thing.

As they said good night, before heading off to sleep for a few precious hours before company class, Carlo held Anders by the shoulders and demanded a promise of absolute secrecy.

"No one can know, Andy. Understand?" His eyes were not adoring then; they were forbidding and dangerous. Anders was aware of their size difference, of Carlo's dominant position in the company, his own lack of status once again. Of course, Anders promised him. He'd tell no one.

And in the morning, just like every other day at the studio, Carlo had eyes only for Lucy and the other female dancers, as if Anders didn't exist. When the three of them walked home to the penthouse together, Carlo walked between them but attended exclusively to Lucy, holding her hand, suggestively bumping her hip while they waited at the crosswalk. Anders had to be content with an occasional surreptitious glance.

On the other hand, if it was a day where Lucy had a late rehearsal, Carlo and Anders walked alone together. As often as not, they'd join the group of company men as they headed downtown to bars. Carlo's manner toward Anders changed, becoming solicitous, his glances lingering. With alcohol in their systems, Carlo claimed him, affection washing away all of Anders's doubts until sunrise brought them flooding back.

And one night, Lucy caught them together. It was very, very late, and the boys, confident that no one else was up, landed on the sofa again—inebriated, unfettered, entwined. All at once, Lucy was there, slim form illuminated by moonlight through the balcony windows. Carlo saw her first, then Anders matched her stare. She betrayed no pain or anger. Only contempt, calculation.

49.

PÄR

Over the next days and weeks, it became clear: how Lucy would exact vengeance, how she would destroy Anders—her erstwhile friend and sidekick, now her rival—how she would win. And Lucy's kind of winning, Anders had always suspected but now learned without a shadow of doubt, did not require a soul, only a will.

He didn't suspect it was Lucy's doing at all initially. It was subtle at first, but Anders felt it in the atmosphere of the studio, the looks he got from the other company dancers—compassionate, pitying, in some cases judgmental. People kept their distance from him as much as possible, giving him more space than he needed when it was time to line up for across-the-floor *enchaînements* in company class. When choreography required closeness or touch, Anders noted that people seemed to wipe their hands as soon as the music ended.

He heard whispering cease when he drew near, saw the clandestine stares in the studio's mirrored wall. But the most obvious difference was in the behavior of Carlo, to whom—it appeared—Anders had ceased to exist.

Carlo no longer walked between Anders and Lucy on the way from the penthouse to the studios behind Lincoln Center. He no longer made furtive eye contact with Anders in the studio. On the rare occasions when their eyes did meet, Carlo's were cold. He no longer waited for Anders to walk home or ride to the Village on the nights when Lucy had a late rehearsal. In fact, he was more likely to stay and watch Lucy dance from the chairs posted just inside the studio doorway.

From the start of their relationship—such as it was, and Anders now wondered whether it had been such at all—Anders had never sought out Carlo but had waited to be approached. He'd never gone to the bars in the Village without an invitation from the older dancer. And now that Carlo no longer accompanied the other company men downtown, Anders remained available but was not sought out by anyone. He had been disinvited from his life yet had no idea of what he'd done. To counter the sense of invisibility, Anders took to dying his hair—red, blond, purple, a different color each month when the company was not performing. Anything to give people a reason to look at him.

Finally Ivan, a friend from Anders's first days of training at the academy, who was drafted into the company along with Lucy and Anders, shed light on what had happened.

"Is it true, Andy?" Ivan asked Anders as they stretched opposite one another at the portable barre in the center of the studio before company class. "Do you have it?"

So Anders knew. What people were whispering, why they recoiled from him, why Carlo was suddenly repulsed by the sight of him. He could feel his face grow hot with shame and fear. But why? Granted, being in constant competition for parts and promotions enhanced the collective tendency toward pettiness and gossip at WynterDance, but to start a cruel rumor? Especially one about the illness ransacking the dance world, robbing them all of friends, partners, mentors? It was worse than inflicting physical harm on a rival, worse than the old legends of competing ballerinas who snuck glass into one another's pointe shoes. How could this have happened? Who would have done such a thing?

Anders told Ivan, no, of course he didn't have it. He told anyone who asked the same thing, the truth. The trouble is that few people asked.

Only Lucy, of all people, swooped in to play Anders's savior during these trying days of denying the lie, of being doubted. She became his confidante—finally—his champion, providing uncharacteristic affirmations when Anders felt most alone and friendless.

Lucy suggested that Ivan or another of Anders's fellow junior members of the company might have started the rumor out of jealousy.

"There's no one else who has anything to gain," she said. Which got too close. Of course Lucy had the most to gain. She'd outed herself by wording it thus, bringing back to Anders's mind something Althea had told him years earlier when he first moved into the Wynter home. *Lucy's fun but watch out. She'll get you.* Now Anders wished he'd asked Althea what to watch out for before it was too late.

He knew now. To watch out for Lucy would have meant anticipating what might have angered her or threatened her place in the company, in her father's favor, in Carlo's arms. Anders could not confront her. He could not accuse her of causing his pain. Instead, he did what he could to stay on her good side—watching out for her after the fact—because at this point, Lucy was his only friend.

She confided in him, head in his lap, arm on his shoulder, offering the only human touch Anders received at that point. She offered intimacies about her romance with Carlo, which burned hot and bright before exploding into bitter conflict. Each word she uttered was a shard of glass in his heart.

Soon Carlo moved out, making it less painful for Anders to be in the penthouse, which was just lonely and quiet then, in the absence of the other girls and Dominique. Anders had endured loneliness before, back in the Berkshire Mountains, but that was before he'd found his home in the world of dance, in the multihued society of fellow artists in the busy, bustling panoramic city. To be ostracized here was excruciating.

When the rumor about Anders's condition reached Tyrone Wynter himself, sorrow overtook the Maestro. He thought of Anders, his Andy, this beloved would-be son of his, being terminally ill, wasting away. But

Tyrone considered the plague now present in his home—the intimacy of it, the closeness, along with the potential sloughing off of infected cells. Was it safe? Tyrone did not know if he could tolerate the uncertainty.

Tyrone mustered his nerve and invited Anders to breakfast one Sunday morning. When the older man gently pressed Anders on the merits of this rumor he had heard, the boy stammered his response. Rage and anguish made Anders's voice shake as he denied the charge, but it was the shaking, not the cause, that Tyrone observed. The dance master could not help doubting his young ward.

And, though Tyrone was loving as he questioned him, Anders registered the care with which his host helped himself from the breadbasket, touching only the side that Anders had not touched, using a napkin to handle the shared cream pitcher to lighten his coffee. Normally tactile and physically affectionate, Tyrone refrained from any such contact with Anders that morning.

In the following weeks and months, though Anders exhibited no symptoms, neither lesions nor evidence of wasting, though the rumor was slowly dispelled, there was no return to the way things were. Though Ivan believed him and made a show of embracing him at length to demonstrate his loyalty and support, Anders could not trust anyone else at WynterDance, could never feel the same love from Tyrone, could never feel safe in his body within the mirrored studio walls.

Though Carlo apologized, wholeheartedly, yet without specifying for what, Anders would never feel the thrill in the Italian dancer's embrace again. Lucy never confessed to starting the rumor.

When audition season arrived, Anders made the full rounds, presenting his polished best technique, elevation, and musicality. And as national dance companies were always hungering for talented males with excellent muscle tone, narrow waists and sloping shoulders, elegant feet and lovely facial bones—the offers came. Anders accepted a contract with Hubbard Street Dance, a prestigious contemporary company in Chicago, where he knew no one.

Britta and her sister Anna visited to help Anders find a modest, clean apartment, helped him furnish it in crisp Swedish style. Anders enjoyed being part of the new ensemble company and remembered himself free of shame. His kindness, his empathy, his gift for being loved. He was as happy as he could imagine being, though his heart still ached when he thought of Carlo and Lucy, of the Wynter family, to whom he was now lost.

As years passed, Anders pivoted toward choreography. He left Hubbard Street in favor of a smaller ensemble dance company, for which he created works with political themes, focused largely around the AIDS crisis. Anders maintained tabs on Lucy, Carlo, and the Wynters the best he could by reading the dance pages of the New York newspapers he bought. He stayed in touch with Ivan on and off and listened to relevant gossip of the dancers in his new company, many of whom had connections to WynterDance members. Anders was thus able to splice together the subsequent chapter of Lucy and Carlo's story.

Tyrone, having learned of Lucy and Carlo's passionate romance, which caused pain for both and distraction from their dancing, schemed to terminate the relationship. Apparently the Maestro had considered firing Carlo, but the Italian soloist sold too many tickets to dispense with. Instead, it was Lucy he encouraged to leave. Operating under the belief that she would benefit from being on her own in a new environment, free from Daddy's influence, Tyrone arranged a private audition for his daughter before the artistic directors of the Pacific Northwest Ballet, who readily accepted her into the corps de ballet. Given that even classical ballet companies were by this time subject to the EEOC's new requirements for diversifying, hiring a Black female dancer (who was pale enough to wash out completely under stage lights) was to their benefit.

In Seattle, alone for the first time but for a sweet Persian cat named Feather, Lucy feared for her future. She remembered the wisdom of her late mother, who had admonished her: "Don't do what I did. Don't lose your head over a man who's a star. Find someone safe. Marry a Jewish doctor who is kind and will take care of you. You don't have to love him. Passion is overrated."

And, as you know by now, coincidence had Lucy reconnecting with Robert Asher, a former Columbia University boy she'd toyed with back in New York. Robert, as you'll recall, had just begun his residency at UDub and would ultimately bring us full circle to Eddie, the twin not taken, the twin mistaken—for the first time in his life, though certainly not the last—for Andy Lindberg, the brother he'd never heard of.

50.

PÄR

Hence, the threads connect. The dust begins to clear, revealing a path from one twin to the other, from Chicago, Illinois, to the Hudson Valley Psychiatric Hospital in Olana, New York. But what of me? Will I be better served by keeping them apart or letting them find one another? While I still have the power of action, how will I decide? On one hand, the prospect of rapprochement appeals to me. What if I could merge with—truly merge as opposed to borrow—one or both of them, enjoy a life more realized than what I have now? On the other hand, I have to credit their separation for my very existence. Isn't it true that I would not be here (where?) at all if our mother had raised them both? If Anders and Eddie had grown up in one another's company, there would have been no need for a vibrant strand of connective consciousness. Because Britta's boys would not have been "Andy and *Eddie*" at all, but "Anders and *Pär*." There would have been no Eddie. Only Pär—his original self, which could not be me.

Contemplating this alternative beginning disturbs me. *Not being* would be a huge load off. But since things went the way they went— and since I frankly *am*—what would reunion mean for me but an excruciating termination?

So it becomes clear what I want, what I need to do: live. The quest for survival at all costs is also natural—even for the noncorporeal among us. And yet, what is natural for me runs counter to nature itself, which will not rest until the brothers are returned to one another. The question being: With only *nurture* on my side—the power to mess with Eddie's will—am I any match for *nature*, the force drawing them together?

Only time will tell.

⁀

Now, doubtless, you're wondering: What will lead Anders to his twin? How will they meet at last?

It starts with a phone call at night. Anders answers, groggily because he's taken a sleeping pill to combat a bout of insomnia that's been plaguing him lately. It's his aunt Anna, his mother's younger sister, gasping through her tears. Britta is dead.

"She's been killed." Anna sobs. "In New York."

"How?" Anders thinks he's misheard her or that he's dreaming. "My mother would not come to the States without telling me."

Anna's words tumble across the wires, but Anders's Swedish is rusty, and Anna's English is compromised by her hysteria. Anders does not understand until he gets a second phone call from a man who identifies himself as Detective Thomas Donaldson, NYPD.

⁀

Despite my extrapolations about her life, I could never read our birth mother's mind. I don't know what made her travel to the States to search for Eddie—still "Pär" to her—in person, twenty-seven years after leaving us. I'll take a guess, which you know I'm good at. Perhaps it was a loss that led her to New York, seeking to fill a new void in her heart. Her mother had died, that must have been it. (Otherwise, why else would she have come? Why now? And how dare she do it this way?)

In any case, Britta is in New York City. We'll say she's been haunted, since her mother died, by guilty thoughts of her lost son. And how does she find him? Maybe back in Sweden, she hired a detective to learn the last name of the family who adopted the boy. She pays the same detective to locate the Ashers: Dave, in Northern California, raising two teenage girls with his second wife; Joanne, residing on the East Side with her second husband, Michael; Robert, who lives on West Seventy-Third Street with his fiancée. Lastly there is Eddie, né Pär, who lives in Brooklyn. So Britta books a hotel room in midtown Manhattan and flies across the sea.

She is not sure she wants to meet him, not sure she has that right. She does not know what he knows, whether he has any idea that there is a twin she chose while leaving him behind. If so, he must resent her. Hate her, even. So be it. Britta resolves to merely study him at first. To learn from a distance what he is like. And maybe then introduce herself, befriending him possibly, if it feels appropriate. Only at this point will she decide whether to reveal herself, her relationship to him. And then, *and then* . . . well, I don't know what. She will see, I suppose, where fate takes them. Britta is not the sort whose eyes will fill with tears as she embraces Eddie, apologizing after all these years. She is not the sort to do much embracing or apologizing of any kind. Unlike her sister Anna, Britta is not versed in the active expression of love. Britta masters her feelings before she feels them, a skill that enabled her to leave each boy: first Pär, in the hospital, and ten years later Anders, in New York with the Wynters.

When she does reconnect with Eddie, Britta imagines she'll share a perfunctory regret or two and then ask how it has been for him all this time. Burning curiosity is what motivates her trip rather than a biological yearning. Perhaps it will be unfair to butt into Eddie's life at this point, but it is something she is compelled to do.

Britta finds him in his Brooklyn neighborhood. She watches him leave his building and walk across the street and around the corner. She watches him return with a large paper cup full of what she decides is coffee. Perhaps he loves coffee as she does, she thinks, with dawning affinity. Britta keeps out of sight. For several days she trails him, keeping her distance, never getting close enough to get a good look at her lost son, but she observes his walk, his build, his posture, like Anders but not. She sees that he's alone, always alone, which makes her wonder: Did she desert him all those years ago to a life of loneliness? But Anders was lonely too, at least until he went to live in New York. It is not leaving Eddie that she feels most guilty about, it is separating the twins. What if she'd left or alternatively taken both?

Britta extends her stay at the hotel.

One evening, our mother considers herself fortunate to be lurking when Eddie leaves his home. She follows him as he walks to the subway station, follows him as he rides into Manhattan. Britta is careful to stay at the other end of the subway car. Eddie has his head down in a book, so she still doesn't get a good look at his face, but she notices how the shape of his forehead, the hairline, is identical to Anders's despite the tighter curl of his hair. She notices the shape of his fingers as he turns a page, long and thin like her Anders's.

She rises when Eddie rises and exits the train at Seventy-Second Street and Central Park West. She follows him north and west to Seventy-Third Street, where he sits on a stoop and stares across the street at the entrance to a building whose address Britta recognizes from the detective's letter—160. It is where Robert lives with his fiancée. Britta conceals herself in a pay-phone shelter on the corner and waits.

It is not long before a young woman emerges from the building wearing a black coat and a decorative green hat with feathers, pulling an elegant suitcase on wheels. Britta sees Eddie's body contract, folding in on itself as if seeking invisibility. The young woman does not appear to notice him. Eddie gives her a head start—about a fourth of the block—then follows her as she steps swiftly away from home. In turn, Britta gives Eddie a fourth of the block and follows him.

The procession takes them to the Seventy-Second Street IRT station on Broadway. Here, Britta mistakenly descends the stairs to the northbound platform, only to discover that Eddie and the young woman are across the tracks on the southbound. No matter. From here Britta is finally able to study her son. She can see how similar he is to Anders. How beautiful. She can imagine Anders beside him, creating a picture of a twindom that should have been. He's arguing with the woman, whom Britta reasons can only be his brother's fiancée; they are doubtless having an affair. In any event, she marvels at the young man's facial expression—the mirror image of Anders's when he has argued with her, the softness of his eyebrows when he is hurt, the way he bites his upper lip and tilts his head.

Britta has a rare and entirely unexpected maternal impulse to go to Eddie, to comfort him, to protect him from this tiny vixen who is clearly in the process of breaking his heart.

At this moment, Eddie glances across the tracks, feeling the power of his mother's stare. And at this same moment, I am seized by a wave of dread and absolute clarity. Britta and Eddie cannot meet. Eddie cannot revisit his origin. For if he does, there will be nothing left to prevent a reunification of my brothers, which may well be the end of me. I am sorry for what I do next, but it cannot be helped.

I take over the body, reaching my arms toward her, meeting her lake-blue eyes for the last time, tears in these brown ones. *Mamma!* I imagine that I love her at this moment, that I love her with this borrowed heart, despite her disgust for our brown skin, despite what she did. She sees me and nothing else as I entice her, *Come to me, Mamma! Here I am!* And—what power I have! To think that Britta's remorse should give me such sway over her mind! I don't know exactly what she sees or which tricks her mind is playing on her, but she steps emphatically in my direction, advancing as if we're separated not by rusted train tracks but by a beautiful sunlit field in Boliden. Arms open, she rushes forth to embrace her lost child.

My eyes are on my mother, but—opportunist that I am—I have the foresight to snatch at Lucy's hat before she dashes off. All I secure are a few feathers, but they'll do. I clutch them in our hand for Eddie to find when he comes back around.

The northbound train arrives a moment before the southbound one. By the time Lucy gets on the latter, continuing her journey to meet Carlo, Britta has leapt onto the tracks to her death. I relinquish the body to Eddie, who returns to himself, disoriented. He is convinced by the feathers that he has done the unthinkable.

At that moment, I believed my act would forever cut the cord between Eddie and Anders. It did not occur to me that the mutual loss would draw them together.

Fuck.

51.

EDDIE

When I open my eyes next, my brother Robert is there, in the single room I occupy now, sitting on the chair beside my bed. My arms are tied up again, for which I blame Pär.

"Hey," he says. It's not a friendly "hey." It's expectant—sarcastic, even. It's a "hey" that means *fuck you.* I don't answer him. "Surprise," Robert says, again with the sarcasm.

I didn't know I was allowed visitors. Who knows he's here? I glance at the monitor in the corner.

"You want to know if I know where she is?" says my brother.

I nod, thinking that this could work if he does the talking for us both.

"I don't." Robert spreads his knees apart, leans forward, like guys do on the subway. Manspreading, Lucy calls it. It's a stance for challenging other men, for intimidating women. Unlike Robert to do either. "Do you?"

I raise my eyebrows as if to say, *Do I what?* Robert is my brother and erstwhile translator. He comprehends.

"I mean do you know where Lucy is?"

I shake my head. I've seen him this pissed off before, but not for a while. Not since we were kids.

"Eddie, what is this bullshit? I found out you were here from some NYPD detective who called you a goddamn mute. Why don't you fucking speak?"

Now I remember Detective Donaldson and the revelation about Lucy. The photograph of the woman who had my Scandinavian jaw and was very much *not* Lucy. I open my mouth, feeling my dry throat crack wide open. Maybe, I think. Maybe now that I know it was not Lucy on the tracks, now that I know myself to *not* be a monster, not be a killer. My vocal cords strain and then: "Sorry." It comes through as a craggy whisper, but it's *sound* in any case, my own voice.

"Sorry?" Robert stomps a foot on the floor so hard, it shakes the room and my bed. I flinch. "So there's something to be sorry for?"

"I didn't push her. They say it wasn't Lucy on the tracks."

"I know it wasn't fucking Lucy on the tracks." My brother shakes his head, rubs his face like he used to do when I exasperated him as a kid. "They told me you were confused."

"I lost time, lapsed again. I don't remember what happened."

"Meaning you don't remember what you were doing in the subway station with Lucy in the first place? And why she had a suitcase?"

I shrug. That part I do know.

"Don't worry—I never thought she was running away with you."

Robert says it derisively, like that would never happen. I find the wherewithal to extend my middle finger, my restraints minimizing the impact.

"The doorman said you were following her. So, you chased her to the subway? Demanded where she was going? Assumed she was taking a trip I didn't know about?"

"Did you?"

"No, dumbass! If I knew where she was going, I'd have looked there."

"Then I guess I'm not the only dumbass, am I?"

My brother pounds his fist against the side of his chair, which makes me flinch again. What if Robert should turn violent while I'm all tied up? Instead he folds his arms, leaning back in the chair.

"I *know*," he says.

"What do you know?"

"What the fuck do you think? I know why you were waiting for her, why you were stalking her. Why you were so quick to help her bury her goddamn cat two years ago. You were in love with her. That's what I know."

"Oh." It's a relief, frankly, to address this. "It wasn't like that. It wasn't *in-love* love; it was more—"

"Shut up, Eddie. I figured it out. Even if I hadn't, Lucy left me a letter the night you both vanished." Robert reaches into his pocket and tosses a folded-up sheet of paper onto my bed. I nod toward my bound hands.

"What does it say?"

"Essentially that you and I are both a pair of fucking dumbasses. That I shouldn't look for her. That you shouldn't either."

I turn my face away. *I'm sorry* is what I mean to say, but Pär swallows the words, whispering in my ear: *He deserves it. Dumbass.*

Robert narrows his eyes, contemplating. "Did you fuck her, Eddie? Did you fuck my fiancée? Or just hallucinate that you killed her?"

"What do you think?" I whisper, but it's loud enough to hear. My brother lands on me and grabs the front of my beige tunic. He's snarling, right up in my face until I force out the words: "I didn't fuck her! I swear!" And he exhales, releasing me.

"Jeez, Eddie." An echo of Lucy. "You could be lying and not even know it. I never know which of your crazy actions you're responsible for and which ones you're not. I only know I hate *her* right now." He gets up and paces, looking just like Dad used to when he and Mom would have their dish-smashing fights. Now Robert lunges at his chair and throws it across the room. His shirt untucks itself, revealing a hirsute swell of abdomen.

"I wouldn't," I say, nodding at the camera. "You could wind up in here with me."

Robert straightens his shirt, reclaiming his dignity. Looks around for and rights the chair, sits.

"So, who is he?"

"Who is who? Oh. The other guy." I can picture him, the Italian, but I can't remember his name. How can I not remember his name?

"Don't fuck with me, Eddie. My fiancée just ran away. That shit happens in old movies, not in real life. Goddamn it!" Robert lands on me again, hands on my throat. "Who the fuck's the other guy, Eddie? Who is he?"

I surprise myself by screaming—more with frustration than fear, or maybe it's Pär screaming, or both of us. Xavier and Jim/John are on my brother in a second.

"Who, Eddie?" Robert says as they drag him away.

"We met him. I can't think of his name," I say as the door closes behind him. "But I know someone who might know."

52.
PÄR

I'm frankly hazy on how it happens, whether Anders reaches out to Althea or vice versa. But why would she? It must be Anders's doing. I'm impervious to the newest medication they're giving Eddie; it's not the pills making me unclear, but the dread.

In any case, Anders and Althea speak. He tells her he is sorry for the loss of her father. He's sorry too that he had to cut her off along with everyone else in the family. Althea is the only one who didn't deserve it. She says she understands. She knows now what happened, how Lucy, and later her parents, betrayed him.

"I wish I'd done something, Andy," Althea says. "Talked sense into them or something. I could have fixed things."

"It was never your fault," he tells her. Then: "Althea, my mother is dead." Before she can offer condolences, he lays it on her. "And I have a brother somewhere, a twin my mother gave up for adoption. I've known since I was a child. He was darker, and she decided she couldn't . . . she kept me but not him. His name was—"

"Stop," says Althea. He can hear in her voice that she's overcome. "Please stop. It's too much now. I can't—" She hangs up.

Althea is a giver, Anders recalls, but not to her own detriment. When she has nothing to give, she retreats, nurses herself, regroups, and replenishes. After a few days, she calls back.

"I know your twin brother," she tells him. "His name is Eddie. Eddie Asher. It has to be."

It's the first time Anders has heard this name. As Althea elaborates, describing Eddie's connection to the family, he breaks down in sobs, sliding down the wall to the floor. "Oh God, he's real!"

Anders tells Althea that he heard from Ivan about the doppelgänger who made a speech at Tyrone's funeral. "I thought it might be him, but it was too much to hope. Eddie? His name is Eddie?"

Anders has only ever thought of his brother as Pär. When he's able to breathe evenly, Anders and Althea put together what they know and contact Robert for assistance, thinking correctly that he might know Eddie's whereabouts.

Althea and Clark meet Anders at the airport when he flies in from Chicago a week later. They will meet Robert at the hospital. There is nothing I can do at this point but observe. I have no agency over which direction I go. My consciousness dances back and forth between the twins without my control. I'm with Eddie, now Anders, now Eddie again. It is to be in flight, hurtling off a skyscraper from which I never intended to leap.

There are limits to the number of visitors Eddie is allowed. Robert has been in already, so Anders, the less volatile brother, is given priority. Robert, Clark, and Althea wait in a lounge downstairs while Xavier escorts Anders to the room where his twin brother awaits.

53.
PÄR

The end of yourself, dying as it were, isn't how you think it will be. At least it's not how I thought it would be for me. The first thing I become aware of is tunnel vision, the room, the world shrinking, moving far, far away. I am on my own moon, orbiting the scene to which I should be an instrumental part. I can hardly see their faces, hear the voices that match in timbre. I can hardly feel their hearts beating in sync at last. It's cruel that, after all these years, I should be robbed of this reunion. Why can't I be there? Don't they need me? From my post, far removed, I have no impact, no capacity to interact.

How I wish I were Anders's fingers as he touches the hair on Eddie's head. Eddie's hair has been touched countless times in his life. But today it's Anders handling it, Anders, whose chestnut eyes are like Eddie's, full of wonder, not scrutiny. I wish I were Eddie's lips as they stretch into a smile, a free, wide smile, characteristic of Anders, not Eddie himself. Such a grin! Unselfconscious, unafraid. For Eddie, that's a coup. And Eddie, being Eddie, defers his anger, learning that he, being brown, visibly *of* Blackness, was left behind while his pink twin was kept. This thought—the thought that has fueled my every impulse—incredibly, won't even cross his mind. Maybe, because I've been the master of his bile for so long, Eddie is incapable of feeling it, feeling anything but gratitude for his twin. The Fish-boy in the flesh.

We—*they*, seeing as I am no longer included, no longer relevant— marvel at one another's existence. At first the slight differences assert themselves. Anders appears rosier, Eddie tawnier, contrast wedging them apart, almost defensively, under threat. The similarities in build, posture, facial features, musculature easily overpower the differences. Anders gives Eddie's hospital gown a light tug to expose the right shoulder. Tears spring to Anders's eyes as he drops the neck of his twin's tunic to cover his mouth.

Their embrace is silent but fills in the gaps in the conversation they began long, long ago. Their tears join to re-create that uterine sea where their bodies formed, the water to which they have tried for years to return, seeking one another in vain. Eddie can summon his courage now, touching Anders's right shoulder, a gesture so natural but impossibly intimate for a moments-long acquaintance. He slips the neckline of Anders's T-shirt to reveal the match to his own crescent-moon scar. Anders's scar is hypertrophic while Eddie's is atrophic, the ridges and spaces of which made extra room for me. Will the scars fade now that I am gone?

Funny. I have imagined this meeting all my life, longer than Anders has known about Eddie, far longer than the hours Eddie has known about Anders. I've been the link between them. I've held space for each of them in each other's lives. For all that, I get no reward? It cannot be. I cannot let it be. With every last bit of will I have left, I make one final push.

Swim, I command myself, *swim!*

PART IV

54.

DR. RICHARD QUENTIN MONTGOMERY

Dear Lawrence,

In addition to being the board chair, you are some-one I consider a dear friend for your constant support of my work. I therefore wanted you to be the first to learn of my anticipated retirement from Hudson Valley Psychiatric Hospital. It has been an honor to serve these twenty-seven years, but the time has come for me to direct what intellectual energy I have left elsewhere.

At this time, I will be focused on new research inspired by the case of Edward A., which I presented at the American Psychiatric Association conference. (My notes are enclosed for your reference.)

Edward's case, as you know, has led me to cast a skeptical eye on my own theories regarding multi-ple personality disorder or dissociative identity dis-order (DID), as it will be renamed in the upcoming

DSM-IV. I've become fascinated with "secret" identical twins and triplets adopted separately for the sake of research. My hypothesis is that dissociative identities standing in for missing twins may arise from the separations. I do not suggest that this is the causal factor in all cases of DID, only in those presenting with a single or very few dissociative identities. Nor do I mean to imply that such separations commonly result in DID.

I will not be including Edward A., or his twin brother Anders L., in the newest study, though I will certainly refer to that case in the introduction to the prospective book. You will recall that Edward and Anders are not identical. Lab work conducted on both twins confirmed that they are extremely rare semi-identical twins, sharing just 75% of their DNA. Additionally, disqualifying them from the current study is the fact that they were born conjoined by a small piece of flesh at the site of their right shoulders. This is evidenced by their scars and confirmed by Joanne S., Edward's adoptive mother, who generously loaned me her files containing articles and hospital records documenting the twins' birth circumstances. It is possible that the detachment surgery exacerbated the psychiatric strain that led to the splitting off of the identity known as "Pär."

While Edward's case is only the first of its kind—where a missing twin is reintroduced to bring about the healing of a psychic wound—the end result of treatment shows enormous promise for our field and for the patients afflicted. Since the reunion with Anders, Edward has shown no evidence whatsoever of dissociation. In a word, he is cured.

In closing, I wanted to share a bit of my follow-up interview with the subject, which highlights his vastly improved functioning.

Edward reports that he will return to Cardozo to complete law school in the fall. Having lost his job as a swim coach, Edward has been doing paralegal work for an adoption agency's attorney. Edward tells me that he would like to pursue adoption law, with an emphasis on ethics and consideration for the child's biological heritage. Additionally, Edward and I have talked at length about the aforesaid twin studies. I have even recommended he read Dr. Thomas J. Bouchard's "Minnesota Study." Edward aspires to use his position someday to reunite as many twins as possible. He dreams of making an impact, as his brothers have—one in medicine, the other in the creation of powerful and socially minded choreography.

In the meantime, Edward and Anders are making up for lost time, learning all they can about one another, their differences and shared traits. They even have a trip to their mother's homeland of Sweden planned. Such a delightful conclusion for Edward, Anders, and myself as well. A more satisfying and successful course of treatment I have not witnessed.

Once again, I must state what an honor these years at Hudson Valley Psych have been. My very best to you and Sarah. Margot and I would be delighted to have you out to the lake at some point before the summer ends.

Fondly,
Rich

55.

BOLIDEN

"I'll hold your hand the entire time we're in the air," Anders has promised me. "And if we fall out of the sky, well, we'll be together and land in the ocean as one." He can poke fun, referencing the bathtub incident and how it unfolded for each of us.

It's still odd, to have another self, who is not quite oneself. A twin. It has enabled me to cut down my anxiety medication by half, enabled me to laugh, to flirt with women in a manner not dissimilar from the way Anders flirts with men—easily, joyfully.

"Jag är inte rädd för att flyga," I tell Anders, though my hand grips the aisle armrest just a might too tightly.

"Bullshit." Anders laughs at me from the window seat. "But I'll cure you of that flying phobia of yours if it's the last thing I do. You'll want to go back to Stockholm again and again."

As we were planning the trip, Anders kept saying that there was no need for me to work so hard trying to master the Swedish phrases I stumble over, the accent I never quite hit.

"Literally everyone in the country speaks English."

Still, I want to learn it as my birthright. The only one I have since we cannot identify the country of our biological father. It's a regret for us both, but having one another is consolation.

We have two full days in Stockholm visiting the summer castle, the old city, and the Nordic Museum before spending a week at our aunt Anna's in Boliden. Walking about the city side by side, I can't help noticing the stares.

"Have you looked in the mirror?" Anders says when I bring this to his attention. "I mean, really looked. We are devastating. And now there are two of us."

I suspect that the stares come from a place other than admiration, but far be it for me to argue. After all that's transpired, I avoid mirrors in any case. What I fear most, more than flying, more than cats or spiders, is going backward to the time when I shared this body. Mirrors remind me of shame and pain.

After Stockholm, we fly to Skellefteå, then rent a car for the forty-minute drive to Boliden, where Anna lives alone with her husband now that their children are grown. She is standing in her garden, beside an open shed, watching us approach with a wide smile and eyes that crease at the sides. She waves, and I have to wonder whether Britta looked like that, stood like that, smiled in that same way.

"Mom was taller and more angular," Anders says without my even asking. "Anna has that cheerful, bubbly thing going on. Mom almost never smiled."

Anna grabs Anders, bear-hugs him, laughing, before turning to me, at which point tears come to her eyes.

"Look at you!" She holds me away from herself, then cups my chin, turning my face from one side to the other. "And you!" She takes Anders's face in her other hand. "You both. Together at last. May I?" she asks before taking me into her arms. Next, she brings us both inside—I follow Anders's lead and remove my shoes—for *fika*, which turns out to be strong coffee served with homemade bread and fresh butter. In the kitchen hang pots and pans on wrought iron hooks. All the dish towels are crisp and white with edges intricately embroidered.

Anna sits at the sturdy round kitchen table, chin on one hand, observing us with flushed cheeks.

"I was the only one Britta told about you, Eddie," she says, eyes still moist. "I was the only one who knew there were two babies. I didn't even know there was *one* until just before you were born, Anders. Pappa had just died, and Mamma was not herself. That's why I didn't want Britta to go away on the exchange program, especially when I learned that I would not get an exchange sister while she was gone. I was alone with our mother, who had become a sad and angry person. With Britta gone, there would have been no joy at all for me if I had not had nice friends around and neighbors who let me visit whenever I wanted. I was looking forward to my sister coming home from her year in America, bringing me goodies and telling me wonderful stories.

"Then Mamma said Britta wasn't coming home. I said, 'Why not?' And she told me that Britta was leaving school because she was going to have a baby. I said, 'Why can't we take care of the baby and Britta too?' And my mother spat. I had never seen her do such a thing. She spat and said that the father of Britta's baby was a . . . she used a very bad word to describe a person who is Black. I'm sorry." Anna nods at each of us in turn. "My mother said that Britta's baby would be—that word—too, and therefore Britta was no longer her daughter. I have never cried more in my life, not even when we lost Pappa. I begged my mother, I said, 'But she will always be my sister.' I did not care what color the baby—well, the *babies* were. I wanted my sister to bring you both home. Of course, the twin was a secret. *You* were a secret, Eddie. Pär, that was your name, after our Pappa—did you know that?

"Britta told me in a letter that she left you. I kept the secret, but it broke my heart.

"My mother and sister did not speak for three years, though Britta stayed in touch with me, sent me letters and photographs of you, Anders, but made me promise not to show Mamma. When I went away to university, my mother wanted to change my room into a writing office for herself and went through my things and found the pictures.

I don't know what happened, but the next thing I knew, Mamma was telling me Britta was coming home to visit, only for the summer, but still, she would be welcome and so would her little boy.

"And you were. Our mother smiled and laughed again when you visited. She said how much you looked like our father. She showered you with affection and baked for you and drew pictures with you. But she never apologized to Britta. Not for rejecting her, not for calling you that word.

"And, Eddie," Anna says, gazing at me now, "I cannot believe how alike you two are. So different, but still so alike. Tell me about you."

I don't know where to start. I tell her that I am a New Yorker, that I'm Jewish, once a law student and will soon be one again. "I have a brother," I add. "A different brother, I mean." I tell her that I grew up loved, "very much, by my mother and father—and by my stepmother and stepfather, after the divorce.

"But all my life I've been—" I struggle to describe myself, the way I was before. "Nervous. Well, odd, compared to most people."

"Odd?" Anna says. "And who are these 'most people'?"

I join her easy laugh. Sitting here in the place from which my Scandinavian jaw originated, I do not feel odd. "I am getting better now."

"What would make us *both* better," Anders says, "is if you could tell us anything you know about our father. Mom swore she knew nothing about him. Not even what country he was from."

Anna frowns, arms folded. "She said that?"

"She got so annoyed when I would press her to remember," Anders says. "I'd beg her to remember anything, anything at all. How tall he was. If he wore glasses. She would say, 'Stop asking me! You are mine and only mine.' So I'd keep quiet until I couldn't stand it anymore and then ask again."

"Oh my." Anna drops her eyes into her lap. "I knew she was secretive, but I didn't know my sister was a liar. How unfair. If I had known I would have shaken her until she told you!"

"About our father?" Both of us stare.

"Anders. How could you not know?"

"Know what, moster Anna? Our birth father was an African exchange student she met at the mixer."

Anna laughs at the absurdity. "What mixer? There was no mixer! He was that man, Anders. You knew him! You lived with him!"

"What? No I didn't!"

"Yes! He was that famous dancer. All the exchange students went to a dance show in New York City and met the dancers afterward. I don't know how all the rest happened. There was a party, I think. My sister danced with the company's director, who was so handsome, she said, so charming, and of course older, in his thirties. My sister told him she was eighteen, you know. She drank and danced and wound up in a hotel room with him. All she wanted her whole life was adventure. She would have said yes to anything that night.

"And you were born to dance, Anders, just like your father. When my sister saw how you loved it, she sent him a picture of you in a costume in some pretty pose." Anna holds her arms aloft in comical imitation. "She sent us the same one, I might still have it. You were so cute.

"Anyway, she wrote to your father, sent him the picture, and waited. She waited years. Heard nothing. And then he wrote to say he was going to hold an audition at a dance festival near where you lived and she should bring you. And so she did. You were ten. I think you know the rest."

"Tyrone!" I welcome this revelation with joy. Another piece of my birthright: that the man whom I grew to love, to whom I wished to belong, was *mine*, truly! I actually knew and adored a biological parent, and even if Tyrone didn't know who I was, he loved me too.

But for Anders, the news is devastating. To learn he had lived as the "ward" of a man who should have claimed him as a true son. The *ward!* To have been so deeply betrayed when he should have been embraced and defended. Anders rises and storms away from the house. Anna and

I let him go. Through a window, we see my brother run down the dirt path that leads to the lake.

"Complicated," says Anna. "Families always are."

I nod and take more bread made by my aunt. I let her pour me more coffee. While we wait for Anders to return, I drink and eat, watching Anna study my face as I study hers. She cannot keep the tears from falling again.

She tells me, "I see her in you."

I smile back at her. "Do you have photographs?"

"Of course." She rises. "You can see all the albums I have. The letters too."

56.

THE SUMMER HOUSE

Anders and I are staying in the "summer house," which looks like a simple, large shed on the property. But unlatched, the door opens onto the most beautiful bedroom I've ever seen. All old wood and stone and delicate embroidery. Blue-and-yellow vases overflow with wildflowers, and a breeze through the open windows stirs pale yellow curtains.

We place the boxes Anna has given us, full of photographs and letters tied up with strings, on a round wooden table. At first each of us is immersed in our own pile of material, silently engrossed. Then Anders shares photographs of himself and family members—Britta, Anna, their mother, and other relatives. In each photograph, Anders stands out, the sole brown face, less brown than I am, but not much. Still, he is smiling in the photos, never without someone's arm around him. Often Anna's, often Mormor's, rarely Britta's. Britta doesn't smile. She is the only one who never seems to be without a distracted frown.

"You looked so much like me," I say, holding up a picture of Anders with his mother, *our* mother, Britta. Who does not resemble Glinda the Good Witch in the least, by the way. I have to recalibrate my brain to take in what she really looked like, reprogramming the image I held of her. Very blond, with bangs, a long face, strong jaw, small, close-set blue eyes that never show joy, as Anders's do. They are on the shore of the lake, which sparkles behind them. In bathing suits. Anders's suit bags and gaps around his skinny waist, like mine always did at the same age. He clutches at it with one hand—again, like I always did. The difference is in the hair, which is stringy with dampness, the curl undone by the weight of the lake water. By contrast, water always beads up on my impermeable curls, shakes off easily, without disturbing the pattern. But otherwise, it's like looking at myself.

"Of course I looked like you," says Anders. "We're twins. We were twins back then."

I have to be told this over and over again. To me it means that, all along, I was part of a *we*. My whole life, and never knew it. Now I ask why Britta looks like that.

"Sad?" says Anders. "She was always like that, as far as I knew. At least until I was older and she returned to Sweden. Partly it was that Mormor was always disappointed in her, critical. You know, that she had me and ran away and all that. But obviously, Mom was disappointed in herself. Her life. She wanted to be an actress, not a mother."

"I didn't know."

"You know, when I first found out about you, I thought, 'Okay, now it makes sense.' Why Mom is sad and weird all the time. I thought it was because she regretted leaving you. I thought she was missing you."

"You thought?"

"Yes. And then, when I went to live with the Wynters and Mom moved back here, she got a little better. If she missed anything, it was this place. And if she regretted anything, it wasn't leaving you; it was that she didn't leave me too. That's what I think now."

I cannot wrap my mind around this: the notion of Anders being unwanted. Guilt, generosity form my next words. "My mother said that if things had worked out differently, she would have taken us both."

"Eddie—" Anders's eyes are still moist. They have not stopped being moist since Anna revealed our father's identity. "There are too many what-ifs between us. Too many ways it all could have gone."

I nod. "And Tyrone. He could have—"

"I don't want to talk about him."

"Sorry." Though I'm not exactly sorry. By now, I know what happened with Anders, Carlo, and Lucy. I know about the AIDS rumor, how Tyrone handled it. And now Anders is facing the fact that his own father did this. But I can't not talk about it. Aloud I blurt, "I think we're different like that."

"Different like what?" Anders says.

"We're both Black. But you're Swedish. I'm Jewish. And Jews—we talk about everything. Even the things that hurt. We talk and talk until things make sense."

"What if they never make sense?"

"We keep trying."

"It sounds exhausting."

"At least we can try."

We return our focus to the piles, untying bundles, spreading out letters, beginning to read.

What we piece together brings us both to a place of disorientation. More than once, I grip Anders's hand or vice versa. There are things that Anders knew and had already shared with me: for example, that we had appeared entirely unlike one another at birth, that, once the separation surgery was over, each of our wounds reflected the color of the opposite twin. Twin A's scar (mine) was pale and raw. Twin B's scar (Anders's) shone in the light, a marbled brown. Almost as if each of us bore an emblem of the other to carry into our severed life.

But there is more. The news story of how the girl (Britta) left the hospital alone initially, then returned and took the fairer twin, whose wound was still draining and at risk of infection. It was an afterthought, taking Anders, expanded on in a letter to Anna, which Anders also translates for me to the best of his ability.

"'I left them both. I felt sure that wherever they wound up, it would be better than with me. I could not tell Mamma. I could not bring them home to her. And Pär, what would his life be like, I thought. He would be ostracized. I could not do that to him. I walked the city. I was sick and I didn't know what to do or where to go. I went back to the hospital. I still had my bracelet. I did not understand that I was being hunted. When I returned to the ward, there were reporters in the nursery. Everyone wanted pictures of them: the Black and white Siamese twins, but by then they weren't Siamese anymore; they'd been cut apart. And sewn up.'"

Britta was sick when they readmitted her. Nurses were bottle-feeding the infants by then, but Britta still had milk.

Anders reads the paper in front of him, lips moving as he attempts to translate. "Eddie," he says, eyes imploring. "Can we skip this one?"

"No. I want to know it all."

"Not this."

"Yes, everything. I need to."

Anders gets water, sits back down, and resumes translating. "Okay. She says here . . . Eddie, are you sure?"

"Yes."

"'A nurse brought them to me. They were easy to tell apart. Anders had an easy time suckling, but Pär couldn't manage it. He didn't want me. Anders did.'" Anders looks up when my breath catches.

"Go on."

"Okay. 'I didn't think it through when I left again. I just did. I took Anders and left Pär behind. I thought he'd be better off.'"

I keep still, staring at the air between us. I would be better off, our mother thought.

"Eddie. Are you okay?"

"Go on."

"There's not much left in this one. It's just . . .'"

"What?"

"About our names. 'You probably want to know why I named him after Pappa, the one I left. Well, I was going to leave them both, remember. Pär is the one who came out first. Like Esau with Jacob clinging to his heel. But they were shoulder to shoulder with this blob of skin between them. I didn't like to look at it. I didn't like to look at them at all. They were a thing. Not babies. A thing. That is what I thought. And I cried.

"'But Mamma wasn't there and you weren't there, Anna. The nurses were nice, but they thought I was crazy. I was crazy. Did you know I lied when I got there? I said that I was twenty-five and that I was Ann-Margret. I guess they didn't know what the actress looked like, because they believed me at first. Then one nurse said she knew I wasn't her because the real Ann-Margret was in Vietnam performing for the troops right then. They knew I was a kid. They didn't know my name, but they did know I was crazy.

"'And when I left with Anders, I thought I might change the babies' names so I would be keeping the one I named after Pappa. The white twin. In the end I was glad I left the Black twin with Pappa's name. It's all he will ever have of me and of our family.

"'Tell Mamma that I'll be in touch when I can. Tell her I'm safe. I have people who are taking care of me and the baby. They said I can stay here for a while.

"'With love, your sister.'"

Anders looks up from the page at my face. "That's everything."

"So that's why I'm Pär—I mean, why I was named Pär."

"You came out first. I never knew that."

"She said we were a thing, not babies."

"She was seventeen."

"I know."

Wordlessly, lost in our private thoughts, we refold letters, retie photographs, replace the items in the first box, and open a second one.

"You changed," I tell Anders.

"What do you mean?"

"You were the white twin." I'm trying for humor, but there's accusation in my voice. Like Anders set us up for different lives on purpose.

"No I wasn't," says Anders. "We were newborn babies. Newborn babies are never their real colors."

I've had little exposure to newborn babies.

"You saw those pictures," Anders says. "You were red. I was pink."

"I did see the pictures. I saw what our mother saw."

Anders shuts the boxes, but the headline stays with me.

Swedish Jane Doe, Believed to be Minor, Disappears with White Twin, Abandons Black Twin at St. Vincent's

But the kicker comes later. Anders finds it, a letter addressed to the family in Boliden from Tyrone, postmarked August 1967, when we were just over a year old. Britta had disappeared with Anders by then, as far as we can tell from other correspondence, and I was home with the Ashers. I *was* an Asher. Apparently, Tyrone learned about us when the world did, read the article, did the math.

"How did he know their address?"

"Maybe he contacted the exchange program?"

"Or her host family?"

This will remain a mystery. As will the question of how Tyrone was able to keep his single night with the sixteen-year-old Swedish girl a secret from Dominique, even after Anders went to live with them. Even as the resemblance between Anders and Tyrone became evident. We can see it in pictures of young Anders. We can see it now in one another.

"How stupid are we?" we keep murmuring, eyes scanning each other's features. "You look just like him." Which is true when you know what you're looking at, looking for. If you don't know, it's possible to chalk the similarities up to coincidence, as Dominique must have done.

The last line of a second letter from Tyrone to Mormor, dated 1968, is what gives us the biggest jolt of all.

"'I will not give up,'" I read. "'I'll tell my wife whatever story I need to tell her. But you mark my words, I will find both of my boys. Wherever they are, they belong with me.'"

Both, Tyrone wrote. *Both of my boys.*

"He knew," I say. "All along. He knew." But the letter's other revelation is what stands out most: Tyrone wanted us. At least at the moment of his writing, he did.

With chills, I recall Tyrone's slip of the tongue that afternoon in the chemotherapy suite.

I never told you about my boys, did I? He meant us. Anders and me.

57.

RETURN

On the flight home, Anders remains somber, with me trying too hard to cheer him up, offering drinks, misfired jokes.

"Eddie, my mother is dead, and the man I didn't know was my father broke my heart."

It hurts me that he says "my" instead of "our," but I don't let on. I tolerate the silence between us for as long as I can.

"Tyrone apologized," I say, surprising him. I add, "I never told you that?"

"No."

"Well, he did. He thought I was you. He sometimes got confused like that. I didn't know what he was apologizing for at the time. But I knew he meant it." Tyrone's exact words about Anders were *I never forgave him for leaving,* but I lean into the burnished narrative, which seems to bring Anders back.

"Thank you. That helps a little." My brother faces forward now, reclines his seat as far as it will go, and shuts his eyes.

I observe him, letting him process for just a moment. It will take me months to fully consider my own relationship with Tyrone, months to regret the missed chance to talk with my biological father about who we really were to one another. But now another thought takes me by surprise—I have to cover my mouth to keep from shouting it.

"Anders!" I'm shaking him awake. "Anders, Lucy is our sister!"

How did it not hit me until this moment? Have I really gone this whole time without Lucy front and center in my thoughts?

Anders seems to mull this over. "Of course she is. So are Regina, Sophia, and Althea."

"Right." They are all our sisters. But Lucy, after all this, after everything. The train, her vanishing, Carlo, she's still mine. No matter who else she belongs to, she is my sister.

"Have you forgiven her?" Anders says.

I think for a moment—how to explain to him what I feel about her. "I will if she comes back." I feel sure that she'll come back. She'll come back, and I'll tell her everything. "Have you forgiven her?"

"Of course not." Eyes still shut, Anders adds, "And we can tell Althea about Tyrone, maybe Regina and Sophia one day, but not Dominique. I think it would be too much for her."

"Okay." I turn toward the window and watch the bright-blue lakes of our mother's homeland grow smaller and smaller.

At JFK, we brothers embrace before Anders dashes off to make his connecting flight to O'Hare. I keep my eyes on him until he turns a corner; then I go on to baggage claim. My mother, Joanne, will meet me there while Michael brings the car around.

"Did you have a nice time?" Mom says on the ride to Manhattan.

"Yes." I don't know where to start. With the pictures, the stories of my birth mother? With the fact that I know the identity of my birth father? Instead, I tell her about the summer house and how much she would have loved all the embroidery and little painted porcelain. "I took pictures for you."

"Oh goody!" my mother says. "I can take the film to be developed tomorrow." Then, after a pause: "Do you and Anders get along well?" It's strange to hear her say the name, my two families, two worlds merging.

"We finish each other's sentences."

"Don't tell Robert. He'll be jealous," Michael says with a wink in the rearview mirror.

Though I suspect it is Joanne who is jealous—of Sweden, of Anders and Anna, of everyone and everything with a biological claim to me. I also know what my mother has been thinking since I told her about Anders: that if she'd adopted us both, if I'd had Anders all along, everything would have been better, easier. It would have lightened everyone's load: her own, Robert's. But then, I think, there would have been no Michael Stern in her life. And Michael, in his quiet way, has been the purveyor of unconditional love to Joanne and me as well.

I am frankly relieved to be taken in by Mom and Michael, now that I'm out of Hudson Valley Psych, now that I'm free from the influence of Pär, on whom I depended in ways I never understood until now. Pär was someone to blame, to retreat into, when life got confusing. But now, thanks to Anders, to Sweden, to Michael and Joanne, I am finding my footing *as myself*, my real self, for the very first time.

I call Robert almost immediately when I get home. Due diligence.

"Hey, Eddie."

"Hey."

"Did you have fun with your real brother?"

"Don't be like that. But yes."

"Nice for you."

I can hear in my brother's voice that he is only joking and still loves me. Loves me again. An awkwardness percolates on the line, as if a confession is nigh.

"Eddie . . ." It's Robert who breaks the silence. "I'm glad you're okay now."

"When wasn't I okay?"

"You know what I mean. That doctor at Hudson Valley Psych. I'm glad he was able to help you get better."

"Oh. Right. Good old Monty!"

"I'm serious, dude." A thickness enters Robert's speech, and I realize he's choking up. "I always felt like it was partly my fault you had so many problems."

"You looked out for me." Which we both know is a half-truth.

"But I lost my patience too," says Robert. "I hurt you."

"I was a little nutjob."

"You weren't the only one," Robert says. "I just kept things in and then took it out on you. That time in the elevator—"

"It's okay."

"I'm sorry, Eddie."

"I know."

Robert doesn't mention the bathtub incident. The brothers Asher leave that in the past.

"I love you, Eddie," Robert says, then blows his nose.

And I—for I *am* Eddie now, unequivocally and perpetually Eddie—have to admit that it's mutual. Remembering certain things, as I do, now that I have full access to myself, I can choose how to feel about this brother of mine. And I choose love. Still. Always. Despite Pär's revelations. There is nothing I cannot forgive now that I am this close to being whole.

"Robert, are you sitting?"

"Now I am. What?"

"It's about Lucy. You'll never guess."

"I won't try."

"She's my sister."

Robert is silent for a moment, then hoots. "Of all the crazy shit I've ever heard out of you." He laughs harder, keeps laughing until I hang up the phone.

58.

TAVERN ON THE GREEN

On the evening of Althea and Clark's engagement party—at Tavern on the Green in Central Park, a few blocks south of The Majestic—I meet Robert at his apartment so we can walk together. Anders will be there too, but not Lucy. Oh, no, not Lucy.

"She called me today," Robert tells me.

Here's the thing about a comeuppance: if properly delivered, it can result in redemption. For Lucy, the jury is out as to whether that has happened. But she sobbed with contrition when relating the following to Robert.

Upon arrival in Milan, Lucy discovered that she was not even close to being Carlo's only girlfriend but part of a veritable bevy. Hired as only a temporary member of a small dance company Carlo's friend had founded, Lucy soon found herself jobless. She remained in the lovely apartment that Carlo rented with two other dancers, women who were content to share him and one another, but Lucy's sense of romance and hedonism did not fit with theirs. And then her period was late. Quite late, as it turned out. Her weight gain was not due merely to a fondness for gelato and lack of dancing but to the presence of an additional inhabitant of her person.

Comeuppance indeed. Her changing shape was a deterrent to Carlo's attentions, especially when Lucy counted back the months. The child was not Carlo's. Lucy first wrote to Althea, who was at that point already too busy planning her own wedding to fly to her sister's side. Robert was the next person Lucy thought of reaching out to, really the first person she should have called. For the baby could only be Robert's—or so she told Robert.

"I was going to hang up the phone before she got to the part about the pregnancy," Robert says. "But then I knew she was pregnant, and I couldn't hang up. All I could think of was this baby. Who's going to be my baby. *My* baby, Eddie! How fucked up would it be if I cut Lucy off completely just for being Lucy? I mean, it's not the kid's fault."

Lucy isn't asking Robert to take her back, though I can tell he is considering it. She only asks that they raise the baby—if not together, then jointly—so it knows both of them. Lucy will return to the States with the child when it's born, and Robert will help support them.

I'm speechless by the time we arrive. Tavern on the Green is full of family—the Wynters, the LaFontaines, and Clark's family as well. Althea is stunning in a pink strapless gown, braids wound up into a glamorous topknot. Clark looks handsome and smart, yet uncharacteristically sheepish in a tan suit. It will be the first time many of those who attended Tyrone's funeral will see Anders and me together, but I'm not thinking about that. All I can think of, as we mill through the crowd in search of drinks, is Lucy's impending return. I scan my body for tightness, fear, anger. But there's nothing but calm resolution. It will be good to have her back, to meet the child who will be my own blood.

59.

CHAMPAGNE

At the wedding, Anders and I stand in for Tyrone in giving the bride away. Althea is splendid in cream-colored satin and lace, a wreath of white roses supporting her veil.

As every head turns our way, I am most aware of Lucy's. She is seated in the second row, among the Wynter relatives, which somehow extends to include Robert today, who is at Lucy's right. Baby girl Tyra is asleep on Robert's shoulder. Lucy catches my eye, singling me out for a special smile, full of meaning.

And I wonder then: Does she know? Because sometimes it feels too good, too real, and too brilliant to keep the full truth to myself. Perhaps one day I will tell Lucy everything from the beginning. She would appreciate it, I think: how I studied him, memorized and internalized him, until I could perform him seamlessly—the way Eddie himself once did with Andy. I'll tell her how it started as a game for me—impersonating rather than simply intervening—and then how it became a matter of life and death. To be and live as Eddie Asher, to replace him perfectly and take this body for my own forever—mine and mine alone. I'd earned it, hadn't I?

Though there are moments, especially in the water, when the guilt overwhelms me and I miss him terribly. No, I miss us. Britta and Tyrone's three boys: Pär-who-would-never-be, Pär-who-would-be-Eddie, and

Anders. When were we ever whole, peaceful, together as one, but in the womb?

Oh, yes! Back in '76, in our respective bathtubs. Each twin was face down in the water: Eddie looking down at Anders, Anders looking up at Eddie. The joy and safety brought each boy back to the organic chamber they'd once shared as a true unit, before the doctor's blade made them two.

It was splendid in the underwater place, the collective bathtub, as I made my transfer from one to the other. How I loved the feel of being a trio once again. God, it was perfect, too perfect to move on from. So I decided for us all: we would stay, bonded together in that two-sided porcelain chamber, together forever. I clutched Eddie by his shoulder, Anders by his. I pulled and stretched and pulled and stretched with all my might, believing I could weld them back together, resurrect myself, and there in the balmy deep we'd stay. I would have drowned them both to have them back for myself. Wouldn't you?

Of course, now that I stand tall in this supple body, I am grateful to Robert for rescuing it, even a bit sorry I saddled him with the blame.

Now Anders, none the wiser, elbows me subtly, beaming as Clark places the ring on Althea's smooth finger. I elbow him back, relishing the community, the view, the scents, the sound of Reverend Lou's digni- fied voice. The couple kisses and the real party begins. My hand accepts a cool flute of champagne; delicate bubbles rise up to tickle my nose. How giddy I am tonight, thinking of the untold joys and possibilities life holds.

I have won. It was fair and final. Though wariness is built into my nature. Part of me will always wonder whether the battle is really over, whether Eddie is truly gone or simply, temporarily submerged. Is he capa- ble of adaptation as I was? Can he learn to manipulate my will as I once did his? Will his bitterness evolve into unanticipated strength and pluck?

Perhaps one day I will pay a price for my victory, but in the mean- time, the champagne is flowing. The band has begun, and I promised Lucy a dance.

AUTHOR'S NOTE

As authors, we mine our lives for ingredients for the stories we tell, starting with what we've lived firsthand, folding in what we've witnessed closely, seasoning the batter with what we've gathered through research. We stretch and mold and bake the thing until it feels right—then hope it rings true for others. In 2024, we are living in an age where readers are more likely than ever to wonder about the author and her relationship to the subject matter. I want to shed some light on that in this note.

I write about the Upper West Side of Manhattan, where I grew up in the 1970s and '80s. I write about ballet, my first career. (Like Lucy, I was one of the first Black corps members in the Pacific Northwest Ballet and even played a cygnet in *Swan Lake*.) When I hung up my pointe shoes and earned a master's degree in social work, I became an adoption caseworker before becoming licensed as a psychotherapist.

The twin backdrops for much of *Mirror Me* are multiracial identity and transracial adoption, both of which have been specialties of my psychotherapy practice for over twenty years. Though my experience with adoption is largely professional, I have lived a multiracial identity for over five decades. I was born to a white, Jewish mother and a Black father who had been married for sixteen years at the time of my arrival—hence, decades older than Britta was when Eddie was born. What I share with Eddie is not only being Jewish and Black but also the experience of walking through the world under the umbrella of my mother's whiteness, taking certain privileges for granted as we ran errands, hurried in and out of Zabar's, Bloomingdale's, the East River Savings Bank, the 92nd Street Y. In most settings, I attracted little attention until Mom let go of my hand and I became, in the eyes of strangers, a small Black girl out of place and all alone. It was different with my father, an art director at Viking Press. Whether visiting Dad's beloved barbershop in Harlem, where I'd sit on a stool, swinging my feet, enjoying the banter and perhaps a lollipop, or attending a book party where Dad was the only Black man present, it was plainly visible that I belonged to and with him. Like Tyrone, my father cut a formidable image. His posture and style of dress commanded a respect often denied Black men of the time.

Unlike Eddie, I grew up valuing Blackness and understanding that it was part of me. Unlike Joanne, my mother valued and respected Blackness as well. And while my mother was not religious, Jewishness was part of our home and my identity. My parents taught me about the joys of each culture, but also about racism and antisemitism they each had faced, the harassment they had endured as an interracial couple in the '50s and '60s. In this respect I grew up immersed in who I was, but as an only child, I was often alone to make sense of it.

Transracial adoption has had a place in my heart since I was in prekindergarten and a group of older girls told me I was adopted. My mother, a teacher, was the one who picked me up from school; she was the only parent of mine these girls had seen. When I asked, my mother explained to me what adoption was and identified several children we knew, including three in my class, who had joined their families in such a fashion. All were transracially adopted but one—a white boy adopted by a white single mother. The latter had me stumped. Wasn't the point of adoption to create a family like my own, with a broad range of skin colors? That was my four-year-old understanding.

Midyear, a boy in my class who was Black, adopted by white parents, moved with his family out of the city. I later learned that they had fled harassment from a group claiming that transracial adoption was akin to genocide. When this happened, Eddie would have been in pre-K as well. I chose to leave the politics of transracial adoption out of the story, though I did address Eddie's lack of connection to both his biological cultures. When I was old enough to understand what had happened to my classmate and his family, it occurred to me that my mother and I were likely observed by some with the same hostility. In this way, transracial adoption was always on my radar.

It felt like kismet that my first job offer out of graduate school came from the Spence-Chapin adoption agency. There I worked in the African American and Hispanic Domestic Adoption programs, and also the International Programs in eastern Europe and East Asia. I also worked in the Post-Adoption department and ran support groups for transracially adopted adolescents, most of whom were Korean and Guatemalan, adopted by white families. By the midnineties, the agency was placing very few Black children with white families as there were always plenty of Black families looking to adopt. I was fascinated by the history and legacy of transracial adoption and began creating and disseminating surveys to adult transracial adoptees and their families about their experiences. When I left Spence-Chapin, earned my license in clinical social work and, later, my certification in family therapy, I continued my work with transracial adoptees and their families.

This note is in part to honor, confidentially, all the transracial adoptees I have worked with in therapy sessions: group, family, and individual. I also honor all members of the adoption triad whom I encountered in my years as an adoption caseworker at Spence-Chapin. And here I must add a word on birth mothers, in light of Britta's storyline. In all my years working in and adjacent to the field of adoption, the majority of birth mothers I have encountered made adoption plans for their children with deep love and awareness of what they wanted for their children but could not offer. Britta—along with her abandonment of Eddie—is purely fictional and in no way should be taken as a statement about biological parents who place their children with adoptive families.

I also wish to honor, again confidentially, clients past and present who have presented with dissociative identity disorder (which was, in

Eddie and Dr. Montgomery's day, known as multiple personality disorder). Their stories enhanced my ability to develop Pär and Eddie's relationship. While Pär is not a dissociative identity, and never was in my mind, his function regarding trauma is similar.

As a licensed clinical social worker and therapist in practice for more than twenty years, I am always curious about how people's histories, losses, inner wounds, and family secrets shape who they are. I credit my psychotherapeutic education to Hunter College School of Social Work (now known as Silberman School of Social Work), the Ackerman Institute for the Family, and the EMDR Institute. For details related to birth trauma, I leaned into the research of the Annie Brook Institute, particularly the Healing Infant Memory and Birth Trauma curriculum. Dr. Montgomery and Dr. Lloyd, as well as Eddie's and Lucy's unnamed therapists, use certain jargon that comes out of my mouth on a regular basis. This shrink-speak is my own, though I never have and never will use my actual clients' stories as material for my fiction.

Mirror Me, as noted, is a work of pure fiction. There is only one character in the novel who is based on someone who actually existed. This is Feather the cat, whom I loved deeply and to whom I am grateful for providing comfort and kindness during my loneliest days in a ballet company. It was you, little Feather, who taught me to believe in past lives.

ACKNOWLEDGMENTS

The very first person I want to thank for helping me see this book through its wild evolution is my husband, Jon. He read the first draft in 2009, when it was called *Acid Shabbat* and bore very little resemblance to the version you hold in your hands. Jon read most of the subsequent drafts, continuing to believe in the book even after I'd put it aside to marinate—while I learned to actually write a novel. Thank you, Jon. I love you for your devotion, kindness, tolerance, and unflappable sense of humor.

Thank you also to our children, Zoe and Theo, for believing in me and tolerating having a writer for a mom. You were both so little when I began writing this book. Watching the two of you grow into the remarkable young adults you are today has been my greatest joy.

Next, I want to thank my agent, Uwe Stender, whose enthusiasm for this book and my work helped keep my eyes on the prize throughout the entire publication process. Thank you to editor Selena James for helping to guide me through the ups and downs of revisions and for giving Eddie, Pär, Anders, and Lucy a chance to shine. And to Michelle Flythe, my editor of heroic skill and insights, thank you for seeing the gold in this story and helping me bring it to light. Thank you to the whole team at Little A—Nicole Burns-Ascue, Jon Ford, Rachel Norfleet, and Heather Rodino—for being so supportive as we turned my manuscript into this book.

Thank you to my beta readers, Jenny Hiraga, William Dameron, Erika Gaynor, and most extra especially Lisa Roe. Lisa not only read early drafts but also provided me with endless moment-by-moment writer support through our near daily stream of texts.

Thank you to my sister-in-law, Audrey Rosenberg, by whom I ran too many ideas to count.

Thank you to my cousin Nancy Soren for virtually guiding me through the streets of Chicago for Andy's walk home. Thank you to Debbie Trotsky Soren for her input on the Chicago scenes. Thank you to Pär Olsson for details about Sweden, the Swedish language, and for the loan of a name. Thank you also to Portia and Carla Poindexter for being my twin muses for so many years. Thank you also to Paul Kogan for giving me extra twin guidance.

I must also acknowledge several sources I turned to for research, including *Multiple Personality Disorder from the Inside Out*, a collection edited by Barry M. Cohen, Esther Giller, and Lynn W., and *Diagnosis and Treatment of Multiple Personality Disorder* by Frank W. Putnam. I selected both volumes because they are contemporaneous with Dr. Montgomery's work, predating the *DSM-IV*. Thanks to the Scary Mommy team for their December 2020 article "What are Semi-Identical Twins?" as well as to BBC News for their February 2019 article "Doctors Have Documented What They Say Is Only the World's Second Known Case of 'Semi-Identical' Twins." Here, I have taken liberties in my fiction, as Britta's twins were born long before the first such case was identified in 2007 (also reported by the BBC). Lastly, for the history of twin separation, I consulted *Deliberately Divided: Inside the Controversial Study of Twins and Triplets Adopted Apart* by Nancy L. Segal, where I learned about Dr. Thomas J. Bouchard's "Minnesota Study," mentioned in Dr. Montgomery's letter.

Additionally, I want to acknowledge the Spence-Chapin adoption agency and the Pacific Northwest Ballet company. I learned volumes during my employment at each establishment.

And of course, I owe a huge thank-you to my expanding writing community:

The Tall Poppy Writers, especially Ann Garvin, Stephanie Burns, Tricia Blanchet, Julie Dalton, Nancy Johnson, and Weina Randel for so much fabulous support throughout the ups and downs of last several months of mom-and-writer life.

Thank you to the Women's Fiction Writers Association, especially Lisa Roe (again!), Suzy England, Emily Barbaro, Thelma Adams, Sharon Ritchey, Nancy Johnson (again!), Lynne Golodner, Sonali Dev, Camille Pagan, and Heather Drimmer.

From the Vermont College of Fine Arts June 2023 writer's retreat, I must give special thanks to Connie May Fowler, Laura Warrell, Luanne Smith, Dahlma Llanos Figueroa, Jessie Ulmer, and others for support and encouragement.

My AWP24 peeps: Ann Kim, Britt Tisdale, Jean Alicia Elster, Lydia Kang, Jenny Qi, Chloe Benjamin, Ebony Stewart, and Christina Chiu.

Finally, I need to acknowledge Amy Rader Olsson, in memoriam. Thank you, my sweet friend, for your friendship, your humor, your singing, and years of wonderful memories. I will never forget our walks in Stockholm and drives through the beautiful Swedish countryside.

QUESTIONS FOR DISCUSSION

1. Though Eddie and Andy are semi-identical twins, they have different complexions at birth. They are mistaken for one another as adults, but there is no mention of them being indistinguishable when they are side by side. Why do you think the author chose not to make the twins identical? How differently did you imagine them appearing?

2. Britta chooses Anders, the fair-skinned twin whom she believes resembles her, over Eddie, who is visibly Black at birth. What do you think it would have been like for Eddie and Anders to be raised together by Britta, the Ashers, or Tyrone and Dominique?

3. Colorism is at play in another sibling relationship. Lucy, who is biracial like Eddie, describes the reception she got from her half sisters, Tyrone and Dominique's daughters, when she joined the family. "If my mother had been Black, I bet they'd just have felt sorry for me. But I represent something political for everyone. Regina and Sophia used to call me Dad's 'little white princess.'" What do you think Lucy meant by this? Why is this hard for Eddie to understand, having grown up as the "only brown Asher"?

4. There are several instances where race and racism are at play in the novel, particularly when Eddie is warned to stay

away from the Black kids or steer clear of dangerous Black neighborhoods. Was there a risk for the Asher family—for Joanne and Eddie especially—if Eddie had been more exposed to Black culture?

5. In one section, Pär briefly implies that Tyrone once reached out to Joanne, asking to meet Eddie when he was about nine. This meeting never happened. What do you think Joanne's reluctance might have been to such a meeting? What impact do you think meeting Tyrone as his birth father might have had on Eddie?

6. In addition to race and class, culture is also touched upon in the book. The Ashers are Jewish but not very religious until Joanne marries Michael Stern. Even so, Eddie (who is at this point actually Pär) points out that he is Jewish, while his twin brother, Anders, is Swedish. Why does Eddie mention this? How is this difference between the twins manifested? Think about your own cultural background, beyond language and religion. How do members of your culture or cultures seem to communicate differently from others? Has this led to misunderstandings or other discomfort?

7. *Mirror Me* has numerous references to water: Eddie's swimming, the bathtub incident, the Puget Sound, which houses Lucy's whales. Why is water significant to the story? How does it relate to the relationships between Pär and each twin? Between Eddie and Lucy?

8. Eddie and Lucy have a complicated, at times ambiguous, and almost romantic relationship. How did you feel upon learning that they were half siblings?

9. Aside from Eddie and Lucy's storyline, there are several other big reveals in the book: the true connection between Eddie and Andy/Anders/the Mountain boy. Tyrone's relationship to the twins. The origin of Pär and

the identity of the woman killed on the train tracks. Which of these were surprises to you? Which did you have hunches about?

10. The book begins and ends in Pär's narration, making him the primary storyteller, though Eddie is technically the protagonist. Did you see Pär as a villain or a sympathetic character, despite being a threat to Eddie?

ABOUT THE AUTHOR

Photo © 2024 Deborah Copaken

Lisa Williamson Rosenberg is the author of *Embers on the Wind*. She is a former ballet dancer and psychotherapist specializing in depression, developmental trauma, and multiracial identity. Her essays have appeared in Literary Hub, Longreads, Narratively, Mamalode, and *The Common*. Her fiction has been published in the *Piltdown Review* and in *Literary Mama*, where Lisa received a Pushcart nomination. A born-and-raised New Yorker and mother of two college students, Lisa now lives in Montclair, New Jersey, with her husband and dog. For more information, visit www.lisawrosenberg.com.